P9-CMW-558

Just this time, can the beast
tame the beauty?

ou'd better stop," he said. "I'm trying to be the sane one in the room, but you're making that exceedingly difficult."

She made it impossible. She was a goddess in a passion. The blaze of her blue eyes and the pale fire of her hair and the crimson glow of her cheeks.

She flung down the hat and grabbed the lapels of his coat. "I wish I were a man," she said. "I would knock you down. I would plant you a facer. I'd break your nose. I—"

"No, really, I mean it," he said. "You're murdering my brain." And he took hold of her shoulders and bent his head and kissed her.

By Loretta Chase

DUKES PREFER BLONDES
VIXEN IN VELVET
SCANDAL WEARS SATIN
SILK IS FOR SEDUCTION
ROYALLY EVER AFTER
DON'T TEMPT ME
YOUR SCANDALOUS WAYS
NOT QUITE A LADY
THE LAST HELLION
THE MAD EARL'S BRIDE
LORD OF SCOUNDRELS
CAPTIVES OF THE NIGHT
THE LION'S DAUGHTER

ATTENTION: ORGANIZATIONS AND CORPORATIONS
HarperCollins books may be purchased for educational, business, or sales promotional use. For information, please e-mail the Special Markets Department at SPsales@harpercollins.com.

LORETTA CHASE

Dukes
Prefer Blondes

AVONBOOKS

An Imprint of HarperCollinsPublishers

PUBLIC LIBRARY
EAST ORANGE, NEW JERSEY

This is a work of fiction. Names, characters, places, and incidents are products of the author's imagination or are used fictitiously and are not to be construed as real. Any resemblance to actual events, locales, organizations, or persons, living or dead, is entirely coincidental.

AVON BOOKS
An Imprint of HarperCollins*Publishers*
195 Broadway
New York, New York 10007

Copyright © 2016 by Loretta Chekani
ISBN 978-0-06-210034-4
www.avonromance.com

All rights reserved. No part of this book may be used or reproduced in any manner whatsoever without written permission, except in the case of brief quotations embodied in critical articles and reviews. For information address Avon Books, an Imprint of HarperCollins Publishers.

First Avon Books mass market printing: January 2016

Avon Trademark Reg. U.S. Pat. Off. and in Other Countries, Marca Registrada, Hecho en U.S.A.
Avon, Avon Books, and the Avon logo are trademarks of HarperCollins Publishers.
HarperCollins® is a registered trademark of HarperCollins Publishers.

Printed in the U.S.A.

10 9 8 7 6 5 4 3 2 1

If you purchased this book without a cover, you should be aware that this book is stolen property. It was reported as "unsold and destroyed" to the publisher, and neither the author nor the publisher has received any payment for this "stripped book."

In memory of Owen,
whose knowledge and love of art and architecture
enriched our visits to England and elsewhere,
and whose affection, wit, and generosity
enriched our lives

Acknowledgments

Thanks to:

May Chen, my editor, for the inspiration, encouragement, and skill in guiding the fragile and sometimes wayward writer ego;

Nancy Yost, my agent, for her enthusiasm, good humor, and phenomenal work ethic;

Isabella Bradford, kindred spirit, for nerdy history co-enabling, leadership through the shoals of social media, and excellent fashion sense;

Bruce Hubbard, MD, friend and ER doc par excellence, for finding a way to not kill the nineteenth-century patient, despite no antibiotics or, really, anything useful;

Sherrie Holmes, horse and carriage expert, for answering my many questions with patience, humor, and splendid clarity;

Colonial Williamsburg milliners and mantua makers and tailors, experts in historic dress, who continue to enlighten and often surprise me with historical matters sartorial;

Paul and Carol, friends, who continue to offer the shelter and peace of a beautiful house on Cape Cod;

Larry and Gloria, friends, who continue to offer a refuge from the winter in their beautiful house in Florida;

My sisters Cynthia, Vivian, and Kathy for tactical and moral support, with bonus thanks to brainstorming partner and walking companion Cynthia, for all the brilliant ideas; and attorney Kathy, for advice about lawyers and how they think;

Walter: the man in my life, for telling me to write faster and asking, "Is it done yet?" and taking me to beautiful places, even if it isn't done yet.

For flaws, faults, errors, and divers atrocities I take full credit.

Prologue

Muse make the man thy theme, for shrewdness famed
And genius versatile.
—*The Odyssey of Homer*, translated by William Cowper,
1791

Eton College
Autumn 1817

To begin with, he was obnoxious.

Oliver Radford's schoolfellows didn't need more than a day or two after his arrival to discover this.

They didn't need much time, either, to administer the nickname "Raven," though why they chose it was less obvious. Maybe his thick, black hair and too-piercing grey eyes gave them the idea, or maybe it was his deep, husky voice, better suited to a grown man than a boy of ten. Or maybe they referred to his nose, although this, while by no means small, wasn't as beaky as many others.

Still, he did always have the nose in question in a book, and some—one of his paternal cousins, in fact—said that young Radford reminded him of "a raven poking into the guts of a carcass."

The cousin failed to mention or forgot or perhaps didn't know—not being observant or clever—how extremely intelligent ravens were, for birds. Oliver Radford was extremely intelligent, for a boy. This was one reason he found the books vastly preferable to his schoolmates.

Especially his unbelievably stupid cousins . . .

At present he leaned against a wall at the edge of the playing fields, well away from the others, who were choosing sides for cricket. Unlikely and unwilling to be chosen, but required to be present at the character-building proceedings, he had his nose in the pages of Homer's *Odyssey*.

A shadow fell over Oliver and a fat hand with grimy fingernails covered the page of Greek script. He did not look up. He was, like his father, more-than-average observant. He recognized the hand. He had good reason to.

"Here he is, gentlemen," said Cousin Bernard. "Spawn of the family's laboring branch: our Raven."

Laboring was meant to disparage Oliver's father. Since the eldest son inherited everything, the others and their offspring had to find rich wives and/or places in "gentlemanly" professions like the military, the church, or the law. George Radford, son of a duke's younger son, had elected to become a barrister. He was successful as well as happily married.

All that Oliver had observed told him the other Radfords had extremely small brains and marriages the antithesis of his parents'.

That a boy of ten knew what *antithesis* meant was another reason to hate him.

He didn't help matters.

"Naturally you find the law laborious," Oliver said. "Firstly, it wants a mastery of Latin, and you barely comprehend English. Secondly—"

Bernard cuffed him lightly. "I'd hold my tongue if I was you, little Raven. Unless there's tales you want told."

"Firstly, if you *were* me," Oliver corrected. "Since you are patently not, you require the subjunctive. Secondly, *tales* is plural. Therefore you want the third person plural of the infinitive *to be*. The correct verb form is *are*."

Bernard cuffed him less lightly. "Best not to mind him too much," he told the small crowd of his disciples, some of them cousins. "No manners. Can't help himself. Mother not quite the thing, you know. Bit of a tart. But we don't talk about it much."

George Radford's family had made a fuss of some kind when he married, at age fifty, a divorced lady. But Oliver didn't care what they thought. His father had prepared him for the vicissitudes of Eton and the less-than-likable relatives he could expect to encounter there.

"You're contradicting yourself," Oliver said. "Again."

"No, I'm not, you little fart."

"You said *we* don't talk about her but you did."

"Do you mind, little Raven?"

"Not a bit," Oliver said. "At least when my mother pushed me into the world, she contrived to keep my brain intact. The evidence shows the opposite result in your case."

Bernard yanked him away from the wall and threw him down. The book fell from Oliver's hands and his head rang and he was aware of his heartbeat increasing and a wild panic. He shoved these sensations to the very back of his mind, and pretended the feelings were miles away. He pretended that what was happening to him happened to somebody quite separate, that what he felt was felt by another self, whom he observed with detachment.

The panic vanished, the world came back into balance, and he could think.

He rose onto his elbows. "I'm so sorry," he said.

"You ought to be," Bernard said. "And I hope it's a lesson—"

"I should have read it as 'in an agony to redeem himself,' rather than 'anxious to save himself.'"

Bernard looked blank, not an unusual expression for him.

"Odysseus," Oliver said patiently. He rose, picked up the book, and brushed away the dirt. "He strove in vain for his fellows, whose own witlessness destroyed them. The witless destroy what they don't understand."

Bernard's face got very red. "Witless? I'll teach you witless, you insolent little turd."

He leapt on Oliver, knocked him down, and started punching.

The fight ended for Oliver with a black eye and a bloody nose and ringing ears.

This wasn't the first time. It wasn't the last. But more of that anon.

Royal Gardens, Vauxhall
July 1822

Oliver was baffled, an unusual condition for him.

His experience with women was limited. Mothers didn't count. His stepsisters were somebody else's mothers already.

The Earl of Longmore's sister Lady Clara was, she had announced, eight and eleven-twelfths years old.

Though nursemaids abounded to look after the dizzying numbers of young Fairfaxes, Clara, according to Longmore, was usually let to tag after the boys. Her brothers treated her like a pet, perhaps because she was the first girl after three boys, and something of a curiosity. Then, too, the young Duke of Clevedon, whose guardian Longmore's father was, doted on her.

But tonight's planned activity was not for girls. Clevedon was moving away, gesturing to Longmore to follow.

The latter gave him a nod and told his little sister, "You're not allowed to go in the boat with us."

She kicked him in the ankle. This only made her brother chuckle, but she must have hurt her toe, because her lower lip trembled.

Then, for reasons unknown, Oliver heard himself saying, "Lady Clara, have you ever seen the Hepta-plasiesoptron?"

He was aware of Longmore throwing him a puzzled glance but more aware of the sister, who turned a sulky blue gaze upward to meet his. "What is it?"

"It's a sort of kaleidoscope room," Oliver said. "It's filled with looking glasses, and these reflect twining serpents and a fountain and palm trees and lamps of different colors and other things. It's over there." He pointed to the building containing the Rotunda and the Pillared Saloon. "Shall I take you to see it?"

While Oliver was talking, Longmore slipped away.

"I want to go in the boat," she said.

"I don't," Oliver said.

She looked about and noticed her brother's back retreating from view as he hurried to catch up with Clevedon. Her gaze came back to Oliver, eyes narrowed accusingly now.

"Your brother doesn't want you along," he said. "He doesn't want to worry about your being sick or falling out of the boat and drowning."

"I won't," she said. "I'm never sick."

"You will be if Longmore's rowing," he said. "Why do you think I'm not going?"

She said, "That rhymes."

"So it does," he said. "Shall I show you the Hepta-plasiesoptron? I'll wager anything you can't say it. You're only a girl, and girls aren't very clever."

Her blue eyes flashed. "I can too say it!"

"Go ahead, then."

She screwed up her eyes and mouth, concentrating. Her expression was so comical, he had all he could do not to laugh.

Longmore and Clevedon had come to Eton the year after Oliver arrived. Very much to his surprise, they made a friend of him. This was more or less in the way they made a pet of Lady Clara. They'd dubbed him Professor Raven, which they soon whittled down to Professor.

He'd come to Vauxhall's Second Annual Juvenile Fête because Longmore's father had sent an invitation to join a family excursion, and Oliver's father said he must accept. Oliver had expected to be very bored and irritated, but Vauxhall turned out to be fascinating. It offered acrobats and rope dancers and trained monkeys and dogs, and all sorts of interesting optical illusions and devices, as well as music and fireworks. He didn't at all mind not joining the other boys in the boat.

He hadn't planned on playing nursemaid to a little girl, certainly. But Lady Clara had turned out to be something out of the ordinary, rather like other Vauxhall wonders. She wasn't nearly as stupid as one would expect, considering she was, firstly, a girl and, secondly, related to Longmore. No one had ever accused his lordship of intellectual prowess.

She'd pronounced *Heptaplasiesoptron* correctly by the time they got to it. Equally important, she was perfectly willing to be taught about reflections and optical tricks.

After exhausting the marvels of the Pillared Saloon, they walked on to the Submarine Cave. After her ladyship had her fill of that, they were moving on to the Hermitage when a disagreeably familïar voice called out, "That the best you can do, little cuz? She hasn't even got bubbies yet."

He was distantly aware of his temperature rising and

his heart beating hard and of seeing the world through a red veil. He heard himself speak as though from a great distance to Lady Clara. "Stay," he said.

He marched to his cousin Bernard and punched him in his fat gut.

The fat must have been more solid than it looked, because Bernard only gave a baffled "Huh," before punching back.

Unprepared for the quick reaction, Oliver was an instant too slow to dodge, and the blow made him stumble. Bernard took advantage, hurling his great carcass at Oliver and knocking him down.

The next he knew, Bernard was sitting on him.

Oliver was aware of Lady Clara shouting something, but mainly he was aware of his ears ringing and trouble catching his breath.

Bernard laughed.

Oliver was trying to dislodge him when he heard a wild cry. Lady Clara launched herself at Bernard in a flurry of punching and kicking. This was so funny that for a moment Oliver forgot he couldn't breathe.

Then he saw her lunge at Bernard, and he saw Bernard throw his arm up to shield his face. Oliver wasn't sure what happened next, but he deduced she'd run into his cousin's knuckles or elbow, because she fell back, her hand over her mouth.

Bernard leapt up and yelled, "I didn't do anything!" And ran away.

Oliver saw blood on her hand. He looked about, but Bernard had vanished. He'd picked his moment, as usual, when no adult witnesses were about.

"The bastard," he said. "The cowardly bastard. At least he could have asked if you were all right. Are you all right?"

She took her hand away, then tested a tooth with her

thumb. "Is it broken?" she said. She displayed her teeth. No blood there. It must be Bernard's blood on her hand.

Her teeth were impossibly white and even. Except for the left front incisor.

"Did the one in front always have a chip in it?" he said.

She shook her head.

"It does now," he said.

She shrugged. "I hope the chip's stuck in his elbow and stays there *forever*," she said. Then, in a whisper she added, "The bastard." And giggled.

Perhaps Oliver fell in love with her then.

Perhaps not.

Whether he did or he didn't, after that night he never saw Lady Clara Fairfax again.

Until.

Chapter One

At the head of Whitehall-street is the noted point of Charing cross; and immediately above it lately opened Trafalgar square, where is to be erected a splendid naval monument; and the new national gallery of the fine arts, now in building, is on the north side of the square.

—Calvin Colton, *Four Years in Great Britain*, 1831–35

Environs of Covent Garden, London
Wednesday 19 August 1835

Stop it!" the girl cried. "Get off! I won't go!"

Lady Clara Fairfax, about to alight from her cabriolet, couldn't hear what the boy said, but she heard him laugh and saw him grab Bridget Coppy's arm and try to drag her away from the building she was about to enter. It housed the Milliners' Society for the Education of Indigent Females.

The horse safe in her tiger's keeping, her ladyship snatched up her whip, picked up her skirts, and ran toward the pair. She struck the boy's arm with the whip's butt end. He let out a high-pitched oath.

He was a mean-looking boy, red-haired, with a square, spotty face. He wore the cheap, showy coat she'd learned to associate with the strutting ne'er-do-wells who infested the neighborhood.

"Get away from her, or you'll get more of the same," Clara said. "Leave this place. You've no business here. Be gone before I send for a constable."

The boy eyed her in an insolent manner. The effect was spoiled, however, by his having to stretch his head back and cast his beady-eyed gaze upward a distance, for Clara was not petite and he was not tall. His gaze dropped to the whip in her hand, then to the dashing cabriolet behind her—from which she didn't doubt her maid Davis had descended, brandishing her umbrella.

With a sneer, he said what sounded like, "You better hit harder'n that, you want me to feel it." He didn't wait for her to hit harder, but set his hat at a very sharp angle and sauntered off.

"Are you all right?" she asked Bridget.

"Yes, your ladyship, and thank you ever so," the girl said. "I don't know what was in his mind to come here. He oughter know his sort ain't welcome here."

The Milliners' Society for the Education of Indigent Females housed and educated girls determined, against prodigious odds, to be respectable.

In the ordinary way of things, girls aiming to learn a trade became apprentices. But London's dressmakers could pick and choose their apprentices, and the Milliners' Society girls were outcasts or rejects for one reason or another: The majority were too old to be apprenticed and/or they were "fallen" or carried some other stigma.

The Society picked them up from the gutter—if they were willing to be removed from that location—and did everything possible to make them fit for employment. With practice, diligence, and good eyesight, most girls would learn to sew straight, tiny stitches at great speed, and they could be placed as seamstresses. Some, though, had the potential to rise higher—for instance, to embroider fine muslins, silks, linens, wools, and these materials' numerous combinations. Perhaps one or two might even possess the wherewithal to rise to become successful milliners or dressmakers.

Bridget was fifteen years old. An unsuccessful flower seller, she had appeared on the Society's doorstep after being assaulted and robbed who knew how many times, thanks to her refusing assorted pimps' protection. She had been completely illiterate. She had turned out to be one of the most diligent students and an especially gifted embroiderer. In the display cases, her work always stood out.

Outside the building, so, unfortunately, did her looks.

"I can tell you what was in his mind," Clara said. "He wasn't thinking much beyond the fact of your being pretty and what males think when they see pretty girls."

Lady Clara Fairfax ought to know. Twenty-two years old as of yesterday, she was the most beautiful and sought-after girl in London, and according to some, in all of England.

Small Drawing Room of Warford House
Monday 31 August 1835

Clara did not run screaming from the room. A lady didn't run screaming from anywhere unless her life was in *immediate* danger.

This was simply another marriage proposal.

The Season was over. Almack's had held its last assembly at the end of July. Most of Society had gone to the country. Yet her family remained in London because her father, the Marquess of Warford, never left before Parliament rose, and Parliament still sat.

And so her beaux lingered in London. For some reason—either they'd joined a conspiracy or had made her the subject of wagers in White's betting book—they seemed to be proposing on a biweekly schedule. They were beginning to wear on Clara's nerves.

Today was Lord Herringstone's turn. He said he loved her. They all said so with varying degrees of fervor. But being an intelligent girl who read more than she ought to, Clara was sure that he, like the others, merely wanted to claim the most fashionable girl in London for his own.

She'd inherited the classic Fairfax looks—pale gold hair, clear blue eyes, and skin that seemed to have been poured like cream over an artistically sculpted face. The world agreed that in her these traits had reached the very acme and pitch of perfection. So had her figure, a model for one of those Greek or Roman goddess statues, according to her numerous swains.

Her single flaw—on the outside, that is—the tiny chip in her left front tooth, only made her human and thus, somehow, more perfect.

She was like a thoroughbred everybody wanted to own.

Or the latest style of dashing vehicle.

Her beauty surrounded her like a great stone wall. Men couldn't see above, beyond, or through it. They certainly couldn't think past it.

This was because men only *looked* at women. They didn't listen to women, especially beautiful women.

When beautiful women talked, men merely made a greater pretense of listening. After all, everybody knew that women did not *really* have brains.

Clara wondered what women were imagined to have in their skulls in place of brains or what men thought women did their pitiful excuse for thinking *with* . . .

" . . . if you would do me the inestimable honor of becoming my wife."

She came back to the present and said no, as she always did, kindly and courteously, because she'd been rigorously trained in ladyship. Moreover, she truly liked Lord Herringstone. He'd written odes to her, and they were witty and scanned well. He was amusing and a good dancer and reasonably intelligent.

So were dozens of other men.

She liked them, most of them.

But they had no idea who she was and did not try to find out.

Perhaps it was quixotic of her, but she wanted more than that.

He looked disappointed. Yet he'd survive, she knew. He'd find another woman he would look at and not listen to, but that woman wouldn't be so unrealistic as to expect him to. They'd wed and rub along together somehow or other, like everybody else.

And one of these days Clara would give up hoping for more. One of these days, she would have to say yes.

"Either that," she muttered, "or become an eccentric and run away to Egypt or India."

"My lady?"

Clara looked up. Her lady's maid, Davis, had been standing in the corridor by the door during the marriage proposal. Though the door stood open, though any number of large footmen lurked in Warford House's corridors, and though none of Clara's infatuated swains would dream of uttering a cross word to her, let alone attempt to harm her, Davis remained ever vigilant. People said Davis looked like a bulldog, but looks, Clara very well knew, weren't everything. Not many years older than her charge, Davis had been hired immediately after one of

Clara's many childhood contretemps, this time at Vaux-hall. She protected Clara from fractures, concussions, drowning, and—most important to Mama—Clara's becoming A Complete Hoyden.

"Where is Mama?"

Her mother usually entered close on the heels of rejected swains to wonder Where She'd Gone Wrong with her eldest daughter.

"Her ladyship is in bed with a sick headache," Davis said.

This was probably because she'd had a visit earlier from her poisonous friend Lady Bartham.

"Let's go out," Clara said.

"Yes, my lady."

"To the girls," Clara said. A visit to the Milliners' Society for the Education of Indigent Females would give her a chance to do some good instead of brooding about men. "Please order my cabriolet."

Clara drove herself whenever possible, partly to reduce servants' spying and tattling, but mainly to feel she was in command of something, even if it was one horse pulling a small, two-wheeled vehicle. At least it was a dashing vehicle. Her eldest brother, Harry, the Earl of Longmore, had bought it for her.

"We'll stop on the way and buy some trinkets for the girls." She glanced down at herself. "But I can't go in this. They must see me in my finest finery."

When a proposal could not be avoided, she dressed as unflatteringly as she dared, to make her rejection sting less.

The girls were another matter. The Milliners' Society's founders were London's premier modistes, the proprietresses of Maison Noirot. They made Lady Clara's clothes, and they had taught her that dress was a form of art and a form of manipulation and a language in itself.

Twice they had saved her from what would have been catastrophic marriages.

And so, for their girls, she dressed to inspire.

Charing Cross
A short time later

L ook out! Are you blind? Get out of the way!"

Clara hadn't time to see what she was in the way of when an arm snaked about her waist and yanked her back from the curb. Then she saw the black and yellow gig hurtling toward her.

At the last minute, it swerved away, toward the watermen and boys clustered about the statue of King Charles I. Then once more it veered abruptly off course. It nicked a passing omnibus, struck a limping dog, and swung into St. Martin's Lane, leaving pandemonium in its wake.

Some inches above her head—and plainly audible above the bystanders' shouts and shrieks and the noise of carriages, horses, and dogs—a deep, cultivated voice uttered an oath. The muscular arm came away from her waist and the arm's owner stepped back a pace. She looked up at him, more *up* than she was accustomed to.

His face seemed familiar, though her brain couldn't find a name to attach to it. Under his hat brim, a single black curl fell against his right temple. Below the dark, sharply angled eyebrows, a pair of cool grey eyes regarded her. Her own gaze moved swiftly from his uncomfortably sharp scrutiny down his long nose and firmly chiseled mouth and chin.

The day was warm, but the warmth she felt started on the inside.

"I daresay you noticed nothing about him?" he said. "But why do I ask a pointless question? Everybody flies into a panic and nobody pays attention. The correct question is, Does it matter?" He shrugged. "Only to the dog, perhaps. And in that regard one may say that the driver simply put the wretched brute out of its misery. Let's call it an act of mercy. Well, then. Not injured, my lady? No swooning? No tears? Excellent. Good day."

He touched the brim of his hat and started away.

"A man and a boy in a black Stanhope gig trimmed in yellow," she said to his back. Clara was aware of the tall, black-garbed figure pausing, but she was concentrating, to hold the fleeting image in her mind. "Carriage freshly painted. Blood bay mare. White stripe. White sock . . . off hind leg. No tiger. The boy . . . I've seen him before, near Covent Garden. Red hair. Square face. Spotty. Garish yellow coat. Cheap hat. The driver had a face like a whippet. His coat . . . a better one but not right. *Not* a gentleman."

Her rescuer slowly turned back to her, one dark eyebrow upraised. "Face like a whippet?"

"A narrow, elongated face," she said. With one gloved hand, whose tremor was barely noticeable, she made a lengthening gesture over her own face. "Sharp features. He drives to an inch. He might have spared the dog."

Her rescuer looked her up and down, so briefly Clara wasn't altogether sure he'd done it. But then his expression became acutely intent.

She kept her sigh to herself and her chin upraised, and waited for the wall to go up.

"You're certain," he said.

Why should I be certain? she thought. *I'm only a woman and so of course I have no brain to speak of.*

She said, more impatiently than she ought to, "I could see the dog was barely alive. No doubt boys would have tortured him or a horse would have kicked him or a cart would have rolled over him soon enough. But that driver knew what he was doing. He struck the animal on purpose."

The stranger's keen gaze shifted away from her to scan the square.

"What an idiot," he said. "Making a spectacle of himself. Killing the dog was meant as a warning to me, obviously. A master of subtlety he is not." When his gaze returned to her, he said, "A whippet, you say."

She nodded.

"Well done," he said.

For an instant Clara thought he'd pat her on the head, as one would a puppy who'd learned a new trick. But he only stood there, alternately looking at her then looking about him. His mouth twitched a little, as though he meant to smile, but he didn't.

"That man, whoever he is, is a public menace," she said. "I have an appointment or I should report the incident to the police." She had no appointment. Her visit to the Milliners' Society was a spur-of-the-moment decision. But a lady was not to have anything to do with the police. Even if she got murdered, she ought to do it discreetly. "I must leave the matter to you."

"Firstly, nobody was injured but a dog it's obvious nobody cared about," the gentleman said. "Otherwise the creature would have been a degree more alive to begin with. Secondly, one doesn't pester the police about the demise, violent or otherwise, of a mere canine unless its owner is an aristocrat. Thirdly, it's now clear the fellow was aiming for me when you stepped in the way. I couldn't see him clearly through the"—he gestured at her hat, his mouth twitching again—"the whatnot rising from your head. But Whippet Face . . ." Now he smiled. It wasn't much of a smile, being small and quick, but it changed his face, and her heart gave a short, surprised thump. "He's been trying to kill me this age. He's not the only one. Hardly worth troubling the constabulary."

He gave her the briefest nod, then turned and strode away.

Clara stood staring after him.

Tall, lean, and self-assured, he moved with swift purpose through the sea of people surging over the streets converging on Trafalgar Square. Even after he entered the Strand, he didn't disappear from sight for a while. His hat and broad shoulders remained visible above the mass of humanity until he reached Clevedon House, when a passing coach blocked her view.

He never looked back.

He never looked back.

Moments later, after she'd calmed both her maid and her tiger, Colson, and was giving her horse leave to start, the gentleman's face flashed into her mind, and his voice with its husky overtone seemed to sound again from somewhere above her head. Like a shadow cast by a guttering candle, an image flickered in her brain for a moment. But it was gone before she could make it out. She shrugged, trying to push the incident out of her thoughts, and went on her way, though now and again she did wonder how he'd known to address her as *my lady* . . . and why he hadn't looked back.

Oliver "Raven" Radford, Esquire, didn't need to look back. In the usual way of things, he would have sized up the tall, aristocratic blonde at the first glance. Fairfaxes being ubiquitous, their handsome features distinctive, even Society's outsiders recognized them, and he calculated excellent odds of her being one of the many dubbed Lady This or Lady That.

Yet he'd given her second and third looks, for three reasons.

Firstly, his mind had refused to fully accept the evidence of his eyes. He was observant to a degree not usually associated with human beings—some said he wasn't, quite—and his memory was equally inhuman. But yes, further examination proved milady's attire to be as complicated and demented as his eyes had ascertained.

Secondly, upon that further examination, he felt certain he'd met her before. But he couldn't dredge up from his prodigious memory the time and place.

Thirdly, he realized she'd surprised him.

He couldn't remember the last time anybody had surprised him.

"Face like a whippet," he murmured, and laughed—startling passersby as he strode along the Strand. "Wait until I tell him. He'll want to kill me *twice*, and by inches."

*D*on't look back, you halfwit," said the driver of the Stanhope gig.

The boy, one Henry Brockstopp, better known as Chiver—for his skill with a knife, or chive—said, "That were her! The bleedin' great bitch what come after me with the horsewhip a week or more back. I wish you'd run her down."

This, in any event, is the way his speech would translate into recognizable English.

"Moron." The driver backhanded the boy. "And have every last blue bottle in London after me? And the army, too? How many times do I have to tell you? Don't touch a hair of a nob's head unless you fancy a slow choke on the end of a rope and a nice lie-down later on a sawbones's dissecting table. With a lot of other 'prentice sawbones watching him pull out your liver and such, and all of them laughing at your tiny precious nuts." He laughed. "Leave it to Raven to use the handiest female for a shield."

Jacob Freame, as all London's underworld knew, had a fine sense of humor. He smiled when he squeezed shopkeepers for more protection money. He grinned when one of his bawds led a bumpkin into a brothel he wouldn't come out of alive. He chuckled when his boys kicked in an enemy's head. Always good for a laugh, our Jacob.

"She's big enough," Chiver said sullenly, rubbing the side of his head.

"She can be as big as she wants, because she's quality," Jacob said. "And when you see quality, you take off your hat and you bow low and you say yes ma'am and no ma'am and yessir and nosir. You kiss their arses, you hear me? Nobody cares what we do among our own sort. But you annoy the fine ladies and gentlemen, and trouble comes down on you like a ton of bricks. Do you understand, or do I have to knock it into that thick head of yours?"

"I understand," the boy said. But he'd teach that Bridget Coppy a lesson, wouldn't he? And the Long Meg wouldn't like it much, neither.

Jacob Freame glanced back though his prey was long out of sight. "Maybe another time, then, Raven, eh?" he said. And laughed.

Environs of Covent Garden
Not long thereafter

*T*oday Bridget Coppy was in charge of the Milliners' Society shop. Here visitors could purchase articles the girls made, with profits going to the organization's upkeep. Made by girls of dissimilar talents and experience, the items on offer varied in quality.

"This must be yours," Lady Clara said as she took up a splendidly adorned reticule from the case the girl had opened for her.

"Y-yes, my lady. Only there's a mistake. That knot. It w-wouldn't—" Bridget burst into tears.

She turned away, her pretty face crimson, and hastily

found her handkerchief. "Oh, I'm so sorry, my lady. So sorry."

A lady was never at a loss in any situation. She took pity on the less fortunate, even when she'd chosen to visit the less fortunate as an antidote to her own vexations.

"My dear, I can't even see the offending knot," Clara said. "Your eyes must be very sharp, indeed."

"Yes, I've— No, I mean, it oughter be *perfect*. You can't— Why, what if your ladyship had a dinner dress embroidered with floor de leezes and your ladyship looked down and there was a thread hanging off of one of them? Or—or the bud was crimson when it oughter be rose? Or—" Tears leaked out of the girl's eyes, now as red as her face, and rolled down her nose. She turned away and sniffed, and vigorously wiped away the tears. "Please forgive me, your ladyship. Oh, if Matron sees me—that'll do it, that will."

"Matron's nowhere about," Clara said. "But if you're so upset you can't contain your feelings, the trouble must be very bad. Why, you're one of the most even-tempered and responsible girls here."

"Responsible!" the girl wailed. "If I was, would I be in this fix?"

Two days later

Clara had never before entered the lair of London's lawyers. When a lady needed legal assistance, her attorney went to her. But a lady must not find herself in any kind of situation involving lawyers. If she was so misguided as to need one, she must put the matter in the hands of her husband, father, guardian, brother, or son.

This was why today she wore one of Davis's dresses, hastily altered. This was why she, Davis, and the boy Fenwick traveled by anonymous—and grimy—hackney coach rather than her distinctive cabriolet. The hackney took them from Maison Noirot in St. James's Street, where Fenwick was employed, eastward into Fleet Street. At Inner Temple Gate they left the vehicle and proceeded into Inner Temple Lane.

Soot-darkened buildings of disparate ages crammed together to loom over the Temple, like a very dirty Greek chorus overlooking a tragedy. Clara knew her object resided on the second floor of the Woodley Building. But which was that? Fenwick was trying to decide between two grim edifices brooding over the Temple churchyard when a boy strolled out from among the gravestones. Fenwick applied to him.

Yes, of course he knew where it was, the boy said. Wasn't he only just coming back from an errand of the gravest importance for those same exact gentlemen? And wasn't some people blind, the name being writ up there plain as plain? He pointed to a row of dirty bricks that *might*, under the coating of soot and bird droppings, have been inscribed with the building's name.

Fenwick took exception to the boy's tone and his remarks.

The boy made an impolite suggestion.

Fenwick hit him.

The boy hit back.

Meanwhile, on the second floor of the Woodley Building

*D*ead," Westcott said. "Dead, dead, dead." He waved the letter in Radford's face. "There it is in plain English."

A cold weight settled in Radford's chest. But by now it was instinct to remove himself from the part of him experiencing feelings—i.e., irrationality. He'd taught himself to behave as though this emotional inner self were another

being entirely, and view the matter at hand with detachment. And so, metaphorically speaking, he elbowed aside
this emotional self and calmly took note of Westcott's tone,
the letter's handwriting, and the type of writing paper.

Not Father.

Not dead.

Not yet.

All the same, it took more than his usual strength of
will to say calmly, "Not precisely plain English. You've
overlooked the fact that lawyers have written it."

Thomas Westcott was a solicitor as well as Radford's
friend. Possibly his only friend. The two men shared,
along with chambers in the Woodley Building of Inner
Temple, a young clerk named Tilsley, whose duties included collecting and sorting the post.

Radford did not accept the duty of reading it. Except
for letters from his parents and stepsisters, he let Westcott, in standard solicitor mode, make what he would of
the daily deluge of paper.

"You haven't read it," Westcott said.

Radford didn't need to read it. The legal hand, the
seal, and *dead* sufficed as clues. It came from the Duke
of Malvern's solicitor, and reported the death of a family
member, most probably the duke himself, given the paper's weight, the message's verbosity, and His Grace's
advanced age.

"I'm a barrister," he said. "I can recognize legal gob-
bledygook at twenty paces. Dueling distance. A pity one
can't shoot it, in the way gentlemen resolve so many dif-
ferences. But then, barristers who thrive on sordid criminal cases aren't quite gentlemen, are we?"

He'd happily followed in his father's footsteps. Since
Radford was very good at what he did, he'd never doubted
he'd rise steadily in his profession, righting what wrongs
and stupidities he could on the way.

What he couldn't right or repair were the other Radfords.

Bernard's grandfather had set his sons and their sons' wives and children against one another. He was a selfish, vindictive, manipulative man, and his offspring carried on in the same style. Radford's grandfather, being intelligent and observant, had observed this destructive family behavior and intelligently decided to have no part of it.

Father felt the same way. Ages ago he'd said, "The only way to keep your mind from being poisoned is to stay far away from them. Live another life, son. Live your own life."

This was exactly what Raven Radford had done. He wanted no part of the ducal vipers' nest, and especially not now.

Three months ago, at Grumley's pauper farm, a place where the poorhouses sent their excess children, five little ones had died. Fever was the ostensible cause. In fact, Grumley's system of neglect, starvation, and filth had killed them. An inquest had found him guilty of manslaughter. This verdict had led to the criminal trial Radford was prosecuting at present, the most challenging of his career to date.

He took the document from his friend and scanned it for loopholes. He was distantly aware of the inner weight's return. His face wore a bored expression.

"Only Bernard left," he said. "How the devil do they do it?"

The previous Duke of Malvern, Bernard's father, had possessed, in the way of near relatives, three brothers as well as, by his second marriage, three sons. Over the years, nearly all the males, young and old, had contrived to die, some of illness, some in accidents.

"One would think they were at least capable of breeding," he said. "Blind sheep can do it."

"The royal family has a similar problem," Westcott said. "King George III sired nine sons. And our present heir presumptive? An adolescent girl."

"A pity the dukedom can't go to a girl," Radford said. "Those they've got a surfeit of. But the girls can't inherit, and it isn't my problem." He tossed the letter onto Westcott's desk.

"Radford, if the present duke dies—"

"Bernard is not thirty years old. His wife is five and twenty. He'll keep trying for sons."

Bernard had better not die for at least fifty years. Radford didn't need the letter to remind him his father had become next in line to inherit. George Radford was eighty years old, and in poor health.

A fever last winter had permanently undermined his health. His chances of surviving the coming winter were not good. He was going to die, sooner rather than later. He ought to be allowed to die in peace, with his wife at his side, at Ithaca House, the peaceful villa in Richmond he'd named after the mythical Ulysses's longed-for home. The last thing Father needed was the annoyance of taking over vast estates whose affairs had been mismanaged for years.

"Her Grace's health, according to the letter, is precarious," Westcott said.

"I'm not surprised," Radford said. "The odds of her dying in childbed are very high, as are those of any woman who endures numerous pregnancies. You may be sure that, as soon as she's dead, he'll wed again, no matter how old he is. His father started a second family in his fifties."

Radford's own father had married for the first time at fifty because he couldn't afford to marry earlier. This was why Radford and Bernard had been schoolmates.

Westcott took up the letter and read it through again.

"Something isn't right," he said. "I can't put my finger on it, but I'm sure there's a meaning here we've overlooked. I can't seem to read between the lines, and you refuse to."

"I'll tell you what isn't right," Radford said. "It only purports to be a legal document. Amid the lawyerly convolutions do you distinguish anything more pressing than a summons from Bernard? Can you ascertain anything to be gained by my heeding it?"

"You might at least take the trouble to find out what he wants."

"Now? Have you forgotten the Grumley case?"

"I could go in your place," Westcott said. "As your solicitor."

"Neither you nor anybody else will represent me in this. You don't know Bernard."

Father could deal with the lack-brained bully if he had to, but there was no reason he ought to. The last thing he needed now was strain and aggravation. Radford had better write to his mother straightaway, warning her.

"He'll only waste your time for the fun of it," Radford said. "You and I have more useful things to do. For the present, I aim to send that villain Grumley to—" He glared at the door. "Who's there? Where the devil is Tilsley?"

"If you refer to your clerk, he's punching a boy in the churchyard."

The voice, though muffled by the closed door, was clearly feminine. And aristocratic.

Westcott, while not as observant as his friend—who was?—had no trouble recognizing the diction of the upper reaches of the upper classes. Some of his clients lived in these exalted realms. He hurried to the door and opened it.

The tall blonde walked in.

Chapter Two

Juvenile delinquents . . . are found in every part of the metropolis . . . Many of them . . . are in the regular employ and training of older thieves; others obtain a precarious subsistence by begging, running errands, selling play-bills, picking pockets, and pilfering from shops and stalls.
—John Wade, *A Treatise on the Police and Crimes of the Metropolis*, 1829

Following a long climb up dark, narrow stairs, Clara and Davis had found, along a passage lined with black doors, the one bearing the name they wanted.

Davis had knocked thrice before the men inside took any notice. They seemed to be arguing, but Clara couldn't be sure.

One of the voices—the deeper one—sounded familiar.

But Clara hadn't placed it by the time she walked in. When the pale grey gaze fixed on her, she started in surprise. Heat sprang from several inner places at once and raced up to her neck and face as well as to areas ladies did not acknowledge to anybody, including themselves.

This was a disturbing development, but a lady always

appeared to be in control, even when she felt as though she'd walked into a lamppost.

"Lady Clara," he said. His keen grey gaze traveled over her, swiftly assessing. "Is that supposed to be a cunning disguise?"

The other gentleman said, "Radford, what the—"

Clara held up her hand, silencing him. If she didn't immediately seize control, they would. They'd treat her like a child, the way men usually treated women, especially young women. They'd murmur soothing things and send her on her way. They might even tattle to Papa's solicitor. She doubted any lawyerly rules of confidentiality applied to women.

Do not show uncertainty or anxiety, she commanded herself. *For once in your life you can do something more productive than decline marriage offers.*

She adopted her paternal grandmother's autocratic manner.

"Thanks to you, I now know who he is," she said to the other man, who was a degree shorter and fairer, and not dressed entirely in black. "It is immaterial to me how he knows who I am. You must be the eminent solicitor Mr. Thomas Westcott. I haven't much time, and I should prefer not to waste it on formalities. As your colleague has so cleverly ascertained, I am Lady Clara Fairfax. This is my maid, Davis. The boy Fenwick, who is trying to kill your clerk, advised me to consult you."

As she let her glance rest briefly on the tall, dark man, the sense of familiarity she'd experienced at Charing Cross returned. "He seems to believe Mr. Radford is peculiarly equipped to assist us with a problem."

"He's peculiar, I'll give you that," said Mr. Westcott.

"This isn't about the mangy dog, is it?" Mr. Radford said. "Because the police have more important matters—"

"It's about a pauper boy," Clara said.

Mr. Radford stalked to the window and looked down. "And you wanted us? Can't mean the fellow down there. He's holding his own. No, wait. Better. He's giving Tilsley a Chancery suit on the nob. That boy of yours looks familiar."

Having spent a part of her childhood with three older brothers, she knew what he was looking at. A Chancery suit on the nob involved getting one's opponent's head under one's arm and punching said head with the free hand.

"You're familiar to him, which is why we're here," Clara said.

"What's the brat calling himself now?" Mr. Radford said.

"He doesn't call himself anything," Clara said. "He could teach clams a thing or two. His employers call him Fenwick. And he seemed to think you could help us find a boy named Toby Coppy."

Mr. Radford turned away from the window. "Friend of—er—Fenwick?"

She'd spent the last two days studying the notorious Raven Radford, no easy task, even had she not had to keep her mission secret from her family.

His name didn't feature in the usual accounts of parliamentary or social doings. Mainly his name appeared in reports of criminal proceedings, some dauntingly lengthy. From what she'd read, he seemed to be sharp-witted, learned, and tactless to a spectacular degree. Though she hadn't had time to read everything, she'd thought it amazing he'd won so many cases, when judges, witnesses, juries, and even his own clients must have wanted to throttle him.

She, for instance, was already growing irritated.

"If I might begin at the beginning," she said. "Rather than proceed along the haphazard route of your questions."

One black eyebrow went up. "Haphazard," he said.

"That was a setdown, in case you didn't recognize it," Mr. Westcott told him.

"I thought so," Mr. Radford said.

"Not that snubs have the least effect on him, my lady," Mr. Westcott said, "even when he recognizes them as such. Brilliant otherwise, of course."

"So I've been informed," Clara said, "else I wouldn't be here."

"Certainly, my lady," Mr. Westcott said. "And since your ladyship has taken the trouble to be here, we ought to proceed in an orderly fashion. Frankly, I'm puzzled why a man renowned for his fanatical attachment to logic has been perambulating into detours in this strange manner. If your ladyship will be so good as to take a chair—here, by the fire—or what is, in colder weather, a fire. It's cleaner—"

He broke off as Davis advanced and wiped the chair with a handkerchief and him with a censorious eye.

"Yes, quite so, thank you," Mr. Westcott said. "And if her ladyship would make herself comfortable, I should be happy to take notes. Radford, we don't need you at present." He gave Clara an apologetic smile. "Only if it comes to trial, naturally, which—"

"It will save time if I listen," Mr. Radford said.

"No, it won't," Mr. Westcott said. "Because you'll interrupt."

"I shall remain as silent as the churchyard denizens under our window," Mr. Radford said. "The ones below-ground, that is."

He folded his arms and leaned back against the window frame.

"Kindly proceed, my lady. I'm all ears."

*I*t was the chipped tooth.

When she walked in and caught sight of him,

her composure disintegrated, her mouth fell open, and for a moment she looked like an astonished little girl.

Radford knew that little girl.

She recovered with remarkable speed, but Radford had seen all he needed to.

The distinctive Fairfax features he'd identified the other day . . . assorted bits he'd read in newspapers and magazines . . . the nagging sense of familiarity.

With the chipped tooth, the last piece of the puzzle fell into place.

This wasn't merely one of the numerous Fairfax family members he'd seen from time to time in his perambulations through London.

This was the little girl to whom he'd shown Vauxhall's Heptaplasiesoptron. This was the little girl who'd tried to rescue him from Cousin Bernard.

She was all grown up and dressed in what she fondly imagined was a disguise.

Unlike the comical hat she'd worn in Charing Cross, her bonnet was dull and dark, boasting nothing in the way of adornment but a darker ribbon. Its large brim did not tilt up in the way the hat had done, to show her perfect face framed in lace and bows. It tilted downward, its shadow concealing her countenance. That was clever, actually. A veil—the usual ruse for ladies—would have called attention to her attempt to appear incognito.

All the same, he would have known her for the Charing Cross female anywhere, even had she been wearing a veil. The drab dress failed to disguise her posture and figure.

Remarkably fine figure, he was aware of his irrational self thinking. It proceeded to imagine said figure in its natural state. Such meditations were not conducive to clear thinking.

He wrestled the other self into a dark corner in the

back of his mind and focused on watching the lady ignore the chair Westcott had offered and her maid had scoured.

Lady Clara remained where she was, posture upright—

Horizontal would be better, said the inner voice of unreason.

He ignored it and listened to a tale told with a conciseness he would have believed incompatible with the female brain, such as it was. In a shockingly few words, she contrived to explain what the Milliners' Society was and who Bridget Coppy was.

"Her father is dead," she said. "The mother is a hopeless drunkard who takes in mending on the rare occasions she's sober. The Milliners' Society has taught Bridget to read and write a little. She persuaded her brother to attend a ragged school. I know I needn't explain to you what that is."

Ragged schools were pitiful attempts to teach pauper children the basics they needed to improve their lot in life. The teachers were unpaid, many of them nearly as ignorant as the children. All the same, it was better than the nothing otherwise available to London's impoverished masses.

Most members of the upper classes had never heard of ragged schools. Being a duke's great-grandson, Radford was, technically, a member of the upper classes. His life had been different from most, though, and he knew all about these schools.

The note of distress in her voice told him the schools were a very recent and disturbing discovery for her.

She had no idea how some people lived in London, practically under her nose.

But why should she? And how odd it was, her having discovered even so much.

She was saying, "With Bridget's help, Toby was learning to read and write and do sums. But as you know, less reputable types hang about the ragged schools. Bridget says a gang of thieves has lured him out of school, and she hasn't seen him for more than a week."

The day, which had brightened remarkably when Her Majesty sailed into his chambers, reverted to its customary grey.

A missing child of the lower orders. Radford knew where this story led. Not to a happy ending.

First the accursed ducal letter.

Now another boy lost among London's teeming thousands of unwanted children.

Why couldn't she have come to him because she'd murdered somebody?

That would have been so much more promising, not to mention stimulating.

"Bridget wishes to remove him from the gang before they get him hanged," she went on. "She's sure the police will take him up in short order. She does not believe her brother has the intelligence or dexterity to be a successful thief—not for long, at any rate."

Oh, better and better.

Very likely there was more to this than met the eye. It didn't matter. The boy was doomed.

She was wasting her time as well as Radford's. She was completely deluded if she thought the brat could or ought to be rescued. But of course she wouldn't believe him. She hadn't the least idea what she was about.

He said, "Do you know which gang, precisely?"

"Fenwick has been unable to find out," she said.

"Does that tell you anything?"

"That London holds a great many gangs."

"And therefore . . . ?" he led the witness.

She regarded him with a polite expression, her gracefully arched eyebrows slightly raised.

By now Westcott ought to have leapt in to state the

obvious or at least give the *don't* signal, warning Radford he went too far. He glanced at his friend.

Westcott was gaping at her as though he'd never seen a girl before.

No, in point of fact, he was doing the opposite: what men always did when they looked at women. He was admiring her breasts in what he must suppose was a surreptitious manner, and had become fully absorbed in that endeavor.

Hers, Radford would readily admit, were uncommonly good. Either that or her undergarments were constructed to make them look good. He'd debated this point with himself when he met her the other day. Whatever the truth of the matter, Westcott had no business drooling over them.

The part of him Radford kept tightly confined was developing a fantasy of pitching his friend and colleague out of the window.

Thrusting the mental image aside, he said, "Does the phrase 'needle in a haystack' signify anything to your ladyship?"

"Let me think," she said. She screwed up her mouth and eyes in an exaggerated effort of thinking. He remembered the little girl learning to say *Heptaplasiesoptron*.

"Yes," she said. "Yes, it does, shockingly enough."

"Good," he said. "Because—"

"Fenwick assured me you'd know how to find Toby if anybody would. And you've made a name for yourself as an advocate for pauper children."

"I suspect that's because advocating for paupers, being unusual to the point of bizarre, makes sensational headlines," he said. "In fact, mainly I appear in court for very boring cases: poisonings and burglaries and assault and libel and such." Few of these cases attracted the more respectable newspapers' attention. The rare cases that did tended to focus on plaintiff, accused, and lurid witness statements, not boring lawyers. Until recently.

"But the Grumley case—"

"Ah, yes, the sensational one," he said. "Which demands my full attention at present. I promise you, the judge will not give me a leave of absence to hunt down this boy, even had I any hope of finding him, with a year to do it in."

An emotion flickered in her eyes, but even he, usually so perceptive of the subtlest facial cues, couldn't decide whether she was disappointed or . . . relieved?

Not that it mattered in the least.

"Yes, of course," she said. "I've read about the Grumley horror. I should have realized . . . How silly of me. You have your work cut out for you there. In that case, perhaps you can advise me how to proceed."

"I strongly recommend you leave it alone," he said. "These sorts of things never turn out—" He broke off because her chin went up another notch and her posture stiffened, and he was forcibly reminded of the girl who'd kicked her brother in the ankle.

"But how silly of me," he said. "You're not going to leave it alone."

"No."

He looked to Westcott. No help at all. Had the dome of St. Paul's slid off and onto his head, he could not have looked more stupidly oblivious. You'd think he'd never seen an attractive woman before.

Admittedly she was more than usually attractive. But still.

His other self had something to say on this point. Radford stifled him.

"In that case," he said, "I should recommend, firstly, that you read Sir John Wade's *Treatise on the Police and Crimes of the Metropolis*."

"Mr. Radford," she said.

"You needn't read the whole thing, but you might wish to skim at least the chapter dealing with juvenile delinquents," he said. "Secondly, in the event Wade leaves you undaunted, I recommend you hire a member of the Metropolitan Police as a detective. I highly recommend Inspector Keeler." A former Bow Street Runner, Keeler was, in Radford's opinion, the best of the best: quiet, persistent, and a genius at blending into his surroundings, no matter what disguise he donned.

Her head tipped slightly to one side, and she studied him with an expression that seemed to hover between patience and exasperation. He wasn't quite sure. Along with maturity, her countenance seemed to have acquired a sort of screen or veil.

"It seems I was misinformed," she said. "I was told you were the cleverest man in London."

Westcott made a choked sound.

"To my knowledge, you were not misinformed," Radford said.

She bit her lower lip, bringing the chipped tooth into sight for a tantalizing instant. "How odd," she said. "Because I should have supposed that even a man with a very small brain and only the dimmest awareness of Society's million unwritten rules would realize that I'm not in a position to engage detectives. Ladies, you see, Mr. Radford, are not permitted to hire professionals, except in a domestic capacity."

"Right," he said. "I wonder how that slipped my mind. Perhaps it was your appearing here in cunning disguise. Most intrepid of you."

"I'm in disguise because ladies are not allowed to haunt the Temple in search of lawyers."

"But you do see how I might have thought otherwise," he said. "Looking at you, I might suppose an upheaval in social mores had occurred while I was busy elsewhere, getting criminals hanged—or not, as the case may be."

"Mores have not changed an iota from what they were in my mother's time," she said. "If anything, they've grown stricter. My grandmother—but I digress, and I know your time is precious. You seek justice for five innocent children, a Herculean task. I apologize for taking you away from that worthy challenge for even a moment. If you have no useful advice for me, I'll leave you to it."

"Might you offer a reward?" he said. "Or is that not allowed, either?"

She gazed searchingly at him this time. She must be trying to read him. That would take some doing, since he wasn't fully present, in a manner of speaking. He stood apart from himself as he always did—or tried to do. Today he was having to work harder than usual at merely observing the proceedings.

"Do you know nothing whatsoever about ladies and the rules they must live by?" she said.

"Your ladyship would be amazed at how little he knows in that regard," Westcott said. "Haven't seen him much at Almack's, have you? Never marked his presence at Court? A person would never guess his father was the Duke of Malvern's heir presumptive—"

"As though that signified in the least," Radford said sharply. "The beau monde and I are not well acquainted, for obvious reasons, I should think, they spending little time in criminal courts, and I being gainfully employed therein."

"Then I had better explain, lest the next lady you encounter decide you are deranged or brainless," she said.

"Do you suppose that's of any consequence to me?" he said.

"I should think a lady's opinion of you would carry some weight were she considering your services to prosecute a villain," she said. "Or, say, in a case of homicide, if she hoped to avoid the gallows."

"If you kill anybody, Lady Clara," he said, "I shall be only too happy to offer my services."

"If I kill anybody," she said, "I shall be far too discreetly ladylike about it to get caught. But I thank you for the offer."

He looked into her unusually attractive face and believed her. "May one ask—"

"One may not," she said. "That would spoil the fun. In the meantime, I ought to point out to you that a nobleman's daughter may not hire detectives or post rewards for missing children. If we were permitted to do such useful things, why, where would it stop? Why should we not hire detectives to help us find husbands? Or post rewards for same? I daresay we should have a better chance of finding our soul mates in that manner than you seem to think I shall have in finding Toby Coppy."

"I should think advertising would save a deal of bother," he said. "All those nonsensical social rituals—"

"My lady, as my colleague has indicated, the chances of finding this boy are truly not at all good, especially in our present harassed circumstances," Westcott said.

Radford looked at him. Westcott made the small, quick gesture of cutting his throat, meaning *don't. Now* he signaled? Just when the conversation finally took an educational and entertaining turn?

"Even if our docket were not full," the solicitor went on, "we should not advise attempting it. In our experience—"

"*However*," Radford cut in before his fool friend could launch into the gory particulars, "in the event your efforts, with or without a detective, prove futile, you're welcome to return to us. When the boy is arrested, that is. Then we might be of real use."

The odds were strongly against Toby Coppy's staying alive long enough to get arrested, but she seemed to have some noble notion of Saving Him, and Radford recognized fatal obstinacy when he saw it.

She studied him for a time, in the way she'd done before.

Nothing in the searching blue gaze told him she remembered him from that long-ago time.

And why, pray, should she? A lifetime had passed since then. They'd spent together perhaps an hour in total. She'd been a child and he'd been merely one of her brother's many schoolmates. She'd seen him only the once. Radfords were common enough in England—or had been. Very likely, she hadn't even known his name. Longmore never called him anything but "Professor." Except for that hour, Radford and she had lived worlds apart. Even when she was in London with the rest of Fashionable Society, she might as well live on the moon.

Not to mention that even he, with his famous memory and exceptional powers of observation, wouldn't have known her if he hadn't had a glimpse of her tooth. The one she'd chipped trying to save him from his idiot cousin.

She said, "Thank you, Mr. Radford, I'll bear that offer in mind as well."

"We do greatly regret that we can't offer your ladyship more help," Westcott said.

Of course he regretted. He couldn't get enough of gawking at her.

She gave a little wave. "I quite understand. My foolish mistake." She started for the door, and Westcott hurried to open it. She paused there and smiled, and a ray of light seemed to brighten the somber room. "Well, then, no injuries, gentlemen?" she said. "No swooning? No tears? Excellent. Good day, Mr. Westcott."

"Good day, my lady."

"Good day . . . Professor," she said. She gave a little laugh, and left.

Professor?

"Professor?" Westcott said.

Radford was staring at the closed door.

He started toward it, then stopped.

"What did she mean?" Westcott said. "About the injuries and swooning? That sounded like you."

"It was me." Radford brought his attention back—from Vauxhall and wherever else it had wandered to—to his friend. "The other day in Charing Cross, when Freame tried to run me down, the lady stepped in the way. Even he could see she was quality. Murdering annoying barristers is one thing, but an aristocratic female is an altogether different article. He swerved away, no doubt cursing vehemently, and plotting future violence."

Radford had been instrumental in sending six of Freame's favorite minions to permanent residence in penal colonies and two to eternity.

"Freame tried to kill you *again*?" Westcott said. "And you did not see fit to mention it to me? Attempted *murder*?"

"Good luck proving he aimed for me." Radford faced a more difficult problem of proof in the Grumley case, one the defense was taking full advantage of, with the lackwit judge's eager assistance.

"You did not see fit to mention the lady, either, I notice," Westcott said.

"The incident did not strike me as important."

Westcott's eyes widened.

"Had she been injured, naturally, I should have had him taken up," Radford said. "The swine killed a cur on its last legs, but the world regards stray mongrels as a nuisance. Scavengers collected it in no time, and the excitement was soon over. The lady and I did not introduce ourselves. She went her way and I went mine."

Westcott gave him one of his looks. It wasn't altogether unlike Lady Clara's—the one of mingled exasperation and patience and perhaps, yes, there was an element of wonder in it, too. On Lady Clara's face, however, the expression was more arresting.

Of course, he was used to Westcott.

And she was prettier. By a factor of six hundred.

"At first, she seemed surprised to see you," Westcott said.

"She came to see *us*," Radford said. "Why should she associate the fellow in Trafalgar Square with the pedant who wastes the court's time with tiresome pauper children? But it happened only the other day. Small wonder she remembered. Clearly it amused her to quote my own words back to me."

"I should like to know how anyone who'd met you would forget," Westcott said. "Unless you kept silent, which I am certain is a physical impossibility. And *Professor*?" Westcott's eyebrows rose in a most annoying manner.

"A nickname her eldest brother gave me when we were at Eton. She must have put two and two together and concluded I was the Radford he and Clevedon called Professor."

He'd been *positive* she hadn't remembered him from Vauxhall. He was deeply, painfully curious how she'd worked it out and how she'd contrived to do so without offering the smallest clue she was doing it.

A most intriguing veil or screen.

He couldn't remember encountering such outside the criminal classes, and even there it was rare. Most criminals were not intelligent. They could be sly, yes, and they lied splendidly, but they were by no means difficult for a practiced eye to read.

She was intelligent and . . .

He became aware of himself following this path of thought and stopped. He hadn't time for pointless speculation, especially about women who belonged to another universe. The Grumley trial was in its very last stages, and matters looked extremely unpromising.

She'd known that, too. How did she—

No, he did not have time to think about her.

He had windmills to tilt at.

The Old Bailey
Three days later

$\mathscr{N}$ot guilty.

Radford glanced up at the visitors' gallery, where Lady Clara Fairfax sat, in disguise once more, the bulldog maid in attendance. Her ladyship had appeared there every day since their encounter in Westcott's office.

She wore more or less what she'd worn that day. But for court, she'd done something to make her silken skin appear rough and dull, and she'd perched spectacles on her perfect nose. Still, he had no trouble recognizing her or the signs she gave of dismay. When the verdict was read, her mouth sagged, and she put her gloved hand up to her eye. Only a moment passed before the invisible screen came down, but that was more than enough time for him.

He became distantly aware of having failed her, and images rose in his mind of tearing the wig from his head and stomping on it, leaping into the dock and throttling Grumley, grabbing the judge and dashing his head against the bench.

That was his other, irrational self.

The rational Raven Radford would have been astounded had the verdict gone the other way.

All the same, it bothered him. He detached himself

in the usual way, but the method didn't work in the usual way. Even detached, he saw her mischievous smile when she'd exited his chambers the other day, and heard the short, light laugh she'd given at the startled expression he must have worn.

He did not understand how she'd found him out then and he did not understand why she'd appeared in court. Her disguise told him she oughtn't to be there, and must have come at some risk. Why?

St. James's Street
Monday 7 September

"Oy! You!"

Radford glanced toward the voice.

A young male in fantastical lilac and gold livery jerked his head toward a passage near the shop window where Radford lounged.

The boy had taken notice of him some minutes ago, but didn't leave his post at the dressmakers' shop door immediately. After he'd ushered in a lady, the footboy or porter or whatever he was casually crossed St. James's Street, summoned Radford in this suave manner, and stepped into Crown and Scepter Court.

Radford followed him into the narrow passage. He saw that from here the boy could keep an eye on Maison Noirot's door and dart across the street, should he be needed.

"Well, then, whatchyer want?" the lad said.

Radford regarded the blinding livery for a moment. Then, "Jonesy," he said. "That's a clever disguise."

"It's my *clothes*," the boy said. "I got a job."

"Ah."

"And it ain't Jonesy, neither. It's Fenwick." The boy's eyes narrowed, daring Radford to laugh.

"I heard something to that effect." Though he advised others to hire detectives, Radford was quite a good one. His profession often required it. His nature demanded it. He was drawn to mysteries and puzzles the way other men were drawn to gaming or drink.

He'd pursued the Fenwick riddle among his numerous contacts on the London streets.

"The French dressmakers," Radford said, nodding toward the shop opposite.

"They stole me right off the street." The boy leaned toward him, his face a picture of shocked innocence.

"I heard it was off the back of a carriage, when you were trying to empty a gentleman's pockets. That was stupid. And you were one of the few of that lot with a brain."

"It's a long story."

"Don't tell it to me," Radford said. "I haven't time. I need to send a message to a female." He explained.

Fenwick stared at him for a moment, then went off into whoops. The hilarity lasted for some time.

Radford waited.

"You!" the boy said when he caught his breath.

"It's not—" *what you think*, Radford very nearly said. He caught himself in time. What the boy thought was immaterial.

"Yer barkin' up the wrong tree, Raven," the boy said. "All her gennelmen is nobs, mainly, and you can get in line behind the other five hundred and sixty."

"Yes, well, I'm cleverer than any of them."

Fenwick cogitated upon this, his expression skeptical.

"It's about the truant boy, Toby Coppy," Radford said. "You do remember? You led her to me the other day." He studied Fenwick's face. "By the way, I notice the swelling has gone down."

"He looks worse'n me!"

"Tilsley does look a good deal worse, and his bruises, unlike yours, don't match his regalia."

Fenwick narrowed his eyes at him.

"Your *ensemble*, I believe the dressmakers would call it," Radford said.

Fenwick looked down at his lilac and gold splendor. "They said I could pick what I wanted."

"And you wanted to look like Louis XIV," Radford said.

Fenwick's brow knit. "I fink I know which one he was," he said. "They been teaching me. I can read and write now. And I can do ands."

"Hands?" Radford said.

"*Ands*," Fenwick said more loudly, as if to a deaf person or foreigner. "What's fourteen and six and six again? Twenty-six. *Ands!*"

"Ah. Well, then, what does sixpence and sixpence come to?"

"Twelvepence. A bob!"

"Exactly." Radford took out a shilling. "Here it is, if you're clever enough to smuggle a message to the lady."

Fenwick folded his arms and eyed the coin with disdain.

"A shilling, you little thief," Radford said. "That's twelve times the going rate, and you know it."

"The other fellers pay me more," the brat said.

"I'm not the other fellows," Radford said. "If you won't do it, I'll find another way, and you know I can."

Fenwick shrugged and started to exit the passage.

Radford told himself to walk away. His was idle curiosity, no more, and he hadn't time for it. He'd a new case to prepare for. He had to shield his parents from the accursed Bernard.

Radford had his own life, and she wasn't and never would be part of it.

Her path would never have crossed his if not for a missing boy who by now was either permanently lost in the thieves' kitchen or already a corpse.

If he sought her out, she'd think he wanted to help. And her mission was futile. It wouldn't turn out as she hoped. Boys went wrong all the time, and the best he could do was spare them the gallows. He didn't always succeed.

He would leave it alone, as he'd advised her to do.

It was the only rational course of action.

"Wait, you little brigand," he said. "Here's another shilling."

Chapter Three

Such a place of filth, and tipsy jollity, and nocturnal rows, and squalid wretchedness, is no where to be found, except on "Saffron Hill" in the vicinity of Fleet Ditch, where a large portion of the indigenous poverty of the metropolis is congregated.
—Nathaniel Sheldon Wheaton, *A Journal of a Residence During Several Months in London*, 1830

The following day

The Milliners' Society for the Education of Indigent Females stood in a row of narrow, grimy buildings not far from the Bow Street Police Office.

The rear of the building looked out upon a cramped courtyard. Undersized and starved for light, this patch of ground strove, like the girls within, to be something better. Someone had created a facsimile of a garden under the stunted trees. Someone had swept every trace of debris from the ground. Only one lonely leaf marred its neat order, and that, Radford felt sure, would soon be dispatched. Here and there a pot of flowers brightened the gloom. A bench, whose paint had been refreshed within recent months, stood under one of the dingy trees.

Head bowed, face in her hands, Bridget Coppy sat on the bench and wept.

Lady Clara chose that moment to arrive.

Actually, calling it an arrival was like calling the eruption of Vesuvius a fire.

Her ladyship wore a pink explosion of embroidered organdy boasting the gigantic sleeves still, against all reason, in fashion. The dress revealed more of Lady Clara's creamy neck than ladies usually displayed by day, and the satin handkerchief, edged in ruffled Valenciennes lace and looped rather than tied at the neckline, didn't fully cover the indiscreet-for-day bits.

Though no fashion connoisseur, Radford had an eye for detail. This and a quickly acquired fluency in the arcane language of dress had proved crucial in two burglaries, one fraud, and one assault with violence.

This must explain why he noticed exactly how low from the shoulder the sleeve was cut, the size of the waist the belt encircled, the snugness of fit above the waist, and the amount of satiny skin, in inches, visible above the handkerchief's loop.

A rice straw hat topped off the lunacy. Blond lace framed the inside brim, where a pink bow fluttered near her right eye. On the outside, flowers, leaves, and sprigs leapt skyward from a bower of ribbons and bows, to add some ten inches to her height.

None of this explained why the wan little garden seemed to perk up and brighten, nor did he choose to pursue the question.

Bridget had jumped up from the bench and curtseyed the instant Lady Clara appeared. Now, though, as she took in her ladyship's ensemble, her mouth fell open and only her gaze moved, up and down and all over the apparition in organdy. This stopped the waterworks, in any event, for which he was grateful.

"Lady Clara," he said. "You're punctual to the minute." He didn't take out his pocket watch. He had an accurate idea of time, especially when it was wasted. Of the last five and twenty minutes, all but four, by his measure, fell into that category.

"I seem to be late," she said with a glance at the red-eyed Bridget. "But your message stipulated two o'clock."

"I wished to speak to Miss Coppy before you arrived," he said. This would spare his having to listen to two females talking at the same time, which females invariably did. "As I supposed, she's told me very little more than what you told me, but in thrice as many words, punctuated by tears."

Lady Clara surveyed the girl, who regained her senses sufficiently to wipe her eyes with the back of her hand.

"It was Toby, your ladyship," she said. "He come by last night. He was so horrid. It come into my mind when Mr. Radford was asking me questions."

Toby was still alive. Given this fact, and what Bridget had told him about an encounter with a nasty piece of work known as Chiver, Radford was beginning to formulate a theory, one he didn't much like.

Meanwhile, he was still trying to detach himself from the news that her ladyship had attacked one of the London underworld's most feared young cutthroats with her horse-whip.

"Are you sure you want to save him?" he said. "We might be able to retrieve him, but you can't expect us to undo the corruption of his mind."

Bridget nodded. "He's led easy enough, and once I have him home again and back in school—"

"He's very likely to be led away again," Radford said. Had the mother not been an inebriate, he would have had more hope. Not much more, admittedly.

"If he does it again, I'll wash my hands," Bridget said. "But I know school's hard for him, and he isn't clever. I'll try to get him a place as an apprentice. But if he won't stick to it, there's no more I can do."

"We'll help you find a place for him," Lady Clara said.

"We?" Radford said.

"Yes." Her ladyship gave him a level look.

He gave her one back, then said to Bridget, "You may return to your duties. I can report to Lady Clara more succinctly as a soloist."

Bridget looked blank.

"It's all right, Bridget," Lady Clara said. "Do go in. But wipe your face properly first. You don't want Matron wondering what Mr. Radford said to make you cry."

The girl found her already damp handkerchief, scrubbed her face with it, bobbed several confused curtseys at them, and finally left.

"I did not make her cry," Radford said. "She wanted no assistance in that regard. The ticklish part was getting her to tell the story in a logical manner."

Lady Clara gazed at him in the way of a patient teacher encumbered with a student of slow understanding. "She's fifteen," she said. "She's barely educated. She doesn't know Euclid from Eucharist. Where do you imagine she would have learned logic?"

"One and one makes two," he said. "She wouldn't go from Whitechapel to Shoreditch by way of Bloomsbury. It doesn't require a knowledge of geometry or Aristotle to understand the shortest distance between two points, whether it's furlongs or words."

"Judging by the speech your honorable friend made in court yesterday, the concept isn't clear even to university-educated gentlemen."

"Right," he said. "Why were you in court, by the way?"

"I was trying not to get married," she said.

He was, momentarily, lost, in an unexpected flurry of emotions too confused for him to sort, let alone name. But he swiftly set aside his bewildered other self, his brain returned to work, and he said, "That would appear to be a brand-new way to go about it. But if anybody would set the fashion, I reckon it would be Lady Clara Fairfax."

"You've been studying me," she said.

"You studied me," he said.

"Due diligence, do you call it?" she said. "You're interesting. You were an interesting boy, I recollect. I had better walk about. Some of the girls will be watching at the windows, and the dress shows to best advantage in motion. I'm told they like to see me in my finery. It's good for their morale."

While he was trying to digest *interesting boy*— *irritating* was the more familiar adjective—she began a slow circuit of the small courtyard.

In motion, the dress did appear to great advantage, but he saw more than that. She changed the atmosphere.

The effect of beauty, he told himself. People experienced strong feelings looking at a fine painting or hearing splendid music. His other self wanted to sit on the bench and drink her in. That, however, wouldn't produce intelligent or useful results. The opposite, rather.

And so he walked with her.

"The Season is over," she said. "Most of the other families have gone to their country places. But Parliament still sits, and Papa remains to the bitter end. And Mama needed time to recover from . . . some weddings that weren't mine."

He glanced at her. Pink tinted her fine cheekbones.

"Some of the gentlemen lingered, too," she went on, "and now they're proposing twice a week. I think it's become the latest sport, proposing to Lady Clara Fairfax. And I know what you're thinking."

"I doubt that," he said. His other self decided the gentlemen ought all to be pitched out of windows.

"But you don't care what people think of you," she said, "and so I won't let myself care what you think of me—that I'm shallow and vain and capricious—"

"That wasn't what I was thinking," he said.

"No, you don't think of me at all, and why should you?" she said.

Gad, was she a simpleton, after all?

"You have *important* things to do," she said. "I know. Even Bridget has more important things to do than I. There she is, trying to make something of herself as well as her brother, who's probably a hopeless cause. Yet she won't give up. And there are those poor pauper children—and their parents . . ." She clenched her expensively gloved hands. "It makes me wild to think of the injustice. I don't know how you bear it. But you *try* to do something. You even somehow make a victory out of failure. And there am I—alas, poor me—running away from my beaux—"

"Straight into the Old Bailey," he said. "So it was desperation that drove you there. I was vastly puzzled. Never would I have theorized anything to do with your lovers. Whose name, I understand, is Legion."

She looked up at him. "That's why you summoned me today? You were curious why I was in court? It had nothing to do with Bridget? Are you completely insane?"

"I'm less insane than most people, if by *insane* you mean irrational," he said. "And it did have to do with Bridget, peripherally."

"But you don't want my help."

"With what?" He studied her, his gaze going up to the mad garden on top of her head down to the toes of her pink half-boots, once, twice, thrice. "As I recollect, you came to me for help. You didn't set out on your own to find the tiresome boy."

"And I'm to do what?"

He gave a dismissive wave. "Whatever it is ladies do." He started away.

She stamped her foot.

He turned back and gazed at the pink-clad foot. "You stamped your foot," he said. "Like a spoiled child."

"I *am* a spoiled child, you insufferable man," she said. "I am only trying to be a little less spoiled and to be of use to somebody."

"You're of no use to me," he said, ruthlessly beating back the other, arguing self. "I'm not overly scrupulous about using people when necessary, as anybody will tell you. And I should use you if there were any sense to it. But I will not enter Seven Dials or Whitechapel or wherever the wretched brat's gone to ground, encumbered by a young lady—and not merely a young lady, but a peer's daughter. You'd only be underfoot, and I should have to look out for you as well as myself. If you think I mean to complicate this asinine business needlessly, because you're bored and too many men love you, then what small brain you might have once possessed has atrophied."

Clara wanted very much to strike him with her umbrella, but she hadn't brought one, and Davis, who always did carry one, was inside, where she'd told her to remain.

Furthermore, Clara knew he was right.

She'd only be an encumbrance.

How on earth had she thought she'd be of any use to him?

This wasn't the scrawny adolescent boy who might have broken his hand when he punched the lumpish bully for speaking offensively in her presence.

Yes, even at not quite nine years old, she'd known what that was about. Trailing after three older brothers, she'd learned things, like what *bubbies* meant. She'd understood, too—perhaps not then, but not long thereafter—that if Harry or Clevedon had been about, they would have done what the Professor did. Probably more successfully, but that made his doing it all the more admirable.

Now he was as big as Harry or Clevedon. And judging by the powerful physique whose contours the well-tailored black coat and trousers outlined, he'd spent the intervening years exercising his body as much as his brain.

She would not think about his physique. He was intolerably supercilious and conceited. She wished Harry had taught her more about fisticuffs. Fighting worked so well for males, old and young, never mind who was right or wrong. How she would enjoy giving Mr. Radford a Chancery suit on the nob!

"I fail to see what's thrown you into such a snit," he said.

"Snit!"

"Do try to use your head," he said. "What other means had I to talk to you? I don't circulate among the haut ton. I could hardly appear at your door and hand a footman my card. Then your family would wonder how we'd become acquainted. Your disguises make it clear they don't know what you've been up to."

She hadn't dared tell even her sister-in-law Sophy, who could have helped her with the disguises. Sophy had married Harry, and Clara didn't want to ask her to keep secrets from him.

"You went to all the trouble of summoning me here, in the most clandestine manner, only to satisfy your *curiosity*," she said as calmly as she could.

"Did I not say so? Did it not occur to you that your appearing in the Central Criminal Court was in any way strange?"

"That's why I was in disguise," she said. "I never dreamed you'd notice."

"That was unintelligent of you."

"It was perfectly reasonable." *You great lout.* "I assumed you'd be concentrating so intently upon your task, you'd never heed the crowd in the gallery except as a crowd. But you did glance up, I recollect, and must have recognized Davis."

"I recognized *you*," he said. "Davis only confirmed the discovery."

She was aware of inner disturbances. She throttled them, wishing she could throttle him.

She kept her temper as best she could and looked up at him, into those keen grey eyes. Such an unusually pale grey, like a winter sky. "You *are* a prodigy, aren't you? I shouldn't have believed it possible to let one's attention stray for even a moment, yet you penetrated my disguise."

"Firstly, my attention did not stray," he said. "It's possible to glance in one direction and pay attention elsewhere at the same time. I took note of the proceedings, though I knew what would be said. Secondly, it wasn't much of a disguise."

"Secondly," she said, "it was a very good one. Mr. Bates passed me in Ludgate Street without a second look."

"Mr. Bates is unobservant," he said. The penetrating grey gaze swept over her. "I should know you anywhere."

She went hot all over. She ignored it. "And firstly—"

"Firstly usually comes before secondly," he said.

"Yes, but the secondly was so provoking," she said, "And so, firstly—"

"You're mocking me."

"Why not? You mock me."

His mouth quirked, more discernibly this time.

She went on, "Firstly, it was a challenging exercise for me. With my tiny brain, you know, it wanted supreme concentration to find chinks in the defense's arguments. Some of the legal hairs were split so very fine, I could hardly make them out. But that was the point, wasn't it? There was no way to prove beyond doubt that Grumley's methods rather than the fever killed those children."

He folded his arms, and the grey gaze became almost painfully acute.

This was a test, she thought. And if she failed, she would have to go back to listening to marriage proposals and fantasize about becoming an eccentric and running away to live in a tent in Arabia.

She began to walk again, not because she needed to pace, but because she knew her clothes would distract him somewhat, and she would feel less like an insect under a magnifying glass. "Your witnesses made a poor show under the defense's close questioning," she said. "The judge's badgering made them more uncertain and inarticulate. The jury had no choice. Naturally, my learned friend, you would have recognized this long before I did."

He stood back and rested one big, gloved hand on the back of the bench where Bridget had sat. He said nothing.

Clara made herself look away from the gloved hand.

"And so I came back the next day, to see if I could discover your strategy," she said.

He only watched her in a brooding sort of way. This was the tricky part, and he was not going to make it easy.

She plunged on, "You gave a fine performance of bumbling and desperation, while at the same time calling attention to each of the defendant's acts that, taken together, ought to have led to his conviction. Day after day, that was what the newspapers reported, because that part wasn't legal hair-splitting, but something all readers could understand, and judge for themselves."

Nearly all the newspapers had protested the verdict in

the strongest terms. Grumley had gone free but he was an outcast, ruined.

She understood now, in her heart as well as her brain, how Radford had earned his reputation.

After a long moment, while she became aware of the dusty leaves' rustling and the distant sounds of the London streets, he said, "You may come with me to the ragged school Toby Coppy attended."

She very nearly staggered.

But ladies never staggered. They stood straight or swooned gracefully.

"The day after tomorrow," he said, "at ten o'clock in the morning, when the more undesirable elements will be asleep or only half awake and less likely to pay close attention to you. But you're not to wear *that*." He waved his hand at her dress. "Nor yet the thing you wore in court. Go in and tell Matron to have the girls run up something for you in her style of dress. Say it's for amateur theatricals. Send me a message via Fenwick, telling me where to collect you."

He touched his hat brim and walked away through the courtyard. She watched him go. She kept on watching long after he'd moved out of view and his long strides would have taken him to the next street.

"I passed," she murmured. "I passed the examination."

Saffron Hill
Two days later

The house looked about to collapse on itself. The buildings in the Temple grounds had been modern, airy, pristine purity by comparison.

Inside was only marginally better, hinting of attempts, against great odds, to clean. To Clara the odds seemed insurmountable. Scores of very dirty, very ragged girls crammed the first room they entered. Some of the older ones loitered in corners much as they must have done on the streets, their garish finery proclaiming their trade. Others, of varying ages, sat bent over scraps of paper or asleep, their heads on their arms. Still others lay curled up asleep on the floor. Very possibly, this was the cleanest and safest place to sleep these girls knew.

Two teachers, one man and one woman, calmly—and stoically, in Clara's opinion—tried to impart some rudimentary form of learning to this mélange. The woman was in charge of reading, and the man patiently led his charges through the simplest arithmetic.

"You'd better get used to this before we go on to the boys," Radford said.

"Get used to it!" she repeated softly. "How is that done, I wonder?"

"You wanted to help," he said.

"I think I can get used to the smell," she said. She didn't think a lifetime would be long enough to get used to the sight.

These girls, crammed into the low-ceilinged room, made up only the smallest drop in London's ocean of impoverished humanity.

"Try not to touch anybody or breathe too deeply," he said. "If you catch a fatal fever, your brothers will take me apart limb from limb—and that will be the most enjoyable part of my untimely demise."

"My brothers will have to stand in line behind Davis," she said.

The maid was muttering to herself, yet when Clara glanced at her, she thought she saw sorrow as well as disgust in the faithful bulldog countenance.

Davis had certainly taken every precaution, dousing Clara's handkerchiefs with vinegar and making sure every inch of her was covered, except for her face. She'd tried to make Clara wear a vinegar-soaked handkerchief over her nose and mouth, but Clara won that battle.

Two of the prostitute-looking girls smiled at Mr. Radford. One started to sashay toward him but he gave a brisk wave, and she retreated with a smirk and whispered something to the other girl.

The male teacher approached them. Mr. Radford led him aside, and they muttered together for a moment. Then the teacher summoned one of the young prostitutes. Mr. Radford jerked his head toward a corner of the room where nobody was lounging at the moment, and the girl went with him. He hadn't invited Clara, but after a moment's hesitation, she went, too, and Davis trailed after her.

He didn't scowl at Clara, as she expected. Instead he gave her the What a Good Puppy You Are look and said to her, "Ah, Mrs. Faxon. Here is Jane, who is acquainted with Toby Coppy."

Jane eyed her suspiciously, top to bottom, then in reverse.

"Jane, Mrs. Faxon teaches at Bridget Coppy's school. They're looking for Toby."

"What's he done, then?" the girl said.

At least, that was what Clara guessed she said. Her Cockney speech was several degrees more impenetrable than Fenwick's.

"You know perfectly well what he's done," Mr. Radford said. "He's left school."

The girl shrugged. "Who wouldn't?"

"You don't."

"Well, no one tole me—" She stopped abruptly, and looked hostile. "Here now, I know your tricks, Raven, like everybody does," she said loudly. "Don't be thinkin' I'll squeak on Toby or nobody else. I don't nose on my friends." Then more softly but with the same truculence she muttered, "Not and ask for a slicing, would I? And you tell Bridget she can thank herself for it." She flounced away.

Mr. Radford shook his head. "Come along then, Mrs. Faxon. I knew we wasted our time with this lot. They stick together. This is what they call honor among thieves, in case you were wondering."

R adford had to give her credit. Lady Clara passed through the first trial without being sick or even showing signs of swooning.

But then, she was Longmore's sister, for all she looked so little like him.

They went on to the boys' classroom, where anarchy seemed to prevail, although the teachers bravely did their business and a few brave boys worked at learning.

There he picked the likeliest lad in the bunch and took him aside in the same way they'd drawn Jane away from the others. Not outside the room, though. That would be the perfect way to learn absolutely nothing.

The boy Jos displayed even more hostility than Jane had treated them to, and in the same vein.

Having left the boys' area with the same kinds of dismissive comments he'd used in the girls' schoolroom, Radford led Clara and her maid outside. He said nothing. They said nothing—shocked speechless, no doubt—but hurried along with him to the hackney stand in Hatton Garden, where they climbed into an ancient coach.

"That's all?" Lady Clara said once the vehicle was moving. "How many more ragged schools must we visit before we learn anything?"

"Were you not paying attention?" he said. "They told us everything."

"They all seemed to know you," she said. "Those girls . . . Jane . . ." She trailed off and looked out of the window, though he'd defy her to see anything through the scratched, dirt-encrusted glass.

"They know I don't need every syllable spelled out for me," he said.

"Speaking of syllables, I could barely understand Jane," she said. "The boy—Jo, was it?—might as well have been speaking Mesopotamian."

"Nor why your ladyship ought to understand, I can't guess," Davis said. "And to think I should see my lady in a place alongside the likes of those creatures, and that insolent girl's rags touching your skirts." She glared at Radford.

He shrugged. "You can burn milady's attire later. In the dead of night, if you like."

"And how should we do that without attracting attention, *sir*?" the maid said, making the *sir* sound like *you fiend from hell.* "Do you suppose I spend any time in the kitchen, that they wouldn't wonder at it? Do you imagine a dress burned in my lady's bedroom fireplace wouldn't set the whole house talking, and her ladyship's mother hear of it?"

"Send the dress to me, or leave it for me somewhere," he said in a bored voice. "I'll burn it."

"Never mind the dress," Lady Clara said. "What did you learn?"

"That Jane referred to a party who liked cutting people."

The maid looked at her mistress. "Why will you not let me kill him?" she said. "This is a horrid man. Your ladyship has got mixed up with some horrid men, ever since—"

"Do be still, Davis," Lady Clara said. "I'll thank you for not airing my dirty linen in Mr. Radford's hearing."

His unwanted self, meanwhile, who'd been meditating upon her virginal bedroom, promptly set about imagining her linen, every layer of it, starting with the uppermost—corset and petticoat—and working his way down to chemise and skin.

"Curdle my blood all you like, Mr. Radford, since it amuses you so much," Lady Clara said. "But eventually I should like to know what you discovered."

"Firstly, it was clever of me to bring you along," he said.

"Clever!" she said. "Of *you*! I was the one who had to pass the examination."

"If you hadn't passed, it wouldn't have been clever of me but unintelligent and counterproductive," he said. "But Jane was jealous of you—"

"*Jealous?*"

"Streetwalkers are competitive about men and undiscriminating," he said. "She wanted to show me she knew what you didn't. The boy Jos showed off because he's a boy and you're an attractive female, even with whatever that muck is on your face."

The composition dulled her complexion and made it seem rough. It couldn't conceal her beauty, though, even from the most unobservant and dull-witted boy, which Jos was not.

"A blend Davis made for me," she said. "Jos was—what? Nine years old?"

"Fourteen," Radford said. "Their bodies might be stunted, but they age more quickly in the rookeries than in Mayfair. He wanted a closer look at you. And maybe he was curious what clean smelled like. He knew he had to pay for the privilege, and so he gave me what he had. In short, your ladyship was wonderfully useful in untying tongues. At last we know who has Toby."

Freame, as he'd suspected. Of all the gangs in London, the boy had to get himself led into that one. Thanks to Chiver, which made the motive plain.

"I don't," she said.

"Maybe you'll solve the puzzle on your own, if you care to waste valuable mental energy upon that rather than escaping matrimony," he said. "But I'm not in a humor to indulge your idle curiosity further."

Lady Clara had taken a great risk going with him this day. He should never have let it happen. He could have learned what he needed without her, though it wouldn't have been nearly so easy.

Very well. He'd made a mistake. He'd correct it.

"Idle! You said a moment ago—"

"Your maid doesn't approve, and all the evidence supports her," he said.

"Davis isn't my *mother*," she said.

"Don't make me tell your mother," he said. "I don't like nosing on my friends any more than Jane does, but like her, I'll do it if provoked sufficiently. You'll soon reach Oxford Street. I'd better disembark here. I need to talk to some fellows at the Bow Street Police Office." He signaled the coach to stop.

"Mr. Radford, you are the rudest man—"

"So I'm told," he said. "Obnoxious, too." The coachman was taking his time about climbing down to open the door. Radford wrestled with the window, muscled it down, and turned the handle.

He had the door open when Lady Clara grabbed his arm.

"Mr. Radford—"

"My lady!" the shocked maid cried.

He was shocked, too, at the intimacy, and that wasn't all.

Lady Clara did not take her hand away.

A small, slender, lady's hand, gloved and weighing next to nothing. He should have scarcely felt her touch, but it shot through him as sharply as a dagger thrust, and his blood seemed to rush to meet it.

"You may not dismiss me so easily," Lady Clara said.

"May I not?" He covered her hand with his, and he felt her tense. Davis turned bright red and grabbed her umbrella, meaning to brain him, no doubt. He didn't care. Indignant women had hit him before, for much smaller cause.

He lifted her ladyship's unresisting hand. She was too shocked to resist, no doubt. He brought it not an inch below his lips, as was proper, but to his mouth. And he kissed—not the air, as politeness required, but the unresisting hand. Lingeringly. And drank in the tantalizing trace of scent that was her and nobody and nothing else.

"Farewell, dear, dear lady," he said. "Thank you for a most entertaining morning. With any luck, we'll never meet again."

He released her hand and stepped calmly out of the carriage, still smiling.

He closed the door and his smile faded. He thrust a coin at the dilatory coachman, warned him not to charge the ladies, shooed him back to his box, and stepped back onto the pavement.

Radford watched the coach trundle along Broad Street, and cursed himself.

Clara stared at the hand he'd kissed.

When she'd touched him, the whirl of feelings startled her so, she'd almost pulled away. She didn't know what to call them. All she knew was that it felt as though she'd come in from the cold and reached out to warm her hands at a fire.

And then. And then . . .

She was not a child, and she wasn't as innocent as she ought to be, but when his hand closed over hers . . .

Longing and longing and longing.

She'd longed for things before—freedom, adventure,

forbidden books and places—but never for a man's company. And this wasn't like the other kind of wanting. Those were perhaps no more than wishing. This was deep and aching and bewildering.

Stay, she'd almost said.

He'd stayed only another moment, only time enough to kiss her gloved hand and shatter her world.

It was the warmth of his mouth through the thin leather. That was all it took. She'd felt it race to her heart and make it beat faster, and she didn't know how he could do that and she couldn't ask him because he'd gone.

She remembered the boy, so long ago, who'd said, "Stay."

"It seems as though I did," she murmured.

"My lady?"

Clara looked up to find Davis watching her. "Nothing."

Davis smoothed her gloves. "Well, if nobody kills him soon, he stands a chance to be a judge or Lord Chancellor, or even a duke, and I daresay you can make something of him."

"As though I'd want to." Clara looked out of the window. Not that one could see anything through the scarred glass.

"Certainly not, my lady, of course. Not wise at all. Better to put the likes of him out of your ladyship's life. And easily done. Parliament's up today, and you'll be leaving for Cheshire the day after tomorrow."

"Davis."

"Tonight will be the parties, and nearly everything is packed, everyone expecting it. Day after tomorrow we leave, and no danger of seeing him again."

Clara turned away from the window to scowl at her maid. Not that it made an impression. Usually, Davis kept strictly to her place and held her tongue, not wanting to set bad examples for lesser servants. But she'd been with

Clara through any number of crises over the years. In private, or if under undue emotional strain, she allowed herself certain liberties associated with longevity, seniority, and the many confidences reposing in her bosom.

"I'm not going to Cheshire," Clara said.

"I didn't think so," Davis said.

"Stop acting like *him*—all-wise and all-knowing. It's tiresome."

"Yes, my lady."

"I will see this thing through."

"Yes, my lady."

"Tell the driver to take us to Kensington. I need to talk to Great-Aunt Dora."

"Not in that dress," Davis said. "My lady."

Chapter Four

On Thursday, the King went in state to the House of Peers to prorogue the Parliament. His Majesty entered his carriage shortly before two o'clock, attended by the Earl of Albemarle and the Marquess of Queensberry.

—*Court Journal*, 12 September 1835

Radford had done, by his count, three very stupid things: firstly, enlisting Fenwick to contact Lady Clara; secondly, meeting her at the Milliners' Society and letting her talk; and thirdly, taking her to a ragged school where she might have easily contracted one of the various ailments floating in the miasma. Unlike the students, she hadn't been toughened by poverty, filth, and disease. She could die of something that wouldn't even give someone like Jane hiccups.

At this rate, Cousin Bernard would win the intelligence competition.

Radford could only hope that kissing her hand acted as a countermeasure. He'd behaved shockingly—more shockingly than usual, that is. She'd have the good sense to avoid him in future. And if his other self objected, well, his other self was irrational or Radford would have remained closer to him.

These logical and sensible thoughts ought to have restored his equilibrium.

He'd made a decision and acted on it. He'd taken control of the situation.

Yet he couldn't detach himself from the *feeling*.

It was like a ghost clinging to him, the feel of her hand clasping his arm. He felt its weight as he made his way along Drury Lane and into Long Acre. He felt it still, after he entered the Bow Street Police Office and asked to meet privately with the superintendent.

The New Metropolitan Police had come into existence only six years ago. Initially, practically everybody had hated them. When one was killed in the line of duty, the coroner's verdict was justifiable homicide. But the public was beginning to take a more neutral if not positive view.

For their part, the police had mixed feelings about Radford. Like so many others, they found him difficult and at times might have wished murder were less illegal. On the other hand, his network of informers made him useful, and he was an excellent prosecutor.

Not wishing to waste anybody's time, Radford reduced the plot to its essentials. "Bridget Coppy's taken Chiver's fancy," he said. He didn't have to explain who Chiver was. "She, trying hard to be respectable, most sensibly rejected him. To soothe his wounded pride or extort a change of mind, he's lured her brother from the straight and narrow. Ordinarily, this would be business as usual in the rookeries, and I shouldn't waste your time with it. But Bridget shelters at present with the Milliners' Society for the Education of Indigent Women."

"The girls' school over in Hart Street, you mean?"

Radford nodded.

The superintendent pursed his lips. No one had to paint a picture for him.

The Society's school fell within Bow Street's police district as well as Jacob Freame's territory. The Society's three founding sisters had married into the upper reaches of the aristocracy. If Freame's gang made trouble at the Milliners' Society, these powerful personages would come down severely on the police. Heads would roll, starting with the superintendent's. On the other hand, ridding the area of its most troublesome gang would win the police friends in high places, which they still needed.

What Radford did say was, "I know you've been trying to get Freame for ages."

"Let me call in Sam Stokes," the superintendent said. "Freame's on his special list. Been at the top of it since Stokes was a Runner."

Once upon a time, Bow Street had been headquarters for the Bow Street Runners, London's thief takers. They'd had their corruption scandals, and this had contributed to the Runners being disbanded with the creation of the Metropolitan Police. But Sam Stokes was honest, patient, persistent, and a great deal sharper and more dangerous than he appeared. Now an inspector, he was the best detective in the division—perhaps in all of London—though police were no longer supposed to be detecting, but preventing crime.

He arrived within minutes of the summons, a nondescript fellow who could have disappeared in any crowd, and whom one might overlook even if nobody else was about. He was of average height and build with a forgettable face.

"Freame again," he said when Raven explained the situation. "I've run up against some slippery ones, but he beats them all. Always seems to know when we're coming for him. We get to his latest den, and he's gone, found another one. We can't even lay hands on his henchmen."

Chiver and Husher. The more feared of Freame's lieutenants, Husher was a man of few words, unlike the swaggering Chiver. The nickname, though, didn't refer to his taciturnity but to his favorite work: hushing people permanently.

"If you're willing to try again," Radford said, "I have some ideas."

For a respectable, unmarried young lady, getting into and out of disguise wasn't easy. In disguise Clara didn't attract much attention. As herself she was as unnoticeable as a fireworks display.

At present she had no choice but to change her attire at home, at Warford House. Fortunately, to screen the property from the Green Park, which it adjoined, the trees and shrubbery about the property grew tall and abundant. With care, she could slip into one of the outbuildings and with Davis's assistance, become herself again.

This was easier today, because Parliament was rising at last. This threw the household into in an uproar of packing for the country, and the women into a frenzy of preparing for the evening's parties. In all the chaos, especially her mother's and younger sisters' temper fits, Clara attracted little attention.

She had the cabriolet sent round, and set out for Kensington and the home of her Great-Aunt Dora, Lady Exton.

Once upon a time, Clara would have confided in her beloved paternal grandmother, who understood her so well. Grandmama Warford had died three years ago and Clara still missed her, especially her no-nonsense advice. She'd warned Clara not to wait for the Duke of Clevedon, and she'd been right.

It was not quite the same with Great-Aunt Dora, but she, too, had grown up in what she called a "less missish" generation. At present, since one could not bring

Sophy and her sisters into it, this relative was Clara's only hope.

Fortunately she'd timed her visit well. She found her ladyship in the throes of boredom and unable to decide how or where to alleviate it. She found Clara's tale the opposite of boring.

"Radford, you say," she said. "George Radford prosecuted a theft for me. Brilliant fellow. But so irritating. The only other man I wanted to throttle quite so much was my husband. The barrister at least made himself useful. But no, it can't be the same man. He retired, I believe, about the time your grandmother died."

"I refer to his son," Clara said. "Oliver. But everybody calls him Raven."

"Do they, indeed?" Great-Aunt Dora's blue eyes gleamed. "How interesting. But of course you must stay with me. Young blood in the house—what could be better? That is to say, young blood not belonging to my children or grandchildren. So prim. They get it from their father's side, I assure you."

"I promise not to be prim," Clara said. "But I'm afraid Mama will want persuading."

Lady Exton dismissed this with a wave. "I'll call on her this day. She'll be frantic, as usual, though I can think of few less tumultuous ventures than rusticating in Cheshire. But since she'll have worked herself into a pet, she'll agree to anything to be rid of me. Better yet, they'll have packed your things already. Yes, this will do very well, indeed."

Clara kissed her and thanked her.

"Never mind, child, never mind," her great-aunt said. "You ought to be allowed to do one disreputable thing before you settle down."

"I've already done two," Clara said. She reminded Great-Aunt Dora of the Broken Almost-Engagement and the Shocking Incident at the Countess of Igby's Ball.

Great-Aunt Dora dismissed these with a wave. "Social mishaps. This is altogether different. Certainly I know you're too intelligent to take foolish risks, and if Mr. Radford is anything like this father, he will have a head on his shoulders with rather more in it than the usual."

A fine head, set off by thick black hair and a rakish curl at the temple . . . eyes like a winter sky . . . a fine, imperial nose . . . and a shockingly adept mouth.

But looks weren't everything, and neither was the ability to stir a woman's senses. He was what he was, and would probably become only more so as the years passed. No good would come of trying to make something of a man with a brain like machinery.

All Clara wanted was to return Toby Coppy to his sister, as she'd promised to do. Maybe Toby was a lost cause. But he had a sister who loved him and wanted a better life for them both, and Clara could at least help give him another chance.

Then, when it was done, Clara would go back to her world, and her normal life would close about her again . . . like a boa constrictor. And then?

She'd suffocate in the most discreet and ladylike way.

After a little more conversation, Clara left, and her great-aunt sent for the butler who'd served her for many decades. Like any other self-respecting head of staff, Nodes maintained an updated mental compendium of the British upper ranks.

"Radford," her ladyship said. "There's a duke in there, I know, but I can't bring the name to mind."

"Malvern, my lady."

"Details, if you please," she said.

He had, as she knew, far more to tell her than did *Debrett's Complete Peerage of the United Kingdom of Great Britain and Ireland*, or any other official listing of the upper orders. These tomes came out only once a year, while her butler faithfully studied the "Births, Marriages, and Deaths" sections of the periodicals.

When he'd finished, she said, "My grandniece Clara is coming to stay. I want all made ready for her. And let the household know they're to keep quiet about her comings and goings if they want to keep their places."

"Yes, my lady." Nodes bowed and departed.

R adford spent the rest of the day and early evening talking to informers, who talked to others.

At three o'clock in the morning, three young men were caught breaking into a house in St. Clement Danes.

They fought the police fiercely. After breaking one constable's nose, they ran away. But the youngest and smallest tripped over a strategically planted walking stick and fell. The police arrested the boy, Daniel Prior, age thirteen. When they'd taken their prisoner away, Radford retrieved his walking stick and went home.

As previously agreed, Radford received the brief to prosecute.

Woodley Building
Afternoon of 11 September

W hen Radford entered Westcott's office, he found the solicitor gazing at a large, lumpy article wrapped in brown paper and tied with string.

"It's for you," Westcott said. "Came by ticket porter."

Radford gazed at the parcel.

"I was about to open it," Westcott said. "It weighs little and doesn't smell, which tells me it isn't a dead animal."

Now and then Radford received messages from friends or foes of persons he was prosecuting or defending. Since these persons' skills didn't include reading and writing, their communications tended to be symbolic.

This time, though, the sender had written Radford's name and direction neatly on the parcel.

"I know what it is," he said.

He untied the string and pulled away the paper.

"Looks like a woman's dress," Westcott said.

"What a noticing fellow you are," Radford said.

It was Lady Clara's. The one she'd worn to the ragged school.

Westcott came around the desk. He studied it for a moment. Then he lifted it up and held it against Radford's chest.

"This color has never become me," Radford said. Her scent, faint but unmistakable, wafted up to his nose.

"Is this a message?" Westcott said, taking it—and the scent—away. He turned the dress this way and that. "Rather less threatening than the usual."

"I'm to dispose of it," Radford said.

"Not evidence?"

Radford looked at him.

"No, of course not," Westcott said. "You'd never destroy evidence. I must have been in the grip of a momentary dispersion of wits."

"So it would seem."

"Shock, undoubtedly. It's not every day you receive a woman's dress instead of a death threat."

"Lady Clara's maid has joined the list of those wishing to kill me," Radford said.

"How odd," Westcott said. "This news surprises me not at all. What have you done this time?"

"I took Lady Clara into a ragged school, where a prostitute's dress had the temerity to touch hers," Radford said.

"Lady Clara." A pause. "Fairfax." Another pause. "The Marquess of Warford's eldest daughter."

Radford nodded.

Westcott put the dress down on his desk. "You took her to a ragged school."

"In Saffron Hill."

"Oh, even better," Westcott said.

Radford explained. Then he explained where he'd been for most of the night and morning. Westcott stared at the dress and listened without comment.

"The maid couldn't burn it herself without starting gossip in the servants' hall," Radford concluded.

"A trifle extreme," Westcott said. "True, prostitutes loiter in insalubrious areas. But it can be cleaned, and I'm sure someone can make use of it. Our charwoman, perhaps."

"Yes. Yes, she well might." Radford took up the dress and went out of the office and into his and Westcott's private living quarters across the corridor.

He took the dress into the sitting room and threw it down on a chair. Then he took it up again and looked at it.

Then he brought the bodice to his face and breathed in deeply the too-faint scent of the woman he must never see again.

Five minutes later, he walked out again into the outer office. He thrust the dress into Tilsley's hands and said, "Give it to the charwoman."

The Old Bailey
Monday 14 September

*G*uilty.

Trials in the New Court having proceeded speedily that day, Daniel Prior had a short wait for his sentence: transportation for life.

He promptly commenced screaming and wailing. He hadn't done it! It wasn't his fault! It was someone else, like he said. He was nowhere near there, but they was all against him!

He pointed at Radford. "I ain't done, Raven!" he shouted as the jailer laid hands on him. "But you're for it now!" He went on shrieking threats while he was dragged away. They could still hear his muffled screams after the heavy door leading to Newgate Prison swung shut behind him.

It was all a show. Or at least partly a show.

Since he'd appeared in court many times, had assaulted a police officer, and was known to associate with bad characters, Prior stood an excellent chance of dangling at the end of a rope. He'd informed on Jacob Freame in exchange for the prosecution's recommending leniency: a sentence of transportation instead of death.

Radford glanced up at the visitors' gallery.

She wasn't there.

And why should she be?

He'd made it clear he had no use for her, and he'd behaved so very badly in taking leave of her, she'd never again have any use for him.

He left the courtroom and went to the robing room, where he exchanged his wig, linen bands, and robe for street attire.

He found Westcott waiting for him in the corridor outside.

"Well done," Westcott said. "The boy put on a fine performance."

"It was only partly performance," Radford said. "While a long, hellish life in a penal colony is preferable to hanging, it's hardly worth celebrating." All the same, the sentence in this case wasn't grotesquely harsh. Daniel Prior had been a hardened criminal practically since the day he was born.

"Given the magic trick you've performed—one of your better ones, by the way—I expected to find you in better humor," Westcott said.

"We don't have Freame yet."

"You'll get him."

"*If* the wretched boy gave us correct information. And *if* Freame doesn't get wind of it before the police get there."

They stepped out of the building and into a driving rain. Old Bailey shivered in a grey blur, and now and again the wind gusted, turning the rain to whip strokes.

"We'd better get a hackney," Westcott said.

"For a half-mile walk?"

"I don't fancy a drenching," Westcott said.

"One can never get a coach when it rains, as you well know."

A boy holding a large umbrella ran up to them.

"Please, Raven, and you're to come straightaway," he said. "She's over there." He pointed to the curb where stood a hackney cabriolet. These vehicles were commonly known as coffin cabs, and not only on account of the funereal shape.

Curtains drawn and apron in place, it concealed as well as protected its passenger from the rain.

"*Who* is over there?" Radford said, while his other self came to sharp attention.

"Her," the boy said.

The other being's heart gave a leap and the wild, dark day brightened several degrees as he strode across the pavement to the cab.

"Get in." A haughty voice, feminine.

"Oh, good," he said. "Drama."

"Get in, Raven," she said.

He turned to the boy, who'd followed him, holding the umbrella over his own head. "Tell my friend I'll meet up with him later."

The urchin only stood there, looking up at him while rain cascaded from the umbrella onto Radford's shoes.

He reached into his pocket. "Pirates, the lot of you. I'll give you a bob, but you'd better give my friend the umbrella."

The boy snatched the coin and grinned. "Fanks, Raven!" he called, and raced back to Westcott. Or in the direction where Radford had last seen his friend. He didn't look that way to find out whether Westcott waited or not.

Radford climbed, dripping, into the cab. The scent of an expensive woman instantly enveloped him.

his is cozy," Radford said.

Four stupid things, he thought.

"I heard you won the case," Lady Clara said.

Though the closed curtain turned the cab's interior into a tomb, it wasn't completely dark. The curtains flapped, and light entered through the narrow opening, especially when the wind gusted. He couldn't make out the details of her dress. He smelled damp wool. Mingled with it was a light herbal fragrance he couldn't quite pinpoint, and the scent of her skin, which he could.

"You might have read the result in the court proceedings instead of coming out in this deluge," he said. "But you seem to have a self-destructive streak. It isn't enough to invite a lung fever, but you must hire a cab, from which you're likely to be expelled suddenly, with fatal results."

Hackney cabriolets were notorious. The drivers felt honor-bound to show how fast they could go. This led to crashing into street posts and other vehicles, and hurling their passengers into the road.

"Better yet, no maid in sight," he went on. "Have you taken leave of what few wits you possess?" He paused and thought. "Parliament rose last week. Why are you still here?"

"Firstly, my maid is to meet me at your chambers. We could not all fit in one cab."

"Then why not—"

"I am trying to answer counsel's questions in order," she said. "Secondly, I am in possession of all my wits, thank you. Thirdly, I am staying with my great-aunt Dora, who knows all about the Case of the Disappearing Toby."

Radford was aware of his other self's ricocheting between elation and alarm. Freame. Chiver. Husher. Still on the streets.

"Was you wantin' to go anywheres, sir?" the driver shouted above the beating rain. "On account this ain't a stand and I'm not to be loit'ring and blocking the traffic and the constable'll stop by to tell me to move along."

"The Temple," her ladyship called back.

"Sir?"

She released a small sigh. "Why is it, when a man comes on the scene, the woman becomes invisible?"

"Fleet Street, as the lady says," Radford said. "Inner Temple Lane." To her he said, "I only wish you were invisible."

The cab jerked into motion.

She said something under her breath.

He didn't ask her to repeat it.

He was trying to get away from himself, with limited success.

It wasn't true he wished she were invisible. He didn't wish, either, that he hadn't entered the cab. No man in his right mind would wish to escape sharing a seat in a narrow vehicle with Lady Clara Fairfax, with the curtains drawn. Any man in his right mind would wish for a smaller vehicle, heavier curtains, and a longer journey.

Radford would have preferred, however, to be *more* in his right mind at present.

He was deeply conscious of every place his body touched hers—a great many places, varying from time to time as the infernal cab jolted along Ludgate Hill. They had a short distance to cover, but the ferocious rain made even a hackney cab driver cautious—relatively speaking, that is, since a hackney cab driver's idea of caution matched the average person's idea of homicidal negligence.

He wrenched his mind to the last relevant matter. "Who is Great-Aunt Dora?"

"Lady Exton, once Lady Dora Fairfax," she said. "Your father prosecuted a theft for her in a difficult case, the thieves being cleverer than average. She said he was brilliant but extremely irritating."

He felt a stab of grief, yet he almost laughed, too. In response to his letter, Mother had written:

> *You know I can't keep your letters from your father. But he says you are not to make yourself anxious on his account. Whatever it is Malvern wants, he'll have to learn patience. Your sire may be loitering at death's door, he says, but no man, no matter how young and healthy, is any match for a wily old lawyer.*

"I'll mention it to him when next I visit," he said. As soon as this wretched Toby business was out of the way, he'd make for Richmond. He hadn't seen his father since consulting with him shortly before the Grumley trial started. What would he do without him? Who would he talk to?

He said, "You haven't told me why you're still here."

"Let me think." She put her index finger to her chin. "Because you're irresistible? Probably not. Because Toby Coppy hasn't returned yet? Most certainly so. It's clear you're in desperate need of my help."

This was so patently delusory that for a moment—possibly the first time in his life—he was speechless.

That didn't last long.

He said, "I realize your ladyship is very bored, being loved to death, but you ought not to let ennui dull your reason. My world is not like the fantasy one you live in. Mine demands I work within the bounds of the law, with the cooperation of the police. We didn't learn Toby's whereabouts until the small hours of morning. I've suggested a plan, and the police are prepared to carry it out. Nobody needs you."

Radford's other self raised an objection. Radford overruled him.

The air in the carriage seemed to throb.

But she said mildly enough, "And you know what Toby looks like, do you?"

"I have a detailed description," he said.

"I've seen him," she said. "And spoken to him, more than once. I've given him money. Which of us do you think he's more likely to trust?"

"Trust doesn't come into it. We—"

"Yes, sir, and it was Inner Temple Lane you wanted?" the driver shouted. "Which this is the gate, sir, and missus."

*H*is hand on the back of her waist, Radford hurried Lady Clara through the gate, along Inner Temple Lane, where the walls of the looming buildings shielded them from the worst of the rain and wind, and into the Woodley Building. Even so, she was wet through. He hurried her up the stairs into the outer office, where they found the clerk Tilsley trying to balance a ruler on the tip of his snub nose.

Tilsley dropped the ruler and gaped. This did not make the green and yellow bruises on his face any prettier.

"Bring coals," Radford said. "We need a fire, before pneumonia sets in. Look sharp, man! You know dead ladies attract unwanted attention."

The boy slid down from his stool. "Yes, sir, Mr. Radford, which I noticed the wet, sir, and took the liberty.

Accordingly making a fire in Mr. Westcott's office, expecting you and him back soon enough."

Lady Clara approached Tilsley and studied his face. "Oh, dear, did Fenwick do that?"

"Thanking you for your kind concern, madam, and assuring you I got my own back, and the other party got in extra only due to cheating."

"Mrs. Faxon, may I present our clerk, Tilsley," Radford said. "He was otherwise engaged when last you called on us. He's far more efficient than appearances would indicate."

Tilsley went red at the unexpected compliment, making a rainbow of his bruised face. Radford virtually never remembered to bestow praise.

"Since you've made a fire, you may now make tea," Radford said.

"Yes, sir."

Radford opened the door to Westcott's office and pushed her in.

The day was stormy and the room, with its dark wainscoting and heavy furniture, was gloomy at the best of times.

She was the only bright thing in it, he thought.

Candlelight and firelight glinted on the moisture sliding from her bonnet to her cheek. And down her neck.

Wet!

He pushed her toward the fire.

"Yes, Mr. Radford, I can find the fire for myself," she said. She started pulling at the ribbons of her hat.

"Not like that!" he said. He went to her and pushed her hands away. "You'll tighten the knot. Does this surprise me? No. Naturally you have no idea how to untie your own hat ribbons."

"You're wrong," she said. "But they're not so manageable when wet and I can't see what I'm doing."

"Put up your chin so that I can see what I'm doing. This brim is monstrous. It looks like a giant duckbill and does nothing to shield the sides of your face."

She tipped her head back and looked up at him.

Her eyes were the clear light blue of aquamarines. The damp on her perfect skin was like dew on rose petals.

The hat was hideous. She was unreasonably beautiful.

A less disciplined man might have found it painful to look at her.

He concentrated on unknotting the ribbons. His hands were perfectly steady. His heartbeats were erratic.

He drew the soggy ribbon out from under her chin. "There. It's done. I should advise you to throw it on the fire, but at present I have no ladies' hats to replace it." He snatched the sodden hat from her head and dropped it on the nearest table. "However, I recommend . . ." He trailed off as he turned back to her.

The room's light flickered over hair the color of champagne.

He'd never seen her bareheaded before.

He tried to detach himself, but his other self clung, and for a moment he felt he'd been launched into the world of the *Odyssey*. She was too cruelly beautiful to be a mere human. She was Calypso or Circe or Aphrodite herself. The mythical bewitchers of men.

But this wasn't a myth and he was a reasoning human being. He could not be bewitched because there was no such thing.

She was fumbling with the cloak's fastenings.

He went to help. "I know it's true, but one must see it to believe it," he said. "You cannot manage even the simplest act of self-sufficiency." He reached for the fastenings.

She pushed his hands away. "I'm perfectly capable—"

"You obviously are not." He tried again.

She jerked away. "Leave me alone."

"You can't—"

"You don't know what I can and can't do. Stop treating me like an idiot."

"I did not say you were an idiot."

"You say it *constantly*," she said tightly. "In a hundred different ways."

"I merely point out simple facts, which you seem unable to accept."

"I'd like to see you accept them," she said. "I'd like to see you try to live my life. You wouldn't last twenty minutes."

"Oh, no, such a trial it is to live in the lap of luxury, where one is endlessly petted and adored."

"You haven't the stamina to endure it," she said. "You'd die of boredom in an hour."

He stepped back, aware of a fraught note in her voice and a flash of something—pain?—in her eyes. "Very possibly," he began. "But—"

"You've no notion how I live in the world you call a fantasy," she went on in the same taut tone. "You've no idea what it's like to spend your life wrapped in cotton wool, with all about you protecting you, mainly from yourself, because you don't behave as they think a girl ought to do, and they believe something's wrong with you. You don't know what it's like to watch your brothers go away to school and make new friends and have adventures you'll never have, even vicariously, in books. You don't know what it's like to be scolded for reading too much and knowing too much—to be taught to hide your intelligence, because otherwise you'll frighten the gentlemen away—to stifle your opinions, because ladies aren't to have any opinions of their own, but must always defer to men." She stamped her foot. "You know nothing about me. Nothing! *Nothing!*"

She burst into tears—and not mere weeping, but great, racking sobs, as of a long pent-up grief.

He started to reach for her and caught himself in time. "Stop it," he said, clenching his hands. "Stop it."

"No! You're such an idiot!"

"You're hysterical," he said calmly, while his heart pounded. "Don't make me pour a bucket of water on your head."

She stamped her foot again. "I'm already w-wet, you m-moron!"

"Oh, good. What I always wanted. An irrational female bawling and stamping her foot, because she can't have her own way."

"Yes, I'm irrational, you supercilious, conceited, ill-mannered—"

"Better and better," he said, aware of heat—inappropriate heat—surging within. "A temper fit over nothing."

"Nothing!"

She whirled away and grabbed her ugly hat from the table.

"Going so soon?" he said. "And we—"

"You condescending thickhead!" She hit his arm with the hat. "You obnoxious—" She hit his chest.

"You'd better stop," he said. "I'm trying to be the sane one in the room, but you're making that exceedingly difficult."

She made it impossible. She was a goddess in a passion. The blaze of her blue eyes and the pale fire of her hair and the crimson glow of her cheeks.

She flung down the hat and grabbed the lapels of his coat. "I wish I were a man," she said. "I would knock you down. I would plant you a facer. I'd break your nose. I—"

"No, really, I mean it," he said. "You're murdering my brain." And he took hold of her shoulders and bent his head and kissed her.

Chapter Five

THE BARRISTER . . . 1. In considering his duty to his client, he reflects upon the propriety of his acting; upon the person for whom he should act; and his mode of acting.
—*The Jurist*, Vol. 3, 1832

Clara knew what a lady was supposed to do when a gentleman attempted to take liberties. She was supposed to fight him off and defend her honor with all her might.

Whoever made that rule had never been kissed by Raven Radford.

His mouth pressed to hers and things happened in her head and spread over her body, alien feelings in a great, overwhelming rush, like a windstorm, and all the rules of ladyship, written in a massive tome in her brain, flew off the pages and vanished.

She did not push him away. She held on for dear life, and gave back the best she could, given limited experience.

Given no experience.

What had previously passed for kisses before compared to this in the way playing with tin soldiers compared to Waterloo.

She let go of his coat to reach upward and wrap her arms about his neck, and her body lifted to fit against his.

He made a sound deep in his throat and moved his hands downward from her shoulders past the barrier of her sleeve puffs, to grasp her upper arms. He started to draw away but she wasn't ready. She held on, and after a heartbeat he slid his hands to her waist and pulled her closer. His kiss grew more fiercely determined, as though he would wipe every recollection of anything remotely resembling kisses from her mind and imprint his, permanently, upon it. And upon her body, where the alien feelings simmered into excitement and happiness and a yearning for more.

Strange feelings, and most likely wrong, as so much was for young ladies.

She let herself swim in them the way she'd swum, in childhood, in forbidden waters. She floated on the rise and fall of his breathing, fast, like hers. She swam in the heat radiating from his big frame and the warmth and strength of his hands, in a sea safe and not at all safe. Beyond it, on some far horizon, lay another realm toward which she was moving on a strong current.

Not safe, not safe.

She didn't want to be safe. She'd been too safe all her life.

She wanted to be in danger like this, caught in his arms and crushed to his powerful body. She wanted not to think at all, simply to be aware of him and everything about him and about this moment. The feel of wool and linen and the faint rustle of her cloak against his coat and the scents of coal fire smoke and damp wool and linen mingling with the smell of male, this male. She wanted to burrow into him. She wanted the heat and the deepening kiss and the feelings pulsing along her skin and through her veins that made her restless, wanting some vague *more* and more still.

She inched her hands upward to tangle in his hair, so thick and black and beautiful, like a raven's wing.

Raven.

She heard the groan, deep in his throat. He pulled her closer still.

A moment later, she felt him tense.

Then she heard it. So quiet the room was, the tap sounded like thunder. She tried to push the sound to the back of her mind, but it wouldn't stay there. She felt him withdraw, though he didn't let go.

A knock. And another, sharper one.

Then came Tilsley's voice, pitched to be audible through the closed door.

"The tea being ready, madam and sir, only wishing not to interrupt at inopportune junctures and breaking a train of—erm—thought."

Mr. Radford lifted his head and looked at her for a moment as though he didn't recognize her. Then he took his hands away and stepped back so casually. She stood, meanwhile, her world upended, and broken bits of the life she used to know scattered about her like a child's discarded toys.

It was only thanks to years of training that she didn't cry out or stagger or even look about her like one stupefied, which she was. All these things happened inside.

She'd never been kissed before. Whatever she'd thought those things were, they weren't kisses. She'd never known desire before. Whatever she'd felt before was merely the thrill of being naughty—and not very naughty at that.

She'd thought she was sophisticated. She was the greenest of greenhorns.

Standing on shaky legs no one could see, she looked up at him, into grey eyes like an approaching storm. Years of training kept her composed on the outside while inside her heart was stumbling about in her rib cage, and all she could think was *I've made a very bad mistake*. And the next thought was *I don't care*.

"Yes, yes, come in, Tilsley," he said. "What are you waiting for?"

The door opened a crack.

"Permission, sir," came the voice behind it. "Having received instructions on two separate occasions regarding the same subject, to wit, not bursting in on those intervals of Mr. Westcott or Mr. Radford being with clients. Them pointing out the degree of urgency to be considered, for instance, the premises not to be equated with Newgate. And as to that, the gentlemen offering the kindly reminder how it's not like anybody's waiting on the scaffold with the rope round his neck and I'm running in with a royal pardon."

Mr. Radford bit his lip. "A good boy, but talkative."

He walked, perfectly steady—while her knees were hanging on by a thread—to the door and opened it fully.

Tilsley, his face scarlet, stumbled slightly over the threshold, but managed not to drop the large tea tray he carried.

He placed it carefully on the table nearest the fire. He livened up the fire with more coals and a deft application of poker. He did not look at her or Mr. Radford once.

After urging them to let him know if anything else was wanted, and promising to stay within easy calling distance, Tilsley went out, closing the door behind him.

A moment's silence followed, while the candlelight and firelight glimmered over the book-filled shelves and the walls and tables and chairs, and made shadows on Mr. Radford's face. And while she thought, *What am I going to do? What am I going to do with him?*

Then, "I'm not going to ask if you're done being hysterical," he said. "It would be plain to the meanest intelligence that you've stored up years of that article, and it's bound to break out at intervals. I'm not going to apologize for kissing you. I'm not going to make excuses for doing so. The facts are simple and obvious. You were in a passion. Lady Clara Fairfax in a passion is very exciting. I'm a man. I succumbed to a normal and natural masculine urge." He met her wondering gaze. "And I will *not* promise never to do it again. If you choose to continue plaguing me, you will have to take your chances. My self-control is above the average, but I am not an automaton, and my mechanism is not clockwork."

"Firstly," she began. Her voice was unsteady and hoarse.

He held up his hand. "I'm going to unfasten your cloak and you will try with all your might to resist impulses to scream at me or do me an injury or demand a *discussion*."

I'm not plaguing you, she'd been about to say. But that was a lie.

She'd plagued him from the start. And it was all very well to tell herself she wanted to see this thing through and help a girl who was trying so hard to make a decent life. But Clara wasn't needed. She only wanted to be needed. She was merely tagging along, the way she'd tagged along after her brothers until Mama put a stop to it.

This is what comes of letting her do as she likes, Mama had raged when, days after the Vauxhall contretemps, she'd discovered the chipped tooth. *This is what comes of letting the boys indulge her. She will spoil all her looks, and never learn how to behave, and then where will she be when she's of age to wed? She'll be a hoyden and a bluestocking and nobody will want her.*

Clara had never told anybody how she'd chipped the tooth.

She wasn't sorry for what she'd done and she didn't care about the tooth. At least she'd done *something*.

And it was a good thing she'd done it, because she'd

been permitted to do almost nothing to any purpose ever since.

She refused to be sorry now for wanting to be needed. She was two and twenty, and her life, it turned out, was a great, big froth of pretty nothing. She was desperate.

She put up her chin, though she still did not seem to have full control of her muscles and wanted very much to sit down. "You may unfasten my cloak, and I will try not to molest you, but I cannot make any promises in that regard, unless you can do the job *without speaking*."

His mouth quirked, very slightly, upward.

The mouth he'd had on hers only a moment ago.

She strangled a sigh.

He advanced, undid the cloak fastenings, slid the garment from her shoulders, and draped it over a chair.

"Firstly?" he said.

"Never mind," she said. She needed a new tactic, but the kiss had fogged her brain and the light wasn't coming through yet. She needed to think, to find a way not to be sent home and told to leave him alone.

She tried to find a clue in what he'd said, but her mind wouldn't cooperate. All she knew was, this was the only man in the world who'd follow a kiss like that with a speech like that.

She walked as steadily as she could to one of the chairs by the table holding the tea tray. "One thing I do know how to do is preside over tea."

"Your shoes are wet through," he said. "You ought to take them off."

She looked at her half-boots. The ribbons threaded through long sets of tiny eyelets, a dozen or more pairs of them per boot. These were not conveniently placed down the front or even the outer side, but along the inside.

She looked up at him. "I know how, in theory. In practice, I should have to be a contortionist." Not to mention she was on fire at the mere thought of exposing her stockinged feet to his view. "I'll put my feet on the fender while I drink my tea. Not that I ever take cold, but I know you've got it into your head I'll expire of a little exposure to damp. It seems I'm not the only one in this room afflicted with hysteria. I may be a lady, and useless in many categories, but I'm not delicate."

She sat and concentrated on the tea tray. A fine-quality black tea. No tea cakes or sandwiches but fresh bread and butter, cut and arranged neatly. Fresh, rich milk, too, a discreet sniff told her.

He took the other chair. "I thought you said your maid was to meet you here."

"Maybe she ran into Mr. Westcott and they were overcome with passion and commenced an *affaire d'amour*. That will be interesting. She'll arrive with her hair in wanton disarray and her clothes buttoned incorrectly."

He smiled, and her heart squeezed.

It was only a ghost of a smile, here and gone in a heartbeat, but it changed his face, and she glimpsed, too briefly, a man just out of her reach.

She performed the hostess task she could have done blindfolded in the middle of an artillery bombardment.

He took a lump of sugar and no milk and made two-thirds of the bread and butter disappear with smooth efficiency.

She'd never thought of him eating. She'd never thought of him hungry. She wasn't sure she'd thought of him as human, except when she recalled the boy at Vauxhall.

And a moment ago, when he'd touched her. When he'd kissed her.

Passionately.

Or so it had seemed. How could she be sure?

She'd wanted passion. She'd rejected the man supposedly meant for her because she knew he didn't feel it for her nor she for him. She still wasn't sure what passion was. She'd only had a chance to experience its possibility.

She drank her tea, but eating was beyond her ability to feign normality. She told him to finish the bread and butter, and he did. And for some reason, her heart ached, watching him.

"It seems I was famished," he said when he was done. "But it was a long night with our young criminal. He held out until the last possible minute, terrified of hanging but more terrified of what Freame—or, more likely, one of Freame's favorite assassins—would do to him if he tattled. Then there was the judge to deal with. He's been wanting to hang Daniel Prior this age. Persuading him not to took more time than was convenient. Time is an article we haven't much of in this situation. But Bow Street is ready to move in. And so we go out tomorrow morning, not long after daybreak, to collect Toby Coppy and, with any luck, a clutch of criminals."

He paused, and she waited for the speech listing the reasons she would not be allowed to participate.

Firstly . . .

He said, "You may join us if you promise, solemnly promise, to do *exactly* as I say."

*A*nd that was Mistake Number Seven.

Five: Taking her to the office instead of telling the hackney cab driver to take her back where she came from.

Six: Kissing her. What had happened? What had happened? He was still . . . unsettled. No, *aroused* was the brutal truth, and he was experiencing an unusual degree of difficulty in calming himself.

That must explain his making Mistake Number Seven.

The color washed out of her face, and Radford nearly sprang from his chair, thinking she'd faint.

But the color washed back in, a shade pinker than normal. She opened her mouth, briefly revealing the chipped tooth. Then she closed it.

Her beautiful, luscious, untutored-in-kissing mouth.

His other self was gnashing his teeth.

If Tilsley hadn't banged on the door and shouted . . .

But what-ifs were nonsensical.

Tilsley had interrupted in the nick of time, and that was that.

"When you say . . ." Her voice had climbed half an octave higher than usual. She paused, lifted her chin, and went on in her normal tone, "When you say I must promise to do exactly as you say—"

"That is precisely what I mean," he said. "If you can't promise, on your sacred word of honor—"

"Suppose somebody kills you," she said. "Then how am I to do exactly what you say?"

"You'd better not try splitting hairs with me," he said. "I do it for a living, and I've been doing it since before I earned a living. I'm requiring you to do what I require clients to do. If they will not be guided strictly by me, if they interfere or question or fail to cooperate, I can't answer for the consequences."

"Very well, I promise," she said. "But—"

"No buts," he said. "I can't believe I've offered to bring you along. I devoutly wish I hadn't. But it's too late. You murdered my brain, and I've said it, and if I go back on my word you'll cry, and I've had enough of that for the present."

That wasn't altogether true.

He was used to women crying. Usually women needed him because they were in trouble. Women in trouble wept. Copiously.

What troubled him was far more upsetting than her tears.

What troubled him was her raging, despairing speech. He couldn't detach himself from it or push it to the back of his mind. It stuck in the front of his consciousness like the sharp instrument she no doubt wished to plunge into him.

He remembered the little girl, intelligent and brave and full of life. And now he saw how the life of a lady had closed about her like a cage. He understood, because he was too intelligent not to, that she was suffocating.

That was why, he realized. That was why he'd made Mistake Number Seven.

"Please," she said. "I promise to do what you say."

Please. Oh, good. Stab to the heart follows stab to the head.

"Very well," he said. "Firstly, you may not bring your maid. It'll be bad enough, my bringing a female into it. Two females is not to be contemplated."

She opened her mouth, and he knew she was going to argue. Then she took a deep breath, folded her hands, and nodded.

"Secondly—"

He broke off because he heard voices in the outer office.

"What the devil do you mean?" Westcott was saying. "It's *my* office."

"Yes, sir, but—"

"Get out of the way."

Lady Clara kept her hands folded and merely looked toward the door, eyebrows very slightly upraised in the manner of one witnessing a gaffe.

The door opened and Westcott strode in, Davis close behind him. "I say, Radford, this is the outside of enough. The dratted boy stood in front of the door—*my* door—and said—"

"Mrs. Faxon, you will remember Mr. Westcott, I believe," Radford cut in.

Lady Clara gave a regal nod. Her hair was coming down and her dress was wrinkled but her damp clothing directed blame to the rainstorm rather than to Radford. Not by so much as a twitch or a blink did she betray the truth of what had happened recently, and not even Westcott would suspect that his friend and colleague had kissed her in a most ill-considered manner, might easily have gone further than was remotely acceptable or safe, and had not yet recovered fully.

"I was beginning to grow alarmed, Davis," Lady Clara said. "I expected to find you here waiting for me."

Westcott did not give Davis a chance to respond. As though she were a client, he went into full attorney mode, and answered for her. "Miss Davis would have been here in a matter of minutes, but for the crowd in Old Bailey when the session ended," he said. "As often happens, her hackney driver made a detour to avoid the crush. But there was an accident near the Fleet Prison. Somebody injured and a vehicle smashed."

"I didn't see it," Davis said. "I couldn't see anything, between the rain and the dirty window. My driver told me why he had to stop. A crowd had gathered. We were obliged to wait for some time."

"Did you make the same detour?" Radford asked his friend. "I'd expected you long before now."

"I decided to wait out the worst of the rain at the coffeehouse," Westcott said. "When it had abated somewhat, I made use of the umbrella you so kindly sent to me, and walked. I met Miss Davis at the gate."

"Then we're all accounted for," Lady Clara said.

"Yes, my lady, and time to be returning," Davis said "Lady Exton will be expecting your ladyship."

"The lady—that is to say, *Mrs. Faxon*—will not be returning quite yet," Radford said. "We have business to transact. We're going to retrieve Toby Coppy, and I require the lady's assistance."

The maid's eyes widened and her mouth opened. Then it snapped shut and set in a tight line.

Westcott, not being a servant, didn't feel any need to subdue himself. "Are you quite mad?" he said. "You cannot take La—"

"Mrs. Faxon is vital to the mission," Radford said, with a glance toward the door. Tilsley, to his knowledge, wasn't a habitual eavesdropper. The door was thick, in any event. Yet he must have heard something, to make him decide to play sentry.

Radford moved to close the door. Then he said in a low voice, "Let's keep our clerk out of this for the moment. The fewer who know, the better." He looked at Davis. "I give you my word no harm will come to your lady. Neither she nor I will participate directly. This is a police matter, and they don't want amateurs bollixing up their plans. But the enterprise will proceed more smoothly and rapidly if the lady is on hand to identify Toby. If he balks, she'll persuade him to cooperate."

"It's all right, Davis," Lady Clara said. "I'll be surrounded by police. Armed with batons."

"Yes, my lady. If you say so."

"If I may say so, I must strongly advise her la—the lady—against it," Westcott said. "If anything goes wrong—"

"I realize there's a possibility of unplanned-for events," she said. "Rest assured I'll bring a weapon. And if that isn't enough, Mr. Radford will be by to talk the villains to death."

It was a good thing Radford had a dictatorial personality. A great deal of arguing ensued—or tried to ensue—before he quashed it.

The maid was furious about not being allowed to come, and he wasn't happy to exclude her, but the last thing they needed was another woman, especially one who might easily make misguided attempts to protect her charge. He'd already complicated matters more than sufficiently.

A dozen times in the next hour he told himself to go back on his word. What was the worst Lady Clara could do? Hate him? Strike him?

He was a rational man. He prized logic. He knew his promise was irrational and he needed to take it back. He tried to do so once, twice, thrice—and each time, her taut speech about her life echoed in his head, and the words, the sensible words he ought to say, stuck in his throat.

Instead, he told Davis what her ladyship ought to wear and what time she needed to be ready. He made suggestions about ways to avoid neighbors' and other servants' notice. The lady was not to bring any sort of weapon with which she might hurt herself—this won him a lethal look from her ladyship—but a walking stick or umbrella, he said, was entirely reasonable in any of the less respectable neighborhoods, day or night. "And, as she pointed out, if worse comes to worse, I'll talk until they beg for mercy."

He'd had all he could do not to laugh when Lady Clara said that.

Though he usually enjoyed jokes at Radford's expense, Westcott didn't laugh. He wasn't smiling when Lady Clara and her maid took their leave.

He followed Radford into their private quarters. "Are you quite mad?" Westcott said. "You can't take the Marquess of Warford's daughter on a *police raid*."

"I said I would. I can't go back on my word."

"You most certainly can! How did she get you to do it? Was there coercion? Because you know—"

"Don't be absurd. What would she coerce me with? Her wet hat?"

Radford moved into his room and started taking off his damp clothes.

"I know you're willing to use whatever and whomever will serve your purpose," Westcott said, "but this isn't your fight. It isn't your job to capture gang leaders and their minions. That's what we have a police force for. To prevent crime!"

"I'm only going to retrieve Bridget's stupid brother," Radford said. "The rest is up to the police."

A silence followed, while he swiftly dressed.

Then, "If anything happens to his daughter, Lord Warford will destroy you," Westcott said.

"Only if his three sons leave anything of me for their father to destroy," Radford said.

"I didn't mean he'd kill you," Westcott said. "For you, there are far worse consequences. If anything goes wrong on this mad expedition—for instance, if the newspapers get wind of it—you're done for. You can bid farewell to your legal career. You may have to leave England altogether."

Absolutely true. His other self was tearing his hair out.

"No harm will come to her," Radford said. "No one will find out. If I thought so, I should have pleaded temporary insanity and told her to go home and stop bothering me."

"I'm waiting to learn why you didn't."

"Don't be an idiot, Westcott. Why do you think?"

"Why, curse you? Why?"

Radford shrugged into his coat. "Because she looked up at me with those big blue eyes and said 'Please.'"

"Radford."

Radford found his hat and gloves.

"Where are you going?" Westcott demanded. "Haven't you done enough damage this day?"

Radford moved to the door. "I'm off to Richmond," he

said. "I should like to see my father one last time before anybody kills me."

He went out.

Ithaca House, Richmond
Later that evening

*R*adford told his father what Lady Clara had said, about talking villains to death. At the time, Radford had needed to keep matters under control, and throw his weight around if necessary. But he laughed with his father, who was delighted with the story.

George Radford was not well, and the drawn look of his face spoke clearly enough of his pain, though he didn't. He half reclined on one of the library's sofas, from which he could look out over the river.

But it was too dark now to see, and Radford knew his visits provided distraction from pain and its attendant low spirits. And so he talked, telling his father nearly everything, as always, and leaving out some details, as he often did. Kissing Lady Clara was one of the left-out details. The way his father questioned him, though, told Radford the paternal brain still functioned at its customary high rate of efficiency.

"But of course you must let Lady Clara help," Father said. "She went after Chiver with a horsewhip, you said."

Evidently unaware of the connection to Toby's disappearance, her ladyship had not mentioned the altercation when she first told the story, in Westcott's office. Not until Radford questioned Bridget had he learned of it, and realized how much it told one about Lady Clara. The incident had made Bridget idolize her, and this was why Bridget had confided in her. And set off this absurd manhunt. Boy hunt.

"She isn't timid," Radford said.

"I've never believed in coddling women," his father said. "As your mother has pointed out on more than one occasion, women are not children, unless they're made to believe they are."

He had more to say about women, and Radford, who'd meant to stay for only an hour or two, stayed on, talking and listening, until his father fell asleep. Then he, too, fell asleep, in the chair by the sofa where the frail old man lay.

Unhappily for his sire, though luckily for Radford, the older man was a restless sleeper. It was he who woke Radford—with a sharp rap of cane against his son's shins. "Get up, get up! What's wrong with you? You'll miss your rendezvous!"

Minutes later, Radford was riding back to London. He arrived at the Woodley Building as the sky was beginning to show signs of lightening. Plenty of time, he told himself as he hurried up the stairs and into the private chambers.

He found Westcott dozing in an armchair.

The solicitor woke when Radford came in.

"Is your father all right?" Westcott said.

"As all right as he'll ever be," Radford said. "Good spirits, at any rate. I fell asleep. I was more weary than I'd realized."

"I'm afraid I have more wearisome news for you," Westcott said. He moved to the fireplace, and retrieved a letter that had been propped between a pair of dueling ceramic toads on the mantelpiece.

He gave the letter to Radford, who quickly unfolded it and read.

Her Grace, the Duchess of Malvern, had died after miscarrying.

Radford was wanted at the duke's residence immediately.

Chapter Six

Why should hackney-coaches be clean? Our ancestors found them dirty, and left them so. Why should we, with a feverish wish to "keep moving," desire to roll along at the rate of six miles an hour, while they were content to rumble over the stones at four?

—Charles Dickens, "Hackney-Coach Stands," January 1835

Kensington
Tuesday morning

Clara paced her great-aunt's sitting room. "I should have known," she said. "It was all a hum. He said it only to pacify me. The wretched man's gone without me!"

She'd risen at a time most young ladies of her station would be arriving home from the night's entertainments. She'd gone to bed early, like a child, and dressed this day like a schoolteacher—and all for nothing.

She looked again at the prim little watch pinned to her prim bodice. "I should have realized. He was much too cooperative—that is to say, relatively speaking. Never mind. I know where we're to meet the police. I'll go on my own."

Davis stood at the window, looking out. "I wonder if Mr. Radford gave you the correct information."

Clara stopped pacing. "You think he lied, on top of everything else?"

"I cannot say, my lady," Davis said. "I'm unfamiliar with the streets he referred to. Maybe he told the truth. Either way, you might wish to take a footman with you."

"I can't take a footman!"

"If you mean to go without Mr. Radford, my lady, you'd do well to take somebody," Davis said. "Only consider what might happen should your ladyship arrive when not expected or wanted. I should not put it past Mr. Radford to tell the police to arrest you. In that case, your ladyship would wish to have a servant at hand, to fetch a solicitor."

"Arrest *me*?" Clara said. "They wouldn't arrest Lord Warford's daughter if I stood over Mr. Radford's corpse with a bloody knife in my hand. No one would dare to arrest me, no matter what Mr. Know-Everything said. Why, Papa . . ." She trailed off as she realized what she was saying, what she was thinking. If Papa found out what she was up to— Oh, never mind what he'd do. It would be a happy party compared to what Mama would do. She'd give herself a heart seizure, and Clara would feel guilty for the rest of her life.

"Quite so, my lady," Davis said, reading her face if not her thoughts. "At any rate, here he is."

Clara hurried to the window. Like all hackney coaches, the one slowly trundling by the house was an ancient relic, once the pride of a great family.

Then—in her great-grandmother's time, perhaps—it had been bright yellow. Now it was a mottled mustard.

While its windows seemed newer and cleaner than most, they were small. The faded coat of arms seemed to comprise a half-plucked goose impaled on a pitchfork in a field of rotten cabbages. The wheels were dingy green except for the one that was dingy red—and the pile of rags on the box must be the coachman.

She couldn't see Radford, but he must be inside, since he'd said he'd be inside. He would not come out, though, or stop the vehicle or even wave. A hackney coach stopping in front of the house would give the neighbors' servants too much to talk about. The coach only slowed as it passed Great-Aunt Dora's house—that was the signal—then continued down the street.

Clara slipped out of the house and walked on calmly until she was out of sight of neighboring houses. Then she picked up her skirts and ran to the meeting place.

*Y*ou didn't need to run," Mr. Radford said. "We've plenty of time."

Clara, in the seat opposite, was still trying to catch her breath. It took her a moment to answer. "I thought you'd decided to leave me behind. Half-past five you'd drive by, you said. It was well past six."

"In my experience, women are always late, even for court," he said. "Consequently, I've learned to set an earlier time. You ought to take it as a compliment, my allowing you only an extra half hour for tardiness."

For a moment she could only stare at him while she seesawed between incredulity and rage. "A *compliment*?" she said. "Have you any idea how condescendingly obnoxious you are?"

"A precise idea, thanks to people endlessly telling me."

"I might have slept for another half hour," she said.

"Does this mean you're going to be tetchy and cross?"

"Only to you," she said.

A lady was always courteous. Even if she had to administer a setdown, she did so in the politest possible manner. Clara had learned tricks for concealing irritation or impatience or any of a hundred unmannerly reactions. She'd learned to present a smooth façade, no matter what happened. She reminded herself she wasn't a child, to throw a fit over every little thing. She was a lady of high station who did not allow a mere male, no matter how annoying, to set off her temper. She folded her hands in her lap and calmly regarded him. And that was when, finally, she noticed something was wrong.

"Is that a disguise or did you sleep in your clothes?" she said.

He looked down at himself. He was dressed in the usual black but was unusually rumpled.

"I slept in my clothes," he said. "I was in Richmond. I rode out from there in time enough, but I was delayed at my chambers. I calculated there wasn't enough time to change, then travel westward again to collect you."

"Rode?" she said. "You *rode*? From Richmond?"

"Yes, I'm capable of handling a horse, my lady."

"I always picture you traveling in a hackney or walking," she said. "You're so . . . citified. London citified. I can't even picture you in the country. Richmond is very . . . green."

"It's green and beautiful, and my parents enjoy one of the finest of many fine views," he said. "I went to see them in case you or somebody else killed me today."

"Your parents," she said.

"I do own a pair of them," he said. "Doubtless you imagined I'd sprung full-grown from Zeus's forehead, like Athena. But no, I'm a mere mortal, sprung from the usual place. I have the customary allotment of progenitors, one of each gender, alive and well—relatively speaking—in bucolic Richmond."

"Yes, of course. Great-Aunt Dora told me your father

had retired." She paused. "You said they were well, relatively speaking. I hope they're not ailing."

"My father married late in life," he said. "He's eighty and . . . frail."

It was faint, so very faint. Maybe it was her imagination, but she thought she heard a note of pain in his voice. Her heart squeezed, and she wanted to reach across and take his hand. She didn't. Whatever else she knew and didn't know about him, she was sure he wouldn't welcome gestures he'd interpret as pity or even compassion.

"And you thought it would improve his health to know you were about to risk your life?" she said as lightly as she could.

He gave a short laugh. "I knew it would lift his spirits. He can't do this sort of thing anymore. In his day, the Bow Street Runners and watchmen were charged with keeping order and catching villains. London, he says, was a smaller yet not so tame place in those days. I know he went into law because it tested his intellect in ways he didn't believe a military or church career could do. That wasn't the only reason. Since, being a gentleman, he couldn't be a Runner or watchman, he decided that acting for or against them was the next best thing."

He told her more about the way the practice of law had changed since the start of his father's career, with barristers more and more representing either the accuser or the accused in court, instead of these persons acting for themselves.

In the middle of a sentence illuminating the politics behind the 1829 law creating a Metropolitan Police Force, he said, "Why are you not dozing? I'm at my pedantically boring best, and you're not even yawning, in spite of the thirty minutes' sleep I deprived you of."

"Were you trying to put me to sleep?" she said. "In hopes I'd doze through whatever is to come? It won't work. I can't remember when last I looked forward to anything so much."

"I refuse to believe your life is so dull," he said.

Dullness wasn't the problem. Suffocation was the problem. And despair.

She looked out of the window. "It's not the sort of thing one realizes until one catches a glimpse of something else. I thought I was more or less content, until the day I saw that nasty boy try to make Bridget go away with him."

It had happened on the day after her birthday.

It was as though she'd passed a milestone and come unexpectedly upon a sign at a crossroads. She'd been traveling unthinkingly in one direction, along the main road—the king's highway, in a manner of speaking. But the incident had made her pause, and look down an alternate route.

She hadn't realized until she said it, and even now she wasn't sure she fully understood. All she knew was that her view of the world had changed.

"Let's hope we catch the nasty boy today," he said. "He isn't one you want running about on the loose, carrying a grudge. And as to that, I have a few points to cover, points I had to leave out of yesterday's discussion because of the other parties present."

"I don't recall any discussion," she said. "I recall your telling me what I was to do, and my being obliged to hold my tongue. I recall Mr. Westcott raising objections, which you overruled."

"Do you mean to lecture me on my personality flaws all the way to the rendezvous?" he said. "Because if you're not interested in the details of what's to come, I should like to prepare myself for death, disgrace, or— worst of all by far—the end of what was to have been a brilliant legal career."

She turned away from the window, sat back, folded her arms, and met his gaze. "Oh, good," she said. "Drama."

The house stood in a crooked alley off Drury Lane, squeezed in with others of a similar ilk. Some were more and some less decrepit but all were uninviting. Its ground floor held a dismal shop bearing no identifying features. The morning light had hard going, trying to illuminate the alley at all. At these shop windows it gave up trying. The objects lurking behind the murky glass might have been furniture or crockery or old clothes or coffins, for all one could tell. A china dealer's shop stood next door, boasting windows marginally cleaner and a legible sign. Apart from a pawnbroker near the alley's western end, the other businesses seemed to carry on anonymously. Presumably the area's residents knew what they were, in the same way they knew what went on in the rooms above the shop with the impenetrable windows.

Radford saw Lady Clara examine the watch pinned to her bodice.

"The police will be here soon," he said.

The alley was narrow. Taking extreme care, a hackney coachman could make it through. But the driver—a police sergeant—had pretended to be stuck. Meanwhile a large wagon blocked the other end.

Stokes and his team had better arrive soon, before somebody noticed the two vehicles blocking the alley's exits, and raised the alarm.

Radford became aware of movement. Peering through the small window, he saw the first of the policemen slip into the alley. Others would be moving to block escape routes—at the back of the house and at the places of egress in the court it overlooked. In any event, he hoped that was what they were doing.

It wasn't easy to sit in the coach and look on. He wanted to be with them. He wanted to lead the charge.

But that would be improper. His place was in the courtroom.

And Lady Clara's was in the ballroom or drawing room, where of course she'd shine as brilliantly as any barrister would wish to shine in court. He understood her feeling . . . constrained. All the same, he knew she was never meant for this world, his world. Even at its best, it wasn't pretty.

"They're here," he said. "Now let's hope nobody bungles."

She leaned forward to look out of the small window. As he'd suggested, she wore a schoolteacher's style of garb: a severe bonnet and more severe dress of dull, dark blue with a starched collar, narrow sleeves, a prim line of buttons, and not one bow or ruffle or bit of lace to soften its austerity. Even the watch was plain and practical.

She'd dressed as he'd advised, and he could blame nobody but himself. It was his fault there was nothing to distract the eye from her figure, nothing to camouflage its splendid curves.

She smelled like fresh greenery, and this made pictures in his mind of the soul-soothing view from his father's house. She smelled like herself, too, and picturesque views of Richmond battled more carnal thoughts.

Her face was inches from his. He could almost taste her mouth. His other self was growing thickheaded. He pushed that unhelpful being to the farthest corner of his mind, and drew back a fraction from her, from her scent and silken skin and soft mouth.

"Let's hope we can get Toby out in one piece," she said. "Oh, no. What's happening?"

Nimble as a monkey, a boy scrambled out of a window and quickly down the front of the house.

"Damn," Radford said. "They heard our men coming."

Another boy followed. A moment later, two more boys burst out of the building next door.

"They're getting away!" she cried. "Can't we stop them?"

"Patience," he said, though he suspected something had gone awry with the plan. "The boys were bound to run, and the first thing they learn is to run very fast. That's why we've blocked the ways out, and why we've so many men on the outside. One or two of the quicker and more agile boys might wriggle away, but not all."

More boys streamed noisily out of the house. There must have been scores of them, climbing down the front of the building or bursting through the door, like rats fleeing a burning warehouse. But with constables in the way, they couldn't squeeze past the hackney coach or climb over it. They turned and ran back to try the other way. Some beat on neighboring doors to be let in. Others tried to fight their way past the police waiting for them. Then a shout rose above the scuffling and cursing and threatening, and another. A chorus of young, excited voices echoed through the alley.

"What is it?" Lady Clara said.

"I'm not sure."

He shoved the window down for a better look. "Stay back," he said. "Do not let them see you. We . . ." He trailed off as he realized what the uproar was about.

He opened the door and climbed out. "Stay," he said.

"Mr. Radford."

But he wasn't listening. He was hurrying down the alley, looking up, as everybody else was, at the figure running across the roof.

The boys had stopped trying to escape in favor of watching the show and cheering Chiver on. His hat at its usual insolent angle, he clambered from the roof of their lair to the roof of the next building. This one had a steep pitch, and he slid twice, but managed to catch hold of something—a rope, it looked like—and drag himself back up again.

A policeman appeared on the roof of the building Chiver had fled. The police inside must have encountered obstacles. A constable was supposed to have gone straight to the roof, to prevent this sort of thing.

"Nowhere to go, Chiver," the officer shouted. "Give it up!"

Radford hurried along the pavement, steps ahead of the boy on the roof.

"Go, Chiver!" one of the boys shouted. "Show 'em how you can go!"

"Don't let 'em catch you!"

"Show 'em, Chiver!"

The others took up the cry.

Holding on to the rope, Chiver worked his way upward. He took hold of the crumbling chimney and managed to work his way to the roof's peak. The rope must have been tied about the chimney at an earlier time, Radford thought. They'd want escape routes. Freame would, in any case, though it seemed a risky choice of route for him.

By now all the alley was awake. People hung out of windows, trying to see what was happening. Their neighbors opposite reported.

"He's got a foothold!"

"Won't hold him!"

"There he goes!"

"No, he's back!"

"He's mad! Where's he goin'?"

Radford strode down the alley on the opposite side, keeping ahead of the boy on the roof.

He watched Chiver straddle the roof's peak, swing a leg over, and start sliding down the other side. The rope slipped from his hands. He grabbed the lower corner of the chimney and clung there while he fought to regain his balance.

The policeman was trying to scramble up the roof on the other side.

"He's comin' for you, Chiver! Keep goin'!"

Chiver slid down cautiously. The next roof was a few feet below him. He jumped down and ran across it—and stopped abruptly, inches from empty air.

Between this building and the next yawned a gap. The two buildings leaned away from each other, making the space between them wider at the top. The roof he needed to get to wasn't level with the one he stood on. He'd have to leap upward across ten feet of space.

"Give it up!" Radford shouted. "You haven't got wings."

"That you, Raven?" the boy called. "Whyn't you fly up and get me, then?" He laughed.

"Go on!" one of the boys shouted. "You can do it, Chiver!"

"You can do it!" The boys began to chant, "Fly, Chiver, fly!"

Chiver pulled his hat to a sharper angle. "I can do it easy!" he shouted back.

He started to back away, for a running start. But the constable was climbing down from the peaked roof. "Stay where you are, boy!" he shouted.

"Don't think I will," Chiver shouted back.

"Don't be a fool!" Radford shouted. "Your legs aren't long enough!"

"Yeah, we'll see. Watch me fly, Raven! Watch me!"

With a laugh, the boy stepped back a pace and leapt, an instant before the constable could grab him, and caught hold of the roof edge. The boys, who'd gone utterly still during the leap, burst into cheers. Chiver clung for an endless moment, legs pumping as he tried to pull himself up. There was a hush as he swung one leg up toward the roof. Then his hands began to slide, and down he went, with a blood-chilling shriek, cut off as he struck the paving stones below.

Clara heard shouting, a sudden silence, another outburst, then silence again. She looked out of the window in time to see Radford round the corner of a building, a policeman on his heels. Other policemen were collecting boys and bringing them toward her end of the alley. She was supposed to stay in the carriage, and call out when she saw Toby, but she didn't see him.

She tilted her bonnet brim downward, opened the door, and jumped down from the coach.

The sour aroma of unwashed boys assaulted her nostrils, and for a moment she thought she'd be ill. But she hadn't time for that. Something unplanned-for had happened. By the looks on the boys' faces, it was something dreadful. Most of these children were hardened in crime, according to Radford. Yet while some struggled with the police and others shouted defiance, their hearts didn't seem to be in it.

"What's happened?" she asked the nearest constable. "What was that noise?"

"It's Chiver!" a very little boy cried. "Gone off the roof, he has."

"Splat!" someone else said with a laugh that sounded patently false.

She suppressed a shudder.

"None of these, is it, ma'am?" the constable said.

She shook her head. "Where's Toby?" she asked the boys.

"Which one of 'em's him, then?" one said.

"Never heard of him," another said.

"Gone off the roof with Chiver."

"No, gone to Billingsgate for oysters."

Laughter and more fanciful answers followed.

She started for the house.

"Ma'am, you'd best not go there," the constable said. "We still don't know who's inside and who isn't. They got all kinds of bolt holes."

If they had bolt holes, Chiver would have used one, she thought, instead of leaping from a roof.

She took a firm grip of Davis's umbrella and marched to the house door. It stood open. A policeman tried to get in her way but she adopted her grandmother's autocratic air and waved him aside with the umbrella.

One of the boys made a run for it then, and the policeman had to go after him.

Clara hurried into the house. This time the smell nearly drove her back out again. The odors of dirt and decay rose to her nostrils, blanketing everything in a suffocating miasma. She blinked, tried to breathe only through her mouth, and started up the narrow stairs.

This was worse, far worse, than the ragged school. She could barely see in front of her, and perhaps that was for the best. The stairs creaked and the whole house seemed to groan, but she heard no signs of human life.

On the first floor, two doors stood open. In both she saw clear signs of recent panic: blankets and clothes flung about, crockery in pieces, a toppled coffeepot, an overturned chair. The fire was nearly out, only one or two coals faintly glowing.

The boys had come in, she knew, shortly before dawn. They slept in the mornings, then went out to pick pockets and steal laundry and such in the afternoon. At night they'd break into houses or commit other darkness-friendly crimes, like assaulting anybody who looked like he or she couldn't fight back, according to Radford. Early morning was the best time to catch them. They'd have gone to sleep by then, and most would wake up groggy, slower to react. That, at any rate, was the hope. By the looks of things, they hadn't been very groggy.

"Toby!" she called. "You know me, I'm sure. Bridget's friend from her school."

No answer. She found a candle and a piece of straw. She applied the straw to one of the feebly burning coals and used it to light the candle.

She looked into the corners and behind ragged curtains, calling for Toby. She checked the other room in the same way.

No response.

Heart sinking, she went out into the gloomy corridor, and climbed the rickety stairs to the next floor. The first door showed her a room smaller than the ones below, but crammed with baskets of metal and wooden objects. Articles of clothing and bed linens hung from ropes. The thieves' booty. A treasure trove of evidence for the police.

"Toby!" she called.

She thought she heard something. It might have been pigeons. Or rodents squeaking.

Holding the candle high, she went out and into the other room.

"Toby?"

A sob. Other sounds. Words, possibly, but unintelligible.

"Toby, it's me, Bridget's friend. You remember, I'm sure."

A groan. A cough.

She moved toward the sounds. They came from a heap of foul-smelling rugs.

As she neared, the heap moved.

"Toby?"

"Help me. I can't run. I'm so sick."

She knelt and drew away some of the rugs. The boy lay curled into a ball, shivering. "Toby."

"They left me," he croaked. "Will I die?"

Some of the smaller boys were wailing about Chiver, and one of the older ones got a clever idea and started screaming, "Murder! Them raw lobsters've killed poor 'Enery!"

Oh, good. Just what was wanted now. A riot.

The other boys took up the cry, then the people in the windows of neighboring buildings. Some rubbish rained down on the police, but no bricks. In any case, they were used to abuse and had on several occasions demonstrated skill in quelling riots.

Sam Stokes appeared, without Freame in custody, which meant the gang leader had slipped away again.

The inspector's bland face gave away nothing. Any disappointment, dismay, frustration, or other emotion he felt did not disturb his unremarkable exterior. He waded into the fray with his usual calm unobtrusiveness.

Radford left him and his men to deal with it and turned back into the alley. His gaze went straight to the coach and its open door. He started to run.

"Where is she?" he shouted.

A sergeant jerked a thumb toward the house. "Went in, sir. I had no way to stop her, not without violence."

"She was armed with an *umbrella*! You can't control one female carrying an umbrella?"

He didn't wait for an answer but ran into the building.

"Clara! I warn you, you'd better not be in here! Clara!"

He raced up the stairs, his heart pounding. These old buildings were notoriously ramshackle. They fell in all the time. Only last week four people had died in a building collapse.

But no. Freame might risk his boys—he could always find more boys—but he wouldn't store his plunder in a shaky building.

Rodents and other vermin would abound, though. And fever-breeding filth. The walls were damp. The place stank of mildew and worse.

And who knew what cutthroats lurked in hidden places.

But that was Radford's other self, in a panic and letting his imagination run wild. He thrust him out of the way and stormed up the stairs.

"*Stay*, I told you," he muttered. "When I get my hands on you, my fine lady, you'll wish you'd remained at home with your needlework and your lovers."

He was starting for one of the open doors when he heard the sounds above. Footsteps, making the floor creak. The rustle of petticoats.

He looked up. She approached the rickety railing.

"Don't lean on it!" he warned. "Don't touch it!"

She drew back a pace. "There you are," she said.

There she was, undamaged, apparently. Before he could draw a breath of relief, she said, "Hurry, Mr. Radford, do. Toby's sick and I need help moving him."

Radford swore once, with great energy, then ran up the stairs and into the room.

He knelt by the boy. He felt his forehead and checked his pulse.

He heard her draw nearer, the floor creaking under her feet.

"Stay back," he said tightly. "I think it's only a chill, but there's no way to be sure. Go make yourself useful for once. Bring me the cleanest sheets or blankets you can find. You ought to find plenty to choose from." He looked about him. "They've robbed clotheslines enough, by the looks of it."

She didn't argue this time. A moment later she returned with an armful of bed linens. He unwrapped Bridget's idiot brother from the filthy rugs and wrapped him in the cleaner things she'd brought. He caught the boy up in his arms—he weighed next to nothing—and rose.

"Lead the way,"' he said. "Watch for sharp objects on the stairs. Tetanus is fatal, no matter what the patent medicine quacks claim."

r. Radford carried Toby down the stairs with a gentleness in complete contradiction to the steady stream of reproaches he directed at Clara.

She was supposed to stay in the coach. She had promised to do exactly as he told her. She had broken her promise. He ought not to be surprised. He wasn't. Not at all. He had trusted her—which was very stupid of him, obviously, and he couldn't believe he'd been so naïve. Like everybody else of her class, she had no consideration for anybody else. She was welcome to risk her own neck—indeed, he hoped she would, at another time and far away from him—but she had no right to risk his *career*. If somebody had garroted her while she was fussing over Toby Coppy, Raven Radford's reputation would be *ruined*. He'd be lucky if he was permitted to practice law in Outer Mongolia.

Near the landing before the ground floor, they met the police going up. Mr. Radford interrupted his vituperation to tell them where the thieves' plunder was.

"No sign of Freame?" an officer said. "We haven't seen Husher, either."

Mr. Radford suggested where they ought to look for hiding places.

To Clara's knowledge, he'd barely glanced at his surroundings. But he must have done more than glance, because he seemed to have memorized the room and its contents. In detail. He'd noticed at least a dozen things she hadn't. But then, she'd fixed her attention on Toby.

"Some of them might still be about, but I doubt you'll find Freame," he added. "If he was here when we arrived, he would have made himself scarce while Chiver was putting on a show for us."

Then Clara saw the risk she'd taken and why Mr. Radford was taking a fit. The building hadn't necessarily emptied when the police came. One boy had run onto the roof. Others might have hidden. Freame might have been there. And someone named Husher. While the police ran after escaping boys, these villains could have been standing behind the clothing and linens hanging from the ropes, looking for a way out.

If they'd caught her, she'd have made a fine hostage.

Her mind swiftly painted a picture of what would have happened next, and after that, and after that. She had to clutch the handrail, because the blood was rushing from her head.

"Don't you dare faint now," Mr. Radford said. "And get your hands off that filthy rail. You'll pick up a splinter. Do you never think? You could get a fatal infection. Why must I tell you everything?"

The blood rushed back, and for an instant she saw herself raising Davis's umbrella and swatting him with it.

Later, she told herself. When he hadn't a sick child in his hands.

But at least he'd made her too angry to swoon.

They'd very nearly caught Jacob Freame.

He'd turned up late to examine the boys' haul, one of their better ones. Then he'd learned that one of the new boys was sick. As if that wasn't galling enough, he'd found out, finally, who the brat really was. He'd woken Chiver and knocked him about for mixing personal matters with business. Between that and debating how to get rid of the sick boy quickest, Freame had failed to notice anything amiss in the alley below. By the time he did notice, police were coming up the stairs and pouring into the courtyard, blocking all the ways out.

He'd sent Chiver up onto the roof, ostensibly to get away. The truth was, Freame needed a diversion. While everybody was taken up with Chiver, Freame slipped into the next building, through a concealed door only he knew about.

He stayed hidden in the china shop until the excitement died down.

He hadn't been able to see much, but he'd heard a few things.

A woman's voice, calling for Toby. A woman who spoke in toff accents.

Raven, shouting to "Clara."

Freame didn't believe in coincidences. He didn't believe in much of anything. He could do ands, though, like putting together two and two. The tall nob female who'd called for Toby and the tall nob female who'd given Chiver a beating for bothering Toby's sister had to be the same "Clara" Raven shouted at.

It was a bad idea, Freame had told the late Chiver, to get mixed up with the upper orders. But Chiver hadn't much in the way of brains. A cleverer man tallied the odds. That man measured future profit against present risk.

Freame was in a risky business, after all. And he didn't much care how he finished Raven Radford, as long as he finished him. Chiver was gone, but Husher wasn't. They'd hush Raven one way or another.

The gang leader grinned.

If Chiver's "bleedin' great bitch" was the way to get to him, that would only add to the fun.

Chapter Seven

THE BARRISTER . . . 2. He considers the principle upon which the profession of an advocate is founded.—From our tendency to err, the utmost caution is requisite in the discovery of truth, both in the natural and moral world.

—*The Jurist*, Vol. 3, 1832

*R*adford turned Toby over to a constable, instructing him to take the boy to St. Bartholomew's Hospital in Smithfield. Unlike other hospitals, which had specific days for accepting patients, St. Bartholomew's would admit him without difficulty. The constable would make sure no one let unauthorized persons visit the boy.

Radford would have seen to the business himself, but he didn't trust Lady Clara out of his sight, and he wanted her as far away from Toby Coppy as possible. Otherwise, he'd have taken the brat to a hospital nearer to their route westward to Kensington, rather than in the opposite direction.

He told her all this when he reentered the hackney coach, which awaited him in Drury Lane, now with its proper driver installed on the box.

"I know I took a risk," she said as the vehicle set out.

"But I could hardly leave him there. He was sick and frightened."

Radford gazed into her beautiful face. He remembered what his father had said about women. What his mother had said, actually.

His two selves fought briefly and fiercely. Then, "That was a brave thing to do," he said.

She had been gazing out of the window, her hands folded tightly on her lap.

Now she turned sharply toward him. Her face was white and drawn.

Panic surged. He crushed it.

"Don't tell me you're going to be ill," he said. "You had a hundred opportunities while you were in that house, and better reason. At least I hope you had better reason then than now." He bent his head to sniff his clothing and caught a whiff of Bad Neighborhood. "Or is it me?"

"It's you," she said. "You said something that sounded like praise. You said it to *me*."

"I could tell you as well, with greater fervor, that it was a spectacularly stupid thing to do," he said. "But I've said that already in a dozen different ways, and the topic is beginning to bore me."

"I didn't feel brave," she said. "I was nauseated and terrified."

"But you did it nonetheless."

"I'm not sure I would have done it if he'd been an anonymous pauper boy," she said. "But he was the brother of somebody I knew, a hardworking girl I wanted to help. I'd met him and talked to him. I thought, What if one of my brothers had got himself into trouble? Why do I say, 'What if'? They always got themselves into trouble. And one or the other of them would go to the rescue." She paused briefly. "They came to my rescue, too."

Radford remembered the little girl attacking Bernard.

"But you're a girl," he said. "Given your upbringing, it was nothing short of heroic. I speak as counsel for the defense. As counsel for the prosecution, I can produce indisputable evidence of reckless stupidity and temporary insanity. Even I would think twice, thrice, ten times, before irrupting into a place like that. We're not like those children, Lady Clara, you and I."

"*We*," she echoed.

"Yes, contrary to appearances, I had a gentleman's upbringing. Frankly, I nearly lost my breakfast when I crossed the threshold. I couldn't believe Freame lived in a place like that, as Daniel Prior insisted. But how would the boys know for certain where Freame lived? He might have his own suite in a brothel or gaming hell elsewhere. But it's simpler to house the boys in a species of dormitory and store the merchandise near trusted dealers in stolen goods."

"The pawnbroker on the corner?"

"Very likely."

She said no more, but turned to look out of the window again.

The windows were clean. He'd had that seen to, and insisted on the coach's interior being cleaned, among other things.

The morning light gave her face a pearly glow, but her pallor remained. He let his gaze skim downward, past the long row of grim metal buttons, to her gloved hands, folded so tightly on her lap. The gloves were soiled.

She had been brave. What other young woman of her position would have done what she'd done? Now the crisis was past, though, all she'd seen and done would become sickeningly clear in retrospect. That was why she was so pale.

He told himself she was obstinate, and hard lessons were the only way she'd learn. All the same, he was composing soothing speeches in his mind. But before he could do or say anything to spoil the lesson, the hackney began to slow. He glanced out of his window.

"Bedford Street," he said. "We get out here, to change vehicles. It's no secret I was on the scene, but there's nothing special about that. None of them know yet who you are, though, and I'd like to keep it that way."

They disembarked and climbed into another coach. At the next hackney stand, they changed vehicles again. Following Radford's instructions, the drivers took circuitous routes. Finally, he and Lady Clara settled into one last hackney and began traveling more directly westward.

They traveled in a silence he didn't try to break.

She was lost in her own thoughts. He had a great deal to reflect upon as well. He'd pushed these matters to the back of his mind, because, as he'd told Westcott this morning, a man couldn't be in two places at once, and one didn't break appointments with the Metropolitan Police, especially in an endeavor one had instigated. There would be plenty of time for dealing with Bernard after Radford took Lady Clara back to her proper world.

That would be the end of this professional detour. He'd return to his sphere and she'd return to hers, and they'd never see each other again.

His other self was demanding to know why, and they were having a furious argument when she said, "I trust Toby will recover?"

"Yes, yes, of course," he said. "Nothing alarming in his symptoms. If he'd had anything resembling a proper home, I'd have sent him there to be nursed."

"It's hard to find places for sick pauper children, isn't it?" she said. "If family can't look after them, a kindly person must take them in. Or else they go to the workhouse. Or a place like Grumley's pauper farm." She touched two fingers to her temple. "Such a world. I'm out of my depth, Mr. Radford."

"I should hope so," he said. He wanted to take her hand away from her face and hold it and comfort her. But he wasn't a comforting sort of person, and it wasn't his job, and it was, in sum, a foolish idea.

"The boys said Chiver went off the roof," she said. "That's why you ran into the alley or whatever it was."

"There was a chance he was alive," he said. "I've heard of some surviving such falls, though not intact. But he broke his neck. He won't trouble Bridget again, or anybody else. Cheated the hangman, certainly. And he'll tell no tales. Very convenient for Freame."

"Do you think he egged Chiver on?" she said. "To run across the roofs?"

"Yes, and easily. Chiver always liked to show off."

A short, taut silence. Then, "I don't know how you do it," she said. She gave a despairing little wave. "How you keep your balance. All the poverty and hopelessness."

"I don't usually spend my time in the rookeries, believe it or not," he said. "I've cultivated informants, yes, because I represent the police from time to time. But as I told you, most of my cases are boring. I receive a brief. I study the evidence and the relevant laws. The Grumley case was an exception."

She met his gaze. "You got involved in this gang's business because of me."

"You did make a pest of yourself," he said. "And it became clear that if I didn't take charge, you'd attempt it alone."

This wasn't the only reason. It wasn't, in fact, the true reason. The day they'd met in the Milliners' Society garden, he'd been . . . What? Bewitched was the way another man would explain it to himself. But that was merely metaphor.

He'd watched her walk in the shriveled garden, in all her organdy and lace, with the flowers and sprigs shooting from her hat like rockets.

He'd watched her walk, everything about her fluttering, while he'd listened to her and marveled at her neat summary of his strategy—the strategy Grumley's counsel had failed to understand until too late.

"Not alone," she said. "I'm not that reckless. But I would have plagued somebody else."

His other self decided that, whoever the somebody else was, he ought to be pitched out of a window.

The rational Radford said, "I looked on the bright side. Here was an opportunity to get rid of Freame. It wouldn't change the world or even a neighborhood. Another gang leader would take his place in no time. No danger of that species becoming extinct. But he's exceptionally keen on killing me, and that's rather a nuisance. Instead of looking upon me as a worthy adversary, he holds grudges. But that's the criminal mind, Lady Clara. A very small thing it is. They see the world through their own narrow lenses."

She looked away from him. "As do I," she said. "I had no inkling, until I saw the ragged school, how very small my world is. Today was even more educational."

"You don't need these lessons," he said.

"Generally speaking, no. But among other things, they've taught me how little idea I have of how to begin looking for a place for Toby."

It took a moment for this to sink in, because he'd been lulled into thinking they were having a rational conversation. For once he seemed to be speaking to a sort of . . . friend. It was like talking to Westcott, but Westcott with a much more attractive exterior. But she wasn't a friend. She was an unusually intelligent and headstrong woman. A *wrongheaded* woman.

"Did I say *temporary* insanity?" he said. "My lord, honorable colleagues, gentlemen of the jury—kindly permit me to point out my own grievous error. The woman in question does not suffer from temporary insanity. It is a chronic condition."

Her blue gaze, quizzical, came back to him. "Now what's set you off?"

"You will not find a place for Toby Coppy," he said. "You'll have nothing more to do with him. You're not to come with a mile of him."

"I promised Bridget I'd find him an apprenticeship," she said patiently. "Where on earth is the harm in that? I'll talk to Matron, and see if we can find lodgings for him near the Milliners' Society after he recovers. Matron will be able to advise me as well about finding work for him."

He gazed at her, into those innocent blue eyes, and found himself wrestling the urge to shake her. He opened his mouth, ready to call her ten kinds of idiot.

Patience, he counseled himself. She was naïve, that was all.

Patience, however, wasn't one of his virtues. He had to work hard to scrape up a few bits and make himself say, with what was for him superhuman forbearance, "No."

She wrinkled her brows at him.

"That is not a good idea," he said. "You cannot bring Matron into the Coppy family's problems. You'll complicate Bridget's situation at the school. The other girls will think she's being favored. They'll make her life difficult. More difficult. You don't understand these people and their world. You admitted as much yourself, and you don't know the half of it. They don't think the way you do or the way you did at their age. You must keep out of it. Permanently."

"I *promised*," she said.

"Then keep your promise in a sensible manner," he said. "Westcott is fully capable of finding Toby employment."

Her brow knit, and it was proof of the extraordinary

power of her features that she only looked more impossibly beautiful.

"I hadn't thought of that," she said. "I must be more tired than I realized. I didn't get very much sleep."

Images rose in his mind of her lying wakeful in her virginal bed. Being a man good at solving problems, he easily imagined ways to help her sleep. He crushed the images.

"Then think of this as well," he said. "Try to apply reason to the situation you've placed yourself in. A reasoning being would grasp the importance of removing herself from the neighborhood until the excitement died down. A reasoning being would understand why she needed to keep out of sight until people forgot what she looked like."

"Here's a refreshing change," she said. "You're the first man who's ever told me I'm easy to forget."

His other self was acutely aware he wouldn't forget her. Ever.

How much farther to the house in Kensington?

He said, "For boys like that, yes. They've plenty of exciting distractions, like trying not to starve to death or get beaten or jailed or hanged. They drink to excess, too. Go away for a month or so, and when you return, nobody will be able to pick you out from a clump of a dozen aristocratic blondes."

"Only a month or so," she said. "Fancy that."

"Six months or forever would be wiser," he said, "but I know better than to propose it."

"You're overreacting," she said. "I've noticed this tendency in you. It comes of having to be dramatic in court, I know."

"Dramatic!"

"Do try to think it through in a rational manner," she said. "Firstly, it's unlikely I'll see any of those boys at

Almack's or the Queen's Drawing Room. Secondly, most if not all of them will soon leave London for a lifelong residence in a penal colony on Norfolk Island. Thirdly, all they know of me is that I'm a lady who was looking for Bridget Coppy's brother. What's remarkable in that? Everybody knows ladies patronize the Milliners' Society. Everybody knows ladies throw charity about, to make ourselves feel useful and virtuous. Everybody knows how bored we get, being rich and pampered and having scores of lovers languishing after us."

She was right, absolutely right.

"You have a point," he said.

"Do I?" She leaned forward to peer into his face, and he caught the faintest whiff of her scent. "Did you find it painful to say that? It looked painful. All the same, I'm all aflutter." She sat back and pretended to fan herself with a gloved hand.

"But," he said.

"There's always a *but*," she said.

"The trouble is, they know you can identify *them*," he said.

She dismissed this with a queenly wave, not at all marred by the dirty glove. "Very silly of them," she said. "Everybody knows we ladies can't tell the difference between one pauper and the next. They all look the same under the dirt and rags. Not that anybody wants to look closely at them, since it means getting near enough to smell them. Everybody knows we're perfectly happy to let cutthroats and thieves go about their business, as long as they stay out of our neighborhoods, and stick to robbing their neighbors and cutting their throats."

He narrowed his eyes at her. "Are you quite finished?"

"Not nearly," she said. "They know we'd never appear in a place as sordid as a courtroom. A lady would never be so vulgar as to stand in the witness box. She might as well stand in the dock, because her reputation would certainly be found guilty and hanged—possibly drawn and quartered, too—and minutely dissected thereafter."

She lifted her perfect chin and gazed at him defiantly.

His other self was painfully tempted to do something the rational Radford was sure would only make matters worse.

"Very well," he said. "Do as you like. I haven't time to play nursemaid. I've a libel to prosecute, a dying father to look in on, a funeral to attend in Herefordshire, and a mad cousin's ghastly affairs to sort out, practically simultaneously. I shall leave you to Lady Exton, with my greatest sympathy."

She would go her way and he would go his.

In a very short time, in fact. At the end of this trip across London.

He looked out of the window, because looking at her was making him unhappy and restless and he was having the devil's own time detaching himself. He was surprised to see how far they'd come already. "Ah, we're nearly at Hyde Park Corner," he said calmly.

Clara wanted to tear her tongue out. She wanted to slap herself. But she did neither of these things because the first was easier said than done and the second was vulgar, and possibly a symptom of insanity.

"What is wrong with you?" she said. "Why did you let me go on with my ranting self-pity? Why did you not tell me? Who's died?"

He didn't answer at once. First he looked out of the window. Then he looked down at his hands, resting on his knees. Then he frowned and said, "A young woman, I'm sorry to say. I shouldn't have spoken of it in that cavalier manner."

A young woman.

Clara felt the way she'd done on the day she'd tried, though expressly forbidden, to skate on a pond, and the ice had given way under her feet, and sent her plunging into frigid waters.

She ignored the feeling. It was too foolish for words. He was a man, an attractive man if one overlooked the obnoxiousness. But women had to overlook men's personality flaws, else nobody would ever wed and/or reproduce and the human race would come to an end.

Naturally there would be a young woman in his life. Did Lady Clara Fairfax think she was the only woman in the world because a lot of silly men acted as though she were? Did she think Mr. Radford would be like all the rest, forsaking all others—or pretending to—to worship at her altar?

What nonsense. She knew she was merely this year's Most Fashionable Woman to Pursue, and that was mainly her dressmakers' doing.

Fashion wouldn't rule him. He'd judge for himself.

He was nothing like the other men she knew.

"After such a morning?" she said. "With so much on your mind? Who'd expect you to watch every single word? But here am I, showing off my skills in argument, when you've lost someone you care for. You shouldn't have let me babble on like that."

"Firstly, listening to you was educational and entertaining," he said. "With discipline you might make a fair advocate, were women admitted to the bar. Secondly . . . I didn't know her."

The frozen sensation ebbed.

"But she was young," he went on. "And she died, I don't doubt, from trying repeatedly to produce an heir for my benighted cousin. Do you remember Bernard? You chipped a tooth on his elbow."

She nodded. How could she forget Bernard? In her

opinion, he was directly responsible for the end of her freedom . . . and her life going completely wrong.

"He suffered an infection, you'll be pleased to know," Mr. Radford said. "But he survived. Very recently he became the Duke of Malvern. At present, it seems, his mind is disordered by grief. Or disappointment. Or something. At any rate, they're all alarmed and want me there yesterday."

"Herefordshire," she said, sinking into the lake again.

"Yes."

"For how long?" Why did she ask? What difference did it make? He'd said only a moment ago he'd never see her again.

"Hard to say," he said. "But you needn't worry that Toby Coppy's affairs will be neglected in my absence. I'll write to Westcott from Richmond, and he'll find a place for the boy. Want of intellect won't be a problem. In some professions, the smaller the brain, the better. Some would say that's true of the legal profession, but they overlook the fact that one must read and write—at least after a fashion. On the other hand, any number of boys are useless at manual trades. Our Tilsley, for instance. More or less a charity case. But our reasoning was, firstly, we got him young and cheap, and could train him up properly without having to break him of bad habits—"

"Mr. Radford."

His cool grey gaze met hers. "Lady Clara."

She swallowed. "I daresay we'll never see each other again."

"I calculate the odds strongly against," he said.

Stay, she wanted to say. *I'm not ready for you to be gone from my life.*

She said, "Then I'd better thank you now for helping me recover Bridget's brother."

"You'd better not," he said. "This entire undertaking was against my better judgment."

"It wasn't against *mine*," she said. "It was difficult and painful and sickening and shocking, but it was what I wanted to do, and I did it. I didn't simply hear about it or read about it. I was there. I was a part of it. I saw a world and understood a few things I could never have properly understood before. And I think I'll be better for the experience."

"I think you're romanticizing," he said. "I think you'll have nightmares. I think your maid had better burn every stitch you're wearing. I'll be kicking myself all the way to Richmond, and parts beyond, for not tying you to the carriage seat. Only look at your gloves!"

She looked at them. They'd become remarkably grubby in a remarkably short time. She peeled them off.

"Even when you were dressed in that imbecile disguise the first day you came to my chambers, you were *unsoiled*," he said. "You won't be the better for this."

"I will be," she said. "And Toby will be, too."

"Yes, poor Toby. You're so fanatical about keeping your promise to his sister. You're mighty whimsical about your promises, I notice. What about your promise to me? '*Please*,' you said, in the most pathetic way—and I of all men should know better than to be moved by pathetics— and big blue eyes threatening tears—"

"Big blue—"

"But no, I'm as slow-witted as every other man in London, it seems. 'Please,' you said. 'I promise to do what you say.' And I believed you."

"Oh, Mr. Radford," she said. She moved to the edge of the seat and leaned toward him.

"Don't oh-Mr.-Radford me," he said. "Impulsiveness, that's what it is. This is how you end up with a chipped tooth. I hope dirty gloves are the worst of today's souvenirs. Thank me, indeed. It'll be thanks to my making one mistake after another if you end up with a splinter infection or tetanus. Seven mistakes by my count. No, eight. Number Eight was believing you when you promised. No, we're up to nine at least. Number Nine was—"

"Stop," she said. "Stop it." She reached across and grabbed two fistfuls of his coat.

Before he could say anything more or she could think twice, she pulled him toward her and kissed him. On the lips. Fiercely. Desperately. In the most unladylike manner.

*M*istake Number Ten, she was in his lap, and Radford didn't know how she'd landed there or who was the perpetrator, and he didn't care. He'd raged at her because he couldn't say what he wanted to and hadn't wanted to think what he was thinking.

He wasn't ready to say goodbye forever.

Kensington was drawing ever closer and he was in turmoil.

He wanted more time. He wanted to turn the hackney in another direction, any other direction, even though his reasoning self knew what he had to do and all the reasons he ought to do it.

But now she was in his arms and kissing him, without doubt or hesitation. She grasped the back of his head firmly and possessively, knocking his hat off and holding him in place—as though he'd be fool enough to try to get away. And she kissed him in a way that showed how quickly she'd learned from him. She showed as well how dangerous were the lessons he'd taught her.

The last time, he'd had only a tantalizing taste of possibilities. The last time he'd tasted surprise and a little shock and uncertainty, along with the innocent taste of Clara.

This time she did damage. This time her soft mouth's pressure vibrated through him, to make his heart vibrate, too, and drum heat through his muscles. His brain shrank to nearly nothing, far too small to form a coherent thought. Instead of thinking, he *felt*—the delicious pressure of her mouth, the heat of her body pressing against his, the weight of her perfectly rounded bottom in his lap.

He wrapped his arms about her and crushed her to him. She fit so perfectly in his arms, and it seemed so exactly right for her to be there, as though she belonged and always had.

She smelled of Bad Neighborhood as he did, but that was irrelevant. The real Clara came through, the light herbal scent that blended so perfectly into the scent of her skin and filled his nose and his head and made a fog where there used to be sharp clarity. The dwindling taint of the ugly world they'd visited gave way to the immediate warmth and scent and taste of her.

He broke the kiss to bury his face in her neck and drink in her scent. He kissed the inch of skin above the stiff collar of her dress, and she gave a little gasp that eased into a sigh. She bent her head and kissed the top of his, and tangled her fingers in his hair. He shivered at the touch. He tipped his head back and looked up at her, into her unearthly face, and she put her hand over his eyes and brought her mouth to his again.

This time her kiss was fiercer, so potent that she made him forget she was an innocent. He pressed for more, his tongue urging until she parted her lips to him. The kiss quickly deepened, his tongue tangling with hers. She moved her hands down to grasp his shoulders, so tightly, as though she'd hold him forever.

He slid his hands over her back, down along her straight spine to her waist. The dress was stiff and severe and forbidding, as he'd insisted it be. Under it, layers of undergarments made a barrier between his gloved hands and her skin. Even in his fogged state, he knew he wouldn't get nearer to the real girl. But for now she was real enough, in his arms.

He slid his hands down to clasp her waist, then upward over the gentle curve to the swell of her stern bodice. And upward again to cup her breasts. He wasn't thinking. It was all instinct, and practice. He slid his thumb to one forbidding button and pushed it through its buttonhole.

Her hand covered his. She broke the kiss.

He stilled, as much as he could. He became suddenly aware of the pounding of his heart and the harshness of his breathing. He was far more heated than the situation warranted. One button!

She was breathing hard, too, her bodice rising and falling under his hand. He thought she'd push him away but she only kept her hand over his, over her breast.

He looked up at her. Her face was flushed, her lips swollen, her eyes shining. Her hat was tipped askew, and under it, a lock of pale gold hair had come loose to dangle near her eyebrow.

He did not want to be rational and sensible because that meant stopping and he didn't want to stop, not yet, not for a long time. He wanted to do unspeakable things to her ladyship, with her ladyship, here in a dilapidated hackney coach.

He made himself come to his senses.

He slid his hand out from under hers and tucked the button back into its buttonhole.

He didn't want her to come to her senses, either, but she did. She eased off his lap and back onto her seat in one smooth movement. She straightened her hat, smoothed the front of her dress, folded her hands, and looked out of the window.

She said, "I'm not going to ask if you're done being hysterical. It would be plain to the meanest intelligence that you've stored up years of that article, and it's bound to break out at intervals."

"Hysterical!"

"I'm not going to apologize for kissing you," she went on. "I'm not going to make excuses for doing so. The facts are simple and obvious. You would not stop scolding me and ranting. I'd had enough. I succumbed to a normal and natural feminine urge to silence a man talking nonsense." She turned to meet his gaze, her chin up, her eyes bright, her cheeks pink. "And I will *not* promise never to do it again. I seem to have stored up a quantity of rebelliousness over the years, and you have the knack of unleashing it. You are extremely aggravating."

"You could have hit me with the umbrella," he said.

"Maybe next time," she said. "Oh, I forgot. There's not to be a next time. Just as well. Here's where we part ways."

The hackney came to a stop.

Radford was still trying to digest *hysterical*. He looked out. They were in the Kensington High Street. Already.

"Thank you for a most educational experience," she said. "I think you ought to write to me, but I suppose you won't."

"That would be . . ." Unwise. So unwise. The sooner he separated from her—completely—the sooner he'd recover.

The coachman opened the door.

She alit and started walking away before Radford could pull himself together.

He rose, about to follow her, then regained his reason. He couldn't follow her. He couldn't escort her to her great-aunt's house. The morning was advancing, and the chances of her being recognized had increased radically.

The coach door closed.

He sat down again, and watched from the window until she turned the corner and vanished from view.

He signaled the coachman to drive on, though Radford was no longer sure where he was going. He looked down at his hands and wondered at them and at himself. His gaze fell to the coach floor, and he saw her gloves, which she must have dropped when she reached out to take hold of him.

He picked them up, pressed them to his cheek, then stuffed them into his breast pocket.

Chapter Eight

THE BARRISTER . . . So our advocate has always the honesty and courage to despise all personal considerations, and not to think of any consequence but what may result to the public from the faithful discharge of his sacred trust.
—*The Jurist*, Vol. 3, 1832

Exton House, Kensington
Tuesday 22 September

A lady was supposed to know how to do these things.

Everybody knew gentlemen could be obtuse, especially when it came to matters of the heart. Everybody knew, as well, that gentlemen needed to believe they were in charge. Therefore, ladies had to learn ways of communicating the obvious without being obvious about it.

Clara did not see how one could be more obvious than grabbing a man practically by the throat and kissing him. She'd even suggested Mr. Radford write to her. But she'd offered a way out, and he was an expert in loopholes and technicalities.

Perhaps the customary subtleties of ladyship were wasted on men like Raven Radford. But what was she thinking? No man existed who was *like* Raven Radford.

She sat at her writing desk, pen in hand, a blank sheet of paper in front of her.

Unmarried ladies did not write letters to gentlemen who weren't family members or intimates of the family at the very least. And the gentlemen weren't supposed to write to these ladies.

Though he'd known enough to send his brief messages via Fenwick, "Be at such and such a place at such and such a time" did not qualify as correspondence, even if it was clandestine. But she'd invited him to correspond, hadn't she? And now a week had passed without a word from him. He couldn't still be traveling. He'd have reached the Duke of Malvern's place in a day, two days if he dawdled, something she couldn't imagine Mr. Radford doing.

She knew where in Herefordshire he'd gone: Glynnor Castle. According to Great-Aunt Dora's butler, the previous, fifth duke of Malvern had started building it at the turn of the century. Clara had found a picture of it in the second volume of *Jones' Views*, which illustrated the homes of Britain's upper ranks.

Great-Aunt Dora said nobody she knew had ever visited. She couldn't remember the last time she'd seen the previous duke in London. "I believe the only time any of the Radfords came to Town was to look for wives, though more often than not they found them elsewhere," she'd said. "His Grace liked to keep the family at his beck and call and he couldn't abide London. I can't remember the last time any of them stopped at the town house, let alone lived in it. They usually let it to foreigners."

Clara found it hard to imagine a Londoner like Mr. Radford happily rusticating in a faux medieval castle. He must be tearing out his hair. She could imagine him doing that—losing his detachment and falling into a passion . . . because that was the way he'd kissed her . . . and she wished . . .

But she wasn't sure what she wished anymore. She hadn't slept well these last few nights, and her head was a jumble, thick as pudding. It hurt to think. She put down her pen and closed the inkwell. She pushed the paper away from her.

When Davis came in a little while later, Clara said, "I don't believe I can join my aunt for dinner this evening. I don't feel well at all."

Then she slumped, and would have fallen from the chair if Davis hadn't caught her.

"I don't feel well," Clara said. Her voice sounded odd and slurred. "My head . . ."

"Yes, my lady. You don't look well, either. You're going to bed."

Glynnor Castle, Herefordshire
Thursday 24 September

𝓑ernard was drunk, still.

His Grace the Duke of Malvern had been drunk when Radford arrived, the day before the duchess's funeral. Radford had managed to sober him up for the funeral. That was a mistake. Sobriety only made Bernard belligerent.

His brothers-in-law took the brunt of it, but the clergymen and even the sexton got their share. Bernard muttered during the reading of the Psalms and fell asleep during the lesson from the Corinthians. When they brought his wife's body to the mausoleum, he sobbed loudly, until the rector came to "for they rest from their labors." Then Bernard burst out laughing.

The other family members did not linger. They were at war with one another, as always, and even a castle quickly became too small for them.

The Duke of Malvern owned half a dozen houses, including what ought to be the ducal home, Radford Hall in Worcestershire. But Bernard's father had wanted a medieval castle. With turrets. He'd spent thirty years building and furnishing it. This enterprise, combined with the ongoing project of fomenting trouble among his relatives, left no time for other business. All the estate and other legal matters had, over the last five years especially, subsided into a state of chaos guaranteed to send the average solicitor to the nearest lunatic asylum. But Radford, firstly, wasn't a solicitor, and secondly, liked solving riddles, the knottier the better.

The castle, on the other hand, was splendid. Handsome and built with every modern comfort, it overlooked fine views in every direction. Radford had caught himself more than once imagining Lady Clara's reaction. He thought she'd be amused, but would probably like it. Yet he felt sure she'd like the ancient pile in Worcestershire better, for its character.

He was making a miserable job of not thinking about her, even though he had more than enough to occupy even his overlarge brain.

With the other relatives out of the way, he tackled Bernard.

He found His Grace in the library—by no means reading a book—but sprawled on a sofa near the fire. A glass and a decanter stood close at hand. A wine-stained sporting magazine lay at his feet.

There being more of Bernard than there used to be, he needed most of the sofa for sprawling space. When Radford joined him, he looked up blearily.

"Do you *want* me to inherit?" Radford said.

Even if preambles had been in his style, he'd waste them on Bernard.

The duke blinked. "That's little Raven, isn't it? Dear, dear little cuz. If I wasn't overcome with grief I'd throw you off the premises. Whyn't they do it, then? Or did I forget to tell 'em?"

"You sent for me, you idiot," Radford said. "You dismissed your agent and your land steward."

"They bothered me."

With estate business: his responsibilities, in other words.

Bernard was a brainless bully. Radford did not love him. But he detached himself from his dislike because the dukedom was more than the one man. It comprised great estates in divers parts of Great Britain and all the people whose livelihoods depended on those properties. The vast majority of these people were far from wealthy and worked hard for the little they had.

To His Grace of Malvern they did not exist. On the other hand, his own comfort concerned him very much. When Radford got him to understand that failing to manage the ducal responsibilities would result in every sort of botheration, including reduced income, Bernard told him, "Then you'd better take care of it."

Radford decided he might as well do so. The libel suit was unlikely to reach a courtroom for another month at least, if it ever did. Working for his cousin would keep his mind engaged in the meantime. Radford would have less time and mental space for wandering into unproductive musings and what-ifs and debates about whether to write to Lady Clara.

"I realize you're a pleasanter person—relatively speaking—when you drink," he told his cousin. "Ergo, for the sake of those who must live with you, I will not tell you to stop altogether. But unless you're eager for me to inherit, I recommend you reduce the quantity of intoxicants by at least one half."

He stepped closer and studied the duke's eyes. They weren't grey, like Radford's, but hazel. The whites were not white, either. It was hard to be certain, even in daylight, because his eyes were always bloodshot, but Radford detected a yellow tinge.

"Your physician believes an excess of yellow bile presents an immediate danger to your health," he went on. "I must, on the evidence, agree with him, although, on the whole, I find medical persons to be backward, superstitious, and given to worship at the altar of antiquated theory, even in clear and unmistakable contradiction to clinical experience."

"Want to say it again in English?" Bernard said. "You always was so talkative. Big words, too. And Latin and Greek. How I stay awake when you talk is a mystery to me. And sit down, curse you. You're giving me a neck ache."

Radford drew up a chair and sat where he could face his cousin straight on. "If you don't become more temperate in your habits you'll die young. Before that, though, you'll become impotent. Meaning—"

"I know what that means." Bernard laughed. "Sad, soggy cock. That your trouble, little Raven? That what makes you such a pain in the arse?"

"It's *your* cock we're talking about, you numskull," Radford said. "Now here's the thing. You want to remarry, right? Want to try again for little boys?"

"Live ones," Bernard growled. He blinked hard, and his face crumpled into quivering folds. "She . . . Two girls only, and they didn't last long. She lost the others before she could birth 'em. Then she was sick. Well, how was I to know? Silly cow. Don't know why I miss her."

"Because she was better than you deserved, which I

am sure will always be the case. Listen to me, Cousin. We both know that many parents would sell their nubile daughters to a duke wanting an heir, no matter if he was covered with warts and boils and succumbing to syphilitic dementia."

Bernard heaved himself forward. But since his great belly wouldn't let him go far, he failed to appear threatening. Comical was more like it. "I ain't poxed, you beaky little turd!"

"For your future bride's sake, I'm glad to hear it," Radford said. "I'm glad as well to know your education wasn't entirely wasted, for you seem to understand some big words."

"If I wasn't sick with grief, I'd land you a facer." The duke sank back onto the sofa.

"I only wish to point out that, no matter what ailments you do or do not suffer from, no matter how young and nubile your next bride is, you will not get another child of any kind if you don't stop guzzling drink and laudanum at your present rate."

"Didn't you notice it was a funeral you were at the other day?"

"Don't insult my intelligence by blaming grief," Radford said. "You've been intemperate since boyhood. Until Her Grace's funeral, nobody had seen you sober for the last six years."

Bernard refilled his glass. For a time he regarded Radford over the rim. Then he tipped his head back and emptied it down his throat.

"Ah, witty repartee," Radford said. He rose. "Well, I've said my piece."

"You ain't going!"

"No such luck," Radford said. "For either of us. I've an appointment with your new land steward."

Finding a replacement hadn't been easy. The last one

had left matters in a disarray not wholly his fault, and not all qualified men were like Radford, enchanted at the prospect of untangling a Gordian knot.

"Oh, I've got one, have I? As stupid as the last?"

"Yes, but you're paying him more to compensate," Radford said. "As well, I've rehired your agent, Dursley, because he's the most competent fellow within fifty miles."

Bernard blinked at him. He probably didn't remember who Dursley was.

"Pray don't trouble your delicate little brain about a thing," Radford said. "We'll endeavor to muddle along without you." He started out of the room, then paused a pace from the threshold. "By the way, as long as I'm doing everything else, does Your Majesty wish me to find a bride for you? Given your present state of health, I recommend you make haste."

"Ha ha. You wit, you. Why, yes, find me a bride, there's a good little Raven."

Radford went out. Someone of strong will and strong stomach, he thought, might whip his fool cousin into shape. He could write to Lady Clara for suggestions . . .

I think you ought to write to me, but I suppose you won't.

No, he supposed he'd better not. He was sure that would be Mistake Number Eleven.

The message arrived a short time later, while Radford was closeted with Sanborne, the new land steward, in the muniments room.

Although it bore Westcott's handwriting, Radford would have tossed it aside had it not arrived express. He knew Westcott wouldn't send a letter express merely to bother him with legal business. Heart racing, he tore it open.

Westcott had folded a second document inside. He'd simply written, "Enclosed letter received today from her ladyship's maid. Kindly read immediately." Both messages were dated yesterday.

Davis had written:

> *Dear Mr. Westcott,*
>
> *My lady went to bed unwell and woke early this morning complaining of a dreadful headache. Since then she's grown feverish and suffers pain in her joints and muscles. Lady Exton's physician says this is a febrile attack, and he promises to bleed my lady the next time he comes, if she isn't better. I am sure this is unwise, but Dr. Marler doesn't know* where *my lady has been, and he would never listen to the likes of me, even if I could bring myself to tell him. He doctors the nobility, and most of them only imagine they're sick. He won't know anything of jail fever, or believe it if I was so bold to say what I think. He's like most every other doctor, not listening to anybody else. Even if he did believe me, I worry he'll make it worse. Lady Exton is clever, but she believes the doctor knows everything. And so my poor lady grows more ill by the hour, with no one by who knows how to help her. You may tell Mr. Radford for me that I thank him for the fix we're in. He promised no harm would come to my dear lady, but here she is, so very ill. If she dies, I promise to make him pay, and I will go cheerfully to the gallows after.*

Ice coated his gut.

Jail fever. Typhus.

But it couldn't be. He, more than anybody else, would have recognized typhus symptoms in Toby Coppy. Who else in that putrid place had she been in contact with?

But what had she breathed or touched?

"I must leave at once," he told Sanborne. He hurried out of the muniments room, found the butler, and ordered a post chaise and his bags packed.

He found Bernard where he'd left him.

"I must return to London," Radford said. "It's urgent."

"No, you don't," Bernard said. "You need to be here. Urgently. On account I'm grieving and my mind's disordered."

"This is more important than you," Radford said.

"You said you'd take care of everything, you little turd!"

"I will, but not now."

"You can't go! You can't leave everything and bolt just because—"

"Bernard, I don't have time for this," Radford said. "I've ordered a post chaise. Pull yourself together, will you? I'm needed much more urgently in London than I am here."

Bernard peered owlishly at him. "My dear little Raven's in a taking. Not your venerable pa, is it?"

"Not yet," Radford said tightly.

"A woman, then," Bernard said, grinning. "Why, Raven's got a sweetheart, what do you know?"

"Cousin, you've had enough drink for this week," Radford said. "You need a bath. You're thirty years old. Grow up!"

Bernard refilled his glass. "Well, then, if you're going to be a bleeding little nagging nursie about it, go on. Go to London. And be damned. But take the traveling chariot. And take Harris as postilion. You'll get there faster." He emptied the glass and started to fill another, but the decanter was empty. "And you!" he shouted at the footman standing by the door. "Get me something to drink!"

Radford went out.

Stopping only to change horses and let Harris take refreshment, Radford reached Kensington by Friday afternoon. Lady Exton's porter eyed him up and down, his expression dubious. Radford's other self wanted to knock him down. He was finding it more difficult than usual to thrust that self away and observe the situation coolly.

The fact was, he looked disreputable. He was unshaven and rumpled. He'd stopped briefly at his parents' house to wash his face. He hadn't changed his clothes. No servant wishing to keep his place would let a man in Radford's state in to see anybody without express permission.

As it was, he only contrived to get into the house by saying he'd come straight from the Duke of Malvern. His other self winced at using his cousin's title to open doors even while that overemotional being stormed about in a frenzy of impatience to see Clara. Radford ignored him as best he could.

The porter sent for a footman, who took his time accepting Radford's card and walked out of the vestibule in the most provokingly unhurried manner.

Radford exerted enough self-control not to knock the man down and walk over him. Instead, he told himself to calm down, and settled for pacing the small antechamber he was taken to. If the footman came back to say Lady Exton was not at home, *then* Radford would knock him down.

After an interminable wait, the footman returned and showed Radford into a drawing room. Lady Exton's pallor and state of distraction told him the maid hadn't exaggerated.

"I must see Lady Clara at once," he said.

"Certainly not," Lady Exton said. "I've sent for Dr. Marler again. He'll set her up in no time."

"I'll lay you odds he's never seen a case of typhus," he said.

"Typhus! My grandniece? Have you taken leave of your senses?"

"I can make a strong case for the diagnosis, but we haven't a moment to lose," he said. "Even if your physician has experience of the disease, he's likely to kill her— with the very kindest intentions and volumes of medical wisdom to prove the rightness of his course. He's bound to bleed her, which even some of the most benighted of his benighted profession know is unwise in these circumstances."

He wanted to strangle the oaf of a doctor. It was bad enough for Radford to have lost a day, when every minute counted. It was worse knowing that every minute of the lost time left Clara vulnerable to others' ignorance and prejudices.

"And you've medical training, have you, Mr. Radford?"

"I've had typhus and lived," he said. This had happened in Yorkshire, after he and his father had visited an infamous school there. It was a case not unlike the Grumley pauper farm, one his father had prosecuted. They'd both caught the disease—from the children or poison in the air. No one knew exactly how it was transmitted, although nearly everybody believed it was contagious.

His father had fallen ill first, and Radford had taken care of him because they trusted nobody else. Luckily they'd studied the ailment in preparation for the trip. The numerous treatises, reports, and lectures offered contradictory theories and treatments. But one or two contained elements he'd deemed more logical than the others, as well as presenting, along with the usual anecdotal evidence, helpful statistics. He'd adopted and adapted the treatments he believed least likely to kill the patient.

"We haven't time to argue, my lady," he said. "Every minute counts." The odds were, he'd arrived too late as it was. Catching the disease in the first stage was crucial. "Tell me where she is and save me the trouble of finding her."

"You may be a famous fellow in the criminal courts, Mr. Radford, but you are not a physician," she said. "You will stay away from my grandniece. For all I know, this is your doing," she added in a lower voice. "She was with you last week, and she hasn't been right since."

It was his fault Clara was in danger of dying. He knew it. But listening to accusations, like berating himself, only wasted time.

He marched out into the staircase hall and shouted, "Davis!"

Two large footmen marched into the staircase hall.

"You're not Davis," he said. "Davis! Where the devil are you?"

The maid appeared at the top of the stairs. "You took your time," she said.

He started for the stairs. A footman lunged at him.

"You, Tom!" the maid cried. "You leave the gentleman be or I'll mend your manners, see if I don't."

Tom retreated.

"Davis!" Lady Exton's voice, behind him. The voice of authority, before which servants quailed, or at least pretended to, if they knew what was good for them.

Davis, the faithful bulldog, stood her ground. "My lady, I sent for this gentleman on her ladyship's account, and I expect him to do what needs to be done. With respect, my lady, your doctor didn't know the ailment when it stared him in the face, and I only hope he hasn't signed her ladyship's death warrant."

Lady Exton gasped.

The lady's maid beckoned to Radford. "What are you waiting for? You had better help my lady, or I shall help you to the hereafter well ahead of schedule, *sir*."

"Davis, I shall write to Lord Warford about your behavior," Lady Exton said.

"Yes, my lady, I expect you will. Mr. Radford, why do you dawdle?"

He ran up the stairs.

There was noise outside the room, horrible noise that made Clara's head throb. But it had been throbbing forever. And the headache had spread to her arms and legs and it was in her stomach, too.

She felt a cool hand on her forehead.

Not Davis's hand.

Oh, no, not the doctor again so soon . . . He'd said he'd cut her, and she doubted she had the strength to fight him now. She felt so cold . . .

Shivering, she opened her eyes.

"How dare you fall ill," he said. His voice was low and rough.

Not the doctor.

She tried to focus but it hurt her head. The room was too bright. There was a blinding glare about his head. The voice, though. She knew this voice. She was dreaming, then.

"You'd better get well," he said. "Davis will murder me if you don't, and then she'll hang. You don't want your faithful maid to hang, my lady, and certainly not on account of a trifling fever."

"Raven," she whispered. Yes, she was dreaming. She closed her eyes.

Dr. Marler arrived a short time thereafter. Since Lady Exton lacked the confidence to keep him out of the sickroom, Radford had to deal with him.

He tried reason, but he might as well have talked to a brick. The doctor objected to being questioned—"interrogated," as he put it—by a *lawyer*.

But Radford had dealt with recalcitrant judges and criminals. He badgered the witness until the witness began to shout. Radford reminded him this was a sickroom. The doctor stormed out. Radford followed him out into the corridor, still questioning: How many cases of typhus had he treated? Was it a common malady among the upper orders? Was the doctor familiar with Richard Millar's clinical lectures on the subject?

"How dare you imply that her ladyship suffers from that vile disease?" Marler raged. "Millar wrote of an epidemic in *Glasgow*. It is a disease of the lower orders. Jail fever. The *Irish*."

"It's a contagion, which may float in the atmosphere or adhere to clothing and other articles," Radford said. "One who visits, for charitable purposes, for example, a schoolroom or crowded and poorly ventilated living quarters may be exposed. If you have not had this disease, sir, I urge you—for your patients' sakes—to turn this case over to a colleague who has survived it. In the meantime, as one who has survived it, I'm in no danger."

The doctor argued on, but the possibility of contracting a low disease—one common among the *Irish*, no less—was working in his mind, Radford could tell, and by degrees the medical man began to climb down from his high ropes.

Very well, Marler said. He would seek out a colleague, one of the gentlemen who attended at a hospital. In the meantime, he would leave his orders for her ladyship's maid. He would expect them to be followed to the letter.

He left in a state of spleen very likely to overset the crucial balance of humors in which he put his faith. It would not have consoled him to know that those who found themselves in disagreement with Raven Radford tended to experience similar symptoms.

"Now who is it you're provoking?" came Lady Clara's voice from the bed. If he hadn't known she was in the bed, he'd have had trouble recognizing her voice, so weak and slurred it was. "Are we in court? Have I killed anybody? But it isn't you, is it? Don't let him cut me, please."

He went to the bed. Her face was white and drawn.

"Don't let him cut me, please," she said.

He swallowed. "Don't be silly. Of course I won't let anybody cut you. No leeches, either, unless you annoy me."

This won him a wan smile. But her voice was weary, and he could see her vitality ebbing.

He turned away from the bed, to Davis, whose face, thankfully, was ruddy with emotion, not pale. If the maid took sick, he wasn't sure what he'd do.

"The other night, when she said she didn't feel well, I worried what it might be," the maid said. "I sponged her with cool water and vinegar. I know some say not to, but she was hot."

"You were right," he said. "We'll have recourse to the method again, you may be sure."

"I tried to keep her safe," Davis said. "For fear of vermin I scrubbed her when she came back from your . . . adventure. Sir, she called it an *adventure*." Tears filled the maid's eyes. "And when I scolded her, and said it was a miracle she wasn't a hostelry for insects, she laughed. She said something about a poem about a louse."

Robert Burns, he thought. Only Clara would laugh and think of that poem.

He remembered her laugh as she was leaving West-cott's office, when she'd called Radford "Professor." He remembered the way her smile had brightened the room, as though she brought her own sunlight with her.

"I read where one ought to shave their heads," the maid was saying, "but I couldn't bring myself to it, sir. My beautiful girl." Her face worked.

"There was no need," he said. "I've no doubt you scrubbed away every last foreign article. Whatever made her ill got into her before you could eradicate it."

"I've looked after her since she was nine years old," the maid said. "A rare handful she ever was. You'd better make her well again."

"I will," he said. *I hope.* "First thing let's do, let's strip the room. Let's start with everything fresh and clean. I want the windows opened. That means we'll need a blazing fire to keep the room warm while we freshen the air."

When the fire was built up, he tossed the doctor's instructions into it.

*R*adford wasn't sure what he'd have done without the loyal maid. He was perfectly capable of intimidating others and controlling situations. Manipulating a jury was a skill he'd honed. But any battle took time and mental energy, which he couldn't spare at present. The task ahead of him would demand all his resources. He needed to focus on Lady Clara. Only with Davis as his ally was this possible.

The rest of the household staff were afraid of the lady's maid. When she gave an order, no one dared to say "I'm not allowed" or "Mistress wouldn't like it" or seek permission from senior staff members. She quickly enlisted a pair of strong housemaids to open windows, strip the room, and make all as clean as could be.

All personal care of her mistress, however, was hers exclusively, and Radford found himself elbowed aside when she sponged Lady Clara's face and neck or tried to spoon a little nourishment into her. She'd given her a few drops of laudanum at intervals, cautiously. She must have judged her doses to a nicety, because Clara remained somewhat alert and seemed to digest the little she ate.

Well aware that their watch would be a long one, he left Davis to her work, and went downstairs to make peace with Lady Exton.

*R*adford found the countess pacing what had once been her husband's study. The decor told him she'd eradicated all traces of the late earl.

"It *is* the typhus, isn't it?" she said when Radford entered. "Dr. Marler tells me it's nonsense, but he went away in a great hurry. He said he'd send a colleague, since he was not to your liking, and Clara was rude to him the first time he came."

"What good sense she has," he said.

"He wanted to bleed her, but she said it was a doctor bleeding Lord Byron who killed him, not fever. And she would not consent to his touching her with his filthy scalpel. She didn't know where it had been, she said." Lady Exton's mouth trembled. "She was so like her grandmother—haughty and despotic even from her sickbed—I had all I could do to keep in countenance, for all I was so worried."

She was anxious, and chattering in the way women often did when confronting one ugliness or another. Radford foresaw at least an hour of time wasted with her talking. His usual caustic remedy, he understood, would do nothing to effect a truce. The opposite, rather.

For Clara's sake, he made a furious mental struggle for a tactful approach. He was a barrister, he reminded himself. He could argue a case from any of a hundred different angles. Dealing with this lady would require the gentler language he'd use with judges of tremulous disposition and slow understanding.

When Lady Exton paused for breath, he said, "Refusing to be bled may well have saved her life, and I applaud your ladyship for so wisely taking her side. I know this has been a worrisome time for you. My bursting in, in all my dirt and incivility, was not likely to soothe. I do beg your pardon. But I must counsel your ladyship to be seated. There's no need to wear yourself out."

The ruffled feathers began to smooth, and the lady sat, inviting him to take a chair as well. She sat ramrod straight, her hands folded in her lap. Only a slight tremor of her fingers betrayed her agitation.

"I can't say absolutely that Lady Clara suffers from typhus," he said. "Experienced physicians can't always be certain. But I see all the signs, and I'd rather not risk her health by assuming it's a more benign ailment."

She inhaled sharply.

"However, Davis has done all that I would have done had I been on the spot when her ladyship first fell ill," he said. "Lady Clara is a strong young woman, mentally and physically. We've reason to be optimistic. But we've three weeks or more ahead of us—"

"Three weeks!"

"Three weeks until we're certain she's safe."

He watched her take this in, and control herself, as some ladies could do as well or better than men. "In other words," she said after a moment, "she might die at any time in three weeks."

"I won't let her," he said.

She looked away, toward the writing desk. "I must inform her parents. I've avoided it, not wanting Lady Warford to fall among us in hysteria."

"Lady Clara needs quiet," he said. "She needs rest. She needs constant attention. What she doesn't need is her whole blasted family descending on her at once, which you know will happen. And then what? While we've done all we can to minimize the risk of contagion, I can't assure you unequivocally that another, weaker, person won't contract the ailment."

He reminded her ladyship that Lady Clara's sister-in-law, Lady Longmore, might well be in a family way. Furthermore, Lady Longmore's sister carried the Duke of Clevedon's child. Would she endanger these women and their unborn children?

Lady Exton was not a stupid woman. Presented with evidence, various examples he produced from personal experience in Yorkshire, and himself and his father as Exhibits A and B, the one-woman jury reached the intelligent verdict.

"Very well," she said. "One must write to them or they'll wonder at the silence. I shall simply write in the ordinary way, though telling lies." She rose and he rose with her. "As to you, sir, I'll have one of the guest rooms made up for you. Then I must contrive more lies to explain your presence here."

"I'm a lawyer," he said. "Why else would I be here but on legal business?"

Chapter Nine

Typhus, after it has reached a certain stage, will proceed onwards in its course (a few rare instances excepted), in spite of every obstacle medicine has yet devised to check its career.
—Richard Millar, *Clinical Lectures on the Contagious Typhus, Epidemic in Glasgow, and the Vicinity*, 1833

After sending a message to Westcott for fresh clothes and other items, Radford returned to Lady Clara's room. Davis sat by the bed, knitting.

The bed was a modern one in the Grecian style, with bare-breasted females supporting the bedposts. Apt enough. Lady Clara ought to have a pair of caryatids at the foot of the bed, guarding the goddess's temple. Other Grecian-style articles looked on from the mantelpiece. An elaborate urn clock dominated the center. Cupid stood on its pedestal, pointing to the time on the revolving band encircling the urn. More usual Grecian urns stood on either side of the clock and a row of familiar figures from classical myth posed next to the urns.

Having had the maids draw back the blue curtains to let air circulate, he saw the disordered bedclothes as soon as he entered. In one of her more feverish states, the patient must have flung them away . . . to offer an unobstructed view of her nightgown from the waist up. A plain, virginal affair, with no lace and only a few ruffles, the garment left nothing to distract from her beauty. Even pale and ill, she put the goddesses and nymphs in the room to shame.

Nothing concealed one fact, either: Her undergarments had not created her figure. All they'd done was support it.

Radford did nothing so nonsensical as tell himself he oughtn't to think about her figure at a time like this. Firstly, he was a man of acute powers of observation. Secondly, he was a man.

Not to mention, she wasn't in any danger from him at present. All the danger was the contagion inside her.

Though the evidence pointed to her having been restless earlier, she seemed to sleep peacefully enough now.

He moved to the bed and gently took her wrist. Her eyes fluttered open.

"It isn't you," she said.

"Of course it is," he said. "Your pulse is strong."

"You're holding my hand," she said. And smiled.

He brought her hand down to the bedclothes and released it. This wasn't what he wanted to do. He wanted to hold on and keep her alive through sheer force of will. He was, in truth, afraid to let go, lest she slip away from him forever.

But that was illogical, superstitious thinking. He had to remain detached. Emotion led to panic, which led to mistakes in judgment.

"Tell me how you feel," he said.

"I'm dreaming," she said.

"That's the laudanum." It wasn't the ideal medicine at this stage of the illness, but it was the only relatively safe way Davis had of relieving the pain.

"Do you really think so?" Clara said. "I don't feel so sick now. Was I disgusting?"

"Entirely repellent," he said. "I couldn't bear it. I ran out of the room, and vowed to find another, less revolting girl to look after."

"Are you looking after me?"

"No one else wanted the job," he said. "Especially the doctor."

He heard a shadow of a laugh.

"Are you hungry?" he said.

She started to shake her head, then winced and stopped. "No."

"I'm going to send for more broth," he said. Typhus caused severe dyspepsia, among other symptoms. He knew she wouldn't want to eat or drink anything, but he needed to get something into her, or the disease would weaken her fatally.

"I'll see to it," Davis said. She set aside her knitting, rose, and went out of the room.

After a moment's hesitation, he took the maid's chair. "You must try to take nourishment," he told his patient. "You must do exactly as I say, and get well, because I've promised you would and if you don't, I shall be disgraced, and then—"

"I know. Your career will be *ruined*. You're so charming."

"Everybody says that," he said.

"No, they don't. Never. No one has ever said that about you in all your life, I'll wager anything."

"Perhaps they did not exactly say *charming*," he said. "Perhaps . . . Yes, now I recollect, the phrase was 'tolerable in very small doses.'"

"And yet I missed you," she said. "Fancy that."

She made it so difficult to stay detached. At this moment, it was impossible. He couldn't stop his other self from getting a word in. "I missed you, too," he said gruffly.

"Of course you did," she said. "Because I'm so lovable."

"You are not lovable," he said. "You are excessively annoying. And managing. But I'm accustomed to hardened criminals and half-witted judges, and being with you reminds me of home at the Old Bailey."

Such a smile, then, more like her usual one.

He hadn't realized how leaden his heart had become until now, when the weight lifted, though not fully. Now he knew the weight would be with him until she was well and going her own obstinate way, challenging him and driving him more than a little mad.

"Only you would say that," she said. "I read about ravens. They're so clever. Even when we don't see them, they see us. The best way to watch a raven is to lie flat on your back."

"Well done," he said. "Though you could be a little flatter."

"He never comes straight on, but by maneuvers, and he's nearly impossible to catch." Her eyelids drooped. "I'm tired, Raven."

"You're talking too much," he said. "You won't have the strength to take your pitiful spoonful of broth."

She closed her eyes. "Yes. So clever of me."

He sat by her while she slept, until Davis returned.

Then he moved away, to a far corner of the room, and looked out into the garden while he listened to the maid coaxing her charge to sip: "A small taste, my lady. Come. Another drop. Yes. A little more. You can. You'll feel better, I promise."

It washed over him all at once, an ocean of weariness. The worry and missed meals and missed sleep took hold of him, and he sank under the weight. He dropped into the nearest chair and was asleep in an instant.

*D*avis woke him.

He didn't know how long he'd slept. Hours, it

must have been. The windows were dark. Only one candle burned, light being painful to the patient.

"She was better for a time, sir," Davis said softly. "But then she had a bad pain in her stomach. I fear to give her more laudanum. It quiets the pain and helps her sleep, but I know it cramps the bowels."

Radford went to the bed.

He laid his hand over Clara's forehead. It was hot. Clara lifted her hand and laid it over his and pressed. Her hand was hot as well. The fever was climbing.

She said something he couldn't understand.

"Your head?" he said. He bent his head, to bring his ear close to her mouth. Her voice was so weak and listless.

"Cut if off, please," she said.

"Does your back ache?" he said.

"Take that, too."

"Legs?"

"Those as well."

He had only a confused recollection of his own miseries during his bout with typhus. His father's sufferings, however, were sharp in his memory. Impossible to find a comfortable position. Every motion so painful.

Though George Radford never complained, he hadn't been able to conceal the evidence of his distress. Radford retained a powerful memory of the aged face, so taut and white, the tightly compressed mouth, and the deep lines radiating from his eyes. Radford remembered as well what he'd felt as he watched: his insides so cold and hollow with the fear of losing him.

"She needs to sleep," he told Davis. "So do you. You've been up with her, I don't doubt, since the minute she fell ill, and if you've had a wink of sleep that's all you've had."

"I can't rest while my lady lies so ill," she said.

"Tell me what good you'll be to her if you're too weary

to think or even see properly," he said. "I've had rest. I can do what needs to be done. I've nursed before, and I'm not squeamish. Has Westcott sent my things?"

They were close by, she told him, much to his surprise. He'd expected to be exiled to one of the cell-like rooms on the upper floors, where hostesses customarily crammed low-ranking bachelors. Instead Lady Exton had given him the next room but one. Doubtless she'd bestowed the privilege because George Radford had won her difficult theft case. He'd called it "quite a pretty puzzle," which meant the average barrister would have deemed it unwinnable.

Radford did not for a minute believe his apology had won her heart. His apologies, Westcott had told him repeatedly, rarely came close to meeting the definition.

Furthermore, Radford had never bothered to learn the art of ingratiating himself.

No, his convenient quarters had nothing to do with his limited grasp of polite address. His father had to be the reason her ladyship hadn't had a brace of footmen throw him out bodily.

But he couldn't think about Father now. Mother was a good and loving nurse. Not to mention he'd seemed in slightly better spirits this last time. Or such was Radford's impression. He'd rushed in and rushed away, giving only the briefest explanation of his errand to Kensington, and he might have only imagined his father brightening up.

Never mind. He'd think about his family later.

The present, critical task was keeping Lady Clara from sinking too far to be brought back.

"Kindly have someone bring me the medicine case," he told the maid. "And sleep now, while you can. I'll need you later."

She did go out, though she paused for a moment at the sickbed, and stroked Lady Clara's forehead.

Before the door closed behind Davis, he heard her

murmur to somebody. Within minutes, the young footman William appeared with the medicine case.

"I'm a step away in the corridor, sir," he said. "Anything you need for her ladyship, I'll be pleased and grateful to help. I stay until daybreak. Then Tom comes. Miss Davis said somebody must always be within easy call."

Thanking him, Radford took the medicine chest his father had taught him to carry whenever he traveled. He set up his traveling tea-making kit at the fire, and brewed a dose of willow bark tea. For once he used his pocket watch, to time it exactly.

When he returned to Clara's bedside, her eyes were closed, but her breathing and her hands' restless movements over the bedclothes told him she wasn't asleep.

"I've a delicious treat for you," he said.

Her eyelids came up halfway. "Nothing is delicious," she said.

"I see," he said. "You've arrived at the surly phase of the program."

"I think you should go away," she said.

"Normally, my ears tingle to hear your opinions," he said. "They're so amusing. But that one's boring. I reject it as immaterial. I've made you willow bark tea with my own dainty hands, and you will drink it. There isn't the remotest chance of my going away until you're well. Since you're not well, you haven't the strength to make me go away."

She turned her head away.

"Clara."

She turned back to glare at him, a flash in the blue eyes of the combative girl he knew. "*Lady* Clara to you. Or my lady. Or your ladyship, *Mr.* Radford."

He bit back laughter. He remembered the first day he'd seen her all grown up. The demented hat. The dress resembling a French chef's delirious idea of a cake. The haughty air with which she ordered him to summon a constable.

He wanted that Clara back.

"If you want respect, you must take your medicine like a brave aristocrat," he said. "Think of the French nobles who walked to the guillotine, double chins aloft."

Her mouth quivered.

"Actually, I had my not-at-all-French cousin's chins in mind," he said. "Did you ever see that old Gillray caricature of the Prince of Wales? 'A Voluptuary under the horrors of Digestion,' it's titled. It was done in your grandmother's time. My father has a framed print on his study wall. The prince slumps back in his chair, picking his teeth with a fork. His belly is so big, his breeches can't cover it, and half the buttons are unfastened. His waistcoat gapes, too, stretched so far, only one button is buttoned. Behind him we see an over-filled chamber pot. Behind that a table heaped with sweets. Empty bottles under his feet. That's what my cousin put me in mind of, last time I saw him."

"Cousin? Do you mean Beastly Bernard?" She looked more alert.

"I won't tell you any of his ridiculous story unless you take your medicine," Radford said.

Her chin went up, and though her head, covered in a wrinkled nightcap, lay on the pillow, the arrogant-aristocrat effect wasn't altogether lost.

"Very well," she said. "You're boring me witless and you won't go away. You might as well poison me. It'll make for a change."

He set the tea on the bed table. Then he hesitated.

He knew what to do and how to do it properly. He'd had to help his father move to a sitting position time and again, in order to feed him. He knew he could do it while causing as little pain as possible. But she wasn't his father.

She was a vulnerable young woman dressed in nothing more than a nightgown. And he, of all people, was suddenly shy.

Suddenly insane was more like it.

She was ill. He'd chased away everybody except her maid and put himself in charge of her care. He'd made himself both nurse and doctor because he didn't trust anybody else not to kill her with good intentions. Before the disease ran its course, he'd probably undertake many, more intimate actions.

It wasn't as though he'd never seen a woman in a state of undress. It certainly wasn't as though he'd never touched this woman before. He'd held her in his arms. On his lap . . .

He ought to have written to her, as she'd asked in the teasing, offhand manner that did such disruptive things to his brain.

Too late for epistles, loving or otherwise.

He slid his arm under her shoulders to raise her, and carefully tucked one of the pillows behind her. Though she didn't cry out or so much as whimper, he saw her mouth tighten.

He wanted to take her in his arms and promise everything would be all right: He'd take care of her. He'd make her well again.

He said, "Can you bear to be propped up a bit more? Or shall I hold your head up? I'd rather you didn't choke. A murder charge will gravely disrupt my plan to become Lord Chancellor."

That won him a weak smile.

"One more pillow," she said. She took a deep breath and let it out, her bosom rising and falling. "I feel . . . better . . . with my head up."

He found another pillow and propped her up.

He waited for her to collect herself, then took up the teacup and spoon.

"Your cousin," she said. "Tell me about your cousin."

He commenced the Saga of Beastly Bernard.

Clara was terrified.

No one said exactly what was wrong with her. This in itself was troubling. She'd heard Radford and the doctor quarreling, but she'd been too foggy-brained and miserable to follow it. All she remembered was Dr. Marler's angry voice, and Radford's, so dispassionate, driving the doctor mad, beyond a doubt.

Still, she understood that she must be dangerously ill, if no one came to visit, if even Great-Aunt Dora had stopped coming to look in on her, and—most frightening of all—if it had brought Mr. Radford from Herefordshire to nurse her.

Not that Clara wanted others. She didn't want to see Great-Aunt Dora's worried expression. She certainly didn't want to hear Mama carry on the way she did at everything that wasn't exactly as she believed it ought to be. Mama had never nursed her, in any event. She wouldn't have the slightest idea how to do it.

Until Davis came, nursemaids had looked after Clara.

But she hadn't fallen ill in years and years.

Leave it to her to sicken in the most spectacular way, with a nasty plague of some kind. Not the cholera, else she'd be dead by now, wouldn't she? How long had it been?

Did it matter?

He had come, and he was here, talking about Beastly Bernard, and making her laugh. Inside, that is. Laughing openly was too laborious. It left her weak and the weakness frightened her. For now she had work enough, drinking the brew he promised would ease the pain and fever.

Yet while he talked, fear receded. Hearing about his youth wasn't the only reason. It was his low voice, with the trace of huskiness she found so compelling. The sound stirred feelings she didn't know the names for. She knew, though, that his voice made her shiver inside, and not with cold.

While he talked, he spooned the tea into her. She wanted to feed herself but she couldn't. She was as weak as a baby. She had all she could do to keep her head up. She hated being helpless, especially with him. And yet she was glad he was the one looking after her. Her Raven. Brusque and caustic. And funny. Unlike her, he said whatever he wanted to say. It didn't matter where he was or with whom.

She, meanwhile, had to closely inspect in advance every gesture, act, and word for possible violations of ladyship rules. Except with him.

He was Raven, nothing at all like the other men she knew. No other man taxed her mind the way he did. Even Clevedon hadn't demanded as much of her intellect and wit.

No other man, either, had made her feel what her Raven made her feel.

He didn't even have to try. She had only to look at him. He had only to touch her hand. To talk.

The Bernard story started with Radford's first day at Eton, when the ridicule commenced. Soon thereafter, his classmates dubbed him Raven, a name he liked, though he never let them know. She had no trouble, sick and muddled though she was, understanding how Radford's not-charming personality and know-it-all speeches would have made matters worse for him at school.

"Are you a glutton for punishment?" she said.

"Ought I to have made myself my cousin's toady instead?" he said. "This way, when he or anybody else abused me, I knew beyond doubt I'd earned it. Moreover, the experience was invaluable in preparing me for the courtroom."

Still, the tale wasn't all about being mocked and knocked down. He had funny stories to tell about Bernard, who was not an intellectual giant, as well as the teachers and other boys.

While he talked, she finished the tea, hardly noticing what she did. She felt better than before, not so hot and achy. When she'd emptied the cup and he eased the extra pillow away, she said, "Don't stop talking. Don't ever stop talking."

His voice was the last sound she heard before she fell asleep.

The days and nights passed, while Radford and Davis strove to keep Lady Clara as well-fed and free of pain and fever as possible. Willow bark tea alternated with senna and ginger tea as her main medicines. Then broths, gruel, and possets—any nourishment they could tempt her to swallow. Keeping up her strength was crucial, because every stage of the disease would sap it.

The household worked to help her fight. Maids came and went with prettily decorated trays laden with tempting meals. The cook addressed his art to making easily swallowed foods as appealing as possible. The housekeeper personally searched the markets for the freshest ingredients. Lady Exton discreetly finagled out-of-season fruits and vegetables from her friends' greenhouses. Anything and everything to tempt the patient's appetite.

Every day the maids came in and helped Davis change the bed linens and air out the room. Still, bathing and dressing the patient was Davis's exclusive privilege.

As the disease continued its siege, barrister and lady's maid settled into a routine. Davis kept watch by day, and he took over during the night.

To keep busy and alert while Clara slept, he worked. He moved her writing desk, positioning it to let him see and hear her while keeping the lone candle out of her line of vision. Her eyes were extremely sensitive to light.

On the Thursday, his seventh night at Exton House, he sat at the desk, making notes on the libel case. The room was quiet, but for the scratch of his pen on the paper, the ticking clock on the mantelpiece, and the faint sound outside of the wind rustling the autumn leaves.

"The season, the season," came her voice, just audible. "Over. How could you, Clara? Even she. Yes, Mama, better her than me."

Radford dropped his pen and went to her side. She moved her head from side to side while her hands pushed at an invisible something.

"Clara," he said.

Her gaze came to him. "I must. Don't let Harry kill him. Don't you understand?"

"Clara, wake up."

"I'm going to be an eccentric in Arabia, and live in a tent."

Gently he took her hands and brought them down to the bedclothes. "Clara, you're dreaming."

"That boy. I'll show him. A Chancery suit on the— I don't know. No, no, no. Portsmouth is that way." She mumbled something else, unintelligible.

She wasn't dreaming. She was delirious.

It was a long night. Her fever seemed dangerously high. Sponging her face, neck, and hands was difficult because she wouldn't keep still. Getting her to swallow anything, like a cooling drink, was even harder. Sometimes she would quiet and seem rational for a while. Then, in the middle of a normal conversation, she'd start talking gibberish. At one point, she thought the bed was her carriage and tried to drive it. Toward daybreak, she calmed and fell asleep.

When Davis came in, he gave a short, optimistic version of the night's events. Though he suspected Clara would sleep through the day, as some patients did, reversing day and night, he wanted Davis prepared in case the delirium recommenced.

He went to his room and told himself delirium wouldn't kill her. It wasn't the best sign, especially when her fever seemed so high, but it wasn't necessarily fatal. All the same, weary as he was, it took him much longer than usual to fall sleep.

When his turn came again, Davis reported that her mistress had done as he'd supposed she would. She'd slept most of the day, coming awake a few times and taking some broth before falling asleep again.

But after a relatively calm early evening, Clara woke up agitated. She sat up to rage at somebody in a low, furious voice.

"You villain," she said. "You lying . . . Why do I always? Don't you— Why? It isn't fair. No, no, nothing's fair."

"Clara, it's me."

She glared at him. "Oh, you say. What everybody does. How could you? How could you, Clara?"

"You're Clara," he said patiently. "I'm Raven."

She stared at him, and he had no idea who or what she saw.

"Lie down," he said. "You need to rest."

"I want to go to Astley's Circus and stand on the horse's back with the flags and go round and round faster and faster until my head flies off."

"Tomorrow," he said. "If the weather is fine. But you'll want to rest first." He tried to guide her back down to the pillows, but she jerked away from him.

"Very well," he said. "As long as you're up, why don't you have a nice, cool drink?"

He left the bedside to pour her a glass of lemonade from the pitcher keeping cool at the window.

"Raven?"

He turned back to her. She was down on the pillows, staring up at the canopy.

He brought the lemonade to the bed.

Her gaze came to him. "It's you," she said.

"I hope so," he said.

"Raven," she said, and smiled.

He let out the breath he hadn't realized he was holding.

It went on in this way. She'd sleep by day, and at night she'd come awake. For a time she'd seem rational, then her mind would begin to wander. Most of the mind-wandering time, she talked in non sequiturs, yet remained calm. Night after night she continued like this. But on Sunday, after a time of calmly babbling nonsense, she grew restless.

Sometimes when he talked to her, she relaxed, but this night she only grew more agitated, rolling from side to side. Then she sat up abruptly and lectured somebody who wasn't there, gesticulating. Little of that made any sense, then:

"That isn't what I wanted! You've changed. What is wrong with them? How could I be jealous? Can't you see? Such a joke. But you must not—he's dear to me. Yes, brandy. Only let me get free of this and I'll know— If you don't stop it, Mama, I'll—I'll— Oh, I don't know what to do!"

"Clara."

She didn't seem to hear him. She began raging at somebody, threatening to run, and claiming nobody would ever find her. Then she laughed and laughed. "But not without my maid! No, indeed! I don't know how to lace my boots or put on my stockings. No! Stay away!"

She was flinging herself about too violently. She'd exhaust her strength and undo all the good done in the last weeks.

"Clara, stop it." He tried to take her hand. Sometimes that calmed her.

"No!" She tried to shake off his hold. He held on as gently as he could while she struggled against him. She was out of her head and liable to hurt herself if not restrained. He ought to tie her down, but he couldn't bear to.

"Clara, please. Try to be calm. It's only me, your Raven. Come, my girl."

"I have to go away. I'm going on the boat. Hurry, before Harry gets here. Make haste, Davis. What is wrong with you?"

Back and forth she rocked. When he'd try to still her, touching a shoulder or arm, she'd pull away.

He climbed onto the bed. "Down," he said gently. "Lie down and rest. You're safe. I won't let anybody trouble you."

"The boy!" she cried. "They left him to die!"

"He's all right, my lady," Radford said. "Toby's safe, and so are you."

"It's not his fault. He's only a bit thick. Like Harry. But Harry isn't as stupid as he pretends. They don't know how cunning . . . Don't you see? They're not like you! Why did I do it wrong? Oh, no, let me find him!"

She was pushing at him, trying to climb out of the bed. She didn't realize how weak she was, and Radford was afraid of hurting her while he tried to control her. But she wouldn't quiet, wouldn't lie down.

He spoke softly and reassuringly about Toby being cared for, even better than she was, because Toby wasn't saddled with Raven Radford, but proper nurses and doctors. He tried to make jokes. She'd pause and seem to listen, then she'd try to get out of the bed. When he got in her way this time, though, she jerked away and tried to escape on the other side.

He managed to catch her by the waist, but she wouldn't stop struggling.

He held her down and straddled her. When she started to roll away, he lay on top of her.

She gasped and fell back onto the pillows, her eyes opening very wide.

He was profoundly aware of her soft, warm body beneath him.

He found his brain and made it work.

Rather more hoarsely than he liked, he said, "Be still, will you? If anybody comes in and sees this, we're done for. I'll be ruined, and I shall never be Lord Chancellor or even a madcap judge, my heart's ambition."

"Raven?" she said.

"Yes, drat you. Have you returned to the world of sane people?"

"Are we lovers?" she said.

A pause.

"You're not that delirious," he said. He rose, bracing himself on his elbows.

"Oh," she said. "I forgot. I'm sick."

"Yes. Your fever is up and I need to brew you more willow bark tea, but I can't leave you alone for a minute."

She blinked hard, and he thought he glimpsed tears. She swallowed and said, "I'll try to be quiet."

He thought quickly. "Do you remember how to say the word?"

"What word?"

"The room with the mirrors and twining snakes and trees."

She frowned. After a moment she said, "Hepta . . ." She paused and bit her lip, displaying the chipped tooth.

His heart seemed to be in a state of strangulation.

He climbed off her and off the bed, aware he was shaking and hoping she couldn't see.

"Never mind," he said dismissively. "You're only a girl. I can't expect you to remember."

The blue eyes flashed. "I do!" she said.

"No, you don't. It's too many syllables for your miniscule female brain. And after all the trouble I took to teach you. Dogs can be taught to heel and fetch, I told myself. Monkeys can be taught to dance while the organ grinder plays. Why cannot a girl be taught to say a word?"

Her eyes narrowed. "Professor."

"That isn't the word."

"Heptaplop— Drat you!"

"You try to make your infinitesimally small brain function at a proper level," he said, "I'll brew the tea."

She tried the word a dozen different ways. She muttered to herself, but she did not sound deranged and did not become agitated.

The tea was nearly brewed when she said, with a laugh, "Heptaplasiesoptron!"

"That is correct."

"Heptaplasiesoptron. Heptaplasiesoptron. Heptaplasiesoptron. So there, Professor!"

"That's *Professor Raven* to you," he said, in the same haughty tones she'd used on him. "Or *sir. Genius* will do, too."

"What about 'most provoking man'?"

"And you are not at all provoking, I suppose."

"Yes, I am," she said. "But you like it, Sir Genius. From his lofty intellectual heights, the Great God Raven looks down upon me with amusement. Don't pretend you don't. I see your mouth twitch. I see the glint in your beady avian eye. Why can't you laugh like a normal person?"

"I'm not a normal person," he said. "I'm vastly superior to normal persons."

He filled the cup and carried it to the bed.

He propped her up with pillows, and this time the movement seemed not to distress her so much. She drank the tea without trouble, and when she lay down again, she was quiet, and eventually drifted into sleep. Her fever seemed to have lessened. The delirium had passed, at least for now.

On the next night, she was tranquil enough, although from time to time her mind seemed to wander and she muttered unintelligibly.

Then, near midnight, she grew restless, and demanded her carriage. She tried to get out of bed. This time, when he took her shoulders and guided her down, she went without trouble. He was smoothing the bedclothes when she tried to push him away.

"Come, my girl, you were better before. You need to rest. You can't leap about."

She bolted up to a sitting position. "I know how to drive. You can't make me stay. We're going to Portsmouth and Egypt and Arabia."

This time she was determined to get out of the bed. He struggled with her. When he tried climbing onto her again, she bucked and kicked. Fearing she'd wear herself out, he got off her. He spoke to her but she didn't hear him. He pushed her down as gently as she could, and she went, and lay quietly for a moment, breathing hard. Then she rolled to the edge of the bed, and nearly off before he caught her. This time she fought wildly. "Let me go!" she cried. "Let me go!"

"Clara, please. This is not good for you. Please, Clara, come back."

He was struggling with her, trying to control her without hurting her, when her fist shot up and she hit him in the eye.

Chapter Ten

Though you do not always see the raven, the raven always sees you; and he will steal along, by the side of your route, in the tractless desert for many miles, though when you get a sight of him, he appears always to be leaving you.
—Charles F. Partington, *The British Cyclopedia*, 1836

*L*ady Clara hit hard for a girl.

She must have put all she had into it, because she sank back on the pillows and fell asleep. Worn out, no doubt. Yet her face wasn't as hot as before.

Since she seemed safe for the moment, Radford went out into the corridor and signaled to William.

"Her ladyship has done her best to black my eye," Radford said. "You will have to wake somebody belowstairs and fetch me a cold beefsteak to keep the swelling down. I need both eyes working properly."

A facial spasm, so minute only Radford could have caught it, betrayed the servant's amusement.

"Never underestimate the power of a woman's fist," Radford said. "Too, they don't fight fair. They strike without warning."

"Yes, sir." Another spasm.

"I think the worst has passed," Radford said.

The footman released his rigid control and smiled. "Very good news, sir. I'll get that beefsteak straightaway."

Radford returned to his vigil. His eye was beginning to hurt, but he smiled, too.

The next time Clara woke, Davis was with her. Clara had no idea what time it was. Daytime? Did it matter? Though she was tired, she was a little hungry, for the first time in a very long time. And for the first time, she finished her cup of broth without Davis's nagging or coaxing. She held the cup, too, with Davis steadying it. But the process tired her, and she slept again, for most of the day.

When she next awoke, sometime in the evening, Radford was at his post. Even before she looked, she could hear his pen scratching over a document. She lifted her head and saw him bent over his work, the pen moving steadily.

She came up gingerly onto her elbows to study him. Except for the day they'd rescued Toby, Radford had always been neatly groomed and tailored. She couldn't remember if this had been true lately. She couldn't distinguish one day from another, and she didn't know what had happened and what she'd dreamed.

This wasn't dreaming, though. She saw clearly enough that he was not fully dressed. He'd hung his coat over the back of the chair, and worked in waistcoat and shirt, his long, black-clad legs stretched out under the dainty desk.

At present, only the single lamp on the desk and the firelight illuminated the room. Even so, she could see the way light and shadow outlined the contours of his shoulders and upper arms under the fine linen sleeves. He'd loosened his neckcloth, revealing his throat, which wasn't usually on view. Beard stubble shadowed his jaw. Unruly black curls sprang from his head, telling her he'd raked his fingers through his hair more than once.

Something in his intent expression and in the way the candle cast shadows over the angles and planes of his strong features made her heart squeeze.

She must have uttered a sound without realizing, because he looked up from his work and toward her.

"I'd hoped I'd have a peaceful night," he said. "No luck there."

She was silly, perhaps, but it tickled her when he said things like that. It was rather like her brothers' joking insults—those male signs of affection—though when Raven spoke, it didn't feel brotherly at all.

She swallowed a sigh. She wished she weren't sick and helpless. She wished she had an idea how to seduce a man. But if she hadn't been sick and helpless, he wouldn't be here. In any case, she knew very well she was far from looking her seductive best, scantily clad though she was.

He wiped his pen and set it down. He closed the inkwell and set the paper aside, on top of another document. He rose and came to the bed. Despite the murky light, when he stood over her, she discerned something amiss with his left eye. Was that bruising?

"Did you walk into a door?" she said.

"No, my lady." He bent toward her. His eye was discolored, beyond a doubt. No trick of the light. He brought his arm behind her shoulders, lifted her head, and smoothly slid a pillow behind her, then another.

"I may not be as observant as you, but even I can see your eye is injured," she said.

"Yes," he said. "It collided with your fist."

She stared at the bruised eye, while her sluggish mind worked to no useful end. "I hit you? You must have deserved it."

"No, I was minding my own business—or, rather, your ladyship's business. I was trying to keep you from hurl-

ing yourself onto the floor or out of the window in your
determination to get to Arabia or Portsmouth."

She looked about the room, trying to remember. The
room did not enlighten her.

"You were delirious," he said.

"Oh." She'd rather not imagine what else she might have
done or said. He occupied her thoughts excessively—the
ones she could remember—and the odds were good she'd
been indiscreet. "I dreamed I smelled raw beefsteak. Not
a dream, then."

After a silence, during which she grew increasingly
uncomfortable, he said, "Where did you learn fisticuffs?"

"Harry. Who else? It amused him. But that was ages
ago, when I was little. I can't believe I did that. I'm sick! I
can't sit up without help."

"I didn't get it at Gentleman Jack's Boxing Saloon, I
promise you," he said. "You did it from a reclining position, when I thought you'd calmed, you deceitful creature. It was definitely you, so don't try to wriggle out
of it. I've witnesses to attest to my not having left this
house since the day I arrived. Furthermore, the footman
guarding the door will testify to my eye being in perfect
order when I arrived in your room last evening, and my
not leaving said room until I went to the door to request
raw beefsteak. No jury in the land would find you not
guilty—unless, that is, you batted your big blue eyes at
them."

Clara put her chin up. "If I did hit you, I'm sure you
had it coming."

"I was trying to keep you from hurting yourself, you
ungrateful female."

"Stop whining," she said. "Come closer, and I'll kiss it
and make it better."

His eyes widened, but so briefly she'd never have noticed had she not been watching him so intently.

He wasn't the only one who was startled. Maybe she was still delirious? Her face felt hot, and not for a minute did she believe fever was to blame.

In a heartbeat he recovered his usual cool manner, and took a step back from the bed. "I thought you were done being delirious," he said.

"It must be the laudanum," she said.

"You haven't had any on my watch."

"Then I must be in my senses. Come closer."

"No kissing," he said.

Right. Why would he want to be kissed by a diseased female whose breath would probably stop a charging rhinoceros in its tracks?

"Very well," she said with a theatrical sigh. "I only wanted to admire my handiwork."

After a time of studying the bedpost, he said, "It isn't that I object to being kissed. Even by you. I am a man, as I've pointed out before."

"I noticed that about you," she said. The strong neck and powerful shoulders and broad chest . . . the way his torso tapered to his waist. Since he wore no coat she had a clearer than usual view of that region . . . and of his narrow hips . . . and long, long legs.

She must be getting better. Or very much worse. Maybe her illness had damaged her brain.

"However." A pause, before his gaze returned to her. "You're still ill and not entirely in your right mind," he said. "My manners might be ramshackle, but even I do not take advantage of helpless females."

"I'm not helpless," she said. "I gave you a stinker."

His mouth twitched. "I take the blow as a sign of improving health."

"Maybe it was for the best," she said. "I've been wanting to hit you for quite some time. Now I've got it out of my system."

"From what others have told me, the condition is not so easily cured," he said.

"How many other women have hit you?" she said. A hot feeling went through her, which she knew was jealousy, not fever.

"A slap here and there," he said. "Mainly, they throw things at me."

She did not want anybody but Lady Clara Fairfax throwing things at him.

"That's a good idea," she said. "That way, I'm less likely to hurt my hand."

He moved closer again. "Does your hand hurt?"

It did, actually, a bit. She hadn't paid attention specifically there, pain being a general constant lately. She slid it her hand under the bedclothes. "Certainly not. I only meant that next time, I would be well when I did it, and would hit harder. But no, you're right. Missiles would be wiser."

"Let me see your hand," he said.

She didn't move.

"Do not make me behave in a masterful manner," he said.

If she had been less ill and less self-conscious about what she looked and smelled like, she would have happily let him be masterful.

As it was, she withdrew her hand from its hiding place and presented it.

He took it and examined it, finger by finger. "Does this hurt?"

"No." What she felt was the opposite of hurting. She was piercingly aware of his touch.

"This?"

He went on examining and she went on melting inside. He checked every bone and muscle. He examined her palm, her wrist, and so on. His hand was so warm and strong. She could smell him, too. He didn't smell sick. He smelled like himself, like a man, and a recently bathed man, too.

She needed every iota of her ladyship training as well as her vanity not to pull him down and make him touch her everywhere the way he touched her hand.

"Your knuckles are slightly bruised," he said as he put her hand down on the coverlet, so gently, as though it were a small Ming vase. "I'll order some ice. I should have ordered it with the beefsteak last night."

"I didn't notice it last night," she said. "Probably in the way your bruises didn't show at once."

"You didn't seem injured," he said. "You went straight to sleep, so peacefully."

"And you didn't want to disturb me, and risk getting punched in the other eye."

"I shouldn't have risked your waking up with throbbing fingers. You've enough to cope with." He paused. "As to that . . ."

The way he trailed off made her anxious.

"I'm better," she said. "I know I'm better. I feel more like myself. Not completely, I admit. Still—"

"Spots," he said.

"What?" She touched her face. "I've come out in spots?" It only wanted that.

"Not there," he said. He gestured at his chest and below. "They usually appear on the torso. Red. Small. " He held his thumb and forefinger barely apart.

Oh, prettier and prettier. Red spots. Foul breath. She hoped Davis had bathed her in the last twenty-four hours. Clara had a grisly idea what her hair must look like. Thank goodness for the nightcap.

"I'll ask Davis to check," he said. "They usually go away in a few days, but you'd be wise not to scratch them and risk infection."

"Ice," she said. "You were going to send for ice. For my knuckles." Maybe she could put it on her spots as well, and freeze them away.

She'd always believed she wasn't a vain woman. Clearly, she'd been wrong. At this moment, she'd give a treasured possession—even her cabriolet—to be well again and properly dressed.

"Ice, yes," he said, and seemed to come back from a great distance. "And you seem well enough to try some broth or gruel."

"I'd rather try something more substantial," she said. "What did you do with the beefsteak?"

The spots appeared on Wednesday. Nonetheless, Lady Clara's appetite continued improving slowly but steadily. Likewise her spirits.

On Friday, the colleague Dr. Marler had promised to send turned up at last. He pronounced her ladyship on the mend and scoffed at the idea of typhus. Had that been her trouble, he said, she would never be doing so well at this point. He left written instructions for her convalescent care. Radford threw them on the fire.

By Saturday, the spots had disappeared.

She was getting better.

By Tuesday it would be three weeks since she'd fallen ill, and she was recovering as speedily as Radford could wish. Already she was spending a part of the day out of bed, in a chair. Her strength was returning. She needed less and less help, with anything.

Very soon she'd need no help at all, and he'd have no excuse for staying.

As it was, what he had for an excuse had grown woefully thin.

Radford had some hard thinking to do, and it ended in a hard decision.

On Monday, Clara sat in a chair by the bedroom window, reading *Foxe's Morning Spectacle* while Davis went about her usual tasks.

When the maid came out of the dressing room with an armful of linen, Clara said, "Measles?"

"I beg your pardon, my lady."

Clara read: "'Lady C____ F____, eldest daughter of the Marquess of W____, remains in London with a near relative of his lordship. Lady C____ has been suffering extremely from an attack of measles, which has lasted unusually long but from which she is now recovering.'" She looked up from the paper. "Did I not have measles when I was a child?"

"Yes, my lady, but that is what Lady Exton has told people who called. It's kept visitors away. She said it would keep the family from hurrying back to London, because nobody remembers who had them and who didn't."

True enough. All the childhood ailments had run through the nursery at one time or another, but not everybody had caught every one of them. Since it was the nursemaids who looked after the young patients, and since nursemaids tended not to stay for long—the Fairfax children being little savages—no one could be sure who'd had what.

"Everybody says it's more troublesome after childhood," Davis said. "Especially dangerous for young gentlemen, they say. Like your brothers." The maid paused. "Lady Exton worried that word would get about of your being ill. I believe measles was Mr. Radford's suggestion."

"Not very glamorous," Clara said. "But more so than . . ." She tried to remember if anybody had ever told her. "What was it I had?"

"Typhus was Mr. Radford's diagnosis, my lady."

"Good grief."

"Indeed."

"Yet I lived."

"So it seems."

Thanks to him. *Typhus!*

"Then measles will do nicely," Clara said calmly. "It won't cause Mama heart failure."

"No, it won't, my lady. He thinks of everything."

Clara looked up, but the maid was carrying the soiled linen out of the room.

Not half an hour later, the three Noirot sisters turned up, obviously unafraid of measles and, in the Duchess of Clevedon's case, undeterred by an advanced state of pregnancy.

Clara told them nothing of the truth, but she did try on the clothes they brought her, their idea of convalescent gifts.

Tuesday 13 October

"I 've come to say goodbye," Radford said.

The weeks of looking after her and hiding his anxiety had caught up with him at last, and he'd slept most of yesterday. At one point, he'd been distantly aware of visitors descending on his patient—who was no longer his patient, he reminded himself.

The callers had been women. They were, moreover, women whose otherwise flawless English betrayed to his sharp ears a Parisian upbringing.

It wanted no brain power at all to deduce their identities. These were the famous modistes of Maison Noirot. They bustled along the corridor, talking, sometimes all at once, and he could hear their voices until, after a few minutes, they closed Lady Clara's bedroom door.

A moment ago he'd closed her bedroom door, too, not thinking about propriety, because he hadn't needed to before.

Lady Clara set aside the book she'd been reading, and folded her hands in her lap.

He'd become so used to seeing her in her nightgown. Later, as she became stronger and able to leave her bed for stretches of time, she'd worn a simple wrap over the nightdress. Now she was dressed in the elaborate disha- bille women called morning dress.

Hers comprised a cloud of embroidered muslin, the sleeves full to the elbow and snug on her lower arms. It fit snugly over her bosom and waist as well. Yards of lace and ribbons garnished the concoction, and a pink sash, tied in a bow at her waist, called attention to her figure's lush femininity. As though any man with working eye- sight needed this pointed out.

Instead of the virginal nightcap, she wore a lacy cap trimmed in pink, from which a pair of lacy pink lappets dangled over her shoulders to point to her bosom, in case one didn't know the way.

In case one hadn't undone a button there, once.

A lifetime ago, it seemed.

With her return to what she'd deem proper dress, he saw the wall between their two worlds go up.

Which was exactly what any rational man would expect to happen.

The rational man knew that everything would revert to what it was before. She'd been ill, that was all. She hadn't changed into somebody else. This was the reason a ratio- nal man stood here, saying goodbye.

"Did my sister-in-law and her sisters frighten you yes- terday?" she said.

"Women do not frighten me," he said. "Even some- what French women."

"No, of course not," she said. "How silly of me. Natu- rally you deem it time to go. You've taken care of me.

Now you must go back to Herefordshire and take care of your beastly cousin."

He advanced further into the room. "You ought to sit nearer to the fire," he said. "After an acute illness, one is more susceptible to chills. Stand up, and I'll move the chair."

She rose in a flurry of rustling muslin. "I suppose you can't help yourself," she said. "It must be in the ducal bloodline, this dictatorial manner."

He took up the chair and set it nearer the fire. Then he drew the screen to precisely the place where it would shield her from excessive heat while allowing sufficient warmth.

"You're every bit as dictatorial," he said. "If I didn't tyrannize you, you'd tyrannize me."

"Of course I'm tyrannical," she said. "I was brought up to be a duchess."

The words struck like a blow to the head and to the heart simultaneously. Inwardly, he reeled. Outwardly he went very still. For a moment only. To collect himself.

Only the fire's crackle broke the room's taut silence. Then she crossed to the chair and sat, muslin whispering, lace fluttering.

"My mother will not settle for less," she said.

He was not in the least surprised. He wasn't cast down. He couldn't be, because he'd told himself exactly this. She wasn't for him. She'd never been for him. He was not a man who deluded himself. He'd seen the facts from the moment he'd recognized her, the day she'd appeared in the Woodley Building, a place where she clearly didn't belong. He and she came from different worlds. She might as well have lived on the moon.

"Perhaps I ought to marry Beastly Bernard," she said before he could step far enough away from himself to fashion a rational sentence. "He sounds as though he needs someone like me desperately. Being despotic, I should not have much difficulty making something of him. In my experience, men like Bernard are not at all difficult to manage."

Radford stared at her. It took a moment for his brain to connect to his tongue.

"Bernard," he said.

"Yes," she said. "He's the duke in the family, is he not?"

Clara's heart pounded so fiercely, she thought it must break through her chest. She needed all two and twenty years of ladyship training to maintain her composure.

"Are you delirious?" he said.

"On the contrary," she said, "I view the matter dispassionately. I've been near death—"

"You were never near death while I was by," he said sharply.

"But had you not been by," she said, "my life would have ended, courtesy Dr. Marler, with my having done almost nothing of value beyond rescuing a not very intelligent boy for his sister's sake. I realized I had frittered away my time."

"You're only twenty-two!"

"It's past time for marrying," she said. "Nearly every girl who made her debut with me is wed. Some have children. I'd hoped for— Well, it doesn't matter, because that was silly. I'd considered never marrying, but that was silly, too. I ought to have realized that being an eccentric spinster could not suit me. Especially living in a tent."

"No one says you have to live in a tent! This is demented."

"I only point out a lady's lack of alternatives," she said. "I've been brought up to do nothing else but become a nobleman's wife, and I've put it off long enough. I don't want to marry a gentleman who asks me because it's this year's fashionable thing to do. Your cousin doesn't sound like somebody who cares what's fashionable. He only wants a wife to give him sons."

The fading green and yellow bruises round Radford's eye showed starker as the color drained from his face.

She hoped he was too shocked to think clearly, because otherwise he'd realize what she was up to.

"Furthermore, if I'm to please Mama and be a duchess, I should like to be one whose life isn't tediously repetitive," she said. "All you've told me proves the Duke of Malvern will present a stimulating challenge to my wits and ingenuity. Clearly he needs someone like me to put his household in order. You'll do for estate business, but that means property and legal matters." She waved a slender hand. "The agent and land steward and such."

"I'm overjoyed to know I'll *do* in some paltry fashion." His voice was choked.

"But His Grace requires a woman to take charge of domestic affairs. I was strictly trained to oversee a ducal household. Because I was supposed to marry Clevedon, you know—"

"My cousin isn't Clevedon!" he said. "Bernard is gross! The day you saw him, all those years ago? That was Bernard at his best. He's *disgusting*."

"So are paupers, yet you undertake the challenge of seeking justice for them."

"I don't have to live with them!"

"His Grace owns several houses, all of them large," she said. "I need not see more of him than I can tolerate."

"He's intolerable!" Radford said. "How can you, Clara?"

She looked toward the fire. "My mother always says that."

Out of the corner of her eye she saw him clench his hands, then unclench them.

"I did not nurse you back to health only to see you throw yourself away on Beastly Bernard," he said.

She glanced at him. His color had returned and he seemed as composed and remote as usual, but the ghosts in his eyes told the same story his fisting hands had told.

"Mama wants me to marry a duke," she said. "She'll be mortified if I don't, and her poisonous friend Lady Bartham will make her life unbearable. It's my duty. The trouble is, I threw over Clevedon, and youngish dukes aren't thick on the ground."

"Drat you, Clara, you don't need a duke."

"But Mama—"

"To the devil with your mother," he said. "You need *me*, you stupid girl."

The silence between them became so fraught that the burning coals' soft crackle sounded like artillery fire.

Heart galloping, hands sweating, she raised her eyebrows, but not very much. "Do I?" she said coolly.

*R*adford realized what he'd said only after he'd said it, which showed the state of mind he was in. Or out of.

He folded his arms and walked to the window and looked out. He saw nothing but what roiled inside his head.

"This is absurd," he said to the glass.

"Certainly it is," she said. "I can't think what on earth I'd need you for, unless I was in dire want of aggravation."

He turned back to her. "You will not marry Bernard."

She sat in perfect duchess posture, spine straight, chin aloft.

"I will," she said. "Unless I get a better offer. I have to marry *somebody*."

Me! his other self shouted. Marry *me*!

He'd all but said it a moment ago. But not precisely.

He glared at her. Then he stalked to the fire. One of the mantelpiece ornaments depicted the naiad Daphne in the process of turning into a tree. He moved her an inch to the left. He remained there for a moment, his hand on the mantelpiece.

It was a pose he'd taken many times before, hand on the jury rail, head bent, as he prepared to speak. The trouble was, this time he was on both sides of the case. He needed to represent Reason. His other self was opposing counsel, aka Throw Caution, Intellect, and Basic Facts of Life to the Wind.

"You're going to try to wriggle out of it," she said. "I can tell."

She could tell a great deal too much. He remembered the way she'd taken note, in no time at all and despite fear for her life, of Jacob Freame and Chiver. She'd noted what they looked like, what they wore, and every detail of the carriage apparently aiming for her in Charing Cross.

"I spoke in a passion," he said. "The notion of your marrying Bernard was so revoltingly imbecile as to cause a temporary derangement of my senses." When she'd spoken of Bernard wanting sons, the image had arisen in Radford's mind of Bernard in the process. With her. For a moment he'd believed his brain would actually explode.

"Your illness has brought about an intimacy that would never have happened in normal circumstances," he said. "I will not deny . . . affection."

Love! his other self roared. *You love her, you pompous ass!*

"If there were no . . . affection, I should take advantage of your confusing, at present, feelings of gratitude with . . . stronger feelings," he said. "I should consider your large dowry and do what I could to compromise you, thus forestalling parental objections. Your family would hate me forever, but everybody hates me. Meanwhile, I should have a beautiful wife who owns the closest thing to a brain I've ever observed in a female, whose influence would further my career, and whose dowry would make life comfortable until I achieved the level of success I intend."

Who would make me happy. Whose face I would be so grateful to see on the other side of the table at breakfast. Whose voice I would be so grateful to hear the last thing at night and the first thing in the morning.

"But," she said. "There's always a *but.*"

"Use your head," he said. He moved away from the mantelpiece, farther away from her. "You're not for me nor I for you. The novelty of living in chambers and being a barrister's wife would soon pall. It's nothing like the challenges you've been trained to manage, and the society is a different class of persons. Not to mention how disagreeable I am to live with. Ask Westcott. One of these days he'll shoot me and the jury will call it justifiable homicide."

"I could shoot you just as well as he could," she said. "And I'd probably have more fun doing it." She waved a hand. "Never mind. You're quite right. I've been foolish."

"You've been ill. Naturally, you—"

"I thought the man who had the courage and stomach to look after me during a thoroughly disgusting disease—a man who'd take full responsibility for my survival— who'd trust only to his brains and wit and patience and c-compassion . . ." Her voice wobbled.

"Clara."

She put her hand up. "I'm not done. This is my closing speech, my learned friend, and you will let me say it through." Her eyes glistened, but she blinked back the tears, swallowed, and went on, "I thought such a man was everything a man ought to be. I thought this was the kind of man a woman could live with happily, whether or not he was a duke and no matter how many large houses he didn't have. Silly me, I wanted the kind of man I could love and respect, one I'd be proud to help advance in his profession—because he'll need a great deal of help, given his complete lack of tact, let alone charm. I wanted the man who saw me not as this year's fashionable beauty, not even as a proper lady, but as I was, and as a friend and companion. I don't see why I'm any less capable of putting up with you than Westcott is, but you seem to think so, and you're a professional arguer. And you seem to think I should never be happy unless I married a duke. And so I will take counsel's advice. I'll marry Bernard."

"You will not—"

"I'm not joking," she said. "This is not an idle threat. I've thought it through. I can do him a *great* deal of good. And don't remind me that he's monstrous, because you've made that abundantly clear. You're monstrous, and you don't frighten me in the least. On the contrary, you amuse me. He's monstrous in a different way, yet I reckon he'll amuse me, too. But, we'll see what I make of him, won't we? Well, then. Not injured, sir? No swooning? No tears? Excellent. Good day, Mr. Radford. Thank you for saving my life."

He told himself that all women were in varying degrees non compos mentis, on account of lacking the intellectual faculties conducing to rational thought. He told himself that if anybody could make something of Bernard, she could, and if the prospect struck him as macabre—if not suicidal—that was emotion speaking.

Had not certain of the King's several sisters, desperate to escape prolonged spinsterhood, married obese old men? At least one of these couples had been reputed to enjoy a happy marriage.

"You're welcome," he said. "Good day, Lady Clara."

He went out of the room. As he closed the door, something crashed against it and shattered. He kept on walking.

Chapter Eleven

This word bar is likewise used for the place where Serjeants and counsellors at law stand to plead the causes in court; and where prisoners are brought to answer their indictments, &c. whence our lawyers, that are called to the bar, are termed barristers.

—Thomas-Edlyne Tomlins, *The Law Dictionary*, 1835

Clara glared at the Cupid.

She itched to throw him as well as the clock he was attached to at the door as well, but then she'd be acting like a spoiled child.

Which she was.

Yet she was a reasoning woman as well, and the reasoning woman knew Mr. Radford was right.

At this point, Mama would have accepted, albeit not delightedly, any gentleman owning a title and some property.

But no, Clara had to become infatuated with a man who had no title and might not get one for years—or ever—depending on his connections among influential men. He lived in chambers, not even a rented town house. His father had property, apparently, but no title. Worse, he'd married A Divorced Woman. Adultery and other marital woes abounded in the beau monde, but ladies quietly suffered or quietly went away without advertising their troubles in costly legal proceedings.

As to rank: Mama had accepted Harry's marrying Sophy Noirot, a dressmaker, but gentlemen were allowed more leeway in marriage as in everything else. As it was, Mama and Papa were ecstatic because Harry hadn't married a ballet dancer. Too, Sophy Noirot had had a lady's upbringing. This, combined with her devastating charm, had made Mama almost affectionate toward her.

To expect Mama to accept Mr. Not-Remotely-Charming Radford was beyond the bounds of probability. And if she didn't accept a suitor, Papa would not, unless *he* wanted to move to Arabia and live in a tent.

Even Mr. Radford, for all his rhetorical skills, would not be able to argue, browbeat, or coax them to accept him.

And perhaps, after all, Clara wasn't a suitable wife for him. She was expensive, frivolous, and shallow. One good deed did not turn her into somebody else, and her good deed was nothing to brag about. Mr. Radford could have rescued Toby Coppy without her, and with a great deal less annoyance, then and afterward.

Her trouble was, she wanted to be somebody she wasn't.

It was the same as she'd always done, wanting to be with the boys, because their lives were more interesting. Their toys were more entertaining. Their books were more intriguing. Their games were more exciting.

Mr. Radford was more entertaining, intriguing, and exciting than any other man she'd known, and so of course she wanted him. But he was a man, not a book or a toy or a game. This man had a career he thrived on. He had a brilliant future—unless somebody killed him—in which she didn't fit. Perhaps he liked and desired her. But one must live in the world, and the world hated large gaps in social positions. Had the chasm been smaller and more easily bridged, their paths would have crossed from time to time in the last thirteen years.

She wouldn't fit in his world and she felt certain her world wouldn't let him in. He was too clear-eyed and logical not to see that.

She was the deluded one.

Very well, then. Perhaps she was overwrought, after being ill for so long. Perhaps she hadn't been thinking as clearly as she'd supposed.

She'd have a good cry—several, more likely—and in time she'd get over this. Over him. Then she might as well marry the Duke of Malvern, for all the reasons she'd given. Why not? Grandmama Warford's husband had been chosen for her. She'd married without love. But in time she'd made her spouse into what she wanted and had become quite fond of him.

According to Cupid's pointing finger, two minutes had passed.

Clara made herself take a long, calming breath, then another. She turned away from the clock. She wished the Noirot sisters were here—with a decanter of brandy, their remedy for all ailments, mental, emotional, and physical.

The door flew open.

Radford stormed back into the room. He slammed the door behind him.

"You will not marry Bernard," he said.

*H*e could not keep himself detached. He'd gone as far as the landing, but he couldn't shut out his other self or stifle the turmoil in his mind and heart.

He was a fool, a great fool, and he'd lose in the end, very likely. But had this been a legal matter, had this been one of the hopeless cases no one else would take on, he would have fought anyway and done what he could.

He could not walk away without fighting.

He was aware of shattered porcelain on the floor near the door. Yet one would never know, looking at her, that Clara was the one who'd thrown it.

She had her screen in place. Every inch the highborn lady, she regarded him with an extremely polite lack of expression. The way a duchess might regard a drunken boor at her party, a moment before signaling for the footmen to remove him. Discreetly.

Still, he'd received more daunting looks from juries and judges.

"You'll be wretched," he said. "Bernard disgusts me, but if I believed he could make you happy, I'd wish you both well." He would, though he'd choke to death, saying the words. "But he won't. He's incapable of caring about anybody but Bernard. You'll throw yourself away on him."

He paused, trying to will his heart to slow down to let him breathe. And think.

"If you must throw yourself away on somebody, Clara, then let it be me. If you must make something of somebody, make something of me."

Her expression changed not at all.

"Dash it, Clara—marry me!"

She scowled. "Is that your idea of a proposal? I've never heard anything so unromantic in all my life. Every other gentleman exerts his intellect—as much as he has of the commodity—to compose a beautiful speech. Every other gentleman sinks to his knees to beg for the honor of my hand. Every other gentleman tells me his future happiness hinges on my saying yes. Every other gentleman speaks of how undeserving he is of such bliss. Every—"

"I'm not every other gentleman," he said.

"Hmph," said she.

He advanced. She didn't retreat. He grasped her shoulders. "Marry me, drat you."

"You're crushing my sleeves!"

"To the devil with your sleeves!" he said.

"You cannot barge in here, after—"

He bent his head and kissed her the way he'd wanted to do all the while he'd stood here before, talking and talking and trying to talk himself into sanity. He kissed her with weeks of wanting, weeks of anxiety, weeks of regret.

She kissed him back, angrily but passionately, and his heart unknotted. He was right, absolutely right, in this. She was right. For him.

She broke the kiss and drew back and glared at him. "If you think one kiss is going to sweep me off my feet— after you rejected me in that callous manner—"

"I'm callous," he said. "And obnoxious. But persistent, too, my lady. And if one kiss won't do it—"

He grasped the back of her head and kissed her again, this time determined to conquer. Her mouth instantly gave way. Her mouth . . . so soft, and the taste of her, like nobody else in this world. Sweet and wild, like the nymphs and naiads and dryads of myth.

She brought her hands up to grasp his arms, and he knew she was melting, too.

He drew away. "Marry me, Clara."

Her eyes drifted open. "I'm thinking," she said, not altogether steadily.

"Don't think." He kissed her, this time with all the feeling he stored deep, deep in his heart under lock and key. But the inner vault couldn't withstand the feel of her mouth and the taste and scent and totality of Clara. She unlocked it, and let loose emotions he'd long forgotten or hadn't known were there.

*S*he thought he'd kissed her before. She'd thought those were grown-up kisses.

She'd been wrong. Again.

His mouth slanted over hers, taking over and taking charge and demanding everything. It didn't matter that she couldn't abide being dictated to. Nothing mattered. Her brain said goodbye and her knees fainted and she wanted to say, *Wait*.

He gave her no time to find herself, let alone recover. He swept her into a raging kiss like an electrical storm.

The world went dark, and lights flashed, but it was all in feelings. Flashes of heat and brightness and soaring happiness.

It was almost more than she could bear. If he hadn't been holding her, she would have sunk to the floor in a little puddle of whatever liquefied article remained of Lady Clara Fairfax.

But no, she was still here, upright more or less, and trying to find herself in the whirlwind of sensations. He was kissing all over her face—her nose, her cheeks, her ears, behind her ears. His hands moved over her and her body was tingling, coming hotly awake. She grasped his arms, holding on for dear life, while the one comprehensible thought in what was left of her mind was:

Ye gods ye gods ye gods.

Yes, he'd kissed her before and she'd kissed him back, and learned some things, but this was beyond it. His hands were everywhere, and everywhere he touched, she vibrated like violin strings under a bow. This was what she'd imagined when he'd examined her knuckles that night. She'd wanted him to touch her in the same detailed way, everywhere. He did it now, but it was more than she'd imagined.

He cupped her head in his hands and tilted her head back and kissed her on the lips once more. It was deep and wicked and dark—his tongue moving inside her, knowing her, claiming her, filling her with the taste of him. It was hot, and turbulent with feelings too tumultuous to sort.

He was kissing her and guiding her backward, and she went, like a dancer following his lead. It was like a waltz, but more heated and intimate, their bodies pressed close together, his legs pressing against hers . . . then his knee between her legs, his hand on her bottom.

She felt the bed against her back but had no time to think because he grasped her waist and lifted her onto the bed. He wedged himself between her legs, and she gasped. This was wicked, indeed, so improper. So wonderful.

Then he was kissing her again, and she brought her arms round his neck and gave back fervently what she received. He slid his hands up from her waist to her breasts, cupping them and squeezing, and she arched back. She couldn't help herself . . . oh, the way it felt . . . and how she hated the layers of clothing between his hands and her body.

He lifted her up fully onto the bed and climbed onto it. Then it was instinct, too, to inch back on her elbows, watching him advance, watching him climb over her while her heart beat harder and harder.

She remembered the dream she'd had of him lying on top of her, and the wonderful weight and warmth and sense of safety she'd felt under his big body.

Then her head was on the pillows, and she was half sitting, the way she'd done when she was ill. Now she was strong, though, and more alive than she'd ever felt before.

He took out the pins from her cap and dropped them on the bedside table. Her heart raced and her breath came faster. He took off her cap and tossed it aside. He undid the ribbon at her throat. She felt his thumb at the hollow of her throat.

He murmured, "I saw that when you were in your nightgown, and I wanted to put my tongue there." He touched his mouth to the spot, then his tongue, and feelings streamed through her, trickling to the pit of her belly and making it ache. She squirmed, and her head fell back, and his mouth was on her throat and her neck and she thought she'd die of pleasure. It was so very, very improper.

And *yes*, she thought. *Yes, this is what I want. This is what I was looking for.*

Then he was straddling her, kissing her, and she was aware of his hand sliding down, dragging up her skirts and petticoats . . . his hand on her knee, his finger sliding up to the top of her stockings, then inching up.

He lifted his head to watch her while he moved his fingers up her bare thigh . . . up and up and up.

She gasped.

He bent his head and slid his tongue over her parted lips.

He kissed her. Such kisses. Long and deep and wild, like passion. Like love.

Then, as she was falling into a beautifully dark, turbulent place, he lifted his head.

He let out a shaky breath.

"That's enough of that," he said thickly.

*H*er ladyship opened her eyes and lifted a sulky blue gaze to meet his.

"No, it isn't," she said.

It was so very like the little girl's voice Radford remembered from so long ago: *I want to go in the boat.*

"Yes, it is," he said.

"No, it isn't."

He was overheated, overaroused, and frustrated to the point of insanity. His other self hated him for stopping and loathed his moral principles. His rational self knew he was in a scrape he likely couldn't get out of. All the same it was all he could do not to laugh at her sulky face and voice.

"I will not debauch you in your great-aunt's house," he said. "It's a moral principle, dammit."

"Oh." Her mouth slowly curved upward.

"Right. Not until we're married."

And how the devil that's to happen is beyond me.

He lifted himself off her. Had he been the sort of man who gave way to theatrics outside the courtroom, he would have torn his hair out.

He shouldn't have let it go so far.

As though he'd had the power to stop it.

The enchantress Calypso was nothing to Lady Clara Fairfax.

She lay back on the pillow, her pale gold hair coming undone, her lips pink and swollen, her eyes soft with emotions he did not want to torment himself by trying to name.

Love or desire or affection or pleasure or amusement.

At any rate, she wasn't hitting him or throwing anything at him.

"Are we to marry, then?" she said.

"Yes," he said. "Unless you want to persist in your stupid fantasy of marrying stupid Bernard."

She came up onto her elbows. "I think you'll be more entertaining. But you're not the one who's the duke. It's going to be a bit tricky, isn't it?"

Damned well impossible. Radford, meet Mistake Number Eleven.

"A bit," he said.

The big house was so quiet, away from the hubbub of London, that the noise from below, distant as it was, sounded like a rioting mob.

Cursing himself for carelessness, Radford slid from the bed, taking Clara with him.

"What?" she said.

"Someone's coming," he said. He grabbed her cap and shoved it back onto her head. "Devil curse me, I should have thought."

From the stairs came footsteps, voices. Two voices, female. No, three.

Davis. Lady Exton.

Another, unfamiliar, rose above the others. "Calm? Who can be calm at such at time? Would you be calm, were she your daughter, and you wondering what was being kept from you? I have not slept a wink since I had your last letter. Where is she, Aunt Dora? Where is my poor child?"

He looked at Clara. She looked at him, blue eyes wide.

"Blast," she said, and hastily arranged her cap, shoving in pins.

*L*ady Warford was not the stealthy type.

She entered the room in full sail, and full speech, the other women trailing after her.

"Measles, indeed! What do you hide from me, Aunt? My Clara had measles when she was nine years old. I remember distinctly, because it was not long after she chipped her—"

She came to an abrupt stop when she saw Radford. Up came her eye glass, up went her chin, and she proceeded to demonstrate the fine art of looking down on a fellow more than a head taller than she.

After surveying him from head to toe, she turned her gaze to Clara.

"And this is the physician, I presume?" her ladyship said. "I can think of no other reason for a man to be in your bedroom."

"No, Mama, this is not the physician," Clara said. "This is Mr. Radford."

"Radford," Lady Warford repeated.

"Yes, my dear," said Lady Exton. "The Duke of Malvern's cousin."

He saw Lady Warford's gaze turn inward while she flipped through the pages of her mental Book of Great Families, trying to determine where he fit in.

He saw no reason to raise her hopes. "The legal branch of the Radfords," he said. "The barristers, my lady."

She sent him one glacial glance before turning to her daughter. "And you have a lawsuit in progress, Clara?" she said coldly.

"No, Mama," Clara said. "Mr. Radford is the normal sort of suitor. That is to say, he has asked me to marry him, and I've decided to put him out of his misery."

The glacial expression warmed exactly one degree. "Certainly you would, Clara. You would not wish to toy with a gentleman's affections."

"In his case, yes, I would, Mama. But I've said yes and meant it."

"You haven't the least idea what you mean," said her mother. "You have been ill. Obviously you are not fully recovered, else you'd remember you may not say yes to any gentleman without your father's consent." She turned to Radford. "Lord Warford has accompanied me to London. You may wish to apply to him in the usual way."

Well, that's going to be a great waste of time.

He thanked her and promised to do so, and took his leave so very politely that anybody who knew him would wonder if he was feeling quite well.

R adford followed the usual forms. He wrote to the Marquess of Warford, requesting an appointment. This his lordship promptly granted—because of course Clara's parents wanted to wash their hands of the Barbarous Barrister without loss of time. Radford appeared punctually at the given time, was punctually admitted to his lordship's study, and was punctually rejected. Exactly as he'd expected.

The day was cold, windy, and wet, suiting his mood perfectly.

He walked back from St. James's, along Pall Mall and through Charing Cross . . . where he'd met her on the day that seemed a lifetime ago. He didn't linger but strode on into the Strand as he'd done that day. On he walked, past St. Clement's, heading to his world, the Temple and the lawyers' hive.

As he passed through Temple Bar, he saw a boy hawking newspapers.

Two thoughts rose in his mind and connected.

Radford walked faster, and broke into a run as he turned into Inner Temple Lane. He burst into the Woodley Building and took the steps two at a time to his chambers.

A short time thereafter, Westcott was staring at him, wearing his You Have Lost Your Mind expression.

"Do it," Radford said.

Wednesday 21 October
Mr. Westcott's office

*H*ave you taken leave of your senses?" Lord Warford said, waving the document. "You mean to bring a breach of promise suit against *my daughter*?"

His lordship had received Westcott's letter on Thursday. The marquess's solicitor, Mr. Alcox, had responded on Friday. Westcott had answered on the same day, explaining that Mr. Radford was unable to make appointments at present, being engaged in a brief for libel whose duration one could not predict. Mr. Westcott would not dream of asking Lord Warford to wait on his client's convenience.

Lord Warford did not wait on anybody's convenience. Why should he, when he had scores of people to do the waiting for him?

Westcott had recognized Alcox's clerk—one of many—in the courtroom. He was there throughout the proceedings. And so nobody was surprised to receive Mr. Alcox's message, within minutes of the trial's ending: Lord Warford would appear in Mr. Westcott's office within the hour.

This left more than enough time to change, but Radford chose not to do so.

He still wore his wig, bands, and robe.

He was a lawyer, well aware of the effect one's appearance and manner could have on juries and judges. He knew his courtroom attire would, firstly, remind Lord Warford of the gravity of his profession and the might of the Law, and secondly, create the impression of Radford's having raced here from court, not wanting to keep the marquess waiting.

"Mr. Westcott, you know as well as I that this is nonsense," Mr. Alcox said. "Breach of promise of marriage brought against women is rare, and for very good reason. Even if it comes to trial, you cannot expect more than token compensation."

"I don't want compensation, token or otherwise," Radford said. "I want to marry Lady Clara, as she promised to do."

"The court cannot and will not enforce this alleged contract," Alcox said, still speaking to Westcott. "Her ladyship had no power to make a contract. You have nothing to make a case with. If your client—or associate—or whatever he is—insists on pursuing this ridiculous suit, he'll make a laughingstock of himself."

"Let us not waste time with pointless legal wrangling," Lord Warford said. "We know Mr. Radford is far too intelligent to wish for a trial that can only damage his professional reputation. Furthermore, if he truly cares for my daughter, as he claims, he will not wish to drag her name through the mud. He will not wish to see her and her family featured in the scandal sheets and print shop window caricatures. The question is, What does he wish? What, in short, is Mr. Radford's price?"

Westcott walked round to the back of his desk and shuffled some papers. He picked up one.

"My client's price," he said. "Let me see." He read the document, then put it down and picked up another. "Ah, here it is. Mr. Radford requests a fair trial."

Lord Warford waved his hand. "Pray don't insult my intelligence. We all know there's no question of going to court."

"The trial to take place in this office, my lord," Westcott said. "The jury to comprise her ladyship's parents, Lord and Lady Warford. Mr. Radford will act as his own advocate. As such he seeks the following: to know the crimes of which he is accused, to summon witnesses, to answer questions or challenges put to him by the other party, and to make a summary speech in his defense."

Lord Warford regarded Radford for a time. Then, "That's your price?" he said.

"A fair trial," Radford said. "I ask no more than what we grant to murderers and traitors and even counterfeiters. I place my future in your and your lady's hands."

"And if the verdict goes against you?" Lord Warford said. "Will you leave it alone?"

"My client pledges to abide by the outcome," Westcott said.

"No appeals," Radford said. "No pleading my case in the court of public opinion. Not a word to anybody. In short, no whining." If he couldn't win over Clara's parents, he most certainly couldn't meet the many challenges wedlock would present. If he couldn't bring Lord and Lady Warford over to his side, he wasn't worthy of her.

Lord Warford walked to the window and looked down into the Temple churchyard. After an eternity of a moment, he said, "I've used due diligence, Mr. Radford, in looking into your affairs and character. You seem to be an unusually clever gentleman. Your courtroom work is spoken of in laudatory terms. Your personality . . . would appear to be of a different order. Clara says . . . But we shall disregard her opinions. Woman think with their feelings, not their intellects." He turned away from the window. "Mr. Westcott, I agree to the trial. I have always prided myself on keeping an open mind—though I shall not speak for any other parties who will be present."

"Thank you, my lord," Westcott said.

"In any event, I don't doubt it will be interesting." The marquess looked at Radford. "Be sure to wear that, sir. It makes precisely the impression you wish."

Leaving Alcox to work out the details with his counterpart, his lordship departed.

Chapter Twelve

He num'rous woes on Ocean toss'd, endured.
—*The Odyssey of Homer*, translated by William Cowper,
1791

Small Drawing Room of Warford House
Later that day

"How dare he?" Mama burst out. "Warford, how *could* you?"

"It must have been the wig," Papa said. Then, as usually happened when he saw omens of a wifely eruption, he claimed to have another appointment and left.

Fortunately, he'd brought the news about the Trial of Raven Radford while Great-Aunt Dora was visiting. Even Mama couldn't enact a tragedy while the older lady was laughing so hard.

"There, you see, Clara," Mama said, while Lady Exton wiped her eyes. "We'll be laughingstocks. The satirists will have a field day."

"Quite possibly, if you go through with this trial," Great-Aunt Dora said. "I shouldn't, if I were you. What

I should do is snap him up. You shan't find another such son-in-law in your lifetime."

"I should hope not," Mama said. "A barrister! And his father! An eccentric, married to a divorcée. No wonder he was never knighted. Clara could not have chosen worse had she started planning from the day she was born."

"You fret about a title, when the young man saved Clara's life?" Great-Aunt Dora asked. "What more proof do you want of his character?"

"It isn't a matter of character," Clara said. "It's a matter of What People Will Say."

Mama gave her the Serpent's Tooth–Thankless Child look.

Clara winced inwardly. Mama wasn't completely irrational. Being the mother of London's most beautiful and most proposed-to girl made Lady Warford an object of envy, jealousy, resentment, and many other unamiable emotions. The beau monde would revel in seeing her humbled. It wouldn't last forever but it wouldn't be over quickly, either, and it would be extremely painful while it lasted.

Lady Exton saw things differently. "You're not fretting over what Lady Bartham will say, I hope? Kindly remember you're the Marchioness of Warford. It ought to be *nothing* to you what anybody says, especially women of inferior mental faculties who spend their time gossiping because they're incapable of doing anything else."

And there, in a nutshell, was one suffocating force in Clara's life: the endless petty gossip that passed for conversation.

"I'm glad you enjoy the luxury of disregarding Society, Aunt," Mama said. "The rest of us, however, must live in it. And some of us do not wish to be subjected to pity or thinly veiled mockery."

Great-Aunt Dora stood up. "Frances, I'm disappointed

in you. Here's a strong, healthy, intelligent, and ambitious young man, ready to mortify himself for your daughter's sake—and you fret about what your friends will say! I can't decide whether to laugh or cry. Clara, you may see me out."

"You're not to take her away again, Aunt," Mama said. "To speak plainly, you've done quite enough damage."

"I! Hmph!" Great-Aunt Dora swept out, Clara in her wake.

"For your sake I pray Mr. Radford will carry off his trial successfully," Lady Exton said as she and her grand-niece continued down the corridor. "I might have gone on arguing, but when I saw it was all about What Society Will Say, I knew I might as well save my breath. There's no terror so immense and so immune to reason as the terror of becoming an object of ridicule disguised as pity. Your mother would rather drink poison."

This was only a slight exaggeration.

"You did your best," Clara said. "We must leave it to Mr. Radford. He's tackled harder cases, I'm sure."

He didn't always win.

She mustn't have hidden her doubts as well as she thought because her great-aunt said, "Don't fret, my dear. If he could keep you from dying, he can win over your parents."

"This might be harder," Clara said. "And if he doesn't succeed?"

"Then you can do something excitingly desperate, of course."

Friday 23 October
Westcott's office

$\mathcal{M}$r. Radford wore his wig, along with the rest of his courtroom attire. Although he was the one on trial, he was his own barrister as well.

Yes, Clara had seen him in court garb before, but she hadn't yet become accustomed to the effect. He was elegant. And intimidating. And somehow the robe and wig and lace made him even more potently *male*.

As she took him in, a little light broke through the black cloud threatening to swallow her.

But only for a moment. The courtroom garb wouldn't win any admiration from Mama. It shouted *Barrister!* A felony, because he was murdering her social prestige and therefore her life.

Papa would be the real problem, though. Unlike Mama, he didn't scold or storm about the house. He only grew quieter and more thoughtful. Not a promising sign.

Since Clara's parents hadn't wanted to bring any more people than absolutely necessary into this "farce," as Mama called it, Mr. Alcox read out the charges. These were more numerous than what Papa had first compiled. He'd merely charged Mr. Radford with being unsuitable in rank and fortune.

This, in Mama's view, was grossly inadequate. The list she'd compiled was twice as long as and three times more incomprehensible than what Mr. Alcox eventually made of it.

As condensed and translated by Mr. Alcox, Mr. Radford's crimes were:

1. Soliciting the hand of a young lady he was unable to provide for in a style in any way approaching that to which she was accustomed since birth.

2. Lack of social standing, which would lead to the lady's becoming an outcast from the society to which she properly belonged.

3. Belonging to a family stained by the scandal of divorce, thereby causing her ladyship to be besmirched by association.

4. Having no social connections he could rely upon to aid him in advancing either in professional or social rank to one more appropriate to her ladyship.

5. Being unlikely to obtain the necessary social connections, due to his consorting with, representing, and/or prosecuting persons of the lowest order, including known criminals.

6. Making deadly enemies among the aforementioned low persons, which circumstance would place Lady Clara in physical danger.

7. Number six increasing the likelihood of Mr. Radford's untimely demise, he would soon leave her ladyship alone and without the protection of friends—he having none to speak of—thanks to items number two and three.

8. While his diligent care was alleged to have saved her ladyship's life, it must be pointed out that she would not have required saving, had Mr. Radford not placed her ladyship in a situation leading directly to her becoming severely ill.

9. In relation to number eight: exploiting a position of trust to gain the affections of an innocent girl.

10. Failure to restrain her ladyship from engaging in unsuitable behavior. It was unavailing to claim, as Lady Clara had done, that she insisted on putting herself in jeopardy. Any gentleman who cannot control a headstrong young woman is unfit to carry out the responsibilities of a husband.

Though more than half the list struck Clara as pure nonsense, and made her want to shake her mother, Mr. Radford listened to it all gravely, quite as though he had been charged with heinous crimes.

In lieu of a judge, Mr. Alcox asked, "How do you plead, Mr. Radford?"

He threw Clara one quick glance she couldn't read.

"Not guilty," he said.

"This is absurd," Mama said, turning to Papa. "How can you—"

"Quite right, my dear," Papa said. "Since this is an informal court, let's waive the formalities. Mr. Radford, you may proceed."

*R*adford set his hand on Westcott's desk, tidied for the occasion, and bowed his head as he always did when preparing to speak.

He hadn't heard the full list of charges until this moment. Apparently, Lady Warford had been adding and changing items to the very last minute.

Not that it mattered. He'd known what to expect. He'd understood he was taking a great gamble. He'd seen no alternative.

He raised his head and briefly met Clara's blue gaze before turning to the parental jury.

He couldn't look at her for very long and keep a straight face, and today of all days he needed to keep his wits about him.

She'd donned a yellow walking dress for the occasion. The high neckline was the only sober thing about it. It was a redingote, closed along the front by large silk buttons, and at the top by a braided rope from which a pair of little silk pinecones dangled. Embroidered scallops ran down the two sides of the front as well as around the short cape that flowed over gigantic sleeves. Her hat was relatively subdued, boasting no more than half a dozen bows and only a few sprigs sprouting from the top, not much higher than the brim. Inside the brim, ruffles and little flowers framed her face.

Keeping her in the style to which she was accustomed

would be a challenge—but then, the result would be so entertaining.

If her stony-faced parents would allow him to keep her.

He said, "Ten charges is a heavy count, indeed. We've sent men, women, and children to eternity on a single charge. However, let us remember that marriage, especially among the higher orders, is a far more serious matter than a mere murder among the lowest ranks."

"I object," Lord Warford said. "We did not come here for satire and a lecture on social inequalities."

"Yet social and financial inequality is what your lordship charges me with," Radford said. "But let us begin at the beginning. Item one: my lack of income. I urge the jury to dismiss this charge. By my own count, at least three of the applicants for Lady Clara's hand—including a gentleman to whom she was briefly engaged—were less able to provide for her than I am. The latter gentleman, for instance, was deeply in debt."

"It's hardly the same thing," said Lady Warford.

"It is certainly a question worth weighing," he said. "It seems the gentleman in question was accepted under duress, because he'd compromised Lady Clara in very public circumstances. A scandal, in short. In that case, may we also strike number three? The scandal of my mother's divorce is quite elderly, having occurred nearly thirty years ago. Lady Clara's occurred only a few months ago. I believe that makes us even, at the very least."

"Warford, I protest," Lady Warford said. "Will you not put this fellow in his place? The idea—to equate a fortune hunter leading Clara astray—"

"He has a point," Lord Warford said. "More than one. We may not like what he has to say, but we've promised to give the gentleman a fair hearing. In fairness, we must consider dismissing items one and three. Several of Clara's suitors were on short allowance or in debt."

"She refused them!"

"It makes no matter. We charged Mr. Radford only with *soliciting her hand*. The law turns on fine and precise points, my dear."

"Then as to that, the so-called scandal with that unpleasant man lasted not a day, thanks to his offering for her," said his lady.

"And the divorce which so troubles you was old news when King George III was still alive," his lordship said.

"Warford, you cannot take this man's arguments seriously."

"I do, indeed," said he. "And it wanted no great leap of intellect to anticipate Mr. Radford's response to the scandal item. I recommend you allow the gentleman to continue. For one thing, matters will proceed more swiftly. For another, I do not wish to find myself obliged to strike item number ten as well."

This sounded promising, but Radford knew Lord Warford was a canny politician. He'd agreed to a fair hearing to accommodate his daughter. On the other hand, he had to live with his wife. But most important, he had rational fears for his daughter's future, which Radford would have uphill work overcoming.

Meanwhile, he'd disposed only of the easiest issues. The other charges were sticky, indeed, and his emotional self was squirming.

He took a moment to make certain he was completely detached and able to look on from a proper distance at the proceedings.

"Item two," he said.

Clara needed all her ladyship training to keep her hands loosely folded in her lap and her mouth shut.

She could feel her parents turning against Mr. Radford more and more with every exchange. Mama resented being contradicted by anybody, let alone a Nobody. Clara could feel her seething, though she was doing her best glacier impression. One couldn't trust Papa's humor. He was good at using it to get the better of the opposition.

"Let me take numbers two, four, and five in order," Radford said. "These pertain to rank and social standing. Firstly, as to rank: I am the great-grandson of the third Duke of Malvern. My father is heir presumptive to the present duke. Men of less lofty antecedents than mine travel in the first circles of Society and are admitted to Court."

Only Clara knew what it cost him to use his beastly cousin's rank, and her heart squeezed.

"The only court you're admitted to is criminal court," Mama said. "His Majesty doesn't know you exist."

"As it happens, my lady, my name is known to His Majesty," Radford said. "I have prosecuted for the Crown more than once, as well as seeking royal mercy in the form of conditional pardons. I have represented or advised six members of the upper ranks of society, all of whom have offered to exert their influence on my behalf. In short, I do have useful connections. I simply haven't used them, out of a possibly misguided desire to make my way on my own merits. However, in the event I marry Lady Clara, I won't hesitate to use all possible means to ensure her continued—"

"You may not make such appalling sacrifices on my account," Clara burst out. "You of all people ought to see how silly it is to claim Society will ostracize me. Really, Mama, I wonder at your proposing it. No hostess will exclude me simply because I was so intrepid as to marry Mr. Radford. On the contrary, the world will flood us with invitations."

"Clara, you live in a fantasy world," said her mother.

"I live in *our* world, Mama," Clara said. "I understand as well as you do how our friends think. Yes, everybody will talk. But they'll be wondering what's so special about Mr. Radford. They'll want to know why, of all the fine gentlemen who courted me, I wanted the one who didn't. Certainly the ladies will want to know what I did to bring the elusive Raven Radford to heel."

Only she caught the infinitesimal twitch of Radford's mouth.

"*Raven* Radford!" Mama said. "The criminals are bad enough, but this vulgar nickname—"

"Enough," Papa said. "I call the court to order. Clara, you interrupt the proceedings."

"I! What of Mama?"

"She must be let to express herself from time to time, to prevent the physical injury she would do herself if stifled."

"Warford!"

"Yet after a time, I did call you to order, my dear, did I not? Can't let anybody think I can't control my wife."

"You are on *his* side, Warford!"

"I'm on Clara's side," he said. "Her happiness is what concerns me."

"Then call me as a witness, Mr. Radford," Clara said. "Why should you answer all these ridiculous charges yourself, when it's my happiness everybody claims to be in agonies about?"

"I'm perfectly capable of answering the charges unaided," Radford said.

"Why should you? I got you into this."

"You most certainly did not."

"I plagued you endlessly."

"I'm a lawyer," he said. "People plague us constantly with their problems, and we're glad to have the work."

"But I was always underfoot."

"Not always," he said. "You proved useful now and again. Or, at the very least, entertaining. Enough to lead me to seek you out, when I ought to have let you go your way. On that point, in fact, I was about to call a witness." He turned to Westcott. "Kindly summon the first witness."

Westcott went to the door and murmured something—to the clerk, evidently. A moment later, Tilsley dragged Fenwick, in all his gold and lilac glory, into the office, not without some scuffling and hostile use of elbows.

*R*adford should have realized matters wouldn't proceed precisely as he'd planned.

Fenwick did take the "stand"—the rug in front of Westcott's desk. He did testify regarding the shockingly large bribe—two shillings!—Radford had paid the little pirate to get a clandestine message to Lady Clara.

But then Lady Clara rose to cross-examine, and asked if it were not true that she had initially employed the boy—for two shillings!—to take her to Mr. Radford, he being, on the boy's avowal, "the only feller which'd find a cove which'd gone 'n done a bolt if anybody could."

Then the boy went out again—and, by the sounds of it, scuffled with Tilsley.

But then her father asked, too quietly, what, precisely, his daughter was talking about.

Ignoring Radford's signals to be silent, Lady Clara took the stand to confess to a hundred crimes and misdemeanors, i.e., the full and true story leading up to her illness (but with the naughty bits left out).

By the time she was done turning her parents' hair grey, Radford's emotional self was banging his head against a wall.

He said, "Did nobody ever tell you never to say a word above what is asked of you when you are under examination?"

She said, "Can't you see it's bad strategy for you to take all the blame?"

"Bad strategy!"

"Yes. It makes you seem a wicked seducer, which won't help your case. You know I started this, Mr. Radford, and you know I used all my womanly wiles on you—"

"Such as they are," he cut in before she made him smile—or, more prejudicial, laugh—and before she could make matters worse, though he wasn't sure that was possible. "And let me assure the jury that, as a barrister, I am of a necessity and by training and experience impervious to womanly wiles."

"Yes, and it's very irritating of you," she said. "But I'm obstinate—"

"Let us say *persevering*."

"Do not start being gentle with me at this late date," she said.

"I'm trying to make a good impression on your parents," he said.

"Which goes against your nature and makes you look a trifle green," she said. "I recommend, for your health's sake, you cease and desist."

And he had all he could do not to say, *I love you I love you I love you.*

"In any case, your gentleness is rather condescending, don't you think?" she said.

"Perhaps. A little. Thank you, my lady. You may step down."

"I'm not done."

"I believe your ladyship has done enough," he said. "We shall move on to number . . . ?" She'd made him forget, more or less everything.

"Six," said Lord Warford. "Deadly enemies. Low persons." He glanced at the closed door. "The lad being an example, I take it?"

"A former juvenile delinquent now gainfully employed at Maison Noirot," Radford said.

"That would explain the costume."

"Warford, must we continue this charade?" the marchioness said.

"I promised a fair hearing," said her spouse.

"Fair? You see as well as I do what goes on here," Lady Warford said. "He views it as a great joke, and he encourages the worst in Clara."

A joke. His future. His life. *Clara*'s life. Encouraging the *worst* in her!

A red mist appeared before Radford's eyes. He tried to blink it away.

"He encourages something," Lord Warford said.

"Her independence," Radford said sharply, unthinkingly. "Her mind. Her courage. She's twenty-two and one-sixth years old. *Someone* ought to encourage her. To be herself."

He heard a collective intake of breath—including his own—and he was aware of the parents' stiffening and Westcott making the throat-cutting gesture: *Don't.*

Radford saw the precipice at his feet.

Annoy the judge, provoke your colleagues, but never, ever, attack the jury.

He tried to retreat.

He tried to attend to Westcott's signal.

He almost made it.

Chapter Thirteen

When a lady marries a gentleman of character
and capacity, and who is in every respect suitable
to her, except that his estate is not equal to what
she might expect, I do not call it unequal.
—John Witherspoon, *Letters on Marriage*, 1834

It wasn't too late to back away and take another tack.

But Radford's inner self dragged to the front of
his mind the image of Clara at Vauxhall, leaping on Bernard. His inner self reenacted her raging speech in this
very office, on that rainy September day.

The brave, clever girl was suffocating. Without obnoxious Raven Radford, she'd be stifled—most expensively
and luxuriously—for the rest of her life.

"If Lady Clara cared about the matters the world wants
her to care about, she wouldn't have come to me," he said.
"If she wanted to be safe and coddled, she wouldn't have
come to me. If she believed pauper children were not her
problem, she wouldn't have come to me, and plagued me
to help her help them. She came to me because she knew
nobody else would *let* her help them. She wasn't trying
to save everybody. She wasn't trying to rescue London's
wretched masses. She set her sights on one girl and her

brother, that was all. But she couldn't come to you, because you'd only tell her that her job was to organize and sponsor charities. It wasn't her job to dirty her gloves rescuing a very sick boy from a nest of thieves." He paused. "It certainly wasn't her job to risk her life saving that boy. But she wanted to do it badly enough to take the risk."

He met her father's gaze. His lordship's face darkened, and a muscle twitched in his jaw. If Radford could be intimidated, this was the time to cower. But he'd faced intimidation from his youth, and he'd spent his life fighting against daunting odds.

"Pray, ask her, Lord Warford," he said. "Will you be so good as to ask Lady Clara now if she regrets her actions."

The marquess started to rise from his seat, and Radford thought, *If he walks out now, we're lost.*

But the marquess glanced at Clara, whose face was white. He paused and sat down again. He drew in a long breath and let it out and said, "Have you regrets, Clara?"

Tears sparkled in her eyes but didn't fall. Her mouth trembled a bit, but she shook her head and said, coolly enough, "If I had it to do over again, I would. It was the first truly satisfactory act I've performed in years— though it was rather fun to help Cousin Gladys, too." She wrinkled her brow. "And it did feel good to make a spectacle of myself when I rejected Clevedon."

"Oh, Clara," her mother said.

"Marry me, Clara," Radford said, "and you may make as many spectacles of yourself as you like. I'm bound to encourage you, because making spectacles is what I do. Marry me, Clara, and it will be difficult. At present I can't afford to keep you in the style you deserve—"

"I can do without style," she said. "I did without it for twenty-one and three-quarters years, until those dressmakers got hold of me."

"Do without, indeed," her mother said. "Oh, yes, I

can see it now. You living in chambers, waited on by two servants—if Mr. Radford's income will stretch so far. You, living on an annual income less than what you can spend in an hour—when you're feeling frugal."

"Money is not the point," Lord Warford said. "We can prattle on about Clara's freedom and her tendency to fall into her little scrapes, usually precipitated by good intentions—"

"*Little* scrapes!" Clara cried. "As though I were a child. Really, Papa."

"You're my little girl, and always will be," he said. "I beg you will not jump on me for every word, child. Let me ask Mr. Radford the essential question."

He turned a steely blue gaze upon Radford. "What happens, sir, when this infatuation fades? And don't tell me it isn't infatuation, because nobody ever seems to diagnose the condition, except in hindsight. What becomes of my daughter, Mr. Radford, a year, two years from now—when she's a barrister's wife, living apart from her friends, in a sphere she was never prepared for and knows nothing about. Whom will she talk to? What will she do with her days and nights? What sort of life do you mean to give her?"

Clara opened her mouth to respond, but her mother didn't give her the chance.

"And tell me this, Mr. Radford," the marchioness said. "What sort of regard can you have for a young woman when you invite her to join you in your world, where you have constant dealings with juvenile delinquents and blackguards of all kinds? A world where you are stalked by criminals?"

"What sort of regard," Radford repeated softly. He took his inner self aside and discussed the question with him. Then he let himself smile. "It must be high regard, indeed, because I believe Lady Clara is more than capable of living her life in my sphere with courage and style."

Clara's face glowed, and her mouth turned up. The room brightened, as though the sun had contrived to force its way through both oppressive grey sky and sooty window.

There. That was it, in a nutshell. Infatuation or whatever it was, he knew he'd move heaven and earth to bring that light to her face, to awaken that smile and the glint of laughter in her blue eyes. He didn't see how he could ever get used to it, let alone take it for granted.

Lord Warford looked at Clara, then at his wife. "I've heard quite enough. We shall not address numbers six through ten."

"Papa!"

"Mr. Radford is unsuitable on a wide array of counts," the marquess said.

"*Papa!*"

"Except the most important one," Lord Warford went on. "He suits you, and you seem to suit him."

"Warford!"

He turned back to his wife. "My dear, I'm far from ecstatic about Clara's choice. In social terms, this gentleman is a nobody and seems content to remain so. But he seems to understand Clara, possibly a little better than we do."

"Understanding won't pay for servants," said his lady tearfully. "Who'll look after her? What's to become of her, my beautiful child—living in chambers!"

The marquess took her hand. "Let us allow Clara and Mr. Radford to work out that difficulty for themselves. Let us take comfort in recognizing how well matched they are as regards intellect and character. Their exchanges have offered, I believe, ample demonstration. One must be blind and deaf to fail to discern a strong attachment. While Mr. Radford is not the man I would have chosen, that does not constitute grounds to break my daughter's heart."

"As though I should consent to Clara's breaking her

heart!" her ladyship cried. "But she doesn't know her own heart."

"She's two and twenty and—what was it?—one-sixth years old," Lord Warford said. "She's an intelligent girl. We'd better make the best of it, my dear." His attention returned to Radford. "I shall call on your father, and we'll set our solicitors at each other's throats and see what happens."

Duchess of Clevedon's boudoir
Saturday 24 October

he three Noirot sisters—Marcelline, Duchess of Clevedon; Sophy, Countess of Longmore; and Leonie, Marchioness of Lisburne—all regarded Clara with no expression whatsoever.

She'd told them, in slightly more detail than she'd told her parents, about the events leading to her becoming engaged to Raven Radford.

"I wanted you to know as soon as possible," Clara said into the silence. "I haven't told my own sisters yet. Mama will do that, in a state of tears and indignation, I don't doubt."

The sisters looked at one another, sphinxes all.

Clara knew they'd counted on her to make a splendid match, which would enhance their shop's prestige as well as ensure her continuing to buy its costly creations.

After a long, taut moment, Marcelline said, "But it's so *romantic*, my love."

"You could never marry a man of ordinary intelligence," Sophy said. "You'd be bored to pieces. You'd go into a decline and expire of ennui."

"He's clever *and* ambitious and good at getting what he wants," Leonie said. "He'll make his way, of that I have no doubt."

"But most important," the duchess said, and looked at her sisters again, her dark eyes gleaming.

"The dress!" they chorused.

They went into rhapsodies, at first about their respective specialties—Marcelline rapturous about the dress she'd design, Sophy euphoric about the headdress she'd create, and even practical Leonie was almost poetic about the bridal corset she envisioned.

Though they'd all begun to transfer their business activities to others since marrying into the upper ranks, they'd make an exception for Clara's wedding. She was their protégée and prize client, and they'd waited months for this opportunity.

"Nothing too extravagant," she said. "Remember, I'm marrying a barrister who's only in the early phase of his career." She wasn't sure Radford could afford even one of their dresses, especially the evening dresses.

"All the more reason for a splendid bridal ensemble," Sophy said. "The more expensive you look, the more you increase your husband's status in the eyes of others. Most men recognize this, and like to see their wives well dressed."

"In any event, Lord Warford will pay for it," said Leonie. "You won't want to make your dear papa seem miserly or anything less than pleased with his prospective son-in-law."

"He isn't pleased," Clara said. "I told you."

Sophy dismissed this with a wave of her hand. "The point isn't what he truly feels. The point is what *seems*. No matter how your parents feel, they won't want anybody to suspect they're anything but thrilled with your betrothed. You may be sure I'll write pieces for *Foxe's Morning Spectacle* to make parents everywhere gnash their teeth in envy. Mothers will be shrieking at their daughters, 'Why could *you* not win such a marital prize?'"

If anyone could turn an awkward situation to positive account, it was Sophy.

They went on to fantasize about a newly married lady's walking dresses and morning dresses, dinner dresses and opera dresses, and everything that went on over and under them. Clara tried to rein them in, but soon gave up, because she knew they were right. As usual.

They'd achieved their success because they understood the haut ton perfectly. Yes, it would cost Papa, but he never fussed about dressmakers' bills and such. More important, as they said, an elegant set of clothes would bolster Radford's status and quiet malicious tongues.

The rest of the marriage was up to her and Radford.

Woodley Building
Monday 26 October

"I trust you've thought about where you'll live," Westcott said.

Radford hadn't had time to think about anything practical. He'd barely been able to carry on his lawyerly duties. His fight for Lady Clara was all he'd thought about.

Immediately after the Trial of Raven Radford, he'd ridden out to Richmond, to report to his parents. He hadn't told his father about the trial previously, concerned it would infuriate him: his son having to defend himself to a pair of spoiled aristocrats! Now, though, he took the entire tale in high good humor. His mother said she was pleased, but she'd looked a little troubled.

Buoyed by triumph, he'd told himself the two sets of parents would meet soon, and the odds were in favor of personal acquaintance overcoming many of the social barriers. His father was a gentleman, his mother a well-born lady. No stickler could possibly find fault with their manners. Well . . . Father could be brusque and rude, but so could any number of noblemen, especially those of advanced age.

And considering his father's advanced age and infirmity, Radford didn't think anybody would be so unreasonable as to object to the marriage taking place in Richmond. And the honeymoon, too, for that matter. A bridal trip at this time of year wasn't wise. Given his current legal responsibilities, it was out of the question.

For the time being, he and Clara would reside in the first floor wing of Ithaca House. His parents had essentially abandoned this part of the house as Father grew too frail to stir much beyond the library and the occasional, very slow, walk in the garden.

Everything had looked so rosy then.

Now, not seventy-two hours after he'd obtained Lord Warford's consent, reality crept in, like the chill fog slinking over London and seeping through every available crack and crevice. It slithered into Westcott's office and mingled with the smoke from the fire to make a sickly yellow indoor haze.

Westcott sat near the fire. Yet another letter from Bernard in his hand, Radford had taken up his post at the window to gaze down at the churchyard. Fog swirled round the gravestones.

"I know Clara's parents will want her to live in a suitably fashionable, and therefore extortionate, neighborhood," he said. He thought this an idiotic use of her dowry, immense as it was.

"Nobody's using the ducal town house at present," Westcott said. "Or for the foreseeable future."

Malvern House had been let until a year ago, but the lessees hadn't renewed. Typically, Bernard hadn't charged anybody with finding new tenants.

"Bernard's next wife might have something to say in that regard." The letter Radford held contained, along with the usual trials and tribulations, three pages describing a young lady Bernard had met recently at a dinner party in nearby Ashperton. Apparently, she hadn't run away or gagged at Bernard's clumsy advances, because Bernard intended to court her. "She has good hips for breeding," he wrote, "and she's the only girl in a family of males. I'll get half a dozen sons on her, and you are out of a dukedom, little Raven. Ha ha."

Radford did not feel sorry for the girl, whoever she was. Bernard couldn't pretend to be anything but what he was. He wasn't clever enough, and there was no disguising his whalelike physique. If she could stomach the sight of him at dinner, slurping up food like a pig, or the sight of him after dinner, drunk and even more oafish than usual, then she must be either excessively charitable or excessively determined to be a duchess. Either way, she was welcome to him.

The important thing was, Bernard's next duchess would not be Clara.

"Do you think he'll marry the girl?" Westcott said.

"She's near at hand, she's young and pretty, and she comes of good breeding stock," Radford said. "If she or her parents had discouraged him, he'd have said so, and abused her looks and family, rather than boasting about them. Yes, he'll marry her—before the year is out, I predict."

"But he won't want to live in London, and if he wants to breed sons, he'll keep her at Glynnor Castle."

"Unless she's very persuasive," he said. "In any event, I'd rather not ask him for favors, even for Lady Clara."

She'd remain Lady Clara after they were wed, taking his surname but retaining her title and her precedence. She would remain who she was, a lady bred to be the wife of a nobleman of the highest rank.

How the devil was he to make two lives, so separate in so many ways, fit together?

Sophy did as she'd promised, painting the engagement in glowing terms in the pages of *Foxe's Morning Spectacle*, for which she wrote anonymously. Like everybody else, Lady Warford read this publication devotedly. Unlike most others, she knew the anonymous writer was her daughter-in-law. While neither intellectual nor literary, her ladyship understood the way Society's mind worked. It took her no time at all to see how brilliantly Sophy had managed the debacle. She'd presented the humiliating engagement as a triumph. Thanks to her, unwed young ladies would envy Lady Clara and their mothers would envy Clara's mother—or at least wonder what she knew about her prospective son-in-law that nobody else did.

Lady Warford not only decided that she loved her daughter-in-law more than she'd realized, but absorbed the lesson as well. She began to crow about the engagement as though it were a great coup she'd personally engineered.

She went so far as to share her pretend rapture with the King and Queen—and was shocked (though not visibly) to learn they held Mr. Radford in some regard, even if at times the King, once a naval commander, had expressed a wish to hang him from the yardarm.

"Brilliant fellow," His Majesty said. "But he can be damned irritating."

"I believe Lady Clara is up to his weight," said Her Majesty.

"No doubt about it," said the King. "Lucky fellow, indeed. With such a wife, he'll go far."

He did not add, "If nobody kills him first," because that went without saying.

Glowing with royal approval, Lady Warford was splendidly armed for her battle with Lady Bartham. Best of all weapons was the very great pleasure of apologizing for being unable to invite her friend to the nuptials, "as it is to be quite private, you know, for Mr. George Radford's health is too fragile to endure crowds. We shall have only the immediate family . . . and a few ministers, as Warford's position requires . . . oh, and the King and Queen have appointed certain members of the royal family to represent them, as Their Majesties' schedule does not permit their personal attendance."

*W*ithin three days, the news had reached every quarter of London. By the fourth day, Radford had to dodge journalists on his way to and from the Temple; Tilsley got into fighting form evicting sellers of this, that, and the other thing indispensable to newlyweds; while Westcott saved on coal by burning mountains of business cards and brochures—for household furnishings, "reasonably priced" town houses, staffing services, etc.

Among the lowest of Raven Radford's acquaintance, matters grew hot, too, as they argued and wagered about what this would mean for the criminal business. Some were sure he'd give up lawyering and become a gentleman, living on his wife's immense dowry—a fortune estimated at anywhere from ten thousand to five hundred thousand pounds, with bets covering the extremes and all points in between. Others said they'd have to pry his wig from his cold, dead skull before he gave up harassing "coves which was only trying to sweat out a living someway or t'other."

Jacob Freame wasn't among those wagering or expressing opinions.

A fever had struck him down not long after Chiver failed to fly. This was deadly from several angles. Both rivals and ambitious associates would be happy to help speed his way to the graveyard when he wasn't in a condition to defend himself.

But two of his boys stood by him, even after he took sick: Husher and Squirrel—the latter one of the newer boys Chiver had named for his large front teeth, over-full cheeks, and sudden, darting way of moving. The two had helped Freame get away—by boat. Though it was a hellish way for a sick man to travel, it was safer than the streets, where his enemies would recognize him.

They took refuge in a hovel in one of the foulest neighborhoods along the river, where nobody who knew him would expect him to be. Everybody knew Jacob Freame lived high. He owned a carriage and horse, traveled in the first circles of London's underworld, and lived in luxurious private rooms in one of Covent Garden's better brothels.

In his own world, in short, he was a celebrity.

Among the river's criminal population, he was nobody, and even the worst of them couldn't be bothered to cut his throat, even if they wanted to come near a man dying of fever. Too, Husher was on guard, in case anybody got curious and foolhardy enough to come close.

And so Freame got sicker and sicker and sicker and came to death's door. But Death changed its mind at the last minute, and Freame came back to life in a pesthole, with no place to go and next to nothing to live on. His boys had run away and joined other gangs. Thinking him dead or as good as, rivals had taken over his businesses.

And now . . .

"He's *what*?" he snarled, as Squirrel set a cracked bowl of slop in front of him.

Squirrel and Husher spoke a version of English only others of their kind understood. Revised for ordinary comprehension, the exchange went like this:

Squirrel said, "Raven's getting hisself a wife. I heard it down Jack's."

Husher nodded. "Me too."

Jack's was a disreputable coffeehouse in Covent Garden.

"You can hear anything down Jack's," Freame said. "Doesn't mean it isn't a steaming pile of shit."

"They was making bets on it," Squirrel said. "On account she's the Long Meg what beat Chiver and come to the house that time when he dropped off of the roof. On account she's a nob. With diamonds as big as goose eggs, they say. And they're going to live in a castle and he's giving up the Old Bailey and going to be a gentleman."

"No, he won't," Freame said. "Not him, swanning with the nobs and chatting with the King and wearing diamond stickpins. Not him. He won't be raising himself up after what he did to me."

Husher said, "What he done to Chiver, too. If it wasn't for that Raven—"

"Chiver brought it on himself, the bloody fool," Jacob said. "Who was it brought the whiny whoreson, that— What's his name?"

"Toby," Squirrel said. "Toby Coppy."

"Him," Jacob said. "Why am I sick, why am I ruined, but on account of Master Toby Coppy—and that squeaking sister of his—Betty or Biddy or—"

"Bridget," Squirrel said.

"Her—prating and squawking, and bringing the quality to stick their noses in. But it's all down to Raven, isn't it? And he's going to have sashes and velvet robes and crowns and such and rub elbows with princes and princesses? Ha!"

Freame smiled now, a smile that made his boys tremble and enemies reach for their weapons or run away.

"Oh, he'll have a crown all right," Freame said. "And I'll crown him myself."

Squirrel and Husher looked at each other and smiled, too.

Chapter Fourteen

Let it be observed, that those who write in defence of marriage, usually give such sublime and exalted descriptions, as are not realized in one case of a thousand; and therefore cannot be a just motive to a considerate man.

—John Witherspoon, *Letters on Marriage*, 1834

Ithaca House, Richmond
20 November 1835

Two princesses, two royal dukes and their wives, four members of the ministry and their wives, three slightly French more or less former dressmakers and their spouses: duke, marquess, and earl, in order of precedence. These, Radford's groomsman Westcott, and what seemed to be thousands of Fairfaxes filled the drawing room of Ithaca House.

While Radford knew each and every name, and could if required have recited them a week or a year hence, at the moment they were no more than a sea of hazy faces amid blobs of color.

He couldn't blame the fog on the previous night's extended celebration with the aforesaid duke, marquess, and earl. He'd begun the celebrating already weary, after weeks of working long hours to keep up with his professional responsibilities and Bernard's stream of pestering letters. Thanks to the duke, marquess, and earl's notions of a proper bachelor's party, Radford had enjoyed about two hours' sleep. He decided that they, like so many others, had been trying to kill him, or at least make sure he didn't make it to the wedding.

The haze had nothing to do with any of this.

It was what he saw at the entrance to the drawing room. Clara.

His bride—*his* bride—on her father's arm.

A bride so beautiful, Radford's inner self wept. And maybe a mist managed to escape from that secret inner chamber, to make his vision somewhat watery for a moment. But he blinked, and the mist cleared, and there she was, radiantly beautiful, a sun goddess shedding golden light upon the mundane world beneath.

His mind was falling into the hands of his troublesome self, and descending into poetry, but he couldn't help it.

In a very short time, she would be his, by law.

His in a deeply personal, intimate sense, too.

He mustn't think about that. Yet. Wits and sobriety were needed at present.

He made himself regard her bridal attire as though it were legal evidence.

The dressmakers had created a fantastical iced-cake madness of Brussels point lace and silk embroidery dotted with pearls. A bouquet of lace rose from the braided knot atop her head. Strands of pearls wrapped about the knot and draped her forehead. A pair of lace lappets flowed from the crown down to the richly embroidered lace flounce of her skirt. Rosettes dotted the flounce and marked her puffy sleeves' gathering, above her elbows, where another mile of lace dripped down past the upper edges of her gloves. A lace- and embroidery-adorned sash with long, flowing ends circled her waist. Another rosette rested cunningly between the folds at the neckline of a very snug bodice, drawing the eye to the lace edging, thence to satin skin and the pearl necklace encircling her smooth throat.

He wished he'd had more sleep. He'd need all his inge-nuity to get all that—and everything underneath—off her in less than a day.

He wanted to lick every inch of that satiny skin.

But he could not let himself think about that. The wed-ding night was hours from now—blast these tribal rituals!

He of all men had to get through the rites in a ratio-nal manner. All the world would be waiting for him to do something inexcusably obnoxious. Someone was sure to object when the minister offered the opportunity, and Radford would have to defend himself as well as pros-ecute the objectors swiftly and irrevocably.

It felt like eons, yet only a moment passed before she was standing beside him.

Then his mouth spread into a grin. He couldn't help it. After all the storms and drama and despair and fear, she was to be his at last.

She shot him a quick glance, and a quick smile, barely enough to offer a glimpse of the chipped tooth. But then she seemed to remember where they were and why, be-cause her smile faded and she became solemn.

He became solemn, too, as it struck him, finally, the immensity of what they were about to do. What this re-markable girl was about to do.

Tie her life to his.

Forever.

"Still time to run," he murmured.

She looked at him then in patent disbelief. "In *this* dress?"

The minister cleared his throat.

They both turned toward him, Radford with pounding heart.

"Dearly beloved," the minister began.

That evening

Clara was going to kill the bridegroom.

Admittedly her wedding dress was not the sort of thing one simply threw on and threw off again. Its numerous attachments and fastenings would have sent the bridegroom directly to an insane asylum.

Still, it was a miracle of a wedding dress. Even Sophy's lavish prose in the Special Bridal Edition of *Foxe's Morning Spectacle* couldn't do it justice.

Radford had looked a little misty-eyed when he first saw Clara in her wedding ensemble.

Or maybe those were tears of laughter.

In any case, it was no small challenge to get out of, and she'd had to retire with Davis into the dressing room.

The process couldn't have taken an hour, if that, and Clara had spent the time in a tumult of anxiety and anticipation.

Last night, Mama had sharpened Clara's vague notions of what went on during the wedding night—but not by much, Lady Warford being slightly embarrassed and greatly tearful.

And so, trembling a little, Clara had entered the shadowy, candlelit bedroom.

And found the bridegroom sprawled on the bed, sound asleep, and still wearing most of the clothes he'd worn to his wedding.

Even her brother Harry, who didn't care much what he looked like, had a valet.

Radford didn't. Still, men's clothing wasn't a fraction

as complicated as women's, though the best coats, tailored to fit like skin, weren't easy to remove without assistance.

Yet he'd got off his coat, undone his neckcloth, and detached the ruffles from the opening and cuffs of his shirt. The coat he'd tossed over a chair and the neckcloth on top of it. His diamond stickpin glittered from a small dish on the bedside table. His shoes lay where he'd thrown or kicked them, one on its side and one upside down, near the chair.

He'd unbuttoned his waistcoat but that was as far as he'd gone.

He lay on his side, his head on the pillow, his black hair tousled. He had flung one arm over his face, and tucked the other under the pillow. Her gaze trailed over the long line of his body, from his shoulders down over his powerful torso and trousered legs. For some reason the sight of his stockinged feet made her heart ache. She stepped nearer.

In sleep, his face was almost boyishly innocent. This must be because his closed eyes hid his too-penetrating grey gaze. In the softly shimmering light he looked almost . . . vulnerable.

Perhaps she would not kill him, after all.

He was exhausted, poor man. In the last month they'd snatched moments together, but rarely without people hovering in the vicinity—as though everybody feared the wicked Raven Radford would ravish and abandon her.

Not that he'd had much time to spend with her, even though he hadn't needed to negotiate a peace between their parents. The parents had taken care of that themselves.

Being handsome, lively, and charming, Anne Radford soon won over Mama. The long-ago divorce scandal faded in the glamor of Mrs. Radford's unmistakable breeding, elegant dress, and handsome villa in a fashionable neighborhood.

After engaging their lawyers in gladiatorial combat, Mr. George Radford and Papa had spent a great deal of time together, happily arguing—one a lawyer, the other a politician, and both delighting in a worthy opponent.

All the same, the social activity tired the older man, and Clara knew Radford took on a great deal on his father's behalf. Too, he had clients needing his help. And Beastly Bernard demanding constant attention.

Then came the wedding festivities, starting last night with a men's party Mama said the bride ought to know nothing about. And the wedding breakfast had gone on for what seemed like forever.

"Oh, go ahead and sleep," she murmured. "Only I wish I hadn't gone to the trouble of trying to look irresistible."

Her nightgown wasn't a proper nightgown at all, but a naughty piece of goods the Noirot sisters had concocted, giving rein, she supposed, to their not-very-deeply-submerged Frenchness. Unlike her simple, sensible nightgowns, this was made of linen as fine and silky as his shirt. Lace bordered the shockingly low neckline. Lace and silk ribbons trimmed the sleeves and hem, and tendrils of silk embroidery adorned the bodice.

Since she didn't feel in the least sleepy, she hunted for something to read.

Radford's parents had moved out of the master bedroom some while ago. Though it was elegantly furnished, the books in the writing desk's cabinet left something to be desired. They must be Radford's, because they included not a single novel or book of poetry. With a sigh, Clara took out a dog-eared copy of Sir John Wade's *Treatise*, the one Radford had told her to read when she'd asked him for help finding Toby Coppy.

If anything could put her to sleep, this would. The title alone made her drowsy: *A Treatise on the Police and Crimes of the Metropolis; especially juvenile delin-*

*quency, female prostitution, mendacity, gaming, forgery,
street-robberies, burglary and house-breaking, receiving of stolen goods, counterfeiting the coin, exhumation,
cheating and swindling, adulteration of food, &c.*

And that was only the first half of the title.

She went round to the other side of the bed, set the
book on the bedside table, and climbed onto the bed.

She took the book in her lap.

Her movement must have disturbed him, because he
moved, too, onto his back, and flung his arm up onto the
pillow beside his head. His waistcoat fell open, displaying the breadth of his shoulders and chest. She could see,
under the nearly transparent shirt, the dark hair feather-
ing over his chest . . . and down, over his belly, where it
disappeared at the waist of his trousers.

Her face grew hot, and her heart went *bumpity-bump*.

She returned the book to the bedside table.

She stared at his arm. The light outlined the muscles
under the fine linen. The thin fabric clung to the line of
his collarbone and fell open at his throat, revealing the
hollow at the base. She remembered the way he'd touched
the hollow of her throat—with his finger, his lips, his
tongue.

That had been only the beginning. There had been
much more . . . his fingers stroking up her thigh . . . almost
to . . .

Then he'd stopped.

But there would be more of that sort of thing. Mama
had called it marital intimacy.

A part of Clara wanted to run away but another, stronger part drew her toward him . . . her husband.

Her husband.

Forever.

Nervousness surged into alarm.

What had she done? What had she done?

She closed her eyes against the mad upwelling of panic and tried to recall the wedding ceremony, but it was a blur . . . of happiness, like a dream.

Happiness. He made her happy because of the kind of man he was and because he saw her as she was. And because . . . she liked the way he looked and moved. And the sound of his voice. He'd made her heart beat faster from the moment she'd looked up at him in Charing Cross. When she saw him or spoke to him or sat near him, the world was different and better.

And she could breathe.

All this was why she'd done this irrevocable thing.

She opened her eyes.

In the candlelight and firelight, his hair gleamed like black silk. She bent over him and let her fingers glide so very lightly over the silky curls. She traced the shape of his shoulder and let her hand linger, for a moment, over his powerful upper arm, so warm. With the same delicate touch, as though he were an object of the finest porcelain instead of a strong young man, she stroked over the tissue-thin linen covering his chest . . . then down . . .

Her face burned, and she grew timid.

She returned to his face, with its uncompromising angles of cheekbone and jaw and the imperious nose down which he'd regarded her on that day in Charing Cross.

She remembered the way, more recently, he'd kissed all over her face, and the way that had made her feel. She bent and dropped feather kisses, mere shadows of what he'd done to her, over his face: his forehead and temple and the top of the arch of his eyebrow. She kissed his nose and the top of his cheekbone and the corner of his jaw. Then his mouth was so close, she had to touch her lips there.

His hand came up and he caught the back of her head

and drew her down to him and kissed her, fiercely, fiercely, and the world caught fire.

Sensing her nearness, Radford had swum up out of sleep, and he'd almost opened his eyes when he felt her fingers drift, feather-light, over his hair.

Wanting to discover what she'd do, he'd tried to be still. He'd tried to quiet his heart's racing, though it beat so hard, they must hear it at the other end of the house. But she didn't draw away or pause. He made himself breathe evenly, as though he were still asleep.

He'd borne as much as he could, keeping still while she explored, though he thought he'd die, keeping his hands to himself. Then came those sweetly innocent kisses, like rose petals wafting down onto his face and along his nose. And when her mouth touched his, she flooded his senses: the scent and nearness of her and the sound of her breathing and the whisper of her clothing when she moved. Though he'd wanted to see how far she'd go, he couldn't remain quiet. He couldn't pretend sleep any longer.

He reached for her and kissed her, deeply, tenderly, hungrily—a mix of feelings, as always happened with her. She made a tumult, tugging him this way and that, knocking objectivity and reason askew. Stay detached and in control when Clara was by? What a joke.

He kissed her with feelings he'd tamped down again and again over the weeks since he'd met her: the delight he felt in her company, the desire he couldn't talk himself out of, the humiliation of knowing she was beyond his reach, the fear when he thought death would snatch her away, and the despair when her father refused him.

He poured all that passionate turmoil into the kiss, and softened it, too, with an affection so deep he'd never have believed it of himself.

She tasted like sunlight, the same sunlight one heard

in her laughter and saw in her smile and in the sparkle in her eyes.

She tasted like innocence and like experience, too. Her mouth and tongue joined with and responded to his as though the kiss were a dance, and they'd been dancing together all their lives.

He pulled her closer, bringing his arm round her, and never broke the kiss while he rolled her onto her back.

She was his at last by law, and what he wanted to do was take her there and then and make her his in physical fact.

But she was not a girl of experience, and if he didn't give her time and make her first time as pleasant as possible, she would get the wrong idea about him and about marital relations, and their future together would be even rockier than it looked to be already.

This was why, though he was already overheated and though he'd waited an eternity for her, he eased his mouth from hers and said, "Well, then, let's see what I got myself for a wife."

He came up, shifting onto his knees, and looked her over.

Long and leggy. Voluptuously shaped. Silken skin. A perfect face, set with aquamarine eyes.

Voluptuously shaped—one couldn't say that often enough or appreciate it sufficiently.

How on earth had Raven Radford, of all men, rated a goddess?

And the thing she was wearing—for once there wasn't much of it: a nearly transparent scrap of linen decorated in all the places the eye—the masculine eye—was naturally drawn to.

"You might have taken a proper look when an escape clause offered," she said, coloring. "When the minister asked for objections."

"I did look," he said. "But you were hard to see properly, under all the bric-a-brac. I decided to give you the benefit of the doubt."

"*Bric-a-brac*," she repeated, eyebrows aloft. "Wait until I tell Sophy and her sisters."

He planted a light kiss on each arch of her perfect eyebrows. "Never mind, never mind, my lady. You'll do. For a barrister's wife." He drew back and tried to detach himself.

"What a tease you are." She put her arms up. "Come here."

"No," he said. "If you start that, it'll all be over before you can blink, and you'll want to kill me afterward."

"I expect to want to kill you from time to time," she said. "Come."

Gently he put her arms down onto the bed.

"No kissing," he said.

"Mr. Radford."

"You may call me Oliver. Or Raven. Or both. We're private now, after all."

"And you may call me Lady Clara," she said loftily. "Or my lady or your ladyship. Or Heptaplasiesoptron."

"Thank you, my lady," he said. "If your ladyship would be so good as to lie there and try not to participate until I suggest it—"

"Lie here and take it, you mean," she said. He saw the way her fingers curled and uncurled on the bedclothes. She was nervous, but putting on a fine show, her screen in place.

"Feel free to comment, as the whim takes you," he said.

"Is there a book?" she said.

"A book?"

"With the rules of how to do this," she said. "You know, with a firstly and a secondly and a thirdly."

"There are many books," he said. "This is a plot of my

own devising. Because I've never done it before with a *virgo intacta*."

"Who said I was?"

He straightened. "Are you or are you not? Because if you aren't, we can dispense with—"

"This is my first time." She sighed. "And given the rate at which it's proceeding, I may not live long enough to do it again."

"Then kindly leave this to me," he said.

She laughed.

And sunshine broke out in the shadowy bedroom.

His heart soared with a happiness so rare he wasn't sure *happiness* was the name for it.

"We'll start with familiar things," he said. He straddled her legs, and bent and kissed her nose. "Like this." He kissed her forehead. "And this and this and this." Between words, he feathered kisses over her face.

He kissed her ear and nibbled at the lobe, and she gasped and squirmed. He kissed a tender place behind her ear and worked his way down her neck.

The scent of her skin was in his nostrils and filling his head. He couldn't get enough of it. He brushed his cheek against hers. Her skin was as soft and smooth as flower petals. He couldn't get enough of the feel of her skin. He kissed the hollow of her throat, and the warmer scent of her wafted up from the low neckline of her night dress. He brushed his cheek over the skin her neckline bared and drank in the scent. He brushed his lips over the place. He pushed away lustful impatience to simply absorb the sensual pleasure of this moment.

She moved under his touch and sighed, and her breath came faster.

He let his hands slide over her skin where his mouth had gone, and over her neck and shoulders and down over the swell of her breasts and down where the bodice's fine linen covered them, but not very well. The cunningly designed embroidery circled the deep pink buds. They tautened under his touch.

"Oh," she said. "That's . . . naughty . . . and . . . not unpleasant."

He loosened the neckline's ribbons and drew it down, baring her perfect breasts. She opened her eyes wide, and a blush spread over her face and downward.

He trailed his mouth over the silken curves, following their shape and reveling in the warmth and scent of her, and the way she moved under his caresses and the way she took the pleasure he gave himself and her. He took one rosy tip into his mouth and lightly suckled, and she gasped and brought her hand up and pushed her fingers through his hair and held him there.

"Oh," she said. "Oh, my goodness." Her voice was soft with surprise and pleasure.

She was too perfect, too responsive, too much altogether for a mere mortal male.

He could not go on like this without having a heart seizure.

"Don't stop," she whispered.

So many people wanted to kill him, but she would succeed.

Raven Radford was going to die on his wedding night.

*H*e'd kissed her before. He'd touched her before. Clara had felt pleasure and excitement.

This was beyond anything she'd felt at those times. Then she'd only been on the border of an unfamiliar realm. Now she moved into that new place. Now it seemed as though she'd been only half aware of herself. Or somehow not fully alive. Her body had kept secrets from her.

Radford kissed her and caressed her, and every inch of her vibrated, outside, inside.

He suckled her, and she felt the tug in the pit of her belly. Then his hands and mouth were everywhere, sending electric sensations over her skin and under. She couldn't keep still. She couldn't help making sounds—little cries and moans, not at all ladylike—as shock after pleasurable shock struck and raced along her skin and inside her.

She hadn't realized her heart and body could feel like this. How could she have guessed what it could be like?— the feel of his face against her skin, the masculine scent filling her consciousness and blocking out everything else. The world narrowed to him . . . and her . . . and to sensations familiar and new. And an aching pleasure that made her restless.

He drew her nightgown down, all the way to her waist, but she was past blushing now. Embarrassment couldn't live alongside these surging feelings. Modesty dwindled to nothing under the movement of his hands and the touch of his mouth.

She clutched at the bedclothes, trying to do as he'd asked—in this he knew better, after all—but he was kissing her belly and she couldn't remain still any longer. She had to touch him.

She brought her hands to his head, and dragged her fingers through his thick, silky hair. She felt him shudder under her touch. He paused, but only for a heartbeat. Then he swirled kisses over her belly, drawing her gown down farther as he went . . . down past her hips . . . kissing her . . . kissing her . . . and moving her legs apart . . . and her knees came up of their own accord . . . and he was kissing her . . .

    . . . *down there.*

Her eyes flew open. She saw the canopy above her head, deep blue embroidered with gold that shimmered in the candlelight and firelight. She saw stars, too, flashing in her mind's eye, as though she'd fallen into the sky. But no. The sky felt like water, the stars reflected in it. She wasn't flying but swimming in feelings, happy and restless and wanting very badly to reach a place she couldn't identify.

Her hands fell away, to the bedclothes. She closed her eyes.

He kissed her and touched his tongue *there*, and heat and excitement ruled her, mind and body. She tried to keep still but her body quivered. Then his fingers were there, too. She grabbed fistfuls of the bedclothes, holding on while shock after pleasurable shock knocked her about and made her mindless.

The feelings sharpened and quickened. A stronger shock flooded her with heat and feelings impossible to make sense of. She cried out—not words, but primitive sounds. Her legs shook. She grasped his shoulders and tried to pull him up. She needed him with her. He understood, and came up and kissed her the way he'd done before, and she gave back passion, love, and a wild longing.

She couldn't keep her hands from roving over him, over his shoulders and back and arms. She caught hold of his shirt, and tugged it from his trousers. She wanted skin. She wanted to touch him the way he touched her.

"Clara," he said hoarsely.

"I don't know what to do," she said. "Get this off."

He gave a choked laugh and rose. He shrugged out of his waistcoat and tossed it aside. He pulled his shirt out from the waistband of his trousers, she helping clumsily.

He pulled the shirt over his head and flung it away, and she reached up to set her palms against his chest. His skin glowed golden in the candlelight, and his body was hard and warm like a marble statue come alive. She could feel his strength under her hands. She could feel his body respond to her, his muscles tensing under her touch. She slid her hands over his skin, discovering him as though she were an explorer and he a new land she'd happened on.

And yes, his body was a new world to her.

She'd had glimpses of little boys' bodies in her childhood, and she'd seen statues in a state of extreme undress—most notably and visibly the Achilles in Hyde Park. She'd never before seen a living adult man's body. It was a revelation, though at present she had no idea what exactly had been revealed to her. She was too overheated and dizzy—and he was touching her again, too, moving his hands over her, exploring her body the way she explored his.

He kissed her everywhere, and she followed his lead, kissing his neck and shoulders and every part of him she could reach. She could hear his breathing come harder and faster, like hers. Her skin seemed to be on fire. She was hot inside, too.

He stroked downward, over her belly and down between her legs, and she parted them shamelessly to his touch, opening herself entirely. She'd discovered an altogether new experience, and she wanted more. Her body trembled with the wanting.

She felt him move, changing his position. His hand came away from her, and she nearly cried out.

He said, "That's as much as I can stand, my lady."

She heard fabric rustle, but she was too deranged to recognize it or care what it was. She cared only that he'd stopped touching her and moved away.

She said, "Please don't stop yet."

He muttered something about trousers. She realized he was taking them off. She wanted to look—she had an idea of what was coming—but shyness overwhelmed her, and she couldn't. She kept her gaze to his upper body, his beautiful–not beautiful face.

He said, his voice low and rough, "Before was the firstly and secondly. This is the thirdly."

He came back to her and stroked between her legs. She felt him spreading her, but all she could do was squirm and tremble, her body obeying something that wasn't her brain—

He pushed into her.

"Oh!" she said, startled, dismayed. Was it supposed to hurt?

What had Mama said? She couldn't remember.

He was kissing her again, deeply, passionately. He was caressing her, squeezing her breasts. Pleasure surged once more, flooding her with heat. The craving—for whatever it was—returned, stronger than before.

She was aware of him inside her, and though the initial hurt was subsiding, she wasn't quite comfortable. Yet somehow her body was trying to make it so, warming her and making her move. She heard him groan.

"My girl, I'm not sure how much more of this—"

"Wait. I think I'm getting the hang of it."

He made a sound, laughter and groan combined.

Her head was spinning and her body had been taken over by a savage, but she tried to think what a lady could do.

Put the guest at ease.

"Yes, I'm quite well," she said, trying for dignity while her voice shook. "You may proceed, Mr. Radford."

He laughed again in that pained way, and kissed her again and again. Then he was moving inside her, and this stirred her up anew, more than before. She could feel her blood rushing through her veins and her heart beating fast and very hard, and with these simple bodily sensations came such transcendent feelings—joy and surprise and warmth and an overwhelming tenderness for him and a craving, too, as primitive as hunger.

She couldn't stop her hands from roaming over his body, down to his waist and below, even over his naked bottom. Longing swamped shyness and she learned the shape and feel of the man she'd wed. She moved with him in the way she'd kissed him, taking his lead and learning as she went.

The feelings grew stronger and stronger until she thought she'd burst. Wave upon wave of happiness seemed to carry her farther and farther toward a distant destination, as though she were a ship drawn to a barely glimpsed shore. Then all at once she was there. She shuddered, and felt him shudder, too, sweet sensations coursing through her.

And after a time, she seemed to float down from the waves' crest and fall into his arms. Contentment swept over her, and it seemed she'd come home at last, and she was safe on that other shore.

Chapter Fifteen

Richmond is a village in Surrey, nine miles from London, and is certainly the finest, most luxuriant, and most picturesque spot in the British Dominions.

—Samuel Leigh, *New Picture of London*, 1834

In time, Radford quieted. He was on the brink of falling asleep when a sound stirred his mind awake again.

Rain.

The day of his wedding had veered between sunlight and gloom, like his emotions in the weeks since he'd met her.

Now rain beat against the windows.

He remembered the rainy day when he'd climbed into the cab beside her, and the scent of Clara had enveloped him.

Her scent was everywhere now, mingled with his and the scent of their lovemaking. She was in his arms and she was warm and soft and perfect.

His wife. *His wife.*

He still couldn't take it in. In any case, he was too bone-weary to think.

Cautiously he eased himself from her. Thinking she'd

fallen asleep, he was about to draw her back into his arms when he saw her eyes were wide open. She was staring up at the canopy.

As he hesitated, completely at a loss for once, her gaze, still wide, came down to his face.

"No wonder Mama was tongue-tied," she said thickly. "How is one to explain something like *that*? To somebody else? It's so *personal*."

He stifled a groan.

He'd wanted to be a good bridegroom—nay, being who he was, he'd determined to be a superior one. He'd been near collapse with fatigue, yet he'd tried to stay awake while she spent eternity undressing. He would have liked to undress her, but knew it was wiser to leave that to the maid. In his state of exhaustion, he was bound to fumble as he tried to disassemble her complicated bridal attire. Fumbling was not permissible. This night had to be perfect for her, considering the life she'd abandoned for life with him.

He'd resolved to make her first time as exciting, pleasurable, and free of pain as was humanly possible. He hadn't had the remotest idea how Herculean a task he'd set himself, trying to maintain control in the face of her innocence and willingness and tenderness, coupled with a beauty that made him breathless.

No, never mind Hercules and his paltry labors. All the gods of Olympus working in concert would have struggled to restrain themselves in the circumstances.

He'd used the last resources of his willpower to keep matters going until he felt sure she was ready.

And all of that had gone well. He'd nearly died in the process, but she hadn't seemed to suffer much, even at the painful part, and for the rest of it she'd been . . . open. And passionate and . . . loving.

But now he could scarcely find the strength to breathe—and she wanted to *talk*.

"Clara," he said.

"Mr. Radford." She smiled.

Ah, that smile. It could turn all a man's resolutions, along with the brain holding them, into melted butter.

He said, "If you would allow me a short nap—half an hour—I should be glad to talk or do whatever you like. But at the moment—"

"I know," she said. "You must be weary to death."

"Not of you, I promise."

"I should hope not," she said. "If, after all we've been through, you'd grown weary of me already, I should certainly kill you."

"And no jury on earth would convict you, whether or not you batted your big blue eyes at them," he murmured, trying to keep his own eyes open. "Justifiable homicide, they'd say, and off you'd go, to kill another fellow and get away with it."

"Well, men make up juries," she said. "I meant only that, after the month you've had, it was a wonder you could remain standing for the nuptials. I know I should have kept my hands to myself and let you sleep, but you . . . Well, I'm not very disciplined, apparently. But yes, of course we ought to sleep. I'm not sure, though. Do we sleep close together or—"

"Close together if you don't mind."

"Thank you, Mr. Radford. I have no objections. However, I shall have to follow your lead in this, too. I never slept with a man before."

"Then we'll start with this." He pulled the bedclothes up over them and turned onto his side and drew her up against him. "Like spoons."

"Yes, that's very nice," she said.

He drew her closer, bringing her rump against his *membrum virile*, which promptly forgot how tired it was.

"Oh!" she said.

"Pay him no heed," he said. "He has a tiny, tiny brain of his own and that tiny brain is trying with all its might to kill me. I am a young and healthy man with a most desirable wife, but the brain in my head being larger, I realize that—"

"Firstly," she said, and he heard the smile in her voice.

"Firstly, a considerate husband gives his new bride time to recover," he said. "And secondly, I shall do a bad job in this state of weariness."

For a moment she said nothing. Then, "I don't know anything," she said very quietly.

"Luckily you married me. You'll learn everything correctly."

"Everything," she repeated.

"Everything you need to know," he said. "And possibly some things you don't need to know."

He was looking forward to teaching her, far more than he would ever have guessed.

He closed his eyes and savored her warmth and softness, and in no time drifted into sleep.

Later

The first thing Radford became aware of was warm, soft Woman tucked up against him. At the realization, his body came fully awake and alert well before his mind took in the distinctive darkness that boded dawn.

His mind caught up quickly enough.

He had a great deal to think about. He had decisions to make.

There was his father, who'd borne the wedding excitement well, but needed tranquillity at present. The trouble was, Radford's marrying so high was sure to bring Radford relatives looking for favors. They'd latch on to the older man first, supposing he'd be more vulnerable.

Radford needed to be nearer to his parents. And that raised the question of where he and Clara would live. Her friends and family had offered houses. Like the Duke of Clevedon, they all seemed to have a residence to spare.

Though Radford had resisted the idea of asking his cousin for Malvern House, he couldn't let his pride rule in this case. It might be best for Clara. And best for the house, for that matter, not to stand empty.

Still, it would cost heaven and earth to live there.

While his income was well above what Lady Warford had imagined—the marquess was less surprised, having used due diligence in all regards—it was not up to staffing and maintaining a palatial London residence.

He needed a plan, and soon. Their stay with his parents was to be temporary. Yet he needed to be close at hand to deal with rampaging Radfords. Between London and Richmond there had to be something. In Kensington or another London suburb.

And the bridal trip? He would not put that off indefinitely. He knew Clara wanted to visit the Continent. Though she never said so outright, he'd discerned the longing in her eyes when anybody spoke of Paris or Venice or Florence. Others wouldn't see it but to him it was as plain as the gold letters over the shop door spelling out MAISON NOIROT . . . where his bride had spent thousands of pounds—what her father would regard as pocket change.

When the better weather arrived, then . . .

Clara snuggled closer.

His thoughts trailed away.

He nuzzled her neck and slid his hand down along her arm and over to caress and cup her breast. She made an *mmmm* sound in her sleep. He trailed his hand down along the delicious inward curve of her waist, then over her belly and lower. She stirred in his arms.

"Are we awake?" she murmured.

"You don't have to be," he said. "I can manage this by myself. You don't have to move a muscle . . . that is, not more than a little."

He stroked down over the sweet place between her legs. So soft she was, the feminine nest like silken threads over velvet. Heat tore through him and his hand trembled.

"This will probably not last as long as the first time," he said.

"Oh, my goodness." She quivered under his touch, and made small sounds in her throat, moans caught in sighs.

He shifted her slightly to slide his knees between her legs. "Not a fraction as long."

Her beautifully rounded bottom rested on his thighs. The rush of desire darkened his mind, as though a storm bore down on it. Even though his wilder self was taking over, driving him, he tried not to hurry. He kissed the back of her neck and her shoulders and arms. He slid his hand along her thigh, upward over her belly and up to her breast, and down again while he savored the way she felt under his hands and the way she responded, moving, murmuring, urging him on without realizing she was doing so.

He couldn't get enough of touching her, and yet he had to have her *now*. In the storm of his mind images swirled of the first time—her innocence and understanding and tenderness and lust, too. She'd begun discovering herself as a woman while he discovered her as his woman, his wife.

His wife.

He brought his hand down to ready her, and found her ready, damp to his touch, and squirming under it. He stroked her and heard the hitch in her breathing—the first, small orgasm. He thrust into her. Oh, she was so tight but giving way like water and surrounding him and moving with him, sensation heightening with every movement. The pleasure of it was at the edge of endurable.

"I think you're getting the hang of it," he gasped into her ear.

"Oh, my Raven," she murmured. "I think you are, too."

One choked laugh, then he moved, stroking inward and drawing away, teasing a little at first, but soon finding himself beyond teasing. They found a rhythm to this, in the same way they'd found their own way to kiss, learning from each other, paying attention and caring.

He cared beyond what he'd thought possible in himself.

Because, how could he not? She'd been meant for him and he for her, though this made no rational sense. But reason didn't signify. Reason belonged elsewhere. Here were a man and his new bride, and here affection mattered and desire and pleasing her and pleasing himself.

Their lovers' dance went faster and faster, and the world grew hotter and darker. And mindless though he was, he had a sense of their traveling headlong, two riders in a beautiful storm. Faster and fiercer, until the storm caught them. He felt her shudder when she reached her peak, and felt his own body shake, too, as though he'd been struck by lightning.

But it was love, only love, and for now, nothing else mattered. The storm quieted, and he drew her into his arms, and once more, they slept.

I can hear you thinking," she said.

She wasn't sure what had woken her. It might have been the distant sounds of the household stirring or the not-quite-silent steps of a maid entering to restore the fire or the someone who'd come in at some point and drawn the curtains round the bed. Whatever had jarred her from sleep—sounds or awareness of daylight or something else altogether—she was awake and aware she wasn't the only one.

"You can't hear me thinking," he said. "It's physically impossible."

"It isn't. I can tell by the distracted way you're fondling my breast."

"Your breast is distracting."

She turned toward him.

"Now it's more distracting because there are two of them in plain sight," he said. He ran his hand over first one, then the other. Heat and longing swirled through her. "And fine ones, too, by the way."

"That's lucky, since you married them." Though she spoke so boldly, she felt a flush spreading over her skin. She still wasn't used to being married.

"So I did. Them and this." He stroked her belly. "And this." He moved his hand down and her breath caught.

He took his hand away. "I'd better not start anything," he said. "I should have given you more time last night. The virgin body—"

"I'm not a virgin anymore," she said. "I'm a married woman."

"The newly initiated," he said, "need respite. Otherwise, sometimes, an irritation develops, which can be quite uncomfortable. I've nursed you through one ailment, yes, but you were weak and helpless then. Even debilitated, you hit me. Hard. This sort of thing could put you in a bad mood, and you might strike me with a blunt instrument. Even if there's no physical violence, you won't want me to touch you for months. Or ever again."

"An irritation?" she said. "No one mentioned that." Not that Mama had mentioned much of anything comprehensible.

"And no one will have to mention it if we can contrive to behave ourselves, more or less, until . . . well, at least later in the day. Though it would be better to wait until tonight. I was thinking of a candlelit supper in front of the fire. Then I would prostrate myself at your feet and start licking your toes and work my way up."

She shivered. "Is that what you were thinking?"

"I had to do something to keep myself occupied, so I planned. The future."

"Interesting plan so far," she said.

"There were others along those lines, but I'd rather spring them on you unexpectedly," he said.

There was a pause, a palpable pause, before he added, "I was thinking about more mundane matters, too."

"I think you were doing much too much thinking," she said. "But I suppose you can't help it, your brain being so large. It wants a good deal to keep it fueled and going. I reckon you must get bored more easily than other people."

He came up onto one elbow and looked at her. "Yes. You'll have your hands full, keeping me excited."

"I don't remember anything about that in the marriage vows," she said. "There was *obey*—I noticed that came first—but I privately added a lengthy footnote to that item."

"This surprises me not at all. But there was the part about serving me."

"It, too, needed a footnote. Then love and honor and keeping you and sticking with you and nobody else. I remember all those. But I don't recall the minister mentioning anything about keeping you excited."

"That was the *serve* part. It had an asterisk and some fine print."

"I did not hear any fine print."

"You weren't listening very closely. You closed your eyes once or twice."

"I was trying not to cry."

"I should hope so. At that point, it was too late for regrets."

"Don't be thick," she said. "I nearly cried because of all the feelings. I wanted to laugh, too, but a lady does not indulge in vulgar emotions at her own wedding in front of all the wedding guests, especially when they include royalty. I hope you didn't mind them too much. Mama had to have them, for the show."

"I know," he said. "Pretending she was delighted with your choice of mate. Clara, your mother is not entirely—or even very much—misguided, you know."

She sat up. She had an idea what was in his mind. They would have to settle some things, sooner or later, but this morning the sun seemed to be shining, and it was the day after her wedding, and her husband had made perfect love to her. Twice.

The arguments could wait for later.

She gave a regal wave of her hand. "I'm not in a humor to talk about my mother. I'm starting to feel hungry, and everybody will tell you I become cantankerous if not fed promptly." She raised an autocratic eyebrow, in the way her grandmother used to do. "I trust your plans include a delectable breakfast for your wife, Mr. Radford?"

*T*he argument started in the afternoon, in the course of a drive in Richmond Park. The drive, if not the dispute, was meant to keep them occupied for a time. Then they'd dine somewhere in the vicinity. After which they'd need to find something else to do, to while away the long hours before the promised supper.

Since debate with Radford demanded all of Clara's mental resources, it was an excellent way to keep her mind from dwelling on what the supper entertainment would entail.

Her husband drove her cabriolet. Like Davis, it—along with her horse and tiger—had come with her into the marriage.

Naturally, he drove to an inch, even though the vehicle had been tailored for her and the seat wasn't the right height for his more long-legged self. But this could hardly incommode him.

He drove perfectly because of course he would have studied the art of driving in the same intently focused and thorough way he studied everything else: facial expressions, the precise distance from here to there and the amount of time required to cover the distance, identifying marks on silver, and so on and so on. Raven Radford was a walking encyclopedia.

Clara was hopelessly infatuated with his intellect. Yes, of course she loved his body, and had admired it even when she had only a hint of what it could do to hers. Still, she was only in the early stages of physical appreciation. His brain was a longer acquaintance. It had captured her attention, perhaps from the first day she'd met him, at Vauxhall. It stimulated her, challenged her, and demanded her utmost.

It excited her to match wits with it. And to match her will against his.

"Malvern House?" she said with calm curiosity, when she wanted to shriek, *Have you lost your mind, the wondrous mind I love?* She silently thanked her years of ladyship training in self-control.

"It stands empty," he said.

"I'm not surprised," she said while she tried to fathom what was in his wondrous mind. "The last tenant was a visiting foreign princeling, one of the rare royal cousins who aren't impoverished. One needs a ducal income to maintain and staff it. But other dukes have their own London residences."

"Bernard hates London, and doesn't care what becomes of anything or anybody but himself," he said. "The house is handsome and spacious."

"Spacious enough to want, at the bare minimum, a staff of thirty servants," she said.

"You know Malvern House, then?"

"Of course I know it. Ducal residences formed a part of my studies. I know what it takes to run them, certainly."

"I thought it would suit you," he said.

She looked at him. Even owning an enormous brain, he could be as obtuse, at times, as ordinary men.

"My dear Mr. Radford, O light of my life," she said.

He gave her a sharp glance, and she caught the slight twitch of his mouth. "Yes, my precious one."

"Were you not attending on that day in Mr. Westcott's office, when I engaged in high drama? Did you forget my splendid imitation of my mother in one of her more highly strung moments? Did the rant about my life simply pass through your brain like a puff of air through an open louver?"

"I remember it all vividly," he said.

"And probably word for word," she said. "And so I'm puzzled. After witnessing that explosion, what leads your powers of logic to think of placing me in Malvern House?"

"You can't live in chambers," he said.

"I don't see why not." She could see very well why not, but she wanted to understand what had set him on this path.

"For the reasons you gave in the course of the drama," he said. "You don't know how to put on your stockings and untying your bonnet is uphill work—"

"I have Davis for that," she said.

His mouth twitched more visibly.

"What amuses you?" she said.

"You, my—erm—treasure," he said. "You come to me with your dashing cabriolet, your splendid horse to draw it, and your tiger to look after the ensemble."

The cabriolet represented freedom and a sort of power. "If you minded, you ought to have said so," she said.

"I don't mind in the least," he said. "Driving provides exercise in the open air, requires a level of skill stimulating to the brain, and allows a measure of independence. I never wished for you to leave your vehicle or your near and dear servants behind. This, however, is merely one aspect of the life you're accustomed to."

"I didn't like that life," she said evenly. "It was stifling me."

"O jewel in the crown of my happiness," he said. "That much I perfectly comprehend. It doesn't change the fact of your having spent your life wrapped in cotton wool, as you acknowledged. You've no notion what it's like not to have an army of servants at your beck and call. Do you expect Davis to do your laundry—or even take it to the laundress? Who'll prepare your meals and see to the clearing and washing up after?"

"Not Davis," she said. A lady's maid never performed such lowly tasks. "But you have a woman who comes in to clean."

"She cleans after a fashion," he said. "But let's talk about cooking."

"No lady can cook," she said tightly. "We're not allowed near the kitchen. Among other things, the servants take great offense at such intrusions. We can, however, plan menus and direct the housekeeper and send notes to the cook and such."

"Then who'll make your ladyship's delectable meals?" he said. "My father has a French cook, thanks to my mother, who's civilized him over the years. But Westcott and I go to the nearest chop house or send there for meals, depending on how busy we are and our enthusiasm for venturing into the streets in foul weather."

"It would make a vastly interesting change," she said.

"It sounds cozy and intimate, and I should enjoy not having servants constantly hovering and watching and listening. They're not nearly as invisible as people like to believe."

"You might have mentioned wishing to be cozy and intimate with Westcott," he said. "I had no idea."

"I know as well as you do that larger living quarters are available for married gentlemen," she said.

"Even so, we might grow crowded, what with Westcott popping in when the whim takes him to plague me with desperate clients. And let's not forget Davis and the groom Colson. They'll need room. Even now, if he's listening—"

"Colson doesn't possess your inhumanly sharp senses," she said. "Firstly, the carriage hood is up, muffling conversation. Secondly, the horse, the carriage wheels, and the outside world are far from silent."

"However he learns of it," Radford said, "as soon as your groom catches wind of any plans to move to chambers in the Temple, he'll look for another position. "You may be willing to come down a hundred steps in the world, but Colson, I promise you, will not like giving up his comfortable berth at Warford House."

She gave a dismissive wave of her hand. "The point is moot, in any event. O sun on my horizon, you know as well as I that chambers won't accommodate a spoiled child like your wife. Malvern House is beyond our means. Why do we even mention these absurd extremes?"

"I rather fancy you in Malvern House," he said. "It would be like your marrying my cousin without marrying him. You'd have a proper scope for your mind, training, and talents."

"Looking after you will offer more than enough scope," she said. "I'm encouraged to know your breed is civilizable, though I suspect the process is a slow one, wanting cunning as well as patience."

"It wants a woman of unusually strong will. I believe you're qualified."

"I know I am," she said, "else I wouldn't have married you. My dear learned friend, may we view the problem logically?"

"Sometimes, when you're by, my logic runs amok," he said. "Especially when thoughts cross my mind about what I'm going to do to you at a more opportune time."

Like some exotic vine, tendrils of heat wrapped about her. To cool her senses, she looked about her at the wild splendor of the park, green even at this bleak time of year. Though so many trees had shed their leaves, the evergreens and hardier shrubs brightened the landscape.

"I know what this is," she said. "It's a ploy to make me witless."

"Is it working?"

"To a point."

"Then let's make for that cluster of shrubbery and misbehave in a furtive manner," he said. "Although . . . hmmm."

"Although . . . ?" she said, more than a little disappointed.

"Feel free to gaze at me adoringly—or at your gloves," he said. "But don't scrutinize your surroundings too closely. Somebody near the shrubbery is behaving furtively."

She gazed up at him, focusing on the errant black curl emerging from under his hat. "Another couple?" she said.

"Only one person," he said. "And one very much out of his element."

Radford had sensed the movement and casually glanced that way. At first he'd thought he'd spotted a deer or dog or squirrel darting among the trees and shrubbery. Now he was sure the figure was human but small. A boy, most likely, given his agility.

As the carriage continued its leisurely pace, the boy dashed from his place to hide behind an immense tree trunk. He was fast. Had Radford not been as keenly noticing as he was, he would have missed their watcher.

"Out of his element?" His wife gazed up at him in an adoring manner so patently theatrical, he could hardly keep in countenance.

O light of my life. She truly was entertaining.

"He's good at skulking and he's fast," he said. "He may merely be a boy amusing himself by spying on couples in the park or playing at some game, or he may be up to no good. But the glimpse I had . . ."

He reflected. He'd caught something familiar about the way their stalker moved. "I thought I'd seen him before, but one sees so many boys. The clothes, though. Those seemed wrong for a child from hereabouts. And he seems to be on his own. Children of the middling and upper classes are unlikely to wander this immense park or anywhere else unattended. At the very least, a boy would have a pack of friends with him. Not that I'm positive it was a boy. It might have been a small, nimble man."

"We're near a turning that will take us more deeply into the park," she said. "If he follows us, that stretch of road will give you better opportunities to see him. There are a few large gaps between the trees and such. He'll need to break cover, and you can watch him out of the corner of your eye."

He was already watching out of the corner of his eye, although his beautiful wife offered strong competition for his attention.

The deep green cloak she wore was styled "*merveilleux*," she had informed him. The capes, ubiquitous in women's dress for both day and night, were in the exaggerated shape of a man's coat collar, and trimmed in velvet. The gigantic sleeves of her dress were barely visible through openings in the cape's sleeves. These were rather like tent openings through which she could extend her hands without disturbing the outer layer.

A relatively small rose acacia branch sprouted from the top of her pink hat. That, a ruffled collar atop the cloak collar, and a bow or two here and there, constituted the sole decoration. The look was altogether spare and severe compared to her normal level of party-cake decoration, yet it seemed as frivolously feminine as everything else she wore.

He looked forward to the fun of taking it off, though he might have to knock Davis unconscious first.

But later.

At present another sort of clothes needed consideration.

Their watcher's attire and movement had signaled *London*.

Why, Radford wasn't yet certain. Sometimes he saw things before he truly saw them. This wasn't easy to explain in rational terms. He didn't attempt to account for the phenomenon to himself. He simply heeded it.

He followed her direction and turned into the road leading to the Old Lodge. "You know the park," he said.

"Grandmama Warford drove her own carriage," she said. "She used to take me on outings. Richmond Park and Hampton Court were two favorite destinations. She had friends in both places, and I loved them. They were so much bolder and . . ." She allowed one slender gloved hand to emerge through one of the tent openings and made the sort of vague gesture people made when words wouldn't come to their rescue. "I'm not sure if there's a simple way to describe them. They weren't afraid to be clever. They could be sharp-witted and sharp-tongued, indeed. They spoke their minds more freely. It might have been one of the privileges of age. But I know, too, that her generation was not nearly so straitlaced as mine."

"They were more plain-spoken and not so tame, according to my father," he said. "He's of an earlier generation, but I think the description applies."

"Yes, he reminds me a little of her," she said. "Why don't we live hereabouts, nearer to your parents? You could retain your chambers as a pied à terre when you need to be in court."

Father liked her. Mother did, too, though she wasn't at all easy about the marriage. All the same . . .

"I've been riding back and forth to Richmond this age," he said.

"But why should you?" she said. "Why shouldn't you be nearer? Your father isn't well, and you may not have much time left with him."

He looked at her. It was hard to believe sometimes that so much character and kindness and quickness of intellect lurked under the wildly frivolous dress. He looked away. He needed to keep one surreptitious eye on their follower, and he needed to keep his wits about him. "My father won't appreciate my hovering about him," he said. "It'll offend not only his pride but his sense of logic and practicality."

"Then let's find a logical and practical middle ground," she said. "Maybe something nearer to him without being quite out of London."

"The slowest part of the journey is getting out of London," he said. "After Hyde Park Corner, the congestion abates somewhat. As long as one is not traveling at the same time the mail coaches set out, the way tends to be clear, and one can move at a fair clip. I vow, sometimes the short stretch of Fleet Street is the longest part of the journey. All the damned lawyers cluttering up the place—not to mention that medieval obstruction, Temple Bar."

"Then let's look at one of the villas near Marchmont House," she said.

The Duke of Marchmont's great old Jacobean mansion stood on the western edge of Kensington.

"If you're sure you don't want to play Duchess of Malvern," he said, "and keep a ducal retinue at your beck and call . . . Ah, there he is. A boy, not a small man." He was less certain about the clothes. He needed a closer look, but they seemed to be of good quality. Secondhand? "There's something familiar about him, but I might have seen him anywhere."

One of the scores of boys pouring out of Freame's lair during the raid? Or, quite as likely, one of thousands of boys like them. Even with a closer look, Radford might not recognize him. New boys appeared all the time, while others disappeared. They ran away, joined different gangs in different neighborhoods, changed allegiances, died. Some even found honest work.

He shrugged. "He may be harmless. Perhaps he simply marveled at your dress, and followed us in order to report to his disbelieving friends."

"He might have been lurking in the vicinity for some time," Clara said. "I know some of the scandal sheets employ nondescript persons to follow quarry and report. They've been keeping a close watch on me for months."

This was a reasonable assumption, too. But the sense of trouble remained.

"Blast," he said. "Then I'd better not debauch you in the park."

"You told me we needed to take a rest from debauchery," she said. "Until tonight."

"I forgot," he said. "This drive has turned out more

exciting than I'd expected. Danger is known to be an aph-rodisiac."

"I didn't know that," she said.

"Maybe we'd better go home," he said. "I can take a cold bath."

"And our follower?"

"He can drown himself in the pond for all I care."

Chapter Sixteen

On one side of me lay a wood, than which Nature cannot produce a finer; and, on the other, the Thames, with its shelvy bank and charming lawns, rising like an amphitheatre: along which, here and there, one espies a picturesque white house, aspiring in majestic simplicity to pierce the dark foliage of the surrounding trees: thus studding, like stars in the galaxy, the rich expanse of this charming vale. Sweet Richmond . . .
—Kitson Cromwell Thomas, *Excursions in the County of Surrey*, 1821

But Radford didn't drive home. He couldn't. Not yet.

This was a mystery. To drive away with no answers, not even a clue, was unthinkable.

Even after he decided to take a longer route, the boy trailed them through the park and did an exceptional job of finding cover or disappearing into the scenery.

Another man might simply stop the vehicle and give chase or find another way of cornering their watcher.

Radford wasn't another man.

"Are you lost?" Clara said.

He treated her to a raised eyebrow.

"Right," she said. "You'd probably have to make a special effort to get lost."

"I might be able to do it in an unfamiliar place after dark," he said. "Though the sun is sinking, we've light yet, and I know this park well. If I didn't, I'd rely on you. It's the boy."

"I didn't think you could leave it alone."

"No, it's a curse at times," he said. "Here I am, newly wed, eager to debauch my bride. But no, I must play cat and mouse with a brat from the London streets—or at any rate a brat from streets of some kind. He's too quick and cunning to be an ordinary child."

"I know you have an excellent reason for not stopping the vehicle and giving chase."

"Two," he said.

"Firstly," she said.

He looked at her. She looked at him, her expression sober, her blue eyes glinting with laughter.

He said, "If he's the type I'm sure he is, he has a better than even chance of outrunning me. Such boys learn speed at an early age. He's smaller than I and closer to the ground. Youth, size, and gravity are on his side."

"Secondly."

"Thank you, my dear, for helping with the counting."

She laughed. What a sound! Easy, unaffected. It was a sound like the look of sun breaking through clouds. And there was the chipped tooth, her little battle scar.

"Secondly, all I'll gain from a confrontation is the exercise of chasing him," he said. "I could shake him, dangle him upside down from a high window, threaten him with the authorities, bribe him, or subject him to the tortures of the Inquisition. The most likely responses are defiance, silence, or Cockney humor."

"The way the boys answered when I asked for Toby,"

she said. She went on to mimic them—with surprising accuracy—and he realized he'd only begun to discover her.

He said, "Instead, I'm going to test his stamina. Odds are I'll get a better look at him, and that ought to jog my memory as to what's familiar about him."

*R*adford led the spy hither and yon until twilight, when he drove into Richmond. "Let's pay a visit to the Talbot Inn," he said. "We can order an early and leisurely dinner. We'll see whether he's waiting for us when we come out."

"How very interesting this day is turning out to be," she said. "In so many ways."

"Not quite what I'd planned," he said. "I meant to take you farther afield, where the locals wouldn't recognize Raven Radford and his beautiful highborn bride. But you're used to people—especially men—staring, and we can claim a private dining parlor. Mainly it'll be the waiters gawking at us and trying to eavesdrop. Or trying to memorize your dress, to astonish their wives and sisters."

Clara thought this was a wonderful way to spend the time before the supper and education in marital intimacy he'd promised. To dine at an inn while setting a trap for a spy, or at least deducing a clue or two, was a most satisfactory, not-at-all-ordinary way to start a marriage. Whatever trials and tribulations lay ahead, she did not believe boredom or suffocation would play a part.

*S*quirrel hadn't ever had to deal with Raven, like some others. He hated him just as much as the others did, though. Chiver was the one who saved Squirrel when he was near beat to death, and Chiver was the one who took him into the gang and gave him the first full meal he'd ever had.

Now Chiver was dead, and everybody knew the police raid was Raven's doing.

Squirrel hated this place, too. Trees everywhere, and hills like mountains. And the bloody great park!

But he had to be here. Husher stole clothes for him and got money from somebody—he didn't say who or how—to pay for the hackney Squirrel had traveled in.

Because Jacob needed a spy, and Squirrel was the only one Raven wouldn't recognize.

"Stick close and tell me what he does and where he goes," Jacob had told him. "Then we'll find a way to get him, so nobody will ever know what happened to him. We'll do for him and slide him quiet into the river." And he'd laughed. How he'd laughed.

Yes, it was all great larks to Jacob, but he wasn't the one running after a carriage through trees and mountains and the carriage going on and on, round and round.

Squirrel had never been outside of London, and this was like a foreign country. Everything smelled wrong, even in the village, which wasn't like a proper town at all.

Now Raven and his Long Meg were in the inn and could be in there for hours, in the warm, eating and drinking, while Squirrel stood outside and froze and starved and took care nobody noticed him.

It was a cold and windy night, but he had to stand away from the inn's warmth because he had to keep clear of the lamps and lighted windows.

Raven had sharp eyes, everybody knew. But he'd never met up with Squirrel, and it better stay that way.

He waited in the stable yard. The ones who worked here were too busy to bother about him. Other sorts loitered here and gossiped. He could tell what they were: a pickpocket or two, maybe, and some girls whose kind he knew. But he didn't know who to trust, so he kept out of their way—had to learn how to do that a long time ago, didn't he, unless he was looking for black eyes or broken bones.

Then Raven came out, and Squirrel had to move fast, behind a wagon.

The lawyer talked to one of the stablemen. Squirrel didn't move, and tried not to breathe. It was dark, but they said Raven had sharp ears, too. Sharp everything. Too sharp by half.

But Jacob and Husher would dull him down, and he wouldn't be hearing or seeing anything, ever again.

A woman who'd been loitering in the yard saun-tered to the carriage as Radford was about to climb into his seat. She murmured something to him in a language vaguely like English. Not enough like it, though, for Clara to understand.

Whatever the woman had to say earned her a coin from Radford, though it didn't make him linger.

"I'll give our follower credit," he said as they drove out of the inn yard. "His reflexes are top-notch, and he's good at making himself inconspicuous. But not to her."

"I didn't know you had informants in Richmond as well as London," Clara said.

"Millie used to ply her trade in London," Radford said. "She helped me now and again. When she ended up in the criminal court for the fifth time, I saved her from trans-portation. The judge's condition for leniency was, she was never again to appear at the Old Bailey. Since one couldn't expect her to make a new life in her old haunts, I helped her move here."

"Has she made a new life?" Clara said.

"She married one of the stablemen. She takes in laun-dry and mending. She helps at the inn. Hard work, but easier than what she used to do. Safer, too, and better conditions overall: regular meals, a roof over her head, and a man who treats her well. She's a help to him and to the inn in other ways. She's good at spotting potential troublemakers, a survival skill acquired during her previous career. She was about to report the boy when she saw me come out to speak to her husband."

"I could not understand a word she said," Clara said. "It sounded like a proposition, and I did wonder at her boldness—when I was sitting in the carriage, not easy to overlook."

"She used that tone to keep our spy from suspecting she'd been spying on him." Radford gave a short laugh. "This hasn't been the most romantic evening, but at least we've had an entertaining game of cat and mouse."

"It seemed romantic to me," Clara said.

"What, half of Richmond descending on the Talbot Inn to get a close look at my bride? The servants seizing every thin excuse to visit our private dining parlor, though the innkeeper himself insisted on attending us?"

"It was romantic because we played cat and mouse with our watcher," Clara said. "And because you assumed I'd enjoy the game, too."

And because he'd told her during dinner what he was thinking, and what theories he formulated about the boy. Because he listened to her theories and answered her questions without calling her simpleminded more than once or twice, and then with the affectionate humor that warmed her.

"I knew you'd object to being kept out of it," he said.

"What did she say, then?"

"She noticed him because he behaved suspiciously. He'd kept to the darkest parts of the yard, but at one point a carriage drove in and the lantern light caught him. He was small and thin—a runt, like a thousand other boys she's known. She said he had a pronounced misalignment of his jaw—"

"*Pronounced misalignment?* Millie said that?"

"I translated," he said. "She sketched his profile in the air with her finger and said he had a rat face, from which I deduced buck teeth. But he had very full cheeks. As she put it, 'He looked like he was saving nuts in them.' Though he was better dressed than boys from her old London neighborhoods, she said he was one of their kind. When she saw him scurry to hide behind a wagon when I came out, she arrived at a logical conclusion."

"Whoever he is, if he's kept it up for all this time, at night, in this cold, one may assume he isn't doing it for fun," Clara said. "He's doing it for pay or hasn't a choice."

"I'd rather see him for myself," Radford said. "The description fits no boy I ever met. There are thousands I haven't met—though I do wonder why he seems familiar."

"He could be someone you saw in passing and had no reason to pay attention to."

He shrugged. "Possibly. If he follows us to the house, I'll accost him. By now he'll be tired and cold. Hungry, too, unless he carried food with him. Even so, cold and fatigue would be enough to slow him."

But within a few minutes of their leaving the inn, Radford said, "He's gone."

Clara knew better than to ask, *Are you sure?* She said, "I was looking forward so much to your accosting and interrogating him. I would have helped."

"Despair not, O queen of all realms of my life," Radford said. "Maybe he'll be back tomorrow. Tonight, meanwhile, I believe I'll interrogate you—quite closely—instead."

That night

She made him wait.

Radford's bride wanted a long soak in a hot bath, she said. She suggested he read a book.

Clearly his lady needed no instructions for developing her skills in the marital arts. The undisciplined being who lived in his brain quivered with anticipation.

Banishing the overeager inner self, he took a leisurely bath, too.

No reason in the world to hurry. They had all the night ahead of them.

He could use the time to plan—and not think about the blasted boy, their shadow. Nothing could be done about him tonight, and it was a waste of mental energy to think about him. He pushed Millie's runt with the stuffed cheeks into one of the cupboards of his mind and shut and locked the door. His lady offered a far more agreeable topic for meditation.

After his bath, he donned a dressing gown and slippers and, shockingly, nothing else.

She might wear all the clothes she liked. All the more fun taking them off.

He made his way to their place of rendezvous, the sitting room, and thought about taking her clothes off and how best to accomplish this and what else he could do to keep things interesting.

Eventually their supper arrived. It was the light collation she'd asked for: cold meats and pastries, fruit and cheese and such. A footman, having erased his face of all expression, set it out on a small table by the fire. When he'd arranged everything to a nicety, he quietly vanished.

Radford got up and replaced one chair with a cushioned one. He collected other cushions and placed them nearby. This was something he preferred to do himself. In fact, he preferred to do most things himself.

That would have to change, a bit.

Among other things, he'd need more servants in his married life. He didn't mind the expense. Firstly, it was for Clara's benefit. Secondly, he could afford it without hardship. Not a ducal retinue, but a handful, certainly. What he minded was having them underfoot.

Still, his father had adapted. So could the son. He was willing to be civilized. To a point.

Clara entered the sitting room, and for a moment he stopped breathing.

She wore a cream-colored lot of froth, nothing like a normal dressing gown. He supposed the nightdress under it was even more abnormal, thanks to the French dressmakers. Though it covered her completely, with ruffles and lace at the neck and fluttering down the front opening—which fastened with ribbon ties, he noted—the fabric was thin and the cut cunningly devised to show all the glorious contours of her body.

"Do you think that's entirely fair?" he said, gesturing at her.

"Don't you like it?" she said.

"Let me see. Turn around. Slowly."

She did. He swallowed a groan. And another.

When she faced him again, she gave two slow, sleepy blinks and said, "What do you think?"

He said. "Very nice. Let's take it off."

Clara had gone to a great deal of trouble getting into the ensemble. That was to say, Davis had done all the tying and hooking and muttering about French dressmakers.

It took Radford very little time to get it off, though he never seemed to hurry. But his hands—those clever, agile hands—worked so quickly and smoothly. In two heartbeats, it seemed, she was wearing nothing at all. Then he sank to his knees . . . and down, further . . . and then it was his tongue and his hands on her bare skin, teasing and heating her. Her knees weakened and her legs shook, and he said gruffly, "Perhaps your ladyship would like to sit down."

She'd like to lie down, but the chair was nearest and her knees were buckling, and she dropped into it and gasped, "Good heavens."

He returned his mouth and tongue and hands to their work. Soon her spine gave way, and she began to slide from the chair. As she began to sink helplessly downward, he pulled nearby cushions onto the floor for her to land on.

She said voice as thick as her mind, "I'm not sure I can survive this. Oh!"

"I promised to worship you with my body," he said. "I said it in front of *everybody*."

His tongue, his wicked tongue. His hands, his artful hands.

He made every inch of her quiver, inside and outside. He caressed her and kissed her. He suckled her and she thought she'd scream with the pleasure of it and the madness, too, knocking away all her lady-ness and the veneer of civilization and letting loose a wanton.

And at last, when she thought she'd die of wanting him, he gave himself to her. His body joined hers, and he moved with her in the way that now seemed so completely right and natural, the union of body and soul she'd been waiting for all her life. She'd had only the dimmest sense, before, of what she'd been waiting for. But she had it now, she knew.

With my body I thee worship. Yes, he'd said that yesterday. Was it only yesterday?

And this is forever, she thought, the last coherent though she had. Then the moment came, the peak of joy she'd so recently discovered, and she swam into forever, and floated there, in his arms, until she drifted into a sweet, soft darkness, and slept.

A maid had delivered their morning coffee and cleared away last night's debris, and Radford had expected to go down to breakfast, as one usually did.

But shortly after the maid, the footman reappeared, this time with breakfast. He set it on the table before the fire, reinvigorated the fire, and departed.

Clara, emerging from her dressing room in a more demure dressing gown than she'd worn last night, said, "Oh, how kind of your mother." She blushed. "She wanted us to have a bit more privacy."

"That isn't wise," he said. "The more privacy we have, the more likely I am to take advantage in lewd and unseemly ways."

They'd both forgotten to worry about irritations, and the debaucheries had continued into the early morning hours.

"If that happens, we won't have time for me to dress to go out again and help you lead our follower on a merry chase," she said. "Well, not so merry for him, I suppose."

He must have looked as torn as he felt, because she laughed and said, "My dear, we have all the time in the world for lovemaking. But we don't want our follower to give up in despair, before we can get to the bottom of the mystery, do we?"

And so they had their private breakfast, after which she went away for the lengthy process of donning a carriage dress. Able to dress in a quarter of the time, though unaided by a valet—a domestic addition he supposed he ought to arrange for soon—he whiled away the time thinking about possibilities for their future residence. And calculating the cost of furnishing a house suitably. And children. Since it was only logical to expect them, one must include them in the calculations.

Life was growing a great deal more complicated.

It was early afternoon before they went downstairs.

The butler met them at the bottom of the stairs and told

them they were wanted in the library. Mr. Westcott had come, he said.

"Who the devil invited him?" Radford said, his heart sinking. Westcott would not have returned to Richmond so soon unless he had urgent business, curse him. Radford wasn't ready for business. But he had to be, he reminded himself. He had a wife he needed to support in a manner somewhat resembling what she was accustomed to.

"Drat the fellow," he said as they walked to the drawing room. "Did I not tell you he'd be endlessly popping in, on this whim or that, with one curst document or another or a client in dire need of me at the most inconvenient times?"

"I'm sure he wouldn't be here if it weren't important," she said.

"That's the trouble," he said. "It's going to be important, and I'll have to attend to it, whatever it is. Ah, well, you were the one who wanted to marry a barrister. It seems we'll have to put our mystery aside, after all."

Minutes later

Father half-reclined on his sofa as usual, near the fire. Mother sat beside him in her usual place. Westcott, who'd occupied a chair on the other side of the fireplace, rose when Clara entered.

Everybody looked angry.

This was odd, an oddness that didn't bode well.

Father took up from the table in front of him a heavy document bearing a familiar seal. "Westcott brought this," he said. "Express from Glynnor Castle."

Bernard, drat him. What now?

"I told Bernard's man of business as well as his secretary to address all correspondence to me, as you and I agreed was wisest," Radford said. It was absurd to dis-

turb George Radford's retirement with business matters
Radford and Westcott could easily handle. Only Bernard
wrote directly to Father these days, but not often. He reserved his long, tedious, boastful letters for his *dear little
Raven*.

"It went to Westcott, but it was addressed to me, as
it was required to be," Father said. "Your cousin—blast
him—" He broke off, glaring at the letter.

"What's he done now?" Radford said.

"That's what he's done." His father threw the letter
down on the table in front of him.

Radford looked down. A weight settled in his chest.

The legal hand, the verbosity, the seal . . .

"Dead," said his father. "Dead, dead, dead."

Chapter Seventeen

DUKE, in Latin *Dux, à ducendo*, signifying the leader of an army, noblemen being anciently either generals and commanders of armies in time of war, or wardens of marches, and governors of provinces in peace. This is now the first rank of the nobility.

—*Debrett's Peerage*, 1831

Through the noise in his head, Radford was aware of Westcott speaking . . . . apologizing . . . to Clara.

"I'm so sorry to be the bearer of this shocking news," he was saying. "I must beg your ladyship to be seated."

"Do sit down, child," said Mother. "You're white."

Radford looked away from the ghastly document to his wife. Though she had her screen in place, the color had drained from her face. He discerned other small signs of distress: the slight tremble of her lips and hands.

"Very . . . surprised, that's all," she said. "But I promise you I won't faint."

"I might," he said. "Do sit, Clara. Westcott has left his comfortable seat by the fire for you. And he'll feel better about ruining your honeymoon if you'd at least deprive him of the chair."

She gave Radford one quick, anguished look, then sat. She composed herself. "I beg your pardon. I can't quite take it in. Does the letter say how it happened?"

He couldn't quite take it in, either. He could scarcely think, his brain clamored so. He made himself stare at the paper in his hand until the blur of ink resolved into words. He scanned the pages.

"The news runs rather longer than my father's announcement," he said.

"A lawyer wrote it, that's why," Father said. "You'd better translate for your lady, son. I can't bring myself to repeat the story. Too infuriating."

"Better you don't, my dear," Mother said.

Better Father didn't, indeed. He was badly shaken, though anger seemed to be displacing shock. All the same, any strong emotion debilitated him.

Even Radford felt as though somebody had struck him with a club.

Naturally, logic had allowed for the possibility of Bernard's dying young. This awareness had always hung in the back of Radford's mind, especially lately, since the other Radford men had become deceased so unexpectedly. But the idea had hung very far in the back of his mind.

Beyond question Bernard was obese and a drunkard. Radford had warned him about damage to his liver, among other health concerns. But overindulgence rarely caught up with a man so early in life. England abounded in men like Bernard, and they lived into old age. The previous King, a glutton who swilled drink and laudanum by the gallon, lived into his sixties.

Thirty years old.

It made no sense. Yet it had to make sense because here it was, written in a legal hand on costly paper, page after page of it.

Radford read it through once, picking out the essentials, then once more, translating and condensing the lawyerly convolutions for his wife.

"He'd been hunting," he said. "A large party, including his chosen lady. It seems he'd come out of a wood and to the edge of a steep bank. It had rained hard the day before and the stream below was swollen. Oh, and better and better: He was riding a hunter he'd bought very recently—to impress the lady, I don't doubt. A new horse, slick ground—and of course he was near blind drunk, though one obtains only a glimpse of the fact through all the careful verbiage dancing about it."

He turned a page and frowned. "Since he got separated from the others, we have no eyewitnesses. No way to be sure whether he tried to leap the stream and his mount balked, or the animal was game but Bernard's weight and the wet conditions undermined the jump. In any event, given the horse's superficial scratches and coating of mud, it's clear the creature slipped and went over the edge. The hunt party found Bernard in the water, with a gash in his head. Either he'd hit his head, and the blow killed him, or he'd hit his head, lost consciousness, and drowned before he could be rescued. The doctor who examined him afterward said the blow killed him."

"He would," Father said. "The victim was a duke. Most physicians would choose the explanation most liable to absolve others in the party of fault or guilt. No one could have saved him, in other words, even had they reached him sooner or heaved him out of the water more quickly."

"I'd better examine the body myself," Radford said. "And question the doctor."

"You'd better," his father said. "And without loss of time."

The wives were too wise to ask, *What difference does it make?*

In the great scheme of things, exactly how Bernard had died didn't matter. Dead was dead, and their world had changed irrevocably.

But in the minds of the Radford men, uncertainty had to be put to rest. Moreover, solving the puzzle would settle one's mind.

"I could forgive him more easily, had it been purely an accident," Father said. "But this is so like his stupidity and arrogance. He should never have mounted a horse—any horse, for any purpose—when deeply intoxicated. He couldn't think clearly at the best of times. Naturally he'd overestimate his skill and underestimate his weight. We ought to be grateful he didn't maim or kill his horse, or any innocent bystanders."

"However it happened, I'm very sorry," Clara said, her voice clear and level. "I'd hoped he'd marry the lady and would be happy, and she would make something of him."

Everyone looked at her, and Radford was startled to discover his throat was closing and his eyes itched. Grief? Over *Bernard*?

No, no. It was the shock, that was all. If anything, the grief was a perfectly rational one, for the life he was about to lose. His career, especially. Clara understood—the look she'd sent him! It was selfish of him, yes, to repine the loss of his career when he would gain so much. Yet he was human, and even normal and less selfish human beings resented having their plans disrupted.

He felt grief, too, for his father, whom he'd wanted to shield from Bernard and the others, from the dukedom's problems and demands.

And yet—here was the madness and the difficulty of it—Radford was pleased for his bride. He would be able to give her the life she ought to have and was always meant for.

She went on, "What you told me about him led me to

believe he had potential to be better than he had been. And then there were the gifts."

Radford could barely make sense of what she said. He was preoccupied with wrestling his emotions into submission.

"I know it will seem a small thing," she said, "but it seemed to me he had taste or at least cared enough to charge somebody with taste to choose our wedding gifts. Generous choices, too. And such beautiful things. The tea and coffee service, with scenes from the *Odyssey*. You said it might have been a private joke, because you'd provoked him with quotations from Homer once upon a time."

Radford came back to the moment, and his mind painted a vivid picture of the wedding gifts. He'd briefly wondered at the extravagant choice, and allowed for the possibility, slim though it was, that Bernard had softened a degree. Perhaps he was, if not in love, in unusually good humor on account of his new lady.

"And the Sèvres, with the Olympians," Clara said.

Apart from the brief and quickly forgotten surmise about motives and state of mind, Radford had not, in fact, given the wedding gifts much thought, except to wonder where they would put everything. Now he considered the splendid gifts Bernard had sent, when he had every reason to send nothing at all to a distant cousin who, in his view, had never done anything but bother him.

Dear little Raven . . . Why, Raven's got a sweetheart, what do you know?

Of all people, drunken Bernard had known.

He'd lent his traveling chariot and postilion for Radford's hasty return to London. Could this have been the drunken boor's way of expressing thanks, or at least appreciation, for his despised cousin's coming to his rescue? Or had he found the idea of Raven having a sweetheart so hilarious, he'd encouraged it simply for the fun of the thing?

One would never know.

Radford gave a short laugh, though his irrational self wanted to weep. "He must have been deeply impressed when he learned I'd won a beautiful lady of high rank. He probably thought I did it through some lawyer's trick. Very likely, the gifts were meant to be a consolation prize for you."

"I thought it extremely generous of him," she said, "considering he might have had me for himself, if not for your wicked lawyerly wiles."

Radford explained to his parents his wife's threat to marry Bernard.

"Did you, really?" Father said.

"Well done, my dear," said Mother. "Men were ever obtuse, even otherwise keenly perceptive barristers."

"Let us agree to give Bernard credit for generosity," Father said. "Then we might say something good of the dead."

"Let's give him a little more credit," Radford said. "Let's say he chose with taste and a degree of—what—humor? Conceivably, even affection."

He glanced at his father. He'd relaxed a few degrees. Interestingly, he was regarding Clara in the pleased way he used to look at his son when the youthful Oliver had demonstrated signs of intelligence.

The new duke sent for wine, and made a toast to Bernard. Being the superior lawyer he was, he made an elegant speech, which neatly balanced annoyance with Bernard for dying untimely, understanding of the way his upbringing and family life had deformed his character, and appreciation of his sense of humor. Perhaps it was puerile and boorish, Father said, but at least Bernard had one. This could not be said of many judges.

Then Father turned to Clara. "Well, my dear daughter," he said, the *dear* startling everybody except her ladyship.

"You were wiser than your parents thought. I've become the blasted Duke of Malvern, and you've married my heir, the Marquess of Bredon. Pray, try to keep his lordship from getting killed before he can inherit, will you, my lady?"

Of course Clara knew what to do. She doubted there was a better-prepared girl in all of England.

Her new family were in turmoil, as was to be expected when an earthquake had overthrown their world.

A lady is never ruffled, and she seeks to put those about her at ease.

First order of business, therefore: Restore calm.

She'd boldly tackled the Bernard issue, and the family had responded well. Her father-in-law had regained his equanimity. Because his mind had been quieted, his wife's was. Clara had seen, from the moment she'd met them, how deeply devoted Anne Radford was to her husband. Her daughters adored the gruff old man, as did their children.

Though she hadn't spent a great deal of time with her, Clara hadn't needed much to comprehend her mother-in-law's character.

When they'd left the men to talk business, and retired to the more intimate surroundings of her boudoir, the lady confirmed Clara's impression.

"Naturally, I'll do my duty," she said. "But you must understand, my dear, I'm sadly out of practice. By choice. I do not love the beau monde. They all turned their backs on me after the divorce, though they all knew I was the innocent party. My brute of a husband did not even want our daughters! I should have thought his eagerness to abandon them and drag all our names through the mire of a divorce would offer a hint to the world of the man's nature . . ." She shook her head. "But no, do forgive me. I never meant to go over that old story. It's an age now."

"An elephant has fallen through the roof," Clara said. "Our nerves are frayed. Even my husband displayed a discernible tremor of distress."

"Ah, you noticed." Her Grace tipped her head to one side to study her daughter-in-law. "You found a way to calm Oliver without saying irritating things like 'Be calm, my dear. It is Fate.' Or some such platitude."

"I should commit a platitude only if I were very, very angry with him," Clara said.

"Very wise." Her mother-in-law looked away for a moment, then said, "It's more than thirty years since that time. Now I'm a duchess, and all my old tormentors still alive will have to give way to me. But it makes no difference. I don't want to return to that world. I've been so happy." She paused briefly before going on, "Radford and I lived a quiet life even before he retired. He had his excitement in the courtroom, and I relished sitting in the gallery or hearing about it when he came home. I don't wish to be a reclusive Duchess of Malvern, and hide in the country as the others did or were compelled to do. But the world will soon descend upon us, and I don't want the world. I want to be with my husband. I do not think that so very unreasonable. He is not w—" Here her voice broke.

Clara said gently, "In your place, it's where I should wish to be as well. But did he not say I was clever to marry Mr. Radford? Well, I say Mr. Radford was clever to marry me. You're aware I was brought up to marry a duke." She could hardly fail to be aware of it. Mama had been unable to resist mentioning the subject. Repeatedly. "I shall be happy to do as much or as little as you choose, in the way of making your life as you wish it to be."

Her Grace gazed at her for a moment, and her eyes misted. But she, too, had been born and bred a lady. She blinked back the tears and, to Clara's surprise—for this lady had always seemed a trifle aloof—leaned toward her and took her hand.

"I had doubts, I admit," she said. "I feared you and Oliver would have a difficult time of it. Disparity of rank is no little problem. But I know you truly care for him and he cares for you, and you are a good, kind girl." She slid her hand away and sat back with a smile. "And so I thank you for your offer, and promise to take full advantage of your goodness, kindness, and youth. I believe I shall be exceedingly selfish and lazy and throw everything on your young shoulders, my dear."

Now Clara had only to make sure Radford did the same.

That night

The talking continued through the afternoon, into evening, through dinner, and after it.

By the time they escaped to their apartments, Radford was done with *discussing*.

As soon as he'd closed the door he pulled Clara into his arms and fell back against it. He kissed her, and perhaps it was a desperate kiss. His trouble wasn't the dukedom and the avalanche of work to come with it. He could deal with that. It was losing time with her that made him wild.

When at length he broke the kiss, he said, "I am going to be masterful, after all. This will be our last night together for a time, and that is *not* what I had planned. I am greatly displeased with the disruption of my neatly laid plots and stratagems." He treated her to a leer, and she giggled. "Therefore," he went on, "I, the Marquess of Bredon, command you, my lady wife, to send your maid to bed and place your person entirely at my disposal and whim."

"Only my person, you shallow man?" She spoke

haughtily but couldn't conceal her blush, or the anticipatory shiver.

"*My lord*," he corrected. "And you cannot be so henwitted as to think I married you for your mind."

She stiffened. "That's exactly what I did think."

"Your mind is a negligible commodity," he said. "I married you for lust."

"Where is that set of heavy silver pots and such that Bernard sent us?" she said. "I mean to throw every piece of it at you."

"That sounds exciting," he said as he started unfastening the back of her dress. "I also married you to save you from yourself. Otherwise who knows what self-destructive course you'd set upon. Run away to live in a tent. Marry Bernard. 'Someone has to save this girl,' I told myself, 'and since she has fine breasts and other womanly parts—and seems capable of learning a few simple skills—the someone might as well be me.'"

"The silver service *and* the Sèvres," she said. "All five hundred pieces of it."

The following afternoon

For their private farewell, Radford and Clara lingered in the sitting room that adjoined his study. In a short time, he'd take leave of his parents and Westcott.

"I'll be gone no longer than a fortnight," he said. "I had everything in train before I left. Sanborne is more than competent. The agent Dursley has worked for the family this age, and he knows his business when let to do it without interference. It's only a matter of the funeral and laying down the law to the family. Everybody will be acting terribly bereaved in between demanding this, that, and the other to soothe their wounded feelings. But they'll have to address their sorrows and discontents to Westcott, who's more than capable of deciding what tone to take with whom. It's a pity you can't come with me, and treat the other Radfords to your terrifying duchess persona, but that will have to wait for another time."

"I'm not in the least terrifying," Clara said.

"Do you think not? When you come all over the duchess with me, I quake in my boots."

"That is not where you quake," she said. And blushed.

She knew he found her autocratic manner arousing.

Well, he found many other aspects of her arousing, too, so it was an easy guess.

He drew her into his arms for one last embrace before they joined the others downstairs. He held her for a long time, burying his face in her neck, and dislodging her silk scarf in the process.

When at length he pulled himself away, it was he, not she, who restored the scarf. While he did so he said, "I'm not such a dunderhead as to tell you what to do while I'm gone. Of all women, you know what needs to be done and how to do it. But I will tell you what not to do."

She gave him a look of innocent perplexity that did not deceive him for a moment.

"You're not to pursue the Case of the Stuffed-Cheeks Boy," he said.

"How on earth would I do that?" she said. "When should I find time to do it? I have a house in London to fit out and staff from eight miles away. I must fight off the hordes who'll be trying to beat down the doors here. I must keep my mother as sane as possible. Or maybe it's better to keep her very busy. I must deal with Their Majesties—"

"I can only hope this is enough to occupy you," he said. "Leave it to the servants to look out for intruders. If you go out, be sure you have Davis and a manservant with you."

"My dear, that is the way I normally travel," she said,

with audible patience. "A lady never goes out unattended. I only made an exception in your case because—oh, I forget why. The wayward curl on your forehead distracted me, perhaps."

A footman came to tell them the carriage was ready.

"You'd better make haste," Clara said.

"You're in a shocking hurry to be rid of me," he said.

"If I were you, I'd be gone before my parents get here," she said.

He knew she'd written to her parents yesterday with the news and urged them to postpone visiting until his father's nerves had time to absorb the shock. She hadn't felt certain, however, that her mother's state of euphoria wouldn't overwhelm any good intentions of respecting the elderly gentleman's nerves.

"I doubt you'll enjoy Mama's smothering you with affection," she said. "But more important—the sooner you get there, the sooner you'll be back."

"Yes." He gave her one more kiss—passionate, desperate, and frustrated—which she returned in the same spirit.

Last night they'd made love, fiercely first, and gently and tenderly afterward. They'd talked and talked. It wasn't enough.

They'd had so little time together as man and wife, and a fortnight seemed a much longer time now, when it meant being away from her, than it used to do.

When they broke the kiss, he didn't let go. "Remember," he said. "No playing sleuth."

"Did I not promise to obey?" she said. "Before witnesses?"

"You had footnotes," he said.

"And when you return, I'll tell you all about them." She cupped his face and kissed him once more, so tenderly. This time he let her go, albeit slowly.

Once more he arranged the scarf whose perfection he'd disturbed.

How he wished . . . but wishes belonged to the realm of magic, a place with which he had no desire to become acquainted.

He stepped back.

"Am I all quite correct now, my lord?" Her blue eyes glinted with humor . . . and something else. Ah, yes, affection that made his heart squeeze tight.

"You'll do," he said.

"Then come, take your leave of the Duke and Duchess of Malvern, Lord Bredon."

Two hours later, Westcott was staring aghast at Clara.

"The Coppys?" he said. "Now?"

They'd adjourned to the sitting room, where she and Westcott had reviewed some general matters relating to Malvern House. Then she'd asked for news of Bridget and Toby Coppy.

"As soon as may be," she said. "I hope you haven't lost them. Mr. Radford—that is to say, Lord Bredon—told me you'd find an apprenticeship for Toby and lodgings for them, well away from their mother."

"I haven't lost them, my lady," Westcott said. "The boy's working at St. Bartholomew's Hospital, where he was cared for. But finding him an apprenticeship isn't easy. All anybody needs to hear is where he'd been before the hospital, and they become leery. The decent tradesmen do, at any rate. The more dubious sort will take anybody, but such positions would not be in his best interests."

"Did you say he was working?"

Westcott explained. Once the boy recovered, he insisted on helping at the hospital. "He isn't the cleverest fellow, but he follows instructions well, and will do whatever is asked of him. He mops the floors or the patients' brows."

"Not with the same implement, I hope," Clara said.

"It's a hospital," Westcott said. "I can promise nothing. I can only tell you what's reported to me: He works hard, is happy to be paid with food and a place to sleep. He's extremely reluctant to leave."

"Who can blame him?" she said. "Anybody who escaped the police raid will know we came looking for him. They'll blame Toby for leading the police to them. One of the escapees, I understand, was Jacob Freame."

"Yes, my lady, and I believe that's a subject Lord Bredon would wish left out of our conversation. In any event, Freame is dead. Fever, we're told."

"Who told you?" she said.

"My esteemed colleague's habitual skepticism has infected your mind," Westcott said.

She regarded him patiently.

"That's what's said on the streets, according to our informers," Westcott said.

"I hope it's true," she said, remembering Stuffed-Cheeks Boy. "Whether it is or it isn't, you'll have to dislodge Toby from the hospital. I want him here with me. Bridget, too."

"I wish you would wait until Lord Bredon returns before—"

"He left me in charge of domestic matters," she said. "I was not five paces away when he told you so. Did he not say to you, 'Give my lady every assistance'?"

"Indeed, he did. However, as the family solicitor, I'm allowed to give advice. It's my duty, in fact. And I advise you to wait until his lordship returns."

"You haven't found a place for the boy," she said. "I can employ him here. But whether I can or cannot isn't the issue. If not for those two children, I should never have met my husband. I'm now in a position to do something for them, and I mean to do it."

Clara told Westcott she'd arrange for removing Bridget from the Milliners' Society. After all, Clara was one of the society's sponsors, and her sister-in-law, Sophy, was one of the founders. While Clara remembered Radford's warning about showing favoritism to Bridget, she knew this was altogether different. Bridget would simply be going on to do what all the girls there hoped to do: find respectable employment.

At present, Clara wasn't sure exactly how she'd employ her, but she knew the answer would come soon enough. She'd made up her mind to have the two siblings. She'd been trained to deal with every sort of domestic crisis. It followed that she'd know what to do when the time came.

Not long after Westcott left, she wrote to Sophy, asking her to help arrange for Bridget's departure from the Society.

Then Clara went down to inform her in-laws.

Sentiment," said her father-in-law, with a wave of his hand, after Clara had explained her reasons for sending for the Coppys. "You would never make a proper barrister, madam. One must look at the facts with a cool, considering eye. One must disengage one's emotions. The only emotions needing to be engaged are those of the judge and jury."

"I don't see what sentiment has to do with this," Clara said. He was, as one would expect, intimidating, and more so than her husband. As he ought to be, considering he'd had several more decades' practice in the theater that was the courtroom. But she could not let him cow her any more than she'd let his son do so. "We post rewards for information. The police and others reward informers. While neither child informed, precisely, they did lead me to my husband—"

"Indirectly."

"And indirectly, I've placed them in danger," she said. "I realize the lives of pauper children are hard and hazardous, conditions no one person can cure. However, I embroiled myself in the Coppys' affairs, and they're likely to suffer as a result. You know what those gangs are like and how ruthless they can be. The boy is frightened, and I don't doubt Bridget is frightened for him— though she would be right to be frightened for herself as well. I cannot in good conscience leave these two children as they are. I promise to make sure they do not disturb your household in any way. If that happens in spite of my efforts, they'll be placed elsewhere. But they must be placed, sir. They have—indirectly or not—changed my life, and I will not turn my back on them."

"You would never sway a jury with that farrago," said her father-in-law.

"She might very well do so, George," said his wife.

"Ah, well, she's prettier than most barristers." He gave a short laugh, so like his son's. "Very well, Clara. Do as you like. You've been charged with sparing us every possible disturbance. We may certainly indulge this little idiocy of yours."

"George."

"Well, it is idiocy, and you know it, *Duchess*," he said.

But Clara knew he was only being irritating for the fun of it. And so she smiled and left them to debate the matter in the way they liked best.

London
Wednesday 25 November

Jacob Freame wasn't smiling. He was pulling at the new whiskers he'd been growing so his enemies wouldn't recognize him. They'd come in pretty thick, but to Squirrel he still looked like Jacob, only hairier.

Hairier and madder than Squirrel had ever seen him. Squirrel made sure to keep his distance from those big fists.

Husher didn't look worried. He never did. He only stood by the door, arms folded, listening.

"A lord!" Jacob said. "*Him?*"

"If it ain't all over London yet, it will be," Squirrel said. "Not but I expect they was talking about it at Jack's already."

Rumors always seemed to get to Jack's coffeehouse quickest. A lot of them started there.

"We should've gone all together," Jacob said. "We could've watched for our chance and done for him quick."

Maybe not, Squirrel thought. In London you had Raven walking the streets day and night and crowds you could disappear into easy. You could lay for somebody in Fleet Street, say, near the Temple Gate, late at night.

In Richmond, Raven was harder to get at. Now he'd set himself up so high, getting at him meant much bigger trouble than before.

"Don't look like no chance now," Squirrel said. "He's off to some castle a hundred miles away. Maybe two hundred. Not but what you always say leave the nobs alone."

"Never mind that. Tell me what the yokels say."

The yokels had a lot to say about everything. Squirrel knew to keep it short. "Everybody knew the minute he hired a post chaise. They was talking about it everywhere, him leaving his bride so sudden. Then word come down about what happened, how he was only going for a funeral and coming back, and how there was more servants coming to work at the house."

More servants meant more eyes on gates and doors and windows and more ears listening for trouble, but Jacob didn't look worried. He was walking from one end of the room to the other, fooling with his whiskers. Thinking.

"If he didn't take the Long Meg with him, he'll be back soon enough," he said. He looked at Husher. "You've seen her. Would you leave her a minute longer than you could help it?"

Husher grinned, showing crooked brown teeth, and not a full set, neither.

"I dunno when he'll be back," Squirrel said. "That's why I come here. You said to watch him, is all, and I can't, can I, him in a post chaise, and me—what?—runnin' after?"

"Don't be a halfwit," Jacob said. "What good is it to me what he does a hundred miles away?"

Not much good in London, or anywheres else, Squirrel thought. It didn't look like the best idea, finishing off a brand-new nob everybody was watching and talking about. Even with Husher helping, it could go wrong. Then the hawks would hunt them down and put ropes round their necks and leave them to dangle slow on purpose while everybody watched. After that, the hangman'd sell off their clothes and the doctors would get the corpses and cut 'em up.

Jacob stopped walking. "We're going back," he said.

Husher grinned and nodded.

Squirrel told himself they owed it to Chiver to finish Raven off. But his voice sounded squeaky when he said, "Now? He won't be back—"

"Not now. Use your head. We're going to get ready first." Jacob smiled. "We're going to make sure nothing goes wrong. Except for him and his fine lady, ha ha."

Husher laughed, too.

Chapter Eighteen

THE BARRISTER . . . 2. Who can tell all the windings and turnings, all the hollownesses and dark corners of the mind? It is a wilderness in which a man may wander more than forty years, and through which few have passed to the promised land.

—*The Jurist*, Vol. 3, 1832

Friday 27 November

Westcott delivered the two Coppys in the early afternoon.

He must have devoted the trip to Richmond to terrifying them. This would explain why, when presented to the duke and duchess, the siblings stood stiff, white-faced, and tongue-tied.

After surviving this ordeal, they went with a footman belowstairs, to meet the rest of the staff—and make a good impression, Clara hoped. If they didn't, the servants would make their lives difficult.

At present, however, she had to pass her own test.

The duke was regarding her with one dark eyebrow

upraised. It was the same way his son would look at her from time to time, as though debating whether she owned anything resembling intellect. It produced the same irritation. But these Radford men couldn't help themselves, and one couldn't expect His Grace, at eighty, to change his personality.

She'd written to Radford about the Coppys. She was sure his reply would question her intelligence and accuse her of sentimentality. But she knew she was right in this, and if she didn't begin her marriage by standing up for what she believed in, his powerful personality would crush her. Besides, had not Grandmama Warford told her husbands could be educated?

Too, Clara watched the way the duchess interacted with her husband. She'd had decades to learn how to manage a too-intelligent Radford male.

"The boy," the duke said. "Not much in the brain box, has he? Another reformed juvenile delinquent like the one the French dressmakers adopted?"

His son must have told him about Fenwick.

"I believe Toby's brief experience in Jacob Freame's gang chastened him," Clara said. She'd been amazed at the transformation. The brashness and insolence had vanished.

"That rarely happens," he said. "Associating with criminals usually makes boys worse. Whippings and stints in prison only harden them."

"He didn't have much time to learn criminal ways before he fell ill," she said. "Then, when he was sick, I suppose what he learned was what it was like not to have Bridget looking after him, only a lot of rough, mean boys who didn't care what became of him. He thought he was going to die. He might very well have done so. He learned a lesson, I expect."

"Perhaps," the duke said. "It's mere speculation—and sentimental speculation at that."

"Perhaps," she said. "Or perhaps looking respectable has changed his attitude. Westcott took him to the baths and got him clean clothes. That seems to have given Toby something to think about. I shall put him into livery, and we'll see if he lives up to his finery."

"Was that the treatment your dressmaker friends applied to the boy they took up?"

"It's amazing what a cocked hat, gold-trimmed coat, and shiny buttons will do for a boy's *amour propre*," she said.

That won her a crack of laughter from the duke.

The duchess smiled.

Clara told them about Toby's hospital experience. "He learned how to look after patients by watching what the staff did. He'll never be one for book learning, but he seems not incapable of learning in some form. I'm not sure how useful that is to you, sir. However, the duchess does need a page or footboy to attend her."

"I certainly do not," said Her Grace. "The idea!"

"I promise you do," Clara said. "The rest of the staff will be extremely busy in the coming weeks and months. I mean to augment them, but I know you won't want hordes of servants underfoot."

The duchess's eyes widened. She hadn't realized. How could she?

No matter how much Clara took on, she couldn't return her in-laws' life to what it had been. While Ithaca House was large, it was a fraction of the size of a great town house—Warford House, for instance. A small staff had always sufficed here. But now the household's work would increase. The new duke and duchess could expect more visitors, more correspondence, more of everything, even though they wouldn't be entertaining.

First and foremost was their relationship with the royal family. Their Majesties were in Brighton at present, but they'd soon send emissaries, as they'd done for Clara's wedding. One couldn't deny these people admission. Eventually, the King and Queen would call here, the duke being too frail to call on them. Certain other formal visits would have to be endured. The Duchess of Kent was sure to turn up with the Princess Victoria.

Clara couldn't keep out everyone, and ought not to, for her husband's sake as much as for his parents'. He couldn't continue as a barrister while managing his father's estates and other business affairs. But he could use his legal abilities in Parliament, among other possibilities. The trouble was, despite reform, even the House of Commons remained a private club. To fully belong to this world, the Dukes of Malvern must recover their proper position in Society, and become functioning members of the nobility.

Meanwhile, Clara had to fit out Malvern House from a distance. She'd minimize the disruption but she couldn't stop it altogether.

"I thought you might use Toby to carry messages and run errands, and do other sorts of fetching and carrying," she went on. "He's a strong boy. Otherwise his illness could have killed him. He could help you when the duke's pillows need adjusting, or when he wishes to move from the sofa to his chair."

She knew the duchess found it increasingly difficult to tend to some of her husband's needs. To his frustration, he grew less able to do for himself, and while not quite as large as his son, he was not a small man. There was a great deal else a boy who'd worked in a hospital could do, but Clara had to exercise caution about venturing into the duchess's territory. When Her Grace grew used to having Toby about, she'd find more ways to employ him.

"You suggest I employ the boy instead of one of the maids or footmen," the duchess said, looking dubious, indeed.

"That would free the other servants for tasks wanting more physical strength or intelligence or both," Clara said. "This would reduce the number of new servants needed."

The duchess considered for a moment, clearly torn. The duke said nothing, only watched her.

Clara waited.

Finally Her Grace said, "If it's a choice between an army of new servants and one boy, I'd better take the boy."

The duke's grey eyes twinkled. "Well done, Clara. Well managed, indeed."

"I merely point out facts," she said.

"So you do, so you do. And that excessively pretty girl? What do you mean to do with her? You know she'll turn the footmen's heads."

Exactly what Davis had said.

"Davis and I shall make sure Bridget has no time to seduce the footmen," Clara said. "I've scores of tasks for a skilled needlewoman. For the present, she can help with the household mending. However, I imagine, Malvern House will need extensive refurbishing."

"You'll find it in a shocking state, I don't doubt," said Her Grace. "The furniture heaviest to shift is likely to be there still, under wrappers. But a great deal will have mysteriously disappeared. Meanwhile the family linens will be stored away and falling to pieces—unless, as I suspect, they were stolen and sold ages ago. None of the family have lived at Malvern House in a century or more, and the late duke's father preferred to put his money into Glynnor Castle."

"I've asked Mama to make an inspection of the house," Clara said. "She'll enjoy that exceedingly."

It would give her mother something to do, to forestall lengthy visits to Richmond. She would brag to her dear friend and foe Lady Bartham about working her fingers to the bone for her daughter, the *Marchioness of Bredon*. Clara could hear her:

But what can a mother do? Poor Clara has so very much on her shoulders at present, assisting the Duke and Duchess of Malvern, among so many other responsibilities. And of course she trusts my judgment implicitly.

"I expect new linens will be in order," Clara said. "That will give Bridget more than enough to do, and a chance to use her embroidery talent on monograms and such. I quite look forward to bringing the house back to life."

The duchess laughed. "Better you than me, my dear. I can think of few more tedious tasks than choosing wall coverings and curtains and all the rest of the fittings. I'd much rather spend my time disputing my spouse's absurd opinions about coroners' verdicts or judges' instructions to the jury or various fine points of law."

"You know nothing of fine points of law," said the husband.

"You see, Clara?" the duchess said. "Dealing with this deluded gentleman demands all my energies." She waved a hand. "Do as you like, dear. Send the boy to us once you've made him gorgeous, and we'll see what use we can make of him."

Richmond
Friday 4 December

Squirrel was still amazed at what whiskers and different clothes could do. Two days ago Jacob Freame, along with Husher and Squirrel, had left London in broad day in a curricle, and nobody took any notice. Squirrel knew nobody followed them, because he'd kept a lookout.

Like Jacob said, once they moved into their rooms at the Blue Goose Inn, it didn't take much. Change carriages, change clothes. Dress like somebody else and people think you're somebody else.

Until Chiver brought him into Jacob's gang, Squirrel had only dressed one way, in whatever rags he could get hold of. Jacob could be a right bastard, but so could hundreds of men. This right bastard fed his boys, though, and kept them in decent clothes, with a roof over their heads.

Today Squirrel wore a suit of almost-new clothes. No missing buttons. No holes or frayed edges. No patched elbows or other parts. He had a proper hat and a neckcloth and even a stickpin with a make-believe gem in it. He knew Husher must've robbed and beaten—maybe to death—somebody to get the money for all the things they needed here.

Maybe this bothered Squirrel some. But he always tried not to think too much about things like that, and just do what they told him to do.

He was the servant, Samuel. Husher had finer clothes, on account of being Jacob's make-believe son, Humphrey. Jacob had even made him clean his teeth.

Jacob was the grandest, the way you'd expect. He was Mr. Joseph Green, a swell from the City, here on doctor's orders. He acted like a swell, too, not hard for him. He talked and lived better than most of their kind. He'd been to school, though what school and where he never said and nobody asked.

While Husher lounged around the town, Jacob drove round the big park, getting the lay of the land, he said. Sometimes he sat in a tavern or a coffeehouse and gossiped. It was easy enough to find out all about Raven and the house the family lived in, by the river.

Richmond was used to strangers, but mainly in the summer. Now, though, they came again. They stood on the towing path and gawked up at the house behind its fence. They came down the road from the village green and tried to see if anybody was in the garden. Jacob, Husher, and Squirrel could stop and look, too, like any-

body else. Mainly Squirrel looked at the fence, and hoped
Jacob didn't tell him to climb over it and let him and
Husher into the place.

Not but what it was an easy fence to climb. What worried Squirrel was the servants. They popped up everywhere—in the garden and coming and going from the
stable yard and hothouse.

The town worried Squirrel, too. So small, everybody
knew everything about everybody. He was sure he'd seen
hawks, though Jacob said the London police didn't come
this far—another good reason for him and Husher to do
for Raven here, where there was only a bumpkin constable and some watchmen.

Today, Husher was watching the house and listening
for news. Jacob and Squirrel were driving in the park,
Squirrel on the seat with him for once, and watching for
trouble, like usual.

Jacob cuffed him. "Here, you stop that!" He didn't
shout. He said it soft enough, but his hand wasn't soft.
"Stop looking everywhere like that."

"I was only watching out, like you tole—"

"Not like that," Jacob said. "It looks like you're up to
no good. You want the clodhoppers to see nothing but
pigeons to pluck. That's us, out taking the air, hoping to
get a look at the brand-new nobs. Nobody else's servant
does it by squinting over his shoulder every two minutes."

Not wanting another knock in the head, Squirrel
stopped watching every shadow and sudden movement
and kept his eyes looking straight ahead, mostly. He tried
to pretend he was only enjoying the air, which he hated
the smell of. Too much of it. Too many trees.

That was why, sometime later when they left the park
and started back up the hill toward the village, he didn't
notice Toby Coppy coming out of a shop. He didn't see

Toby stop dead, his mouth opening and closing like a fish, and his face turning as white as his neckcloth.

Toby stood there for a good while, conspicuous in his new livery, but Squirrel saw nothing more than somebody's fancy servant idling on the pavement. He didn't know Toby was watching the gig as it moved up the street, and he missed Toby's facial contortions as he thought as hard as he could until he finally reached a conclusion.

Later

*B*ridget and Toby Coppy stood before Clara in her study.

"Squirrel," she said.

"That's what they called him in the gang," Bridget said. She did most of the talking for Toby because he was far from articulate. He'd come back from an errand, all in a quake, according to her, and she'd dragged him to report to Clara.

"On account his teeth and his cheeks, like he had 'em filled with nuts," the sister explained. "And on account he fidgets like a squirrel and on account he's fast, not only running but getting up into windows and out again. For, you know, housebreaking."

"He must have been one of the boys who got out of the building so quickly on the day the police came," Clara said to Toby.

He nodded.

Bridget elbowed her brother.

"Yes, your ladyship," Toby mumbled.

That must have been where Radford had spotted him— running away down that narrow street. He'd seen the boy's back and the way he ran. One boy among many fleeing the house. Yet Radford had remembered, enough for the boy to seem familiar. What was it like to own such a mind?

"He was in a curricle with a man," Bridget said.

This roused Toby to eloquence. "I fought he were Jacob," he said. "Cos why? Cos there weren't none of 'em never drove in no carriage but him. But this one weren't him. He had whiskers and clothes like the flash coves. And it weren't no gig but a curricle 'n two horses. And Jacob's dead, everybody says. But he made me fink of Jacob. T'other one were Squirrel. He were dressed proper fine, too, but I knowed him." He puffed out his cheeks.

"What's he here for, then?" Bridget said. "That's what Toby asked himself. He was scared and wanted to run away, on account they hate him. But they hate Raven—I mean his lordship—worse than anybody, and Toby thought he oughter know."

"Followed 'em," Toby said. "But not close."

"He followed them all the way to the Blue Goose Inn, where the carriage went into the yard," his sister said. "He didn't go into the yard, though. I told him he did right, because what if they saw him?"

Some might wonder how anybody could miss Toby. While his livery was not as fantastically glorious as Fenwick's, it was splendid, green and gold with epaulettes and gleaming brass buttons.

But if the pair had spotted Toby, would they know him in his finery? Probably not. Had Squirrel possessed a less memorable face, Toby might not have recognized him in his new clothes. While he had something of his sister's good looks, Toby's face wasn't nearly as attention-getting as his attire.

As to the man with him . . .

Clara had her suspicions.

She thanked them both. She told the boy he'd done very well, and she was proud of him.

All things considered, Toby had been brave, indeed.

He'd lived up to his livery.

After they left, Clara debated what to do. She had a long list of items needing her attention. Moreover, Radford would be back soon, and he'd take a fit if she pursued the question of Squirrel and his whiskered friend on her own.

You're not to pursue the Case of the Stuffed-Cheeks Boy.

This was not unreasonable.

She had no experience dealing with cutthroats. She did not know how to organize a police raid, even if she had legal grounds to do so, which she did not. The odds of her getting into difficulties were high.

Her husband had his Radford relatives to contend with. He did not need his wife causing him worry and adding to his trials.

Very well, then. She wouldn't pursue it . . . exactly.

The following day, she drove into the heart of Richmond with Davis and Colson.

Tuesday 8 December

Radford arrived at Ithaca House very late, with a barely functioning brain.

He had just about enough sense remaining to let his father know that, according to all physical evidence, Bernard had died when he cracked his skull on a rock.

Having settled his father's mind with the postmortem, Radford adjourned with Clara to their apartments. He found a bath awaiting him. Of course she'd thought ahead and arranged for it. She'd been trained to be the perfect hostess.

Though a long soak would have done him good, he made quick work of it. He wanted to go to bed. With her. He'd missed her to an uncomfortable extent. Had she been with him at Glynnor Castle, they could have argued

and laughed about his relatives. He would have had somebody to talk to who owned a brain. Who cared for him.
He'd written to her and she to him but it wasn't the same
as talking to her and watching her face and the way she
moved. A letter didn't offer the small clues her ladylike
exterior concealed so well from most people. One couldn't
have marital relations—as she called them—via letter.

When he returned to the bedroom, he found her sitting
in bed, reading . . . Wade's *Treatise on the Police of the
Metropolis*?

She was studying in order to out-argue him, beyond a
doubt.

He climbed into bed beside her.

She set aside the book. "Was it very bad?" she said.

"Which part?" he said.

"All and any of it," she said. "But what am I saying?
In your last letter you promised to be home by today. You
kept your promise, though you had to have sacrificed
meals and sleep to do it. You're tired. You can tell me
tomorrow."

He was deeply weary, to the bone and to the soul. He
sank back onto the pillows. She put out the candle and
slid down, too, and snuggled against him. He drew her
into his arms and touched his lips to her nightcap. That
wasn't satisfactory. He pulled off the nightcap and pressed
his mouth to her hair. It felt like silk and it smelled like
flowery soap and like her.

"It wasn't nearly as much fun as being with you," he
said. "You're vastly more entertaining. And prettier."

"Entertaining?" she said. "Like a court jester?"

"No, like a tricky murder trial."

She laughed softly. "High praise, indeed, my learned
friend."

"It's true," he said. "Dullards are everywhere. I always
know what most people are going to say and do. The other

Radfords, for instance, were exactly as demanding and quarrelsome as I expected them to be. The only surprise was the dead man."

He paused, trying to marshal his thoughts. Reason was so much easier than emotion. "I found the funeral rather more distressing than I would have supposed."

"You must have had some hopes for him or you wouldn't have tried to help him or pestered him about changing his ways," she said.

"I did that for the dukedom and the people he was responsible for. Not for him."

"Yet you were pleased when you learned he was courting a lady."

"I'd be an idiot not to be pleased. I didn't want my father to inherit. I didn't want to inherit. I *liked* my life."

"But it's happened," she said.

"Yes."

And the reality had turned out more complicated and demanding than he'd anticipated. So much to do and think about, even he hardly knew where to begin.

"I'd hoped he'd do better," she said. "I didn't know him, yet I was so disappointed. And angry at him, too, for mucking up his chance."

The feelings about Bernard, like so many, huddled in the farthest reaches of Radford's brain, being brooded over by his other self. They were so deeply packed in that mental lumber room, he wasn't sure what he felt. He wasn't sure he wanted to find out.

"I missed him," he said. "It's completely irrational."

She brought her hand up to his cheek and simply laid it there. He turned his face into her palm and kissed it.

"Feelings," she said. "Not your strong suit."

"I loathe them. More your department."

"I see little value in your cluttering up your great brain with feelings," she said. "I recommend you leave the feelings to me, along with domestic matters. Then you can give your attention to—to—" She waved a hand, and the ruffles at her wrist fluttered. "To what you're good at. Logic and business and such. Henceforth consider the big, nasty feelings my responsibility."

He had to laugh. How could he help it? He caught her wrist. "Come here," he said.

"I am here," she said.

"Closer," he said.

"I do not see how I could be any closer."

"Think harder," he said.

Wednesday 9 December
Marchioness of Bredon's sitting room

*D*ash it, Clara, you promised!"

"I did not, technically, promise," she said.

"Do not split hairs with me! I told you specifically to leave it alone—and you ought to have the intelligence to understand why."

She bristled at this, but Radford went on heedlessly, "Yet you go out, exposing yourself to known villains—"

"That's nonsense, and you of all men ought to recognize it," she said. "Villains are everywhere. We're all of us exposed to them every day. And what should anybody think, if they did see me? 'Ah, there goes the brand-new Marchioness of Bredon—*with her groom and lady's maid.*'"

He held on to his temper with a thread, and that in itself was infuriating. He never gave way to temper, except by design, in the courtroom.

But his heart was pounding with fear—for her—and a thousand thoughts beat in his brain, making chaos there. He moved away, to the window, and stared out.

In the garden, Toby pushed his father's invalid chair

along one of the footpaths. The day was mild, for December. Father was well wrapped in a shawl, a rug over his legs. Mother walked alongside, talking.

They'd taken to the fool boy, amazingly enough.

Clara's idea. She'd been busy, indeed, while he was away.

But this . . .

"Why should they suspect me of anything?" she said. "I'm only a woman. Helpless and incompetent and lacking in intelligence. Even lowborn persons, even criminals, think that. Women don't count."

He closed his eyes and fought for detachment. The other man, in the shadowy corner of his brain, was in a frenzy of rage and fear and memories of last night and this morning . . . their lovemaking and—oh, who knew what else and who cared? *Feelings.*

Her department.

This is a criminal matter, he told himself. *You're in a courtroom of sorts. Consider the facts and the facts alone.*

And my marriage? he wanted to argue. *Does your lordship expect me to ignore my wife and the duty of a husband?*

Of course he remembered every word.

. . . the causes for which Matrimony was ordained. . .

Thirdly, it was ordained for the mutual society, help, and comfort, that the one ought to have of the other, both in prosperity and adversity.

Mutual . . . help . . . comfort.

He waited until the noise in his head quieted to a hum.

He turned back to his wife. She stood by the mantelpiece, where any number of missiles stood conveniently at hand. At the moment, she did not look as though she contemplated throwing any of them. But her blue eyes flashed and he noticed the tension in the hands folded at her waist.

"Clara, it was Freame with that boy," he said.

"So I concluded," she said. "That is why—"

"Do you think a London banker or speculator or whatever he's pretending to be would collect someone like Squirrel on charity? The boy's hard as nails. While at Glynnor Castle, I wrote to Inspector Stokes about Stuffed-Cheeks Boy. I had a full report. Though new to Freame's gang, Squirrel had already made a name for himself as a cracksman."

His wife looked blank.

"Housebreaker," he said. "And Chiver's prize protégé."

"Then it's as well Toby spotted him," she said. "Only imagine if Bridget had gone out."

"She would have had the good sense to run in the opposite direction. Unlike you, driving straight for trouble."

"I did not go near that curst boy! None of us did. You are being exceedingly irrational."

"I!"

"Let me tell you again because I know you were not listening properly before."

"I heard every—"

"Colson went to the stable yard and gossiped," she said. "As grooms do. He didn't have to ask questions. The stable men were only too happy to tell him everything about everybody, including the so-called Mr. Joseph Green, in Richmond for a rest and to take the healthful waters. He's come with his son, Humphrey, and a young servant, Samuel. I was safe with Davis, streets away, in a shop. There's no reason to throw yourself into a pet."

"A pet!" A son named Humphrey, and a servant. Who was Humphrey? Half a dozen gang members remained unaccounted for, according to Stokes . . . including Husher.

Radford's gut knotted.

"You remind me exceedingly of Mama," Clara said.

For a moment he thought his hearing had failed him. His ears seemed to be ringing.

She gave him no time to respond but went on: "Such histrionics are all very well in the courtroom, but it won't do in a marital situation. Unless you are angling for a divorce."

Had he suddenly taken a delirious fever? He could not have heard the words he thought he'd heard. It took him a moment to speak. "Are you quite mad? A divorce?"

"You're right," she said. "It's early days yet. An annulment."

"Stop talking rot."

"You started it," she said. "You flew into a rage because I sent a spy to obtain information necessary to the family's safety."

He had not flown into a rage. He never did. He was the calmest and most rational of men. He said very calmly, "The family is not your responsibility."

"It most assuredly is," she said. "Especially when you're not here. As to spies, you didn't hesitate to use Millie, I recollect. But I couldn't approach her without causing talk, which of course would go round the town. Everybody knows everything about everybody, sometimes before one knows it oneself. Really, my lord, you are behaving quite irrationally. I realize this is a difficult time for you but—"

"It isn't difficult. I'm perfectly capable of managing a dukedom, thank you—and of doing so more competently than my father's predecessors."

"You're making a sad job of managing me, in the present instance," she said. "But I suspect you're excessively troubled by feelings. Unfortunately, I'm too much out of humor with you to attempt to intervene or translate. I recommend you find something productive to do. Or somebody else to rage at. I have letters to write and one hundred fabric swatches to look at, and both want a tranquil mind."

He opened his mouth to retort, then changed his mind.

He stormed out of the room, slamming the door behind him.

He heard something shatter against the door.

Chapter Nineteen

The mildness and inviting appearance of the
weather has induced her Majesty to walk out several mornings this week. Her Majesty has also
taken carriage airings with the King and her
Royal relatives.

 —*The Court Journal*, Saturday 5 December 1835

Heart pounding, Clara dropped into the chair at
her writing desk.

She would not make herself wretched thinking about it.
He was impossible.

She snatched up her pen and started yet another list,
but her hand was shaking and she was so angry, she tore
the paper and spoiled the pen.

She took out a penknife and tried to mend it, but she
only ruined the nib. She pushed the chair back, got up,
stalked to the door leading to her husband's study, and
stomped in. She'd tidied his desk after he left, and it had
comforted her to touch his things. It had also comforted
her to know he'd object to her touching his things, and she
could tease him about it.

Her throat tightened.

She stole a pen from his desk. Not satisfactory. She was still so angry. And hurt.

She'd thought he understood.

Someone *ought to encourage her*, he'd told her parents. *To be herself.*

She opened drawers and started rearranging his neat order. She moved the ruler to the small tray where he kept pencils. She took all the writing paper out of an upper drawer and opened a bottom one to put it there.

She reached down to remove what was in the bottom drawer . . . and paused.

Because there, instead of paper or notebooks or anything else related to his work, rested a crumpled bit of tissue paper, loosely wrapped about something.

She set the writing paper down on the desk and took out the parcel from the drawer. The loose tissue paper opened further, giving her a glimpse of soft leather.

She sat in her husband's chair and set the parcel on his desk and fully opened the flimsy wrapping.

Gloves.

A lady's gloves.

Very dirty gloves.

They were plain but of good quality. They still smelled of lavender . . . the scent Davis always kept in among Clara's clothes.

Her clothes. *Her* gloves. Her plainest pair, the ones she'd worn on the day they rescued Toby.

Only look at your gloves! Radford had said, so bafflingly furious about such a small thing.

She'd taken them off and—then what?

When she returned to her great-aunt's, Davis had said, "Has your ladyship lost another pair of gloves?"

Clara had assumed she'd dropped them in the street when she'd climbed out of the carriage, pretending to an insouciance she'd been so very far from feeling. Or else they'd slipped from her lap and onto the floor of the coach . . . when she and Radford had kissed. She'd supposed the coachman or the next passenger had appropriated them.

She'd assumed incorrectly.

Radford had found them. And kept them.

Her throat hurt.

She heard returning footsteps.

She wrapped the gloves, thrust them back into the drawer, and slid it shut. She dropped the writing paper into its proper drawer and hurried back into her sitting room, taking the fresh pen with her.

She was in the chair at her desk a moment before the door flew open.

By the time Radford stormed back in, she had the pen in hand and a list of some sort—she had no idea what it was—in front of her on the desk. Her heart raced and her hand gripped the pen too tightly. She wanted to throw it down and put her face in her hands and sob.

She placed her grandmother's image firmly in the front of her mind and refused to let the tears fall or her mouth so much as tremble.

He closed the door and stalked to the desk. "Dash it, Clara, have I hurt your feelings?"

"Certainly not," she said. "I take no notice of your irrational ranting and raving."

He set his hands on the desk, leaned toward her, and looked her in the eye. She met his gaze, chin aloft.

"I've hurt your feelings," he said.

"You *promised*," she said.

"Promised."

"That day. At your trial. I needed to be myself, you said. You'd encourage me to make a spectacle of myself. You—"

"I remember."

To her amazement, a tinge of red spread over his cheeks and jaw.

"You spoke of my mind," she said. "But a little while ago, you behaved as though I hadn't one. You—"

"Yes, yes," he said impatiently. "I may have overreacted somewhat."

"*Somewhat?* You insulted my intelligence. On *no evidence.*"

"Flimsy, I acknowledge."

"Not flimsy," she said. "None. Aught. *Nihil.* Unless your great brain is malfunctioning, you ought to know I did my spying as cleverly as you might have done, though you—"

"I should not have done it quite in that way."

"Of course not," she said. "You're a man. You can act more freely. I'm hampered by a strait-waistcoat of rules."

"Except the ones I'm so lost to reason as to try to make."

She wasn't ready to be mollified. "I took no risks," she said. "I could not have been more discreet. I did not pursue your criminals in any way or acknowledge their existence. I simply *gathered information*, which I presented to your ungrateful self as soon as you'd had time to recover from traveling. And if I had it to do over again, I should do it again, because I'd rather nobody killed you at present."

"Not *at present*?"

"I'm not in a humor to wear mourning for you," she said. "I'm already in black for your cousin—whom I dearly wish I had married instead—and it doesn't become me, and I'd rather not extend the length of time I must go about looking like a scarecrow, especially on your sorry account."

He studied her dress. "Black only makes you look a

little pale, though your present rage heightens your color. I should not call it unbecoming."

"Do not try to turn me up sweet." He was doing it, though. She was hopeless. She wished she hadn't found the gloves. He uttered a few vaguely complimentary words and she commenced melting.

"Clara—"

"I'm not *Clara* to you. To you I am *my lady*."

"Your ladyship is doing it too brown. Marry Bernard, indeed."

"I might have made something of him! I can do nothing with you! Your obnoxiousness knows no bounds."

"You knew I was obnoxious when you married me. All the world knows it. My picture is in the dictionary next to the word."

"You're not even *trying*," she said.

"I don't actually have to try to be obnoxious," he said. "It comes quite naturally."

She wanted to throw herself in his arms. She didn't want to quarrel anymore. She loved him, with all his faults. She loved his faults, too.

She reminded herself that the only way to get the marriage she wanted was to fight for it. They could have a partnership, like the one his parents had built. They could have the marriage she'd always supposed was a fantasy. But it wouldn't simply happen because she wanted it.

"I refer to your learning how to be a tolerable husband," she said.

"Tolerable! My dear girl, that's asking a great deal."

"I realize we're in the catastrophe phase of this inheritance," she went on ruthlessly because *my dear girl* made her want to fly into his arms. "But you don't seem to realize that the earthquake has happened to *both of us*. Yes, I trained to be a duchess. But I was not prepared to enter a household that had never been a ducal household or had anything to do with Society or had any thought of doing either, and is completely unprepared—and in many cases, *unwilling*—to change its ways." She added quickly, "You're not to think I blame your parents in the least. It's perfectly reasonable of them to want their peace. But I've been carrying on single-handedly for this last fortnight— and you come back only to find fault!"

His head went back as though she'd slapped him.

He straightened away from the desk, and she thought he'd storm out again, but instead he drew in a deep breath and let it out and said, "You have a point."

"A point!" she said. "I have a hundred points! I could write pages on the topic, had I time. But I must think about curtains for Malvern House. And Mama cannot find half the furniture listed on the last inventory, not but what she says we shouldn't attempt to retrieve it, judging by what remains."

"I do realize—"

"You don't, not a fraction of it. The staff at Malvern House is not only too small, but incompetent as well. We'll have to replace all but one or two. Have you any notion how time-consuming and tedious that is?"

"Surely you don't need to—"

"It's a house of some forty or fifty rooms. We don't know the precise number because we can't find the most recent floor plans. There are five floors in all, and even Mama's stamina could not withstand more than the main ones."

He turned away from her and walked to the fire. He folded his hands behind his back and stood there for a time, staring into the burning coals.

The silence stretched out. She could hear the crackle and hiss of the fire and the anxious beating of her heart, which seemed louder by far.

She gazed at him, taking in his tall physique and broad

shoulders and the strength and confidence of his long, lean frame. She remembered the lanky boy from so very long ago, defending her honor against a bully who, at the time, had seemed to her the size of an elephant.

She thought of the gloves.

She remembered last night and this morning, in bed, their bodies twined. How she'd missed sleeping with him! Though they'd had so little time to be intimate, she'd grown accustomed to the warmth and strength of his body alongside hers, and the sense of having found at last a place where she truly belonged.

She did belong with him. She'd wanted him and nobody else, and while she wanted a partnership, it ought to be a fair one on her side as well. She needed to take into account the strain he was under, far worse than what she felt.

This wasn't the life he'd trained himself for.

It wasn't the life he'd wanted.

I liked *my life*, he'd said.

"It's possible I'm not behaving in the most reasonable manner myself," she said.

"True enough," he said. "Given the circumstances, it would be more reasonable for you to be in fits, weeping and tearing your hair out. My parents are content to let you do everything, our future home wants an army to put it to rights, and your husband is completely blind to everything but his masculine pride and medieval notions of protecting his property. This, in his primitive view, includes his wife."

He turned back to meet her wondering gaze. "You see what happens when my emotions take charge," he said. "I can't see straight, let alone think straight. I react irrationally. What I should have done was congratulate you on your clever form of investigation. Had I known of the situation and you asked for instructions—and supposing myself in a sane state of mind, which it appears I cannot take for granted lately—I should have instructed you to do what you did."

The ache inside eased. "Well said, my learned friend."

"Does that mean you'll set aside the divorce proceedings, at least for the time being?"

"I'd better," she said. "Divorce is time-consuming, and I have so much to do." Divorce, in fact, was impossible, unless the husband initiated it. All the more reason to sort out sticky marital matters at the beginning.

"Kindly set the blasted house aside, too," he said. "We need to deal with these villains first, and quickly."

"We," she said, and her heart grew light enough to fly.

"Freame's the sort who'll sacrifice even his lieutenants to save his own skin," Radford said. "No honor among thieves there. I can't say why Squirrel has stuck with him instead of finding another berth, as the other escapees did, but his reasons will not be saintly. As to the third party, I have a likely candidate, and he's not the vicar, I promise you. They sent Squirrel ahead for surveillance. Now all three are here. I don't like the odds. However, it seems it would be grossly unfair and unkind of me to exclude you."

"Oh, Raven," she said. She rose from her chair, ready to launch herself at him.

"But first, Lady Bredon, you will be so good as to tell me what else you've done."

*H*er eyes widened and her mouth fell open, displaying the chipped tooth: the permanent reminder of her courage and willingness to defend him, no matter what the odds.

She was willing to fight him, too, and that in itself was heroic.

Obnoxious was the merest understatement.

His cold logic had at times reduced battle-scarred colleagues to tears. Never mind the witnesses.

If he reduced her to tears, those would be tears of rage, and a missile would swiftly collide with his skull.

But she collected her composure in the blink of an eye, and gave him a cool stare.

"I haven't had the chance to tell you," she said. "My first course of action required so much defending and argument. In fact, I suggest we walk in the garden. The day is mild, and the fresh air will clear our heads."

"My head is perfectly clear."

"You may think so," she said. "I shall send for our hats and coats."

By the time the outer garments arrived and were satisfactorily arranged—hers, not his—he was nearly dancing with impatience.

Then they stepped out of the house into the handsome garden his mother had created, which pleased the eye even in winter. He felt Clara's hand tuck into the crook of his elbow, and his impatience dissolved.

He wore his customary black and she wore mourning for stupid Bernard.

"Today we look exactly like Mr. and Mrs. Raven," he said.

She gave him a sidelong glance. "You always look well in black. Dashing and dangerous."

"You look better than well," he said. "Dramatic. I can picture your dressmakers swooning when they learned you'd need mourning clothes—and not the usual run of weeds, but the violently expensive kind, befitting a marchioness."

"They know I don't look well in black," she said. "They had to make an extra effort."

He did not think any special efforts were required to make the Marchioness of Bredon breathtaking.

"It was inexcusably inconsiderate of my cousin to die on us," he said. "On the other hand, this gave him no time to decimate his inheritance. When the bills arrive, elegantly engraved 'Maison Noirot,' I shall flick my gaze over them without feeling the smallest desire to cut my throat."

"Had your father not inherited, I should have economized," she said. "But now I'm obliged to do credit to your rank."

"My lady, you do me very great credit. And I'm quite, quite sure that what you're about to tell me will do you credit, too. Undoubtedly I shall suffer a heart seizure or collapse, foaming at the mouth, but it seems we'll simply have to learn to live with that sort of thing."

She pressed nearer. He was aware of the movement's placing her breast against his arm, but he knew this only because he knew exactly where her breasts were, relative to the rest of her as well as to him. She wore far too many garments for truly satisfying sensory experience.

"Look about you," she said.

He took in their surroundings. They walked along one of the winding footpaths. In warmer weather these would be bounded by flowerbeds whose color changed according to the varieties they held and the time of the season. The property was small, a sliver of land compared to those southeastward, belonging to the Earl of Cadogan, the Marquess of Lansdowne, the Duchess of Devonshire, the Duchess of Buccleuch, and other notables. However, Richmond held numerous other modest villas, and Ithaca House was entirely suitable for a successful barrister.

At this time of year all but the evergreens were bare, and more of the neighboring properties was visible than in other seasons.

Which meant that passersby, in the road leading to Richmond Green or the lane bordering the property to the east, had a better view than at other times of his father's house and garden.

"We're rather exposed," he said.

Nothing unusual for the countryside. Quite a bustling countryside in the summer, when scores of boats plied the river, including steamboats dropping off hordes of visitors from London. Until now, he hadn't needed to consider the implications. Until now, he hadn't had time—or the reasoning powers—to think of them.

"Nearly everybody is exposed," she said. "Especially along the riverside, where all that stands between us and trespassers is a not very tall fence. When Bridget told me about Squirrel, I longed for a high wall. But one can't build that in a day, even if it weren't impractical as well as ugly."

Tall walls would make a small property like this feel like a prison, as well as spoil the view.

"Instead, I hired additional outdoor servants," she said. "I've given orders for frequent and unpredictable patrols of the grounds. So as not to arouse our criminals' suspicions, I expressed a concern about London journalists entering the grounds and spying on us for their scandal sheets."

Surprised, he looked at her. Her cheeks were rosy with pride, he supposed. She ought to be proud and he ought not to be surprised.

"That was clever," he said. "Because it's true. We may be sure they're skulking about Richmond and probably getting in our would-be assassins' way."

"*Clever*," she said. "I feel a swoon coming on."

"Not yet," he said. "You've more to tell me, judging by your self-satisfied expression."

She threw him an amused glance, and went on, "As you'd expect, word went round Richmond in no time. The parish constable called and promised to have an eye kept on the property. In passing, he let me know that the Metropolitan Police Act did not extend to this part of Surrey."

"It's rather a patchwork in the counties neighboring London," he said. "Some parishes are included and some are not."

"In any case, it made no sense to fuss with the local authorities about juvenile delinquents from London lurking in the area, in company of a whiskered man."

He'd underestimated her, which was inexcusably stupid. She was beautiful yes, but he hadn't married her solely for her beauty—though nobody on earth would blame him if he had. Among the more obvious attractions was her complexity. She was interesting and she surprised him and that, he ought to have remembered, was because she could *think*.

"Do you know, Lady Bredon, I do believe in time, with the proper guidance, you might become almost . . . intelligent," he said.

She put a hand to her head. "Where are my smelling salts?"

"No time for fainting," he said. "Now I'm back, Freame will strike at the first opportunity. We need a plan, and we need it soon."

Friday 11 December

*B*reakfast time in the Blue Goose Inn's public dining room was Squirrel's favorite time. It was more like London then: busy, crowded, and loud. Better yet, in all the to-do of people coming and going in the coaches and such, nobody paid attention to Jacob and Husher. They sat at their usual table by a window, where they could watch the village green and the busier roads thereabouts. Squirrel stood by them, like a servant would do, waiting to fetch this or that from their room or run an errand.

And all three of them listened to what was going on

around them. Raven was back, like Jacob said he'd be. The
trouble was, newspaper coves swarmed like flies, and because of them, you could hardly get near the place without
some watchman or constable telling you to move along.

Like Jacob said, they didn't have the hawks here, like
in London. But they had private watchmen on account of
all the grand palaces. Lords and ladies had their houses
all over—down by the green and along the river and up
on the hill and in the park.

Jacob was boiling to get to Raven, but not enough to
make Squirrel go over the fence to break into the house
and let them in. Too easy to get caught, Jacob said.

If any of them got caught, the others would bolt. Had to.
Everybody hereabouts knew they'd come here together.

The watchmen and the newspaper culls put Jacob in bad
skin. He was hacking at his beefsteak like it was Raven's
innards. And thinking so hard you could practically hear it.

"Naturally we hope for a full commission." Somebody at the big table close by was talking over the others.
"Malvern House is one of London's finest palaces—in
an unfortunate state at present, else we should not have
been consulted. But Lady Bredon means to make all as
it should be. Down to the stables, you know, though that
isn't my province."

The talker was an old cove, some kind of tradesman.
The expensive kind, going by the cut of his old-fashioned
clothes and the big ring on his right hand. He wore spectacles and a wig, like old coves did.

Jacob stopped hacking so hard. You could practically
see his ears aiming at the talker.

Somebody else at the table said something, but Squirrel couldn't hear over the other talk.

"Not at present," the first man said. "However, his
lordship told me they've brought the present duke's mail
phaeton out of retirement."

"More suitable for a family man," somebody said. "And more convenient for traveling to and from Town with her ladyship."

Not convenient for us, Squirrel thought. Mail phaetons had a box behind the hood, where you could store parcels and luggage—but more important, there'd be a seat on the back of the box, big enough for two servants.

Before, Raven always traveled on his own, whether he rode or drove.

We lost our chance, Squirrel thought.

"His lordship was so gracious as to inform me the carriage had been well maintained these last few years," the first man said. "It needed little work to bring it up to snuff."

He'd been in the house yesterday and talked to Raven and the Long Meg. About curtains or furniture or some such. So people asked him questions, and even the serving maids made excuses to come by and jaw.

Jacob sneaked himself into the general jabber, like he knew how to do. He wanted to know about the shined-up mail phaeton, and the old man was happy to show off all he knew about the brand-new nobs up the river.

Then he was making a bustle—had to meet with her ladyship, and it wouldn't do to be late.

But as he was leaving the dining room, Jacob caught up with him and got him talking in the passage.

And the end of that was, the fellow's name was John Cotton, and Jacob was having supper with him tonight, and Husher and Squirrel could look after themselves.

Richmond Park
Tuesday 15 December

It was going to be here, like it or not, and Squirrel didn't like this park.

Too much of it—ponds and fields and woods and hills.

Only good news was, the weather was turning colder, so Raven didn't drive his lady all over for miles and miles, like the first time. They went round like the swells did in Hyde Park, taking the same route from the house every day. No servants with their arses parked on the seat behind the box, neither. Just them two.

Every day they came down Richmond Hill into the park and took a turn there, then back again.

Thanks to his friend Cotton, Jacob knew they'd be driving out every day. Thanks to Squirrel following them two days in a row, he knew their route.

Had to be here, Jacob said. In Richmond, everybody watched everything and told everybody everything. Practically nobody came into the park this time of year, especially late in the afternoon.

Jacob had his plan worked out, step by step. They came early, to the spot Jacob picked, and practiced. Then Jacob and Husher left Squirrel to mind the curricle. He hid with the carriage and horses a short ways down the road, round a turning at the bottom of a hilly stretch, behind a thick clump of tall bushes with shiny green leaves.

Husher said it was going to be fun.

Squirrel wished it was over.

He waited and waited, and it felt like days.

Finally, he heard the carriage—two horses, four wheels—coming.

Radford caught the movement out of the corner of his eye, an instant before a familiar, wiry figure ran out from the bushes into the horses' path, spreading out the front of his greatcoat and flapping it while shouting, "Help! Help!"

Birds flew up from the trees, setting the leaves rustling while they squawked warnings to their friends. Spooked, the horses reared up, while Freame—it was he, new whiskers and all—went on shouting and flapping the coat, though keeping out of the way of the hooves.

Come and get me, he seemed to say, and Radford longed to go after him and stop him, whatever he was up to—Freame and the others Radford knew were there.

But the horses would bolt. He had to get them under control first

"Give me the reins!" Clara cried.

Another, much bigger figure burst from the shrubbery. He lunged up at Radford, grabbed him, and pulled him off the carriage seat and into the road.

D *on't panic*, Clara told herself.

She focused on grabbing the ribbons as Radford toppled from the carriage. She made herself concentrate on threading the reins through her fingers and getting the horses under control. She had no idea what was going on behind her or how many assailants had burst from the woodland, and she couldn't take the time to look back. If she jumped or fell from the carriage and broke her neck, she'd be no good to Radford. They'd be no good to anybody if the horses trampled them. She had to keep her mind on what she was doing, focus on managing the panicked creatures with voice and reins. She could do it. She had to.

H usher was young but large and strong as a blacksmith. He had solid ground under his feet, while Radford had nothing to stop his being launched into air and thrown onto his back, hard. His ears rang. Panic washed in. The world started to darken and in the shadows he saw Bernard's face, taunting, mocking.

Dead, dead, dead. The bastard.

The world flashed with bright lights. Radford was going somewhere, quickly. Where? Away, far away. Forever? He was aware of the taste of blood and hard ground under his back. The blackness still swirled toward him, an irresistible tide.

No. Something more.

More to be done. Said.

Clara. I love you.

No time for that! Get up! Fight back! Do something*!*

He scrambled to push himself up—Bernard had knocked him down, time and again. He knew what to do. Or did he?

His hand . . . on the ground, no, something there, solid. He closed his fist around it. He opened his eyes and saw a big hand upraised. Husher's face, a wide, gap-toothed grin.

The lowering sun struck the knife's blade. A blinding gold flash. Radford rolled away as the blade slashed downward. He heard a roar of rage, then Husher fell on him, hard and heavy, made of bricks. Radford gasped for breath but he held on to the solid thing in his hand—the whip handle—and as the knife came at him once again, he knocked it aside. Husher swore and grabbed Radford's hand, the one holding the whip, squeezing painfully.

Laughter. "For Chiver," Husher said. "Ha ha."

The Long Meg had her hands full, that was plain to Freame. She was struggling with the horses, and sure to lose the fight. That was good.

But not good enough. Better if the horses overturned the carriage. Better still if the damned lawyer broke his neck when he went down. But no, he was putting up a fight.

Time to give Husher a hand—or better yet, a knife.

But before Freame could move, another cove jumped up from the box, launched himself at Husher, and took him down.

The bloody damned box! Why hadn't Squirrel gone up one of the hills or into the trees, to see what was in there?

Freame didn't wait to weigh the odds. He ran.

*W*ith all the strength he could muster, Radford shoved the huge hand gripping his against Husher's face. The whip handle cracked against Husher's nose, and he roared and let go, clutching his nose as blood poured down his face.

Something thundered nearby. A flurry of movement, then Husher went down, over to one side into the road, Stokes on top of him.

Radford dragged himself to his feet. Another tide of darkness swirled in. But that was the park, whirling about him. Shadow-filled now. He struggled to get his bearings. He caught a glimpse of dimming sunlight through tree branches. He heard a noise he recognized, of a carriage in motion.

He turned toward the sound, in time to see the mail phaeton moving, gaining speed as it rumbled away.

Clara.

In a runaway carriage.

*C*lara had got the animals to stop rearing and dancing but they were still jittery, dragging the carriage along the road. Ahead lay a downhill stretch, with a dangerous turn near the bottom. She held on, fighting for calm while she tried to remember what Longmore had taught her about panicked horses. Stay calm, yes, but what else?

Then she spotted Freame. She'd been too focused on the horses to notice much else, but there he was, running as though the devil himself were after him.

"No, you don't!" she shrieked. "Raven! He's getting away!"

Chapter Twenty

.

In ravens' weather, that is, when the sky lowers
and portends storms, or after the storm has just
passed, they may be seen upon the more open
parts of the woods, sitting on a dark mass of stone
and eyeing the desolation around them with keen
and cautious glance.
—Charles F. Partington, *The British Cyclopedia*, 1836

Freame heard the Long Meg's scream. He ran for
all he was worth. He wouldn't let himself look
behind him. He heard it all: the hooves thundering too
close behind, the chains rattling, the wheels rumbling. But
he daren't leave the road. It was all trees, rocks, bushes on
either side. He wasn't sure how much woodland there was
or where the water was. He didn't fancy breaking a leg or
stumbling into an icy pond or bog.

Never mind. Not far to go now.

Squirrel waited with the curricle, only a little farther
down the road. Freame could make it—though he might
have to jump out of the way of the bloody damned horses.
But they'd end in a crash, and the long Meg would end in
pieces.

Next turn on the carriage road from there would take

him and Squirrel to the Sheen Gate. From there, they'd be on the road for Putney in no time, then on to Putney Bridge. Then London, not four miles from the bridge.

He made himself run faster.

Make them think running is your idea, Longmore had said. *Be in command. Pretend it's a race.*

The horses were already worked up. They needed to run. The rest was up to Clara.

All she had to do was stay calm and in control, watch for obstacles, hope nothing else alarmed the creatures, and keep them following Freame. Trees flew past her, pebbles flew up from the roadbed. The way ahead looked perilously steep and the horses were picking up speed, racing headlong down, toward the wicked turning and the thick stand of trees, stumps, and rocks it held.

But he whistled, then shouted something and signaled with his hand. She noticed movement in the stand of tall shrubbery not far ahead of him.

After a moment, she caught a glimpse of something, partly hidden in the shrubbery. It seemed to be a boy. Behind him, something else. Large animals. Horses. And more: the black hood of a carriage.

Freame was running toward them, about to round the bend in the road.

She couldn't let him get in that carriage and get away. He couldn't be let to run loose, to keep plotting against Radford.

She urged the horses on.

Freame looked back over his shoulder. His narrow face was white. He turned forward again and shouted something to the boy. But the boy had stopped short and he was gaping at Clara bearing down on them, wheels and horses' hooves like thunder above the rustling leaves and the birds' cries. Freame roared something

and turned abruptly toward the boy—and escape—and
she screamed, "No!"

The scream went through Radford like a knife. He
watched the carriage list precariously to one side
as it entered the turning. His racing heart stopped, and
for one icy instant, he saw in his mind's eye the vehicle
slowly toppling, toppling, unstoppable, over and onto
her . . . tree branches and stumps and rocks—all deadly
weapons if she landed on them.

Bernard's head . . . striking a rock . . . instant death.

Radford pushed the image away and beat back panic.

He heard her scream. Then another. Not hers this time,
but male. The mail phaeton teetered, then came fully upright again. Gradually it slowed and stopped.

Radford dragged in what air he could and raced to the
spot.

Clara was looking down and to one side of her, but
she must have heard his footsteps because she turned and
looked at him, and smiled. Tremulously.

Tremulous or not, it was a smile, and it was like sunshine breaking through the deepening gloom of the park.

She was alive and unhurt, by the looks of it. But she
had to be shaken. He was shaken, limbs trembling now,
heart pounding against his chest wall.

Radford started toward her.

"Never mind me," she said. She nodded toward a
crumpled heap, a few feet from the horses' hooves. "I
was trying not to run him down, only keep him in view
and running, but the road here is so narrow . . . then he
jumped out of the way. He must have tripped over something. He cried out as he fell, then he didn't get up again.
I don't know if he's dead. But please take care he doesn't
get away."

The words were hardly out of her mouth when a boy

irrupted from the patch of woodland ahead and ran, at stunning speed, along the road leading to the Sheen Gate.

Radford could only watch him go. Had he been fresh, he'd have a devil of a time catching him. As it was, he hadn't a chance. But he didn't need to try. By the time the boy reached the gate, even he would be winded. He'd have to slow down—and stumble into the arms of the constables waiting there for escapees.

More police waited at the Putney Bridge. The Metropolitan Police district didn't include Richmond and large segments of the park, but it covered the parish of Putney, where the boy was obviously headed. Stokes's colleagues wouldn't let Squirrel slip through their fingers this time.

Radford moved toward the prone figure of his would-be assassin.

A short time later

They had arranged beforehand to meet the police at the Sheen Gate.

Thence Radford, Clara, and Inspector Stokes—aka John Cotton, Purveyor of Fine Furnishings to the Nobility—proceeded with their captives. The brutal young man Stokes called Husher, handcuffed, and Freame, immobilized, his shattered leg on a makeshift splint, shared the mail phaeton's box, with Stokes on guard on the servants' seat at the rear. Everybody was bloody and bruised, except for Clara, who was merely dusty.

Radford's coat hung in filthy shreds. The rest of his attire matched it. In the dusky half light, even with the lamplights' illumination, she couldn't identify the stains on his black clothes. Dirt, yes, but bloodstains, too, most likely. She could make out the marks on his face as well—more dirt, bruises, cuts—and signs of swelling. He probably had lumps on his head. He'd fallen hard.

She was used to seeing the results of males' fighting. This was different. This opened a cold, deep space in the pit of her stomach. He might have been killed, so easily. He might have died, in a moment, like his cousin.

Freame's accomplice Husher was loose-limbed and muscled, with big, thick-fingered hands. She'd seen a blacksmith who looked like that: tall, lanky, and apparently clumsy. But he could lift an anvil or an ox without breathing hard, and he could shape the smallest piece of metal into whatever form he wanted.

The mail phaeton's hood muffled sounds from behind and the rattle of wheels and clatter of hooves tended to drown out other noises, but she was aware of Freame, alternately moaning and raging, though she couldn't make out what he said. Now and again she caught a whiff of Stokes's pipe.

"That did not go quite as planned," she said.

"It never does," Radford said. "As Stokes warned us." His voice was hoarser than usual, and that made her want to grab the horsewhip from his hand and beat Husher senseless, for whatever he'd done to her husband.

They'd planned so carefully. Radford had written to Scotland Yard—via Westcott, because all of Richmond knew where their post came from and went to. He'd described the situation. He'd hired Inspector Stokes, a highly regarded former Bow Street Runner, as a private detective. Everything had been arranged so as to involve the London police without offending local sensibilities and while allowing as few locals as possible in on the secret, gossip being what it was.

Stokes had arrived within hours of being summoned, and he and Radford had made several plans to cover the most likely scenarios.

As John Cotton, Stokes had passed to Freame the information needed to manipulate him into appearing at a certain time of day, along a predetermined route.

On the daily drives, Stokes had curled up under a rug, out of sight of those spying from the bushes.

Even so, even prepared and braced for an attack, and even having limited the possible attack sites, they couldn't know precisely when or where.

Freame's bursting out of hiding had startled humans and horses enough to throw everybody off balance and give the criminals an advantage.

"You knew the police were waiting at the gate," he said. "And we agreed, did we not, that you would not involve yourself unless it was to stop somebody killing me—and then only if it didn't endanger you."

"We didn't allow for your being pulled from the carriage and knocked down so quickly or the horses panicking."

The cattle were well trained, but they weren't London trained, accustomed to constant hubbub and people, horses, and vehicles coming at them. Freame had known what to do: burst into a tranquil scene and make a big commotion, flapping his greatcoat about him and shouting.

"It might have been worse, I suppose," he said. "At least you didn't jump out and try to kill Husher. Or Freame. Though I daresay Freame will claim in court that you tried to run him down."

"Here's what I'll tell the jury," she said. "I was left alone in a runaway carriage. I did my best to get the horses under control. But it was difficult for a mere woman. Freame had the misfortune to trip when he leapt out of the way."

"Difficult for a mere woman," he muttered. "I can hear your brother Longmore laughing now. No, all of your brothers. We'd better keep them out of the courtroom."

"I probably could have stopped the horses by then, or

at least slowed them," she said. "But that wasn't what was in my mind. Though I wasn't aware of thinking in a logical manner at the time, all the practicing and talking with Stokes must have prepared me."

"You had a great many what-if questions, I recall."

She knew he remembered each and every one. She remembered that he hadn't interrupted or dismissed a single question. He and Stokes had taken her seriously. They'd responded as though she'd been another man. She wasn't sure either man would understand how important that was. Men took for granted that sort of respect. They had their pecking orders but still they were men, and in the great scheme of things, men and what they said mattered. Women didn't. They were to be looked at and not listened to.

She hadn't called attention to it then and wouldn't now, but she cherished it in her heart. Later she'd find a way to tell her husband what it meant to her.

She went on, "While the front of my mind was on keeping the horses under control, in the back of my mind I was thinking, too. I knew the police were at the Sheen Gate and at the Putney Bridge. But Freame was escaping. I saw he aimed for the Sheen Gate, where the police were waiting. But that didn't mean they'd catch him. In his place, I would have jumped into the curricle and driven like a madman, straight at them, the way he drove straight at us in Trafalgar Square. The police would have given way instinctively, as we did. Only for a moment, perhaps, but that could be all the time he needed. And who's to say he'd make for the Putney Bridge? He might have turned off the main road sooner and made for the Hammersmith Bridge. It's a long way about—but for that reason, no one would expect him to go that way."

"You have a point," he said. "An excellent point, by the way. Do you know, I was cleverer than I thought, when I decided to marry you."

"*You* decided!"

"Yes, after you left me no choice."

After a pause, he said, "I hope this was adventure enough for you. I'm not sure how many I'll be able to provide in future."

She gave a careless wave of her hand. "I'm not in the least concerned. Whatever you do with your new position, I know I can count on you to alienate and enrage any number of people, and we can always depend on somebody or other wanting to kill you."

"Do you know, I hadn't thought of that," he said. "But then, I've had no time to consider my future. If it isn't one thing, it's another. First Bernard goes and falls on his head. Race to Glynnor Castle, and get them sorted. Race home to find assassins lurking in the shrubbery. Alert Scotland Yard. Bring in Stokes. Form a counterplot. Foil the villains— which it turns out is easier said than done. Now we've got to make sure they get to London safe and sound for a trial next month, for which I must plan a case I can't prosecute."

He spoke coolly enough in spite of what she was sure was a near brush with death. But it was his habit to view the world through the spectacles of logic and reason. Emotions were her department, and she ached for what he'd miss, though he seemed to dismiss it so calmly: to stand in wig, bands, and robe in the courtroom and ask his questions and make his arguments and joust with the judge and opposing counsel.

"That must be . . . annoying," she said.

"Hmm." He frowned.

"But of course you'll give Westcott detailed instructions as well as tell him which barrister is to represent you," she said.

"No." He looked at her, and she caught the wicked glint in his grey eyes. "I don't need a barrister. I must have suffered a minor concussion—"

"A concussion!"

"A minor one," he said. "The only explanation for my failing to remember a fundamental fact of law: victims of crime have the right to prosecute their own cases. They've done so for most of our history."

"But a concussion!" she said. She didn't care about the blasted law.

"I did fall on my head. But unlike Bernard, I survived—and you can nurse me tenderly later. I quite look forward to that. And then so much fun to look forward to next month at the sessions. I shall be Lord Bredon, with everybody bowing and scraping—including the judge, possibly." He laughed, then winced.

She wasn't able to find out where else, besides his head, he'd been injured, because they were nearing the Sheen Gate, where the police waited.

There Radford and Clara learned that Squirrel had eluded the police.

He hadn't come through the gate. Everybody there would swear to it.

Yet he might have done, Radford thought. The boy was so quick. Or he might have hidden in the park, waiting for the excitement to die down. He'd shown patience enough that first time, following Radford as he led him on a long, tedious chase.

Still, it would be hard to prove much against the boy, and the two men they knew to be deadly were in custody.

Radford spoke briefly to Stokes, who sent a pair of constables back to collect Freame's curricle. That, at least, might offer useful evidence.

Leaving the police to finish their various tasks, including, at Radford's insistence, taking Freame to the nearest surgeon, Radford drove home. Though the twilight was deepening into night, he went by way of the park. He could drive this road blindfolded, and it spared their facing gawkers. He knew he looked a great deal the worse for wear. Normally this wouldn't trouble him, but he wasn't in a humor to be gaped at.

He needed some time to collect himself—or rather, detach himself from recent events and the accompanying avalanche of emotions. Then, when it came time to traverse Richmond Hill, he could regard any staring multitudes with cool objectivity.

His mind swiftly turned to familiar, logical spheres: the case against Freame and his associates, for instance.

"It's a pity the sessions don't come on for weeks," he said. "I'll be healed by then, and the jury will think a great, healthy aristocrat, in all his finery, was in no danger from anybody except, possibly, a Mongol horde. Freame and Husher will claim I tried to run them down, you may be sure. And when Husher tried to prevent me, my wife tried to run Freame down."

"Evidence," she said. "So difficult to prove intent—as in the Grumley case."

"Unless somebody squeaks," he said. "Even so, if the informant is one of the conspirators, the jury may not deem him reliable. I'd better warn you: It's unlikely either of them will go to the gallows for assault, even violent assault. Some years of hard labor is more like it."

"I'd rather transportation for life," she said. "I want them both gone from England."

"Not impossible," he said. "Still, we must consider this: If Freame had the money to get himself a curricle and horses and a new wardrobe, and spend weeks in an inn, he might be able to squeeze somebody for funds for a good lawyer. But it's no use trying the case and fretting over the sentence now. There's time for a confession as well as for the police to gather further evidence about Freame's various criminal enterprises. A good case may win a sentence of transportation for life. Not to mention I'm counting on the effect of your big blue eyes and the tears you'll shed, speaking of your terrifying experience."

"I! Do you truly mean to let me testify?" She'd spoken boldly enough of what she'd say in court, but she knew as well as he did that ladies did not stand in the witness box of the Old Bailey, of all places.

"You'd better, or we're too likely to lose."

"Oh, Raven."

"Your parents will take a fit, certainly," he said. "However, if you cared about that sort of thing, you wouldn't have married me."

"Oh, my dear Raven," she said. "I could kiss you witless."

"Could you, indeed? But I'm filthy and bloodstained and one side of my face is growing larger than the other."

"It's dark," she said.

He glanced about him. "So it is. I remember having thoughts, at one time, of luring you to a sheltering patch of woodland and misbehaving in a furtive manner."

"What were those thoughts, precisely?"

They were near the Richmond Gate, but night had descended—and even if it had been full day, he wouldn't have cared. He drew the carriage into the shelter of a stand of trees, and pulled her into his arms and onto his lap. He buried his face in her neck and inhaled the scent of her, rather musky now from fear and excitement, but it was Clara, and she was alive and so was he, battered but all in one piece. And he wanted her.

He raised his head and grasped the back of hers and kissed her, fiercely.

I was so afraid of losing you.

She answered with passion, pressing her lips to his, and parting instantly thereafter, drawing him in, and this was more than homecoming. It was the end of the world and the beginning. *Nonsense*, his logical self would have said, but his logical self knew what they'd lived through, together. The logical self recognized fear and rage and the threat of death. It recognized the joy of surviving and triumphing, too.

They'd won.

And they'd come so very close to losing.

It was all in their kiss: terror and rage and relief and joy. Feelings.

He pulled at the ribbons of her hat, and it fell back, down her neck, and still her mouth clung to his, her tongue coiling with his. The taste of her coursed through him as though he'd drunk fine old whiskey. It burned and exhilarated and it seared away the fear and anger and confusion as easily as it seared away his body's aches and stings.

She moved her gloved hands over him, along the sides of his face and his neck, her touch light but inflaming. A lady's hands, in their fine gloves—he didn't know why this aroused him so, but it did. He broke the kiss and grasped her hand, and peeled back the glove from her wrist. He brought her hand to his mouth and kissed the inside of her wrist. She trembled.

"Oh, Raven, your wicked mouth," she said softly.

He drew the glove down further, exposing her palm. He kissed there, too, with his lips, and caressed the soft skin with his tongue. She moaned softly. He tugged it back further, then eased it off, finger by finger. He let the glove fall from his hand while he kissed each finger, each knuckle, and each fingertip. He took off the other glove in the same way, but more quickly, because she was moving her bottom against his thighs, and his intellect narrowed to a pinhole.

He slid his hands under her cloak, to her narrow waist and upward, to her breasts, so tightly encased. But that was only teasing himself.

He reached down and dragged up the cloak and the skirt of her dress together, miles of material whose rustling sounded like fireworks in the now-serene park. He was aware of the wind soughing through the trees, and the rustle of dry leaves as they ran before the wind, but all that was a distant dream. Under the mountain of clothing he found her legs at last, her long, beautiful legs, encased in silk that whispered under his hand. Her leg quivered under his touch and he felt her hands cupping his face, and he heard her voice, low and soft as a sigh: "Yes, oh, yes."

She drew her tongue along his lips and teased while he stroked up her thigh, above the garter, and upward. The way he'd done that day, the day he'd asked to marry her in that stupid way.

Yes, she'd said then.

Yes, she said now.

He slid his hand between her legs and found the place, warm and soft and slick with desire. For him. He caressed her and she opened to him so easily, and "Don't wait," she said. "I can't wait. I'm so wicked."

"Yes, you are," he said. He unfastened his trousers, and dragged his shirt out of the way, and his swollen cock sprang free. Then her hand was there, holding him, and it was all he could do to keep from giving way then and there. Her hand, her soft, warm hand, the hand he'd kissed so lovingly—and this was the first time she hadn't been shy, but touched him all on her own.

He had no mind left. It was all love and lust and the whiskey fire racing through him. Her hand closed round him, and he groaned. He drew her hand away—her touch would send him over the edge—and pushed into her. She cried out softly, then eased herself down on him, and he thought he'd die of it, of the feel of her, closing about him and squeezing . . . letting go as she rose a little . . . riding him . . . smooth as she would have ridden her mount, and killing him by slow degrees.

"By gad, my dear, I think you've got the hang of it," he managed to gasp.

She laughed a little, and that set off feelings he couldn't describe and wouldn't try to. The world was dark and hot and filled with the scent and taste of her, his beautiful girl. The most beautiful girl in the world, and she was his.

He kissed her, ferociously and tenderly, and they rode together, faster and faster, until they could go no farther. Release came, like a rainstorm of pleasure, and they clung to each other while the storm passed.

And when at last they'd quieted, and he began to help put her clothing to rights, he said, "I love you, Lady Bredon. You know that, don't you?" He'd thought she'd be killed, and would never know, because he'd never said it to her, fool that he was.

She said, "I deduced as much, Lord Bredon."

Later that night

No, you don't!" Freame shouted.

"Your lower leg is badly shattered," the surgeon said. "It had better come off."

"It better not! Don't play your games with me. It's the hawks' doing. I know them. You set it."

"No reputable surgeon would attempt to set this," the surgeon said. "No one would risk trying to save it. Any medical man would tell you infection is bound to result."

"Bugger your eyes, you lying clodhopper. Stokes, get me out of here! I want a London surgeon, none of these bumpkin quacks."

Against the bumpkin quack's advice, Stokes took Freame to London. The Marquess of Bredon wanted the man alive and well for his trial. He'd pay the costs. Stokes hoped Freame would listen to a London surgeon.

He wouldn't.

Stokes wrote to Lord Bredon, "The doctor in London said the same as the one in Sheen. Freame wasn't having it. He demanded another surgeon. Same verdict. Freame wouldn't give in. You ask me, my lord, he's more afraid of being a cripple than dying. In the end, the two doctors set it the best they could and told him he was signing his death warrant. They made me be a witness, so he couldn't blame them later, if he had to lose the whole leg."

Reports continued to arrive from London. Inflammation soon set in, as predicted.

"He has good reason to fear being a cripple," Lord Bredon told his wife, after they'd read the latest report. "He won't last long on the streets, defenseless, and he has enemies who'd make sure he died slowly and painfully. But I suspect he's considering, too, the advantage he'll have in court, looking sick and weak and pathetic."

"It's rather a risk," Clara said. "It looks more like suicide to me."

Her husband shook his head. "He knows his way round the justice system. If he didn't, we'd have tried and transported him years ago. He's counting on making his pathetic appearance at the January sessions. No doubt he's hoping to win damages from me, given the lawyer he's hired. Then he'll decide about amputation. Well, he'd better calculate again. I'll make sure he isn't tried in January."

Husher was, though, and found guilty on several counts, including: "feloniously assaulting and striking and beating the Marquess of Bredon, putting in fear the Marchioness of Bredon, feloniously assaulting with a sharp instrument Police Inspector Sam Stokes, striking and beating him and stating his intent to be to resist and prevent his lawful apprehension and detainer."

This, as Radford had predicted, might not have amounted to much. However, at the same sessions Husher was tried for two separate incidents of robbery with violence. The police found eyewitnesses as well as a victim willing to testify.

He was sentenced to transportation for life.

L ate in January, Freame was taken to St. Bartholomew's.

His case, put off to the February sessions, was put off again.

His condition continued to worsen, and he began to show symptoms of what he claimed was jail fever. According to the surgeon who wrote to Lord Bredon, these were symptoms of gangrene.

Bredon went to see him.

"You'd better give up the leg," he told the gang leader. "I'll keep putting off the trial until you're fit."

"Fit!" Freame said. "When you set them to torturing me? This is your doing, Raven. And you'll pay."

"Try thinking with your head. Minus a leg, you'll win a bit of jury sympathy. Your favorite accomplice got off with transportation. You must know we haven't as much solid evidence against you as we'd like. What we have, a good lawyer will raise doubts about. The odds of your going to the gallows are small."

Miniscule was more accurate.

Freame could claim Husher had tried to assault him, and he'd run into the road for help. He could claim the Bredons tried to run him down. It would not be terribly difficult to raise doubt in the jury's mind. He knew how to look and sound more or less respectable. Even if they found him guilty, the penalty was unlikely to be harsh, since he had no criminal record.

If Freame knew this, he didn't let on. "Oh, smooth

words," he said. "You think I was born yesterday? You think I don't know what it's like for nobs? You whisper a word, drop some coins where the right people find them, and they'll make sure I dangle."

"If it worked that way, my lady would have made sure Husher's neck had a snug relationship with a rope."

"Your *lady*," Freame snarled. "I wish I'd run down the pair of you when I had the chance."

"You didn't, and it was a mistake," his lordship said. "Try not to make another. The leg badly needs to come off. Judging by what the doctors tell me and what I see for myself, you might have left it too late already."

As Lord Bredon later told his wife, he might as well have talked to the chamber pot.

He had the case put off again.

More weeks passed, and the pain grew to beyond what Freame could endure in spite of large doses of laudanum. At last he consented to the amputation, but by then it was too late. The gangrene had spread, up his leg and into his pelvis.

It took him agonizing weeks more to die, on the fourth of April.

Westcott brought the news to the Marquess and Marchioness of Bredon, now residing at Malvern House.

Though still undergoing refurbishment, the house was livable, and they'd recently moved in with a modest retinue of servants.

Most of the main floor was completed by this time. Clara and Bredon met with Westcott in the library.

Though the news wasn't unexpected, it took Clara a moment to digest it. She hadn't realized how much the villains had troubled her until now, when she wanted to weep with relief. Then came her husband's sharp, logical voice, like a brisk breeze breaking through a sultry fog.

"What an idiot," he said. "If only he'd consented to the amputation at the start, he might have got off with a few months in prison. Still, it does save the police the trouble of building additional cases against him."

"He's gone," Clara said, her voice perfectly steady now. "That's what matters. He can't harm you or anybody else again. And it seems a satisfactory justice, his having brought it on himself."

"That's one more would-be assassin out of the way," Westcott said. "Only a few score more to go."

"You underestimate his lordship," said Clara. "In the years to come, I confidently expect great numbers of highly placed persons to nourish murderous fantasies."

"I'm not worried," said his lordship. "I have Clara to protect me."

"And as her ladyship pointed out some time ago," said his friend, "if worse comes to worse, you can always talk them to death."

"You might as well know I was thinking of doing that, regardless," said Lord Bredon. "Clara has dropped unsubtle hints about my standing for Parliament. I think it'll be fun."

"All you have to do is win over the constituency," Westcott said.

"All I have to do is have my wife stand beside me on the hustings and bat her blue eyes," said his lordship. "The voters are men, after all."

"That's your election strategy?" Westcott said.

"It's probably better if he doesn't speak," Clara said.

"You have a point," Westcott said.

"In any event, I'll have plenty of time to speak once I'm in the House of Commons. You may be sure I'll make use of the time."

"In that case, I should move assassination from the 'possible' to the 'probable' column," said Westcott.

"By no means," Clara said. "There's a small difference between Society and the London underworld. Gentlemen may cultivate elaborate fantasies or even challenge my husband outright. They may *wish* to kill him, but they won't be sneaking and plotting about it. Too, if all goes as I intend, their ladies won't let them kill him."

Westcott smiled. "Lady Bredon, I admire and appreciate your affection for your husband. However, speaking from experience, I ought to point out that he can stir the gentler sex to violence without even trying."

She smiled back. "Not when I'm done with them."

"You're in over your head, Westcott," said her husband. "Clara has a plan. A mad, beautiful plan. She's going to bring me into fashion."

"You're roasting me," Westcott said.

"Not at all," said Bredon, his face sober but for the infinitesimal twitch at the corner of this mouth. "She's throwing a ball for me. I'm to be a debutante, you see."

"I certainly shall have to see it, with my own eyes," said Westcott.

"Of course," said Clara. "You're at the top of the invitation list."

"Just before the King," said her husband. And laughed.

Chapter Twenty-one

At length, with conjugal endearment both
Satiate, Ulysses tasted and his spouse
The sweets of mutual converse.
—*The Odyssey of Homer,* translated by William Cowper,
1791

The King's levee commenced promptly at two o'clock on Wednesday the fifth of May. Fairly early in the proceedings the Duke of Clevedon presented the Marquess of Bredon to His Majesty.

"About time," the King said. "You must stop loitering about the Old Bailey, you know. Make yourself useful elsewhere."

"Indeed, sir," said Lord Bredon. "My wife has some ideas about that."

His monarch smiled. "I look forward to seeing Lady Bredon tomorrow."

Their Majesties were coming to look at Malvern House, which they, like nearly everybody else, had never entered.

The King went on to ask after the Duke of Malvern's health, and promised to visit him as well, before next he returned to Windsor.

Then it was on to the next presentation.

Those near enough to hear the conversation repeated it, and word soon traveled through the vast company of men, who went on to repeat it later to their wives, mistresses, mothers, and sisters. The gentlemen offered as well detailed reports on what Lord Bredon wore to the levee: as much black as Court rules could accommodate, naturally.

At Almack's that night, as a result, heads turned to the entrance time and again, only to be disappointed.

As Lady Warford explained to her friends, "Oh, no, it was out of the question. Clara gives her supper ball tomorrow night, you know, and she must try to get as much rest as possible beforehand. The King and Queen visit Malvern House in the afternoon, to view the improvements. They've always been fond of Clara, and His Majesty has a regard for the Duke of Malvern." Though the King and Queen would not attend the supper ball, she explained, other royals would.

If Lady Bartham was gnashing her teeth, she did this invisibly, in the most ladylike way, and even she couldn't invent a suitably poisonous retort—not that she could have got a word in edgeways, with the other ladies so busy currying favor with Lady Warford.

Not everybody had received an invitation to the ball, but those who hadn't could hope to be invited to another event before long. The Marchioness of Bredon was expected to carry on in her mother's style of superior entertainment.

As the King had noted, Lord Bredon's presentation had come rather late after his rise in rank. He'd spent most of the time since he'd acquired his courtesy title overseeing work on the neglected house, building a case for a villain who took forever to come to trial—and then didn't live long enough, after all—putting the Malvern estate affairs in order, and completing his legal responsibilities. He hadn't had time for Society.

Though the lengthy delay was rather irritating, it did mean that all those privileged to receive an invitation to Clara's supper ball accepted promptly. All the beau monde was curious about the new marquess. They'd read about him, yes, from time to time, if they read criminal proceedings. Those connected with the courts had encountered him now and again. But except to those who'd attended the wedding, he was a mystery, all the more so because Lady Clara Fairfax had chosen him in favor of so many amiable, fashionable young men.

Too, everybody wanted to see the house, into which hardly anybody had set foot in a century.

Malvern House
Thursday 6 May

The two drawing rooms were beautifully fitted up for dancing—and indeed, Lady Bredon's exquisite taste was evident everywhere, and the refurbishment of the house greatly admired. Three hundred guests attended. Weippert's band waited to play. The supper would be magnificent.

But all Lord Bredon saw or cared about was his wife.

She'd dressed in the sumptuously simple style that was one of Maison Noirot's specialties. Made of ivory organdy, her dress was very closely fitted in the bodice, displaying her splendid endowments. The plaited tulle fell over the neckline in a single sweet curve, showing off her perfect skin and smoothly arching neck. A pink sash was fixed to the front of her waist, rather than circling it, the ends hanging to the flounce at the hem. A few pink roses dotted the neckline, the ruffled inner elbows of the snug-fitting sleeves (narrow sleeves—at last!), sash, and hem, but the overall simplicity made her stand out in a sea of busier gowns and blinding jewels. In any event, she might have dressed in a nun's habit and still rivaled Aphrodite.

Bredon, to nobody's surprise, wore black—but rather more expensive black than usual.

"The women are swooning," she murmured, when they'd finished receiving their guests.

"That's because I said very little," he said.

She looked up at him. "You're not to stifle yourself. You know I only tease about your talking."

"I know an element of truth when I see one," he said. "Besides, I'm a debutante, supposed to behave modestly. Not to mention, it hardly mattered what I said. Everybody was preoccupied with staring from me to you—and wondering what you saw in me."

"That isn't what the ladies were wondering," she said. "But you go on thinking that." She glanced about her. "It's time," she said.

"It's about time," he said. "You look like a party cake. I can't wait to get my hands on you." He lowered his voice. "And later, my mouth."

She flushed a little as she signaled to the orchestra.

The first notes of a waltz wafted across the room.

He looked at her. "Ready to make a spectacle of yourself?"

"Always," she said, and smiled.

His heart soared, but he gave only one very quick smile, before leading her out to their first dance in public.

The fête, which had commenced at eleven o'clock, ended at four. Their guests had obviously enjoyed the supper and nearly had to be dragged bodily from the dance floor.

That, Clara told her husband as they prepared for bed,

was because she and he had started off the dancing so beautifully.

"You were beautiful," he said. "I was content to form the backdrop."

"You must have been a graceful backdrop," she said. "I noticed you never lacked for a partner after that."

"Nor did you. Do your lovers mean to continue following you about?"

"I think they wanted to show there were no hard feelings," she said.

"In the event you came to your senses and ran away from me, they wanted you to know they'd be available," he said.

"I came to my senses when I met you," she said.

He looked at her, his grey eyes serious now, and searching.

"I thought it was my life that stifled me," she said. "But I see it makes no difference what world I live in. The difference is the man at my side."

He cleared his throat. "It seems you needed a particularly difficult one," he said.

"Much more entertaining," she said.

She untied the ribbons of her dressing gown.

He slid it from her shoulders. He kissed her shoulder then, and draped the dressing gown over a chair.

Then the serious look returned, more intent now. He turned her toward him again, and studied her for a long moment.

"Lady Bredon," he said at last, "have you something to tell me?"

She'd examined herself carefully in the mirror. Only Davis was aware, but a lady's maid had to keep track of such things. Clara had felt reasonably sure it didn't show—that is, it didn't show to a normal person.

"About what?" she said.

"Your breasts," he said. "And your belly. And your face. And the way your eyes shimmer. I thought you looked more beautiful tonight, but logic told me that was impossible."

"I was waiting to be absolutely sure," she said.

"How much surer do you need to be?" he said. "Am I or am I not to be a father?"

Her eyes filled. She didn't know why. "I believe you will be," she said.

His mouth twitched. "A father. Me." He gave a short laugh. "Who'd believe it?"

"Well, then," she said shakily. "Not injured, my lord? No swooning? No tears? Excellent."

He pulled her into his arms. "Excellent, indeed. Oh, what a laugh. Me, a father! I do love you, you amazing girl."

"Well, it is not so amazing, given certain basic facts of biology," she said.

"This is no time to be logical," he said.

He closed his mouth over hers. The kiss was long and deep and joyful and filled with promise of future joy.

But before it was quite over, she made herself draw her head back. "I do love you, my Raven," she said. "I never said so, but—"

"My lady, I deduced as much," he said.

He pulled her close once more, and they returned to finish what they'd started.

Postscript

When I have closed or sent off my daily register of events, I always recollect a number of things which I ought to have mentioned. Then it is too late,—what I have omitted finds no appropriate place.

—Friedrich von Raumer, *England in 1835*

News of Jacob Freame's death soon reached Jack's coffeehouse, and by degrees made its way to a wretched hut by the river. Here Squirrel bided his time while getting to know the members of the river's underworld. Not long after Freame's demise, Squirrel began to work for a dredgerman, one of the scavengers who plied the river between Putney and Gravesend. Eventually, having established himself as reliable, he worked his way out of the river and into one of the riverside taverns. Some years later he married the tavern owner's daughter and lived, if not as luxuriously as Jacob Freame had done, then certainly more securely. Now known as John Stiles, Squirrel grew a little fat, from not having to run so much or so fast, and in time he stopped looking over his shoulder.

he elderly seventh Duke of Malvern did die, but not as soon as he and everybody else might have expected. His son always said it was Clara's doing: The old man's spirits had improved from the time Raven first mentioned her, and continued cheerful as he got to know her better. Good spirits, as everybody knows, make good medicine. This proved to be his case, certainly, for his pain diminished noticeably from the time of his son's marriage.

He lived long enough to delight in a grandson, named George after both grandfathers, as well as a granddaughter, named Frances Anne after her grandmothers. Then one night, some hours after a most enjoyable dispute with his wife about the merits of the Prisoners' Counsel Act of 1836, His Grace died peacefully in his sleep.

Raven Radford, to the amusement or dismay of many, became the eighth Duke of Malvern. He proved to be as great an irritant in the House of Lords as he'd been in the House of Commons and the criminal courts, and continued—aided and abetted by his wife—to acquire friends in low places.

Among their many philanthropic activities, before as well as after he inherited the dukedom, he and his wife took a special interest in the ragged schools. Their first fund-raising fête was held at Vauxhall, and the money raised was used to provide desperately needed bathing facilities for the school in Saffron Hill.

Yes, Lady Clara Fairfax did become a duchess, after all, and her mother—perhaps on account of this or perhaps on account of her increasing brood of *perfect* grandchildren (vastly superior to any of Lady Bartham's whiny lot)—became a truly happy woman.

At least for a time.

Endnote

If our Stranger's mind be of a lively inquisitive nature, his imagination thus fills up the chasm that wonderment has created with ill-assorted suggestions, or he seeks to obtain information from his fellow-travellers, some of whom know as little of the passing scene as himself.
—*A Living Picture of London, for 1828, and Stranger's Guide*

Legal matters

For story purposes, I took some liberties with police and judicial proceedings, e.g., sending felons to trial when convenient to my plot, rather than waiting for the Sessions, during which their indictments would have been reviewed. For a readable survey of the history of the criminal justice system in London, I recommend the Old Bailey Proceedings Online. (http://www.oldbaileyonline.org/index.jsp)

My fictional Grumley pauper farm is a thinly disguised version of an actual case of 1849.

Ragged Schools

hough the Ragged Schools Union wasn't established until 1844, ragged schooling was known
before this, although not necessarily by that name. "It
was with the establishment of the London City Mission
in 1835 . . . that the ragged schooling got its name," according to infed.org (http://www.infed.org/youthwork/
ragged_schools.htm). I took some artistic license in mod-
eling mine on a ragged school that did exist in Saffron
Hill at a later date than that of my story.

Cameo appearances

arcelline, Sophy, and Leonie's stories are told
in my Dressmakers trilogy: *Silk Is for Seduction*, *Scandal Wears Satin*, and *Vixen in Velvet*.

The Duke of Marchmont's story is *Don't Tempt Me*.
His house in Kensington features in *Lord Lovedon's
Duel*, a novella in *Royally Ever After*.

The Broken Almost-Engagement and the Shocking Incident at the Countess of Igby's Ball are episodes in *Silk
Is for Seduction* and *Scandal Wears Satin*.

Yes, the clothes are for real

ashions are based on images in early nineteenth-
century ladies' magazines available online. Among
many other sartorial thefts, I stole most of the description
of Clara's wedding dress from the November 1835 *Magazine of the Beau Monde*. On my Pinterest page (https://
www.pinterest.com/lorettachase/) you'll see the fashions
as well as other illustrations for my stories.

Pounds, shillings, pence, and other old money

Money equivalents: Once upon a time (until 1971) English money wasn't based on a decimal system. It went like this:

> Twelve pence in a shilling (*bob*, in slang).
> Twenty shillings in a pound or sovereign.
> Twenty-one shillings in a guinea.

There were numerous smaller and larger units of these denominations, such as:

> Ten shillings in a half sovereign.
> Five shillings in a crown.

For more, see:
http://en.wikipedia.org/wiki/Coins_of_the_pound
_sterling#Pre-decimal_coinage

Other odd bits

Robert Burns's poem about a louse:

> *Ye ugly, creepin, blastit wonner,*
> *Detested, shunn'd by saunt an' sinner,*
> *How daur ye set your fit upon her—*
> *Sae fine a lady?*
> *Gae somewhere else and seek your dinner*
> *On some poor body.*

—Robert Burns, "To a Louse, On Seeing One on a
Lady's Bonnet, at Church," 1786

You can hear a recording here:
http://www.bbc.co.uk/arts/robertburns/works/to_a_louse/

A tiger is a groom in livery who travels with owner/driver of carriage to hold horses, etc.

If anything else puzzles you, please e-mail me (author@lorettachase.com). I love nerdy history questions, and might even write a blog post about it.

ENTER THE SCINTILLATING WORLD OF
USA TODAY BESTSELLING AUTHOR

LORETTA CHASE

DON'T TEMPT ME
978-0-06-163266-2

Lucien de Grey, the most popular bachelor in the Beau Monde, can easily save Zoe Lexham's risqué reputation . . . if the wayward beauty doesn't lead him into temptation.

LAST NIGHT'S SCANDAL
978-0-06-163267-9

After surviving the perils of Egypt, Peregrine Dalmay, Earl of Lisle, is back in London, facing the most dire threat of all: his irrational family . . . and Miss Olivia Wingate-Carsington.

SILK IS FOR SEDUCTION
978-0-06-163268-6

The Duke of Clevedon is ripe for seduction . . . but Marcelline Noirot's passionate heart could make this game quite dangerous indeed.

SCANDAL WEARS SATIN
978-0-06-210031-3

Turning a scandal into an advantage requires all of Sophy Noirot's skills, leaving her little patience for a gorgeous, reckless rake like the Earl of Longmore.

Discover great authors, exclusive offers, and more at hc.com.

LCH 1015

ENTER THE SCINTILLATING WORLD OF
USA TODAY BESTSELLING AUTHOR

LORETTA CHASE

NOT QUITE A LADY
978-0-06-123123-0

Lady Charlotte Hayward is not about to let a rake like
Darius Carsington entice her to do everything she shouldn't.
But the rules of attraction can easily overpower the rules of
manners and morals.

LORD OF SCOUNDRELS
978-0-380-77616-0

Sebastian Ballister, the notorious Marquess of Dain, wants
nothing to do with respectable women. He's determined to
continue doing what he does best—sin and sin again—until
the day a shop door opens and Jessica Trent walks in.

YOUR SCANDALOUS WAYS
978-0-06-123124-7

James Cordier is a master of disguise, a brilliant thief, a first-
class lover—all for King and Country. His last mission is to
"acquire" a packet of incriminating letters from one notorious woman.

THE LAST HELLION
978-0-380-77617-7

Vere Mallory, the Duke of Ainswood, can't resist a challenge. Especially when it comes in the beautiful female
form of Lydia Grenville.

**Discover great authors, exclusive offers,
and more at hc.com.**

LCH1 1015